CROSSING
THE
Lines

SJ HOOKS

Cover by Graphics by Tammy.
Formatting by Tammy

Who says second novels are terrifyingly difficult?
I did.

Who encouraged me to write one anyway?
You did.

Thank you to my online friends around the world.
Fandom is family.

Always.

CHAPTER ONE

"Please. There has to be something you can do."

The chair creaks as the woman behind the desk swivels it around to face me, looking at me rather than her computer screen. There are deep-set lines on her forehead and streaks of gray in her hair. It's her eyes that age her most of all, though—*world-weary* is the term.

"Look, Miss ..." Her eyes dart toward the ceiling for a second.

"Winters," I supply, as patiently as I can. It's not her fault. In her system, I'm probably just a number. One in a seemingly endless line of women who turn up at her desk with the same story to tell.

"Miss Winters." The social worker folds her hands and leans forward. "The state has several programs for single mothers, but the problem is that you don't qualify for any of them at the moment."

"But—"

"I'm sorry. I really am." Her gaze darts to my right for a second and when she looks at me again, I see a genuine spark of pity. "You have a beautiful son."

"Thank you," I mumble, running my hand over Luke's hair. He looks up from his picture book, smiling at me before diving back in. It's a new book, borrowed from the small stack in the waiting area.

"Until the state launches an investigation into your ex ... husband?"

"Boyfriend."

"Sorry." She rubs her forehead. "Until it's determined that he's no longer providing for you and your son, we can't get you into any of the programs."

"When will that be?"

"I can't say. It doesn't help that your home is still his only registered address."

"But his mail stopped coming months ago. He must have a P.O. Box or something somewhere."

"Probably," she admits. "You're sure nothing happened to him?"

"Yeah, I'm pretty sure. He posted a few things on Facebook at first. Just stupid videos and stuff like that. But he didn't answer the messages I sent him, and one day I was blocked from seeing his account."

The social worker sighs, her lips tightening briefly. "Is there anyone else who can help you until you can get into some programs?"

I shake my head. There's Jo, but I can't keep taking her money.

"Your parents? The father's parents?"

"No. There's no contact. They've never even met Luke, and my ex was raised by his aunt. She hasn't been around either. There's no one." I blink to keep my eyes from watering.

"I'm sorry," the lady says, sighing softly again. "I assume you've looked for work?"

"Everywhere. Anything. Turns out I'm qualified for nothing."

This time the pity in her eyes is more than a spark. "I wish ..." She trails off. There's nothing she can do, and we both know it.

"Yeah, me too," I mumble, pushing back my chair. "Let's go, hon."

Wishing gets you nowhere, I know that all too well. And life isn't fair at all.

∽

"Mommy, I'm hungry."

I look up from the Help Wanted ads and try to smile at my son. I hope I'm successful. I hope he doesn't see the anxiety that flares within me at his simple request.

"Okay, baby. Grilled cheese sandwich?" *Please, say yes.*

Thankfully, he does, and I'm able to relax just a little as I rise and begin assembling what I need: bread, the last two slices of cheese, and a stick of butter. The empty cavern of my fridge stares back at me as I take out the few items and quickly make Luke a meager dinner. I know it must taste a little stale, but he starts eating enthusiastically anyway.

"What about you, Mommy?"

"I'm not hungry," I lie.

The truth is that I'm starving, and not just for food. I'm starving for more than this—for more than this run-down apartment, for more than this life of barely getting by.

"Finish up, hon," I say. "You're staying at Mrs. Watt's tonight."

His face drops, but he nods. I know he doesn't want to go, but I have no choice. I have to find work and there aren't a lot of options for a twenty-two-year-old with no job experience and no marketable skills. In the bathroom, I put on too much makeup and tease my long hair before changing. My nice outfits won't do tonight. I've tried every diner, restaurant, and shop I can think of with no luck. I have to go elsewhere tonight and with a small sigh of defeat, I pull out a short, tight skirt and a low-cut top, pairing the outfit with stilettos. I bought the whole ensemble long ago in a pathetic act of rebellion against my parents but have never had the courage to actually wear any of it.

Looking at myself in the mirror, I don't recognize the girl staring back at me. That's good, I suppose. This is so far from the person I am—normally I wouldn't be caught dead in something this revealing. I hide myself underneath a coat before going back into the kitchen. I don't want Luke to see me dressed this way.

Ten minutes later, I knock on Mrs. Watt's door, just down the hall from our apartment. She's always home.

"Abbi," she greets me, looking me over with a frown, eyeing my tousled hair, red lipstick, and hooker heels.

"Hi, Mrs. Watt. I have to go out. Would you mind ...?" Luke is hiding behind me, clutching the hem of my coat in silent protest.

"Come on in." She sighs, reaching out her hand to my son.

"Mommy," he whispers, looking up at me with wide eyes.

I kneel down as best as I can in my restricting outfit until we're at eye level. "I'm coming back, baby. I promise. It's just for a few hours."

He's terrified of me leaving and no amount of reassurance on my part seems to help. I understand why he's scared, though. Fucking Patrick and his promise to come back soon—it's been six months and Luke's still waiting. Luke wraps his little arms around my neck and squeezes until I can hardly breathe.

"Listen," I whisper. "I love you, baby, and I swear I'm coming back. I'll never leave you, not ever."

"Not ever?"

"Not ever," I promise, and I mean it with my whole heart. "I'll be back before you know it."

"Okay," he sniffs.

Mrs. Watt huffs impatiently above us. She's a no-nonsense lady and I'm sure she thinks I'm coddling Luke, but I don't care what she thinks. I'm grateful for her help, though. Her apartment smells like stale cigarette smoke and her cat, Buster, scares Luke, but underneath her tough exterior she's a nice woman who always takes good care of my son.

"Come on, young man," she says as Luke reluctantly releases me. "Did you have dinner?"

"Yes, ma'am."

"You have room for dessert? I bought cookies. They're in the kitchen."

"Yes, please." Luke wanders into her hallway, giving me one last look before getting his dessert.

"Thank you, Mrs. Watt," I say, hobbling to my feet in the stupid heels.

She looks me over again, obviously noticing how different I look tonight. "Where're you off to?"

"I have to get a job. There's a, uh, gentlemen's club that's hiring."

She nods slowly, taking a drag of her cigarette. "You be careful," she warns, waving it at me.

"I will. I'll be back in a few hours. If he falls asleep, don't wake him, okay? I'll just carry him home."

She closes the door with a small shake of her head. I know she doesn't approve, but what else can I do at this point? Steeling myself, I pull the strap of my nearly empty purse over my shoulder and walk out of the building into the night.

"Well?" The club manager leans back in his chair, a bored expression on his face, as if he didn't just ask me to take my clothes off in the middle of his office. I'm very aware of the large man standing behind me by the door and shoot him a nervous glance. He meets my eyes with an impassive stare, which tells me he's not going anywhere.

"Look, if you can't get naked in front of me and Benny here, how the hell do you think you're gonna do it in front of an audience?" the manager asks.

He's got a point. My hands shake as I peel my clothes off, my eyes fixed on the vomit-colored carpet beneath my feet.

"Nope. Sorry."

My head jerks in surprise and I look at the manager again. "W-what?"

"I can't use you." He waves his hand dismissively. "You've got a pretty face, but you're skinny as a fucking rail and you look scared to death. The innocent girl-next-door routine only works if you look like you've got a naughty side."

Panic wells up inside me. "Please. I ..."

He tilts his head to the side, looking behind me. "Benny, you wanna fuck her?"

"No." The answer comes without hesitation, chipping away my last shred of dignity, and I start pulling my clothes back on.

"Quit starving yourself and maybe we can work something out," he calls after me as I stumble out of his office, fighting a losing battle with my tears.

The back of the club is dark and the music deafening. I rush past the bar, looking for the exit through blurry eyes, when I barrel straight into a solid wall of muscle, losing my balance. Before I can fall, I'm hoisted to my feet by two strong hands on my naked shoulders. I look up, recoiling when I realize I'm being held by a man. His brow is furrowed and his gaze dark, sweeping across my face. I'm a complete mess to look at, I'm sure, and I redden in embarrassment at my disheveled state and revealing clothes.

"Thank you," I mumble, unsure if he's able to hear it. I retreat, making a beeline for the exit, the music masking my choked sobs. I don't linger outside, wanting to get away from here immediately, and I wish I'd brought my sneakers with me as I hobble down the sidewalk, the pain in my feet only eclipsed by the dread I feel.

I don't know what to do now. There's no more money, and there's food for maybe two more days. The rent is long over-due, and if we get kicked out on the street, what will happen to Luke? Will they deem me unfit and try and take him away from me? My heart twists in fear and I have to stop walking and concentrate on breathing.

"How much?"

I startle and nearly trip as I lose my balance. A dark car has pulled over and the passenger-side window is open. "W-what?"

"How much?"

How much for what? Then the proverbial ton of bricks hits me. He thinks I'm a hooker! Well, I guess I do look like one. I should have put my coat back on. "I'm not—"

"I don't care," the voice interrupts. "How. Much?"

"Look," I snap. "I'm just trying to get home."

"I'll give you three hundred dollars."

Whoa! I don't know the going rate, but to me, that's a lot of money. I can almost taste the food I'd be able to buy with it, feel the heaviness of the grocery bags in my hands, and see the brimming shelves in the fridge. I could make a real hot break-fast for Luke in the morning.

"F-for what?" I ask, stepping closer to the car. The door opens and I catch a glimpse of a suit sleeve and a large hand.

I know I shouldn't do this. It's dangerous. But I can't lose Luke. Cautiously, I lean down, peering inside the car. It's him —the man from the club. He followed me.

"Hello again," he says. "Get in."

I look him over: nice suit, clean-shaven, nothing that screams danger. I lock eyes with him, trying my best to assess him. I don't get a bad feeling from him. He also looks like he might actually have that three hundred dollars.

Climbing into the car with my heart in my throat, I don't know if I'm about to make a huge mistake, but I have no choice. I'm desperate. I'm crossing the line.

CHAPTER TWO

Up close, I register that the man in the car is good looking in a corporate sort of way, like a lawyer on a TV show. His dark hair is neatly styled and I can smell his cologne from where I'm sitting. It's nice. He's a lot older than me, probably in his late thirties or early forties. He doesn't seem like the kind of man who'd have to solicit a girl in order to have sex, but what do I know? I've never done anything like this before, so I really don't have a clue what type of men solicit sex workers.

"Close the door," he says.

I hesitate. Am I really doing this? I can't get out if he decides to lock the door. "You're not a cop, right?" I ask. "You have to tell me if you are. It's the law or something."

"Is it?"

"I ... I saw that in a movie once."

He chuckles. "I'm not a cop. And you're obviously new at this."

"Uh, yeah."

I notice he speaks with a slight accent, but I can't quite place it. He's not from the Pacific Northwest, I'm fairly certain, but it doesn't sound like any other American dialect I know either.

"So what do you say? Are we doing this or not?" he asks.

I swallow back the tears I feel approaching. I *have* to do this. "Yes," I answer, closing the door. "I need the money."

He eyes me speculatively for a moment before nodding to himself. "Yes, you do, don't you?" he says, steering the car back onto the road.

We drive for a little while, saying nothing to each other. I pull my coat on and keep a close watch on him, but he just drives, steering the car through traffic with practiced ease, the picture of calm.

I notice as we enter an industrial area of the city, abandoned at this time of night, and I feel a spike of panic as I look around. No one will hear me if I need help.

"It's all right," he says, apparently picking up on my state of mind. "I won't hurt you. This is just more private."

Finally, he turns the car into an alley between two large warehouse buildings and shuts off the engine. I guess this is it.

"So, uh, what do you want?" I ask, glancing over at him.

"I'd like a blow job." He says it as if he's ordering a cup of coffee from a waitress, like it's no big deal at all. Still, I'm relieved. I thought he was going to demand a lot more.

"I should get the money first, right?" *Why the hell am I asking* him?

His lips twitch as he pulls out his wallet, taking three hundred-dollar bills from a large wad of cash and handing them to me. I stare at all of the bills still left in his hand and try to imagine having that kind of money. Stuffing the three hundred dollars in my purse, I resist the urge to thank him. I know I'll have to earn that money now, doing something I've never, ever imagined doing.

"Take off your coat," the man demands.

I manage to wrestle my way out of it, rubbing my bare arms as the coolness of the AC hits them. My mouth goes dry with fear as he gently grasps my wrists, straightening my arms out in front of me and turning them slowly, eyes fixed on my exposed skin. After a moment he releases me with a nod.

"How old are you?" he asks.

"Twenty-two."

He frowns, pursing his lips. "I don't like liars," he says, his voice a bit gentler. "Are you being truthful?"

I nod. Why would I lie about my age?

"Good," he says.

"Good?"

"Yes. You look younger, and I'm really not into the whole underage thing. Take off the top too."

For the second time tonight, I find myself showing my nakedness to a stranger. I look away from him as it comes off, the words of the strip-club manager still echoing in the back of my head.

"Eyes to me," the man directs.

I force myself to meet his gaze.

"You're a beautiful girl," he says, looking me up and down.

I breathe a sigh of relief. There was a good chance he'd want his money back if he didn't find me attractive and I can't deny that it feels good hearing him tell me that. "Thank you," I whisper. I flinch slightly when he reaches out and runs his large hand up my arm and then across my chest, fondling my breasts. My nipples have hardened in the cold and he tugs on both of them, making me gasp.

"C'mere," he says, pulling me closer.

I tense up. We're face-to-face and he's looking me over with unmistakable desire. I imagine I must appear to him as a deer caught in the headlights with my wide-eyed frightened look. He cradles my jaw and runs his thumb across my mouth, smearing my lipstick.

"None of that shit," he whispers. "You don't need it."

He leans in and I close my eyes, thinking he'll kiss me. Instead, I feel his lips against my cheek as they slide across it and reach my ear. "Now, suck me off like a good girl."

His words hit my system with the force of a sledgehammer, shocking the hell out of me. No one has ever talked to me like that before. My heart hammers in my chest as I watch him move his seat back. He flicks his tie over his shoulder, getting it out of the way, his movements slow and measured, as though this is business as usual for him. He turns his head to look at me, raising his eyebrows expectantly.

As I lean forward, he tilts his head back against the headrest and lowers his arms to rest next to him, exposing his lap. All I have to do is unzip him and get it done, and the money's mine.

Do it. Do it!

My fingers are stiff and uncooperative as I try to open his pants, so focused on the task I don't notice he's moved his hand until it's stroking my hair down the length of my back. I freeze up, trembling underneath his touch.

"Hey." He touches me underneath my chin, making me look up at him as he examines my face closely. After a few seconds his lips tighten and he shakes his head. "We're not doing this."

His words hurt just as badly as those from the club manager and I can't hold back the tears I've been repressing all night. He stares at me, eyes wider than before.

"Why are you doing this?" he asks, plucking my top up off the floor of the car and handing it to me. "You aren't just new at this. You've never done this before, have you?"

"I'm hungry," I whimper, my mental filter completely obliterated. "I'm so hungry."

"Fuck." He runs his hand through his hair. "Look, put your clothes back on, and I'll get you something to eat."

I suck in a breath, nearly choking on a sob. I'm so hungry, the promise of something to eat makes my stomach twist in pain. "Y-you will?"

He nods, looking straight ahead. "Get dressed."

I pull my top and my coat back on, and the moment my

seatbelt is fastened he puts the car in reverse, quickly maneuvering us out of the abandoned area and onto a busy street. He pulls into the drive-through of the first fast-food place we come to and turns to me.

"What would you like?"

I lick my lips. "A-anything's fine. A cheeseburger?"

He orders a combo meal with fries and a milkshake, as well as a cup of coffee and an apple turnover in a separate bag. Paying at the window, he hands me the shake and looks inside the larger bag for a second, before thrusting it back into the hands of the worker.

"I ordered a cheeseburger. This is plain. Fix it." His words are clipped, impatient.

"It's really okay," I whisper.

He ignores me, focusing on the clerk who quickly replaces the burger, apologizing. Handing me the bag, he drives to the farthest end of the parking lot and turns off the engine. His behavior is intimidating, but all I can focus on right now is the gratitude I feel toward him.

"Thank you." I clutch the brown paper bag to resist the urge to tear into it immediately.

He glances at me briefly, nodding. "Go ahead," he says. "But don't make a mess."

"I won't."

I force myself to eat slowly, knowing I'll make myself sick if I don't. It's been days since I've had a full meal. The milkshake tastes like heaven, fat and creamy, and I savor every mouthful. The man turns on the radio and sips his coffee. After a few minutes of just sitting there watching me eat, he holds out the turnover.

"You want this afterward?"

"No thanks, I'm almost full already."

He shrugs and takes a bite of it but makes a face and stuffs it back into the bag.

"Not good?" I ask.

"Awful. I hate fast food. It didn't even taste like apple."

"They probably overcooked it." I'm nervous, so I keep talking. "That's the challenge when it comes to pie: the balance between not overcooking the apples and not undercooking the crust. Finding that perfect balance is key."

He turns and looks at me, his eyebrows raised.

"Sorry. I'll ... be quiet."

I finish my meal in silence, aware that he's still staring at me.

"Do you feel better?" he asks after I've wiped my mouth, inclining his head toward the paper bag.

"Yes, thank you." I force myself to look at him, knowing I can't sit here and stall forever. I'm acutely aware of the money in my bag—money I haven't earned yet. Drawing a deep breath, I send him what I hope looks like a flirtatious smile.

"Should we go back to that warehouse area now?" I ask. I put my hand on his thigh, feeling his muscles twitch underneath my touch as I lean closer to him. He looks me over, but then he shakes his head.

"No. We aren't doing that."

Nausea threatens to make me lose the meal he just bought me. I have to find a way to keep that money he gave me. "Please? I want to, I promise. I'll, uh, be with you."

He sighs, shaking his head. "Look. It's obvious to me now you're not a sex worker. Why did you go with me?"

"I needed the money. I *need* the money. Please. I'll do anything you ask."

That gets his attention, his eyes flaring with emotion. But he says nothing, does nothing. Biting the inside of my cheek to keep from crying, I grab the money from my bag. My hand is shaking as I hold it out to him. "Here."

He cocks his head to the side and stares at me, ignoring the bills in my hand. Then he turns and faces forward. "Keep it."

The sense of relief that floods my system is staggering in its intensity. "Thank you. Thank you so much."

"I'll drive you home," he says, starting the car. "Where to?"

"R-really?"

"You thought I'd just dump you here in the parking lot?" His scolding makes my face heat up. "I'm not a complete monster."

"I'm sorry. I've never—"

"I know. Believe me, I know."

I tell him my neighborhood and notice his slight frown. Obviously, he knows it's in a bad part of town, but he doesn't comment. We don't talk on the way there until I tell him to pull over at the twenty-four-hour market two blocks from my building.

"Thanks for the ride," I say, undoing my seatbelt.

"Wait."

Shit. Does he want the money back after all? Cautiously, I turn to him.

"Did you mean what you said before, that you wanted to be with me, as you put it?"

I nod my head. I wanted to earn those three hundred dollars, at least.

He purses his lips, nodding to himself. "How'd you like to earn some more money?"

"Doing what?"

"You said you'd do anything I ask," he reminds me.

I did say that, but it was a desperate plea at the time. Now I'm not so sure. "You won't hurt me, will you?"

"No," he says, his voice softer now. "I won't hurt you. Whatever I do to you, I can promise it won't hurt."

I feel pulled in two different directions. Whatever he does to me he promises won't hurt, but that doesn't mean I'll like it. He obviously has a sexual motive. After all, he picked me up tonight believing I was soliciting. Could I have sex with this man, this stranger? I'm not sure. Then again ...

"H-how much money are we talking about?" I hear myself ask.

"Five hundred dollars for tomorrow night."

Holy shit.

He reaches into his pocket, pulling out a pen and a card, and quickly scribbles something down before holding it out to me.

"Be at this address tomorrow night at eight."

"This is your place?"

He nods.

Can I trust him? He could've hurt me tonight, but he didn't. The fact that he saw how upset I was and stopped me from going through with it, bought me food, and let me keep the money—at the very least it means he has a conscience.

"Okay," I whisper. "I'll be there."

"Good girl."

What a weird thing to say. "Um, good night."

I climb out of the car without looking back and rush into the market, feeling safer underneath the familiar fluorescent lights, and knowing that I can finally pay for everything I throw into my cart brings a genuine smile to my face for the first time in weeks.

CHAPTER THREE

"Mommy, you came back," Luke mumbles as I gently lift him off the couch.

"Of course I did, honey," I whisper, cradling him in my arms. He smiles and falls asleep again almost immediately, his head on my shoulder.

"How'd it go?" I ask, turning to Mrs. Watt.

"Just fine. He doesn't like my cat much, though."

I nod, glancing at it. It's watching me with narrowed eyes and when I look at it, it hisses for no apparent reason. Demon spawn.

"Listen, I know it's a lot to ask, but could you possibly watch him again tomorrow night? I have someplace I need to be at 8 o'clock."

Mrs. Watt watches me closely. "You get a job?"

"Yeah." It's not technically a lie. I'll be getting paid for whatever I have to do.

"All right."

"Thank you so much. You're a lifesaver."

Mrs. Watt doesn't pry, thankfully. I'm not sure what I'd tell her if she decided to ask for more details.

Luke is getting heavy in my arms and I leave quickly, carrying both him and the bags from the market. After I've tucked him in, I put the groceries away and take a much-needed shower. Under the lukewarm spray, I start to cry. I'm both relieved to have a bit of money and food, but at the same time ashamed of what I almost did to get it. I never thought I'd find myself in such dire straits. Thankfully, Luke can't hear me and my tears are washed down the drain without anyone the wiser.

After I've calmed down, I dry off and settle on the couch. Tonight was scary, but I don't regret my decision to get into the strange man's car. I remind myself that I can feed my son and that's all that matters. Besides, it could've been a lot worse. The man wasn't violent or crazy, he fed me, and he even drove me home. If I can earn the five hundred dollars from him tomorrow, I can pay at least part of what I owe the landlord. That's a big "if," though. He barely touched me tonight and I almost jumped out of my skin. Tomorrow, I'm sure I won't get the money he offered if I can't do what he wants.

Even if I somehow *can* go through with it, I know it won't be enough. I need a steady income. My parents aren't going to help and neither will Patrick's aunt, who never liked me much in the first place. After we told her I was pregnant, she blamed me—like I had done it on purpose or something. But we were being careful, so it came as a complete shock to both of us. Patrick mentioned going to a clinic, but I wouldn't hear of it and he came around after a little while. Maybe he felt guilty. He was the one who wanted to have sex, and he was pretty relentless about it until I finally gave in. Two months later, I was pregnant.

There's no one to help me—except the man in the car. Christ, I don't even know his name.

Climbing off the couch, I check on Luke, who's fast asleep, and then look through my coat, locating the card the man handed me. All it says is his address in Medina, a rich suburb of Seattle. I know the neighborhood by reputation only. It's really swanky and my suspicion that he's loaded was apparently spot on. He probably works in an office in the city and spends his nights and weekends in suburban bliss. I wonder if he's married. I didn't notice a wedding ring, but those come off easily. Putting the card back in my pocket, I push all thoughts of him from my mind. No need to deal with the reality of the situation until I have to.

The rest of the night I spend watching blurry TV, too tired to commit to putting a DVD in the ancient player no one wants to buy. Believe me, I've tried.

~

The next morning, I wake up still on the couch. My back is sore, but that's quickly forgotten when I remember what I'm about to do: cook my son a big breakfast for the first time in months. Our kitchen is small and old, but I keep it tidy and clean, so it's not so bad. I work fast, putting together pancakes, bacon, and fruit. I'm making myself a cup of instant coffee when Luke shuffles in, rubbing his eyes.

"Morning, sweetheart. You hungry?"

"You made pancakes and chocolate milk?" Luke is now wide awake, staring at the small feast on the table. The joy on his face makes me so happy. "Is it my birthday, Mommy?"

I laugh, kneeling down to hug him. "No, silly. You know your birthday isn't for another couple of months. Come and eat."

And he does, probably way too much, but I don't have the heart to cut him off. Who knows when we'll be able to splurge like this again? But if I can go through with it tonight, do whatever he tells me to, the man in the suit might consider seeing me again, which means more money for me and Luke. It's a means to an end until I can find a real job, at least.

It's not the best plan in the world, but at this point it's all

CHAPTER FOUR

Getting to Medina is a real hassle. I dropped Luke off at Mrs. Watt's in plenty of time, but he was once again scared of me leaving and it took a bit of convincing to get him inside her apartment. Now I'm running for the bus stop. I'll have to transfer at the station downtown and hope I make it. I have a feeling the man I'm about to see doesn't care for tardiness.

Half an hour later, I'm frazzled and out of breath, but at least I'm standing in front of the right bus, which is headed out of the city in just a few minutes. I shuffle in and tell the driver where I'm headed. He looks me up and down.

I'm grateful I decided not to dress as revealing as I had yesterday. Tonight, I'm simply wearing my nicest jeans with a white top underneath a light jacket. I pay the driver, then head to the back, not interested in making conversation. After many stops in the city, it's a short trip across the Evergreen Point toll bridge and soon the driver calls out my stop. I step off the bus and it's like I've entered a new world. Medina is located across Lake Washington—a haven for wealthy people, filled with golf courses, country clubs, and million-dollar homes. Rows of lakefront property stretch down along the coast as far as the eye can see, each house grander than the next. Taking a deep breath, I start walking, trying to imagine what it must be like to live here. The small town where I grew up didn't have neighborhoods like this one.

It scares me, what I'm about to do. The guy was really nice last night, all things considered, but tonight I'll have to earn that five hundred dollars. I look up, realizing that daylight is fading, and check my watch.

Fuck, I'm late!

I take off running, probably looking like a madwoman, but I don't care. I can't afford to lose this job—or whatever the hell I should call it. Mindful of the addresses on the houses and properties I pass, I reach my destination and turn onto a smaller road leading down toward the lake. The house I arrive at looks big enough for three families. Located right on the edge of the lake, its three stories overlook the water and are surrounded by tall trees.

I don't stop to admire it, instead hurrying to the front door and ringing the bell. Moments later, the man from last night opens it. He's in a suit again this evening, but he's loosened his shirt collar and taken off his tie and jacket. The sleeves of his white shirt are rolled up, revealing a large, very expensive-looking watch on his left wrist and lean, muscular forearms. In the fading light, most of his face is in shadow, but I can tell that he's displeased. His frown deepens as he looks me over. I'm panting for breath, flushed and hunched over, which is definitely not an attractive look on anyone.

"I'm sorry ... I'm late," I manage.

"How did you get here?"

"I, uh, I took the bus and then I ran the rest of the way."

"I can see that," he says, pursing his lips. "Why not get a cab?"

Is he joking? "I-I couldn't afford one."

He doesn't respond and doesn't move, blocking the entrance with his tall frame, his jaw ticking.

"Should I leave?" I finally ask, my stomach churning at the thought that he might have changed his mind.

He inhales deeply through his nose and lets it out again, his eyes locking with mine for a second before I look down, embarrassed by my tardiness. "No, come on in." He steps aside and holds the door open for me as I enter.

"Wow," I exclaim, turning in a circle to take in the huge hall and the sweeping staircase. The man is still watching me, so I try to dial down my gawking at the fancy surroundings and instead look down at the polished hardwood floor, hoping he'll say something. I feel like shrinking away when he moves to stand in front of me, placing his index finger underneath my chin.

"Tell me your name," he orders, tilting my face upward. For a second, I consider giving him a false one, but then I remember how he feels about liars.

"A-Abigail," I stutter. "Or Abbi, if you prefer."

"I don't," he says, and just like that, the discussion is over. I don't really mind. We're on his dime, so I guess he can call me anything he wants. "Abigail. You'll refer to me as 'Mr. Thorne' or 'Sir' at all times. Is that understood?"

"Yes, Sir," I whisper, hoping I'll be able to remember. I don't want to disappoint him.

"Good girl." He smiles for the very first time in my presence. I don't know much about him, but deference is apparently something he enjoys a great deal. His smile reveals tiny wrinkles at the corners of his eyes, but they don't detract from his good looks—quite the opposite.

Now that I'm inside, I can see how attractive he really is. He's tall and lean with lightly tanned skin and thick dark hair. His eyes are hazel with long lashes, and the sharp angles of his face compliment his rather long straight nose. His only softening feature is his lips, which are now smirking at me as I stare up at him open-mouthed. There's something a bit haughty about his face, and I change my impression of him from TV lawyer to English aristocrat in a historical drama –the lord of the manor. The fact that he's so handsome doesn't put me at ease. With his good looks, if he has to hire a girl to have sex with him, he must want something out of the ordinary. Something *way* out of the ordinary. I shiver at the thought and he notices immediately, the amused look in his eyes replaced by a serious one.

"Would you like something to eat?" he asks, surprising me.

"No, thank you."

"If you're hungry, I want to know," he says in a firm tone.

"I'm not, Sir, I promise. I already ate."

He watches me closely for a few seconds before giving me a small nod. "Come with me, then," he says, leading me upstairs. We pass several doors on the first floor before entering a huge, luxurious bathroom.

"I want you to take a shower," he directs. "Use all the products I've put out and dry your hair afterward. Then put this on and come join me in the kitchen. Understood?" He points to a pretty white dress on a hanger by the door.

"Uh, y-yes, Sir."

"Very good."

I feel a bit shell-shocked after he's left. He wants me to shower? I sniff under my arms but can't find anything wrong with the way I smell. I showered at home right before dropping off Luke, so I'm already clean. What a weirdo.

Regardless, I do as I'm told, locking the door to the bathroom first and removing what little makeup I have on before getting into the shower. Mr. Thorne has put out both shampoo and conditioner, expensive salon brands that I could never afford myself. Turning to the third bottle in the shower, I frown and try my best to read the label, but my high-school French isn't proficient. I pour some of it in my hand and the texture tells me it's some kind of exfoliating body scrub, which I use all over. It smells like flowers. After I've rinsed myself, I quickly dry off with a fluffy towel and wrap a smaller one around my head. On the table next to the sink, I spot a comb, a brush, and a bottle like the French one in the shower, this one labeled *Lait pour le corps.*

Use all the products.

Dropping the towel, I apply the body lotion carefully all over, wondering why Mr. Thorne wants me to do all this in the first place. It's creepy.

It rubs the lotion on its skin.

"Stop it," I whisper to myself as I start on my hair. It's weird that I have to go through all this preparation, but it doesn't mean Mr. Thorne's a serial killer. He's probably just neat and prefers his women really clean. After I've blow-dried my hair, I turn to the dress, faced with a dilemma. Mr. Thorne hasn't provided me with any underwear, so does that mean I should wear my own or forego them completely? Since my own clothes apparently aren't up to his standards, I decide that my inexpensive underwear probably isn't either and decide to go commando. Hell, I'm probably here to have sex with the guy, after all. Slipping it over my head, I stand in front of the mirror, turning slowly. I look sweet and innocent, practically virginal in the white sundress with its delicate lace trimmings. Is this what he likes? Taking a deep breath, I unlock the door and make my way downstairs, barefoot and feeling very exposed. I find him at the kitchen table, poring over a stack of papers. I clear my throat softly, but he doesn't respond.

"Mr. Thorne?"

He looks up, piercing me with his gaze. "Never interrupt me when I'm working."

My mouth drops open. *God, he's so rude!* "I'm sorry, Sir."

He stands and approaches me, looking me over with interest. "You're forgiven," he says. "Did you want to ask me something?"

"Well, yes. What ... should I have done when I came down here?" I don't want to annoy him. I need him to be happy with me, so he'll want to see me—and pay me—again.

"You should have waited for me to address you first. You're here for *me*, not the other way around. Tonight, you're mine to do with as I please. All you have to do is obey."

"Y-yes, Sir." I can't keep my nervousness from showing through my voice.

"Don't be scared," he says in a surprisingly gentle voice, tucking a lock of hair behind my ear. I draw a deep breath, willing myself not to let my emotions get the best of me.

Mr. Thorne smiles at me, running his fingers across the apple of my cheek. "There's a good girl. You ready to let me be in charge?"

I nod, bracing myself for whatever he might inflict upon me.

"Very good," he says, nodding. "Abigail, I'd like you to make me an apple pie."

What. The. Fuck?

CHAPTER FIVE

"A-an apple pie, Sir?" I stutter. *Is that slang for some sort of sex act?*

"You commented on the apple turnover last night," he reminds me. "You *can* bake, yes?"

"Oh, yes, Sir." I nod eagerly, beyond relieved that he really is just talking about pie.

"Good." He makes a sweeping gesture with his hand toward the cooking area. "Feel free to make yourself at home in my kitchen. You may begin."

Still unsure, I rummage through the cupboards and the fridge, gathering bowls, utensils, and ingredients, and do my best to ignore the hawklike way Mr. Thorne watches me. After a minute, he finally takes his seat again, and I feel as though I can relax a bit more. His kitchen is every chef's dream, but I can't enjoy the surroundings. I feel as though I'm auditioning for a part, but I have no clue what role I'm up for. I thought he was just looking for sex, but it seems I'm here for more than that.

As I begin to make the crust, Mr. Thorne stands up and walks over. I can feel him behind me, observing, and it makes me nervous. I jump a little as his hands thread into my hair,

27

gathering it and wrapping something around it to sweep it up. He leans down and inhales deeply against the skin on my now exposed neck.

"Lovely," he murmurs.

I don't know if I should respond, so I stand perfectly still, my hands still buried in the flour mixture, my heart in my throat. I wish I knew what he wants from me.

"Keep working," he urges.

I do as I'm told, gently mixing the ingredients while he watches over my shoulder. His warm fingers fiddle with one of the thin straps of the dress I'm wearing and, suddenly, he pushes it all the way down to the crook of my elbow, exposing my left breast.

"That's perfect," he whispers in my ear. "Just like that."

I'm mortified. He walks back to his seat and starts working again, as though nothing is out of the ordinary. Meanwhile, I have no choice but to keep baking, very much aware of the fact that it makes my breasts jiggle with each move I make. It feels obscene. We're in the kitchen! I glance over to where Mr. Thorne is sitting and find him watching me, yet again, while tapping his pen against his lips.

Doing my best to suppress my sense of modesty, I remind myself of the money and start peeling and slicing the apples. After I've placed them on top of the crust, I mix granulated sugar and cinnamon in a small bowl. But before I sprinkle it over the apple slices, I pause. Not everyone likes cinnamon in their apple pie. Does Mr. Thorne? I don't want to take a chance on this. It seems like this pie is important, and I can't risk making something he won't enjoy. I look over at him, but he's not watching me now.

"M—" I press my lips together, stopping the sound immediately. *Shit! Don't interrupt him while he's working. Did he notice?*

I look over again, but thankfully he's still bent over his papers. Picking up the small bowl, I approach the table and stand still next to his chair, saying nothing. The urge to cover myself is strong, but I suppress it. For a few minutes, I'm rooted to the spot while he ignores me. I feel like an object, standing here with my breast hanging out, not moving or saying a word. Finally, he looks up at me, smiling.

"Yes, Abigail?" he asks, clearly pleased at my behavior.

"Excuse me, Sir. I was wondering if you like cinnamon in your pie?" I hold the bowl out to show him. You know, in case he doesn't know what cinnamon is. God, I'm an idiot.

"Well, let's see now," he says, wrapping his long fingers around my wrist, pulling me closer to him. He opens his mouth and taps the tip of his index finger against his tongue before dipping it in the bowl and then tasting the sugar and cinnamon mixture.

"Hmm," he says, looking up at me. "What do you think?" Putting more of it on his finger, he pushes it between my parted lips. "Suck," he orders.

I do as I'm told, hollowing out my cheeks.

"Well?" he prompts, leaning in to nuzzle my breast.

"I like cinnamon," I whisper. The gentleness of his touch, and the fact that I don't hate the sensation of it, shocks me.

"As do I."

I gasp as he wraps his lips around my exposed nipple, flicking across it with his tongue. His eyes meet mine and he grins around my sensitive flesh as his hands start trailing up the length of my thighs, slipping underneath the dress. I turn red as his large hands cup my bottom, giving it a gentle squeeze.

"No underwear," he murmurs after he's released my nipple. "You naughty girl."

He starts exploring underneath the fabric. His touches are slow—lazy almost—while he watches my face the whole time. My breath hitches in my throat as he parts me, and a fingertip comes in contact with my most sensitive place. His touches bear witness to his level of experience. There's no fumbling around—he knows what he's doing.

29

"I'm sorry," I whisper. "You didn't give me any, and I didn't think you'd like the ones I have."

"You wanted to please me?"

I nod, inhaling as his fingers brush against my entrance. The teasing little touch causes a tiny spasm inside me, a reaction I did not expect. As he leans in to kiss my breast it happens again.

"That's good," he murmurs. "You really are a sweet girl, aren't you, Abigail?"

"Yes, Sir." *Well, at least I used to be. Now I don't know what to call myself.*

He looks up at me, still gently caressing between my legs. "Have you had sex before?" His voice is soft, soothing almost. I nod, surprised at how my response makes his features relax. I guess he didn't want a virgin.

Mr. Thorne removes his hands from me and pulls the other strap down, which makes the dress fall off me completely. Once again, I can't help but recall the words spoken by the manager and bouncer at the strip club, and I curl my shoulders, wanting to hide my nakedness.

"Don't," he orders. "Let me look at you."

I draw a shuddering breath, forcing my back to straighten. His eyes scan me from head to toe, pausing on areas that are of particular interest to him before looking at my face. Blindly, he moves his paperwork as well as the cinnamon sugar aside, never taking his eyes off me. When he suddenly rises, I take a step back, overwhelmed by his height. Standing naked in front of him while he's still fully dressed makes me feel especially vulnerable, and I yelp when he grabs me, spinning me around to press himself against me from behind.

"I won't hurt you," he whispers in my ear, stroking my arms. "Relax."

His hands move up and down my body, gentle and firm at the same time, and his lips caress the side of my neck. I feel him taking my hair down and inhaling its scent deeply.

"I'm going to fuck you right here on this table."

I inhale sharply at the roughness of his voice. A startling feeling of satisfaction rushes through me, knowing he wants me this badly, knowing this beautiful man finds me desirable.

"You'll let me do that, won't you, Abigail?"

"Y-yes, Sir."

"Good girl. Bend over."

I obey, trembling lightly as I place my upper body on the cool surface of the table and close my eyes.

"Spread your legs."

Drawing a deep breath, I move my feet apart, exposing myself to Mr. Thorne.

"Beautiful," he says softly. His hands are back on me again a second later, caressing me with certain touches. His fingers rub gently, exploring me. They disappear, but a moment later they're back, wet from his saliva, dipping inside me while his thumb moves to rub tight circles on my outside, making me breathe faster. It feels good, but I don't understand why he bothers.

"That's it," he says, sounding very pleased. "Get my fingers nice and wet."

I sort of hate that my body seems to like what he's doing. It makes it a lot harder to remain detached from this. On the other hand, I'm grateful he hasn't just plowed into me, which would undoubtedly hurt. A moment later, he stops touching me and I hear him rustling around, followed by the sound of his zipper. The crackle of the condom wrapper relaxes me; I have a good inclination that Mr. Thorne's sexual past is very different from mine, and I know I'd have to insist on him wearing one.

"You want this, pretty girl?"

I feel him sliding against me, through my wetness, caressing my hip with his free hand. I nod my head, puzzled that he's even asking at all. I'm here for *him*, just as he said.

"Tell me," he orders. "I want to hear you say it."

31

"I want it." The words are barely out before he pushes inside, making me gasp loudly. He's very big, stretching me to the point of discomfort at first, and he has to ease his way in and out a few times before he's able to penetrate me completely.

"Fuck, yes," Mr. Thorne moans. "You'd better hold on to something."

Two seconds later, I understand why. He fucks me like he's trying to move the sturdy table across the kitchen floor, and my arms flail out as I manage to hold on to the edge of it, protecting my poor thighs from colliding too hard with the wood. A moment later, he grabs my hips, pulling me back against him, our skin slapping together each time my backside meets his front. It's better this way—much better. My body certainly seems to think so.

I cry out, more from surprise than pain, when Mr. Thorne pulls my hair, forcing me up on my elbows. He reaches underneath me, kneading my breasts, while he leans in to groan in my ear.

"So sweet, so tight around me. You're my good girl, right, Abigail?"

"Yes, Sir."

"Louder!" he commands, fucking me harder and faster.

"Yes, Sir. Yes, Mr. Thorne!" I cry, obeying him.

"Fuck, yes!" His hands return to my hips, moving my body with his, taking my body with his as he pulls me back onto his thick cock again and again. I've never experienced sex like this before—so aggressive and wild. It scares me a little even though it doesn't hurt at all. I can feel how wet I am, and it embarrasses me how positively my body is responding to him, how easily the feeling of him inside me switched from strange to welcome. Mr. Thorne comes with a loud groan, his body sinking down on mine as his hips still thrust slowly. I lay down flat on the surface, feeling his shirt buttons against my naked back.

"Mmm," he pants, delivering a gentle bite to my shoulder. "So sweet."

My face feels hot and my body is restless, but I make myself lay perfectly still while he recovers, nuzzling my hair and breathing deeply. I remain still as he gets off me, removing the used condom and zipping his pants.

"Up you go," he says, patting my hip. He turns me around and makes me look up at him. "You've never done that before —been fucked like that."

It's not a question. I shake my head, feeling tears pool in my eyes.

"Stop that," he says firmly, but not unkindly. "No shame, no guilt. You're here for me. To please me."

I nod slowly, drawing a shaky breath.

"And I am," he adds.

"You're what, Mr. Thorne?"

"Pleased."

I breathe in again, deeply, through my nose. Unexpected warmth spreads through my chest, surprising me. He hands me the dress, helping me slip it back on, and then puts my hair back up, his touches slow and gentle as he fusses over me. The contrast between this and the way he grabbed me while I was bent over is startling.

"So, Abigail," he says, sounding formal once again. "I believe that's a 'yes' on the cinnamon query."

"Um, yes, Sir." *What a freaking weirdo.*

An hour later, I've cleaned up the kitchen and the pie has cooled off. Nervously, I serve it to Mr. Thorne. He takes a bite and looks up at me.

"Delicious, Abigail," he praises.

I can't help it—I smile widely, and before I can hide it away, Mr. Thorne returns it. He lifts his hand but retracts it again before it touches mine, his smile vanishing.

"You can go now," he says. "I'll call you a cab."

I'm about to protest when he holds up his hand.

"Do not disrespect me. I will, of course, pay the fare, since I'm the one who's ordering it."

"I'm sorry," I mumble.

"Put your own clothes back on," he says, dismissing me.

I run up to the bathroom and change as quickly as possible, eager for this confusing night to be over. I look at myself in the mirror. I just let a virtual stranger fuck the living daylights out of me. For money. And I may have enjoyed it a little. *Who the hell am I?*

Downstairs, Mr. Thorne's back to work. I wait quietly until he receives a text, telling him that the cab's arrived. Walking out into the hall, he reaches into his pocket and pulls out a manila envelope, handing it to me. Again, I resist the urge to thank him. I've performed a job, and now I'm getting paid.

"Good night," I whisper and turn my back to him, wrapping my fingers around the door handle.

"Abigail, do you cook?"

I close my eyes, trying to prepare myself for what I know is coming.

"Yes."

"I'd like for you to make me dinner on Wednesday night." Again, it's not a question.

"All right." I nod my head, feeling unsure.

"Eyes to me."

I just want to go home, but I turn to face him, forcing myself to meet his gaze.

"You did everything I asked of you," he says calmly. "You earned that money. There's nothing wrong with that."

"Yes, Sir," I whisper, wishing it were really that simple.

"Good girl. Be here at six on Wednesday and take a cab. I'll pay the fare when you get here."

I stare at him. He really wants to see me again. I've done it. It's what I wanted, but it also means that this isn't over. I can't just go home and wash the experience off me, knowing it was a one-time thing.

"Thank you, Mr. Thorne."

"Get home safely, Abigail."

I nod and he leads me out to the waiting taxi, where he holds the door open for me. He hands the driver a bill and tells him to take me wherever I want to go in the city. Then he heads back inside, not looking back.

The cab driver doesn't try to make conversation, which is a huge relief. I glance at my watch, surprised that it's only eleven o'clock, which means I've been at Mr. Thorne's for just three hours. Discreetly, I open the envelope he gave me, feeling my mouth drop open in surprise. Instead of the agreed-upon amount, I count ten—not five—hundred-dollar bills.

One thousand dollars. He paid me one thousand dollars!

I feel dizzy with happiness, and my uncertainty about seeing him again starts to fade. Maybe soon I'll be able to pay off everything I owe, and Luke and I will be able to stay in our apartment. I clutch the envelope to my chest, feeling tears drip down onto my hands. My hair and skin smell like apple pie and Mr. Thorne's cologne, a reminder of what I've done tonight, but in this moment, I don't feel any guilt or shame.

"Hey, you okay, lady?" the driver asks, looking at me with concerned eyes in the rearview mirror.

"Yes," I croak. "I think I will be."

CHAPTER SIX

Jo is the only person I still speak to from my high school,
which is strange since I didn't really talk to her back then.
I've realized that had more to do with my parents not
thinking she was "good company" than any dislike on my part,
but there was only so much I could get away with. Jo was wild
back then. She partied a lot and became pregnant our junior
year, leaving town to have her baby. We found each other in
the city, one year after Luke was born, both of us in similar
circumstances. She kicked her boyfriend Thomas out last year
and has been raising her two girls on her own since then. She's
my only friend in the world.

On Wednesday around noon, Luke and I head over to the
diner where Jo works. I'm being frugal with the money I've
made, but I decide to treat us to a hot lunch since I need to ask
her about watching Luke tonight. I can't keep burdening Mrs.
Watt and I know Luke would much rather stay at Jo's if given
the choice.

Jo looks a bit worn in her hideous pink uniform, but perks
up at the sight of us. After Luke is settled in with an order of
fries and a coloring book, I join her at the counter, which is the

most privacy we can hope for at the moment. It's on a day like today that I wish I could afford preschool for Luke.

"So," Jo starts, pouring me a much-needed cup of coffee. "Still no word from the douche?"

I shake my head. As far as I know, Patrick could have left the country. But odds are that he hasn't. It's more likely he's with another woman somewhere, since I suspected he was seeing someone before he left.

"We really know how to pick 'em, huh?" She laughs, but it's not a happy sound.

"Yeah." We've had this conversation before and I don't feel like having it again. I like her ex-boyfriend. Thomas is a screwup, I can't deny that, but he has a good heart and it's in the right place. He loves Jo and their daughters, and he's never left them. I know he still helps out and wants to be in their lives, even though Jo ended things between them. He's nothing like Patrick.

I change the subject quickly. "Jo, I need your help."

"Shoot."

"Can you watch Luke for me tonight? Can he have dinner at your place?"

"Sure. When are you dropping him off?"

"I have to be somewhere at six, so probably half an hour before that."

Jo nods and wipes off the counter.

"You're not going to ask me where I'm going?" I blurt out after a few seconds.

She gives me a curious look. "Well, I wasn't," she drawls, "but it sounds like you really want to tell me."

I realize she's right. I do want to tell her. I know Jo won't judge me; she's not that type. And maybe her acceptance will assuage the indecision I'm starting to feel again. Mr. Thorne made it sound so simple: I'm doing a job and getting paid, no shame in that. But it's less convincing now that it's been a few days, and I have no idea what to expect of my visit at his house tonight.

"I sort of got a job," I confess. "But it's not exactly something to be proud of."

Jo frowns. "You're not in trouble, are you, Abbi?"

I shake my head, looking over to check on Luke, who's happily eating his greasy lunch. The sight makes me smile. "No, nothing like that. I'm ... I guess I'm a call girl, or whatever you call it," I whisper. "But just for one guy."

Jo's lips part and she inhales sharply. "Holy shit! Of all the things you could have said, I never would've—holy *shit*, Abbi!"

"Yeah, I know," I mumble. "I needed the money. I'm doing this for Luke."

I see the pity she feels for me all over her sad expression. "Why didn't you ask me?"

"Because you would've given it to me. And you're barely making ends meet as it is."

"Oh, Abbi." Jo excuses herself to help a customer and then returns, pouring herself a cup of coffee. "Okay, you need to start from the beginning."

I tell her everything: the failed audition at the strip club, getting picked up by Mr. Thorne, the visit to his house, baking pie for him, and finally, getting screwed on his kitchen table before he paid me twice what we'd agreed on. By the time I'm done, Jo's eyes have widened to near-comical proportions.

"And I have to be at his house at six tonight," I add.

"Yeah," she says. "I figured." Still wearing a shocked expression, she leaves again to help another customer. I check in on Luke, who's happily coloring and looking at his comic books.

"You want my opinion?" Jo asks after she comes back. I nod. "I think you're in way over your head, hon. That guy—well, he sounds pretty weird."

I frown. Mr. Thorne definitely has some quirks, but that doesn't mean he can't be nice too. He wasn't so bad.

Now I'm defending him?

"I mean, it sounds to me like he might be one of those ..." She glances around and leans in. "You know, those guys who get off tying up women and whipping them."

"W-what?" I sputter. "He's never mentioned anything like that!"

"Yet," she says in an ominous-sounding voice. "Come on, Abbi. He said he wanted to be in charge, you have to call him Sir, he held you down and fucked you, *and* he paid you double."

"What does that have to do with—"

"To lure you back, to get you hooked on the money, so you'll let him do more of that stuff. How do you know he doesn't have a dungeon or something in the basement?"

"I don't," I admit. I don't know anything about Mr. Thorne except that he likes cleanliness, punctuality, and women who do what he says.

"Look," Jo sighs. "I'm not saying you shouldn't keep doing this. I mean, I *know* how badly you need the money, so I totally get it. But, it's like you said—he's a good-looking, rich guy. Why is he paying for sex in the first place when he could just use a hookup app?"

I don't have a good answer for her.

"If he's looking for someone to do that S&M stuff with, would you do it?"

I shake my head. I don't know much about that kind of thing but being tied up and whipped sounds awful. There's no way I could ever do that. What if Mr. Thorne really does have a dungeon in the basement of his house? The thought makes me shiver.

"Hey, are you scared of him?" Jo asks, placing her hand on top of mine.

"No. I don't get a threatening vibe from him, if that makes any sense? I wouldn't have gone with him in the first place if I did."

Jo nods.

"But if he really is into tying me up and hitting me, that's not something I can do. I have to tell him that."

"Give me the guy's address when you drop Luke off this afternoon, okay? At the very least, I'll know where you are."

"I will. Thanks, Jo."

"I'm glad you told me."

"Me, too."

"So, how long do you think he wants to keep seeing you?" she asks.

I shrug. "I don't know. He hasn't said anything about that. For all I know, tonight could be the last time I ever see him. It's not like we're on a schedule. I need to get a real job. Maybe the strip club will work out once I gain a bit of weight. I used to be pretty."

"Oh, I remember," Jo chuckles. "The teen dream. And you're still pretty. Why else would your Sir pay so much?"

"I make a mean apple pie?"

Jo snorts into her coffee. "I think it's your other pie he's after."

I roll my eyes. "Don't remind me."

"Was it awful?" she whispers, all traces of humor vanished.

"I don't know. Not really. It was different. You know, sort of rough, I guess. But it didn't hurt or anything like that. It was ..." *Pretty okay. A little exciting, even. God, what's wrong with me?*

"Worth the money?" Jo asks.

I look over at Luke and nod. "Absolutely."

A few minutes later, I join Luke at the table and try my best to eat my lunch. However, the thought of telling Mr. Thorne there are some lines I won't cross is making me far more nervous than when I was just going over there to cook and have sex. All I know about S&M is that there's pain involved, and he promised he wouldn't hurt me, so he can't expect something like that from me. Or can he? Jo is right. I need to tell him. Now I just have to figure out a way to do that.

CHAPTER SEVEN

Getting to Mr. Thorne's on time is easy now that I only have to hail a cab to take me there. As promised, he comes outside to pay the driver the moment we pull up. He doesn't turn his attention to me until the cab has left.

"Good evening, Abigail," he greets. "You look lovely tonight."

"Thank you, Sir." I'm wearing my prettiest skirt and blouse to get on his good side, and I'm glad to see that he approves. I wonder if this means I can skip the shower-and-change routine.

"Come inside." He leads me through the door, his hand resting on the small of my back. The gentlemanly gesture takes me by surprise. The moment we're behind the closed door, his hand slides lower, giving my ass a squeeze before pulling me against his tall frame. Both hands slip underneath the fabric, skimming my naked thighs.

"Are you going to be a good girl for me tonight?"

"Wait, Mr. Thorne—" Nervously, I take a few steps back, out of his arms. "Can we please talk about something before we—er, start?"

"Abigail, is something the matter?" he asks, frowning.

"Well, no. I mean, not exactly. Mr. Thorne, I don't have a lot of experience with this."

"I realize that."

"Right. But I have to ask. Are you ..." I can't get the words out. He's looking at me, his eyebrows raised, hands buried in his pockets. His stance isn't threatening, but his presence is intimidating.

"Am I what, Abigail?"

"Um, do you like, you know ... S&M?" I squeak out the last syllable and then hold my breath. *I can't believe I just asked him that.*

He shoots me a roguish grin, his obvious amusement making him look much younger. "What do you know about S&M?" he asks, taking a step closer.

"Very little," I whisper. "It's about getting tied up and whipped or beaten, right?"

"It can be," he answers calmly.

"And do you want ... that?"

"No."

"No?"

"I won't deny that my inclinations are a bit different than the norm, but I don't define my preferences like that. There are some aspects of the BDSM lifestyle that I do enjoy, though."

I gape at him. He's *so* casual about this.

"W-what aspects?" I ask, feeling my eyes tear up. "'Cause the whole whipping thing—I can't do that! I'm really grateful that you paid me all that money, and I do need it, but I'm scared you'll hurt me—"

"Abigail, easy," he soothes, producing a folded handkerchief from his pocket. Gently, he dabs my eyes with one hand while he runs the other one down the length of my hair.

"Listen to me," he says, tilting my head up so I'm forced to look into his eyes. "I won't deny that I like submissive women, because I do. And I might find it enjoyable to tie you to my bed before I fuck you."

I gasp.

"I may even want to spank your pretty little ass sometimes."

I start to shake my head, but he stops me, holding my chin between his thumb and index finger. "But, Abigail, I can promise you: It will be for pleasure, *not* punishment."

"I don't see the difference," I admit.

"It's really very simple," Mr. Thorne says, taking my hand and giving it a gentle tug. "Come with me."

Obediently, I follow him into the kitchen, where he sits me down before pouring me a glass of water. He stands behind me, gently kneading my shoulders while I take a sip, and I can't help but notice how it's almost affectionate.

"I enjoy submission," he tells me, "but not punishment. Playrooms and instruments do very little for me. I don't want you to fear me; I want you to show me respect. Doling out pain doesn't turn me on—neither does humiliation."

"What *does* turn you on?" I know how the question sounds, but I'm not trying to be coy. I genuinely want to know if I'll be able to do the things he likes.

"You," he answers simply. "Doing what I say."

"Oh." I breathe out with relief before I turn my head and glance up at him. "So if you tell me to jump, I ask how high?"

His lips twitch. "No, Abigail. If I tell you to jump, you start jumping until I tell you to stop."

I nod, swallowing reflexively as a twinge of fear passes through me. Holding my gaze, he leans down until we're eye to eye.

"I already told you, I don't get off on inflicting pain. That's not what this is about."

"So, you don't have a d-dungeon in the basement?"

His warm breath wafts across my skin as he laughs softly, giving my shoulders a small squeeze. "No. Nothing like that."

"Okay."

"You gonna be my good girl from now on?" he asks.

"Yes, Sir."

He leans in closer, his lips touching the shell of my ear. "You won't regret it," he whispers.

Well, that remains to be seen. Knowing that he's not interested in hurting me is reassuring, though.

He moves to stand in front of me, reaching out his hand. When I take it, he pulls me up, back into his arms. "Anything else you'd like to ask me?"

"Are you married?"

His eyes narrow and his voice turns glacial. "Why would you ask me that?"

Oh, shit. "I'm sorry. You're very ... I mean, most men your age are ..." I avoid his eyes.

He draws a breath, letting go of me. "I'm no longer married."

I look at him, relieved to see his expression warming again. I won't ask if he has children, worried that he might turn the question on me if I do. He can never know about Luke. I've had guys hit on me at the park only to practically run away once they realized I'm not Luke's older sister or babysitter. I don't know if Mr. Thorne would find me being a mom unattractive, but I can't take that chance with him.

"So, Abigail," he says. "Would you like a shower?"

"Not really." *Oops, that's probably not how I should put it.* "I mean, I just showered before coming over here, but if it's something you'd like for me to do, I'll do it, Sir."

He smiles. "Good answer. No, that's quite all right. I wasn't sure if you had access to one where you're staying."

Does he think I'm homeless? "I have an apartment."

"That's good." He looks relieved. "I'd like for you to wear the outfit I've put out in the bathroom. You remember where it is?"

"Yes, Sir." I resist the strange urge to curtsy as I exit the kitchen and hurry upstairs to change. Once again, there's no underwear, so I strip down and run a brush through my hair while I check my makeup. The dress is green with white polka dots. I pair it with the modest kitten heels he's left me and look myself over in the mirror. I guess I'm playing a 1950s housewife tonight, which is definitely the type of woman that Mr. Thorne likes.

Submissive.

I know the word, but I can't really identify with it. I guess it doesn't matter, as long as I can do a good job of pretending while I'm here. When I come back downstairs, Mr. Thorne is working at the table, and I stand quietly, waiting for him to address me. I'm nothing if not a fast learner. After a minute, he looks up, smiling appreciatively as his gaze wanders up my body.

"Wonderful," he says, standing up and leading me to the kitchen island. "Now, you said you could cook?"

"Yes, Sir. That is, as long as it's nothing too fancy."

"I'm sure you'll manage. I'd enjoy a home-cooked meal. Feel free to make me whatever you like," he says, gesturing toward the refrigerator.

"Yes, Sir."

He reaches into a drawer, pulling out a white apron which he ties around my waist. "Perfect," he says, nodding to himself. I don't miss the way his lips curve up in a satisfied smile. He must really like this outfit on me. As he leaves my side, he winks, giving my ass a playful squeeze.

"I'll be watching."

CHAPTER EIGHT

M r. Thorne sits back down at his table with a seemingly unending stack of paperwork while I begin the task of cooking his dinner. Inside the fridge, there are lots of choices, and I wonder what I should make. This feels like another test. For a moment, I consider a meatloaf, which is probably what Donna Reed or June Cleaver would make for their TV husbands but decide that might be too cliché. After all, I don't want him to think I'm making a joke out of this 1950s thing, unusual as it may be. His taste seems old-fashioned, so I decide on roast chicken with a side of mashed potatoes, gravy, and peas.

Putting the stuff I need out on the counter, I glance at Mr. Thorne and, unsurprisingly, find him observing me, apparently riveted by the fairly mundane tasks I'm performing. As our eyes meet, he smiles and stands up, walking over to stand behind me.

"Looks wonderful," he comments. I'm not sure if he's referring to the ingredients or me in the housewife getup.

"Thank you, Sir."

His hands trail up my bare arms, leaving goosebumps in their wake, before running back down to my waist and tugging

47

gently on the knot holding the apron together. "Someday, I think I'll tie you to my bed using this," he whispers, brushing his lips against the side of my neck.

"Y-yes, Sir," I whisper, gripping the edge of the counter as my stomach does a nervous flip.

"But not tonight," he continues. "We have plenty of time, don't we, Abigail?"

"Yes, Sir," I lie. As soon as I'm able to land another job, I'm out of here. I can't let him know that, though.

"I'm going up to my office," he says. "You're far too distracting. It's on the third floor, first door on the right. Come find me when everything's in the oven, okay?"

"Yes, Mr. Thorne."

He moves away, but a moment later he's back, pressing his lips against my cheek. "Thank you, Abigail," he whispers.

I watch as he gathers his papers, then walks past me into the hallway and up the stairs. As soon as he's out of sight, I draw a deep breath, pressing my fingertips against the spot he just kissed before getting to work.

Once everything except the chicken is ready, I check my watch and head upstairs, as I was told. Passing the second floor where the bathroom I've used is located, I continue up to the top of the house, following the soft sound of opera music. Although I was asked to come up here, I knock just the same, remembering how Mr. Thorne feels about interruptions.

"Come in."

I enter, drawing a quick breath. *Wow*. Mr. Thorne's office is breathtaking. Furnished with dark wood, there are bookshelves lining the walls, and a real working fireplace in front of a comfy-looking couch. My eyes are drawn to the large floor-to-ceiling windows that lead onto a balcony overlooking the bay. I can almost imagine curling up on that couch, sipping tea and reading a good book on a cold night while enjoying the warmth of the fireplace.

What it must be like to live in a place like this, to have this kind of money. I don't think of myself as a particularly materialistic person, but one day, I'd like to not worry where my son's next meal will come from, and know I have a steady income along with enough to save a little money each month. Hell, even living paycheck to paycheck sounds good to me at this point.

When we brought Luke home from the hospital, I promised him and myself that I'd give him more than our old, run-down apartment. I'd make a real life for us in which he'd have lots of friends and hobbies, go to a good school, and have a yard to play in. Now he's almost five and has none of those things. As far as I know, there are only two other kids in the building, and they're a lot older than Luke. Most days, he's stuck with me. I know he doesn't see it that way and I do my best to come up with fun activities that also have an element of learning. Still, I'd like for him to get out more, play with other kids. We used to go to a nearby park, but a few weeks ago he picked up a syringe near the monkey bars and we haven't been back since. I hate that we live in such a shitty neighborhood. I hate that one day he'll realize what a crappy deal he's been handed in life—no grandparents, a father who left him, and a mother who can't properly support him. He'll never experience a view like this, or a life without financial worries.

"Abigail?"

Instantly, I'm jolted back to reality. "I'm sorry, Sir." Mortified, I realize I'm on the verge of tears, and turn away from Mr. Thorne.

"Come here." It's not a request. "Come on," he beckons, holding out his hand to me.

As soon as I reach him, he pulls me down onto his lap, a surprisingly soft expression on his face. "Want to tell me what happened just now?"

"I'm sorry," I whisper, shaking my head. "I was overwhelmed. It won't happen again. I've just never been in a house like this before. You have so much."

"You've been having a rough time, haven't you?"

I look up, meeting his eyes. They're so kind right now. Slowly, I nod.

He nods back. "You don't have to worry anymore," he says. "You take good care of me, and I'll take good care of you."

"How do I do that?" I feel like I'm constantly screwing up, always crying in front of him. I'm supposed to be here for him, not the other way around. "I mean, what is it that you want from me, Mr. Thorne?"

He settles me more comfortably in his lap, cradling me in his embrace. "In a word," he says, "worship."

"Worship?"

"I don't want you to merely cook and bake for me, Abigail. I want you to *want* to do those things, because you know they bring me enjoyment. I want you to *want* to please me. It's not about just taking orders from me. I like having you obey, but I'd like it even more if you did those things on your own."

I draw a deep breath, trying to gather my thoughts. He's never revealed so much about his motives before. "So ... treat you as if I worship you?"

"Mmm," he hums into my hair. "When you're here with me, I want that to be your only focus: how to make me happy."

He tilts my head up. He's so close, I can feel his breath against my lips.

"Abigail, tell me the truth. Are you afraid of me?" His eyes scan my face. "I know you were the first night in my car, and I don't blame you. That was a scary thing you did—going with a stranger like that—but I know you probably have a very good reason for taking that risk."

My heart slams against my ribcage. Could he possibly know about Luke?

"The money," he says after a few seconds, and I relax a little. "It's making things better for you?"

I nod my head, unwilling to elaborate.

"Good. That's good. Now, back to my previous question: Are you afraid of me?"

"Not really," I whisper.

"That's a very weak reply," he says in a stern voice.

"I'm sorry. I'm not afraid of you, like that you'll beat me up or kill me."

"But?" he prompts.

"The stuff you want—the sex stuff, saying you want to tie me up ... it scares me a little, yes."

"Thank you for your honesty," he says softly. "You seem very inexperienced. How many sexual partners have you had?"

My face flames, and I really want to tell him it's none of his business. But it is his business—he's paying for me to obey him—to *worship* him. Plus, like it or not, I'm now in a sexual relationship with Mr. Thorne and he'll likely want to do a lot more than I've ever done before. Honesty probably is the best policy, if this strange arrangement is ever going to work out.

"Two," I mumble, looking down. "Including you."

"I see."

I search his face, but his expression gives no clue as to what he's thinking.

After a beat he continues. "Thank you for telling me. So can I assume nearly everything will be a first for you, then?"

"Yes," I admit. "I haven't really done much of anything. On the table last time, that was adventurous for me."

"For me, as well."

I look up to see if he's joking, but he looks perfectly serious. Does that mean he hasn't done something like that before either?

"I'd like to do that again sometime," he whispers.

"Yes, Sir." Remembering what he said a minute ago, I add, "I'd like that, as well, Sir."

He draws me close and I rest my head on his shoulder. A

new song comes on, replacing the opera, and it's not what I expect.

"Springsteen?" I ask.

"You don't like him?" He strokes my hair all the way from the top of my head down my back. It feels nice, I have to admit.

"No, I like him. I just imagined you only listening to opera and classical stuff."

"I'm not *that* old," he chuckles.

"No, you're not," I agree.

His arms feel good around me, the music is nice, and the room is so warm. For a moment, I can almost pretend that everything is fine and someone else is taking care of me for a change. I close my eyes, melting into his caress. He doesn't ask anything of me, no sexual favors or acting like something I'm not. He just holds me. It doesn't feel like I'm worshipping him. It almost feels the other way around. I don't understand him at all, and while I still think he's sort of a weirdo, I could get used to this.

"Mmm," Mr. Thorne sighs, running his fingers through my hair. "My sweet girl."

Yes, I can be his sweet girl. At least I think I can. For a little while.

CHAPTER NINE

The Springsteen song ends and the silence breaks the spell I'm under. Mr. Thorne's arms, which felt comforting a moment ago, now make me feel claustrophobic. What am I doing, snuggling up with him? I'm his goddamned escort, and here I am, acting like a clingy girlfriend in need of comfort. I can't help but tense up and he notices immediately.

"Abigail?"

"I'm sorry. I should probably go check on dinner, Sir."

Mr. Thorne tightens his arms around me for a moment and then lets me go. I climb off his lap, standing next to his chair with my hands folded in front of me. Now I feel like a servant again, which is exactly how it should be. I wish he hadn't been so affectionate with me, and I wish I hadn't liked it so much.

"How long until it's done?" he asks.

I need to check on the chicken, which should be done by now, and reheat the side dishes. "Fifteen minutes, Sir," I say, looking down to hide my discomfort.

"I'd like for you to set the table in the dining room. I'll expect to be served in *precisely* fifteen minutes." His voice is stern now. I guess he, too, has realized that I crossed a line by cuddling with him.

"Yes, Sir."

"You're excused."

I practically flee the room, my exposed skin chilled from the change in mood. Rushing downstairs to the kitchen, I pull the chicken out of the oven and check it, sighing with relief that it is, in fact, done. I cover it to keep it warm, set the dials on the stove to low, and go in search of the dining room, which I've never seen before.

When I locate it, I find myself once again gaping at the beauty of this house. The room is very large and could host twenty people for a dinner party, but looks like it's rarely used. I wonder why Mr. Thorne wants to eat in here all by himself instead of sitting in the kitchen where it's somewhat cozier, but it's not my place to question him. I'm merely the hired help.

In one of the cabinets, I find what I assume is the fancy china and wine glasses, and make up a single place setting at the end of the table. Back in the kitchen, I load the food into pretty serving dishes and carry them with me, hoping everything will be hot enough. I realize I have nothing to pour into his wine glass, but I can't do much about that without his instructions. In the kitchen, he has some kind of special wine refrigerator, and I'm sure those bottles cost more than—well, me. No way am I messing up by opening the wrong one.

Two minutes later, he arrives, just as I'm leaning over the table to light the two tapers I found in the cupboard along with the cloth napkins.

"Perfect timing, I see."

I look over and can't help but smile at his pleased expression, happy that he's seemingly forgotten my clingy embrace upstairs.

"Everything looks and smells wonderful," he praises, walking over to where I'm standing.

"Thank you, Sir. I do need your opinion, though."

"Oh?"

"I don't know much about wine, and I didn't want to open the wrong bottle," I explain. "They look ... very expensive?"

"They are," he says, nodding. "That was very thoughtful of you. I'll go get one."

I breathe out as he leaves. Everything I do seems like a test, but at least it feels as though I'm passing some of the time. Mr. Thorne returns with an open bottle of red wine and takes his seat. Then he looks up at me, as if he's waiting for me to do something.

Am I supposed to serve him? It seems I am, so I start by pouring him some wine before loading food onto his plate, being very careful not to spill anything. All the while, he watches me, a small smile on his face. He *really* likes this whole serving bit.

When I'm done, I turn to leave, only to have him pull me back.

"Stay," he orders, taking the first bite of his dinner. He hums appreciatively and looks up at me. "Delicious. You're a very good cook, sweet girl."

I flush with pleasure. Another test passed.

"Thank you, S-Sir," I stutter, feeling his free hand slide up the back of my leg, underneath the full skirt of the dress. He continues eating with his left hand, while the right gently kneads my naked cheeks. I'm too stunned to feel embarrassed.

"These potatoes are very good," he comments, loading another forkful. "Spread your legs."

His command is given in the same pleasant voice he used to compliment my cooking, and I don't have to look at him to see that he's smiling to himself. I can hear it. He loves this.

I move my feet apart, pressing my lips together to stop from gasping as his fingers slip between my legs. He starts out slowly, warming me up, I guess. His touch is gentle, stroking the sensitive skin on my inner thighs before moving to part me, playing me like a well-loved instrument. I know it shouldn't feel good to me, but I can't deny that it does. My libido, which has been pretty much nonexistent ever since Luke was born, seems to have been awakened, and I don't know how to feel about the fact that it's happened at the hands of Mr. Thorne. He's very handsome and obviously knows what he's doing, but he's so weird at times and this isn't supposed to be about me.

For a few minutes he eats in silence, pausing only to taste his wine. His fingers are now sliding in and out of me effortlessly. Every ten seconds or so he pauses, spreading my wetness around, making me want to squirm. Wordlessly, he removes his hand, and I feel both relief and a twinge of regret.

"Clear the table, please."

I grab a plate and a serving bowl and hurry into the kitchen, drawing several calming breaths. As I make the trips back and forth to clear away everything except his wine, I do my best not to look directly at him, although I'm sure he can see how flushed my face is anyway. After placing the tray with the chicken on the kitchen counter, I walk back into the dining room, filled with trepidation, and stand quietly next to his chair. Now that the meal is over, he'll want sex. I'm sure of it.

"Eyes to me."

The look in his eyes, dark and lust-filled, twists my insides with nervousness, and I watch wordlessly as he pushes his chair back, making room between himself and the table and pointing to the space. I step in front of him, wondering if he wants me to kneel there.

"Lift your dress up, bend over the table, and present yourself to me," he orders in a rough-sounding voice.

Present myself? I wonder if I look as shocked as I feel, because he raises his eyebrows in a challenging way, as though he expects me to protest. I don't. My face burns, but I obey, placing my elbows on the table while fisting the hem of the dress. Somehow, I feel even more exposed than if I were completely naked. It feels so lewd.

"Mmm, so pretty." Mr. Thorne runs his hands over my

exposed thighs and backside. "So soft and pale. Spread your legs, Abigail."

I do as I'm told, cringing a little at the knowledge that Mr. Thorne will see how his touch affects me. He sighs contentedly behind me, his fingers slipping through the wetness I've created before dipping inside me.

"Such a good girl," he murmurs, turning his fingers so that his thumb finds the exact spot where I feel the most. His left hand kneads my buttocks and I close my eyes, not sure how to react. What he's doing to me feels good, but I don't want him to know. I can't give him that part of me. It's too private. Suddenly, his left hand is gone, and I startle as it connects with my skin, making a loud slapping sound.

For a few seconds, I'm frozen. The only sound in the room is his harsh breathing behind me. I hardly dare to draw a breath. Then his fingers start moving again, causing me to inhale sharply. I can't believe he did that. Well, actually, I can. This *is* Mr. Thorne, after all. Still, I thought he would have waited to do something like this and maybe prepared me in advance. Then I realize I wasn't apprehensive because I wasn't expecting it, and it didn't really hurt.

"Such a good girl," Mr. Thorne repeats, spanking me again.

I'm ready for it this time, and I try to focus on his fingers and his thumb, which are working me over like I've never experienced before, creating sensations I'd almost forgotten existed at all. I try to stop my hips from rocking, but it's nearly impossible.

"Uh!" I gasp as he spanks me for the third time, pressing my lips together immediately, as if that can somehow withdraw the sound. But Mr. Thorne must like hearing me, because his fingers move faster, causing me to bury my face against my arms to muffle my heavy breathing. I can't remember the last time I felt like this. I didn't know I was even able to feel like this anymore.

"Mmmf," I moan, squeezing my eyes shut against the pleasure as he continues to rub and thrust and slap in perfect harmony. My hips gyrate, silently begging him for more as his hand connects with my ass again ... and again ... and again.

Oh, God! Oh, God! I'm so close!

Abruptly, he stops. He turns me around and pushes me to my knees, reaching behind me to unzip my dress, and yanks it down, causing my breasts to pop out. I tremble as my body is denied what it wants, but I'm not sure if I'm disappointed or relieved that he stopped. I don't want to share something so intimate with him. I'm not ready for him to see me like that. This is a job, and my pleasure is not part of the deal.

Mr. Thorne stands, then unbuckles and unzips his pants, letting them drop to the floor. He's not wearing any underwear, either. I can't help but stare. He's long and thick, and so hard it looks almost painful. I look up at him, licking my lips nervously. I can guess what he wants, why he has me kneeling, but last time I didn't go through with it.

"I-I haven't done this a lot," I admit.

His answering smile is gentle. "I know." He reaches down to pull back my hair, angling my face upward.

"Open," he orders, tracing the outline of my mouth with his thumb. "And put your hands behind your back."

Drawing a deep breath, I comply.

"Use your tongue," he instructs, sliding in between my lips. "And no teeth."

I do my best, caressing him with my tongue as he thrusts slowly, going a bit deeper with each pass. His hands tangle in my hair and he moans.

"That's it. Good girl. Suck me."

His encouragement emboldens me and I pull him in deeper. He tastes good—clean and masculine. It isn't as scary as I thought it would be, and I'm shocked that I actually like doing this. My body warms and I have to suppress a moan.

"You want this?" he asks suddenly, pulling out to stroke himself right in front of my face.

"Yes, Sir." My answer falls from my lips without hesitation. It isn't until it's out there that I realize it's the truth.

"Do you want me to fuck you?"

I stare up at him, a resounding *yes* echoing in my mind.

"I think you do," he says, sliding back in between my parted lips. "I think you want to be fucked so badly. I think you're nearly dripping on my carpet right now."

I flush, because he's probably right.

"But you know what, Abigail? You won't get it until you beg for it. Can you do that for me?"

I close my eyes. I want to, but something holds me back. I'm not supposed to want this, and especially not from someone like him, a man I barely know.

"That's okay, sweet girl. In time," he tells me, tightening his hold on my hair. "Now, look at me."

He fucks my mouth with vigor, keeping his eyes on mine. When I gag around him, he tells me to breathe through my nose. It helps, but my eyes still water as I fight to take all of him. Still, I try. Sucking and moaning around him, I can't help but get into it, wanting him to come, to enjoy this.

"Fuck," he groans, his hips bucking uncontrollably. "Swallow me. Take it all." His movements still as he pulses in my mouth, and I try hard to obey, only coughing once as he finishes. Even so, it's a lot better than I thought it would be to have him come in my mouth, which is something I've never done before. I keep him in my mouth as he calms down above me, and his hands move from my hair to my cheeks. His thumbs wipe underneath my eyes and I look up at him. He has a serene smile on his face, and in that moment he's even more attractive than before. I feel the oddest sense of pride, knowing I've made him smile like that.

"Perfect," he tells me. "You were perfect."

CHAPTER TEN

Mr. Thorne is all smiles as he pulls out of my mouth and starts putting his clothes back in order. I remain kneeling on the floor, unsure what to do. Well, what I really want to do is brush my teeth—or at least drink something—but I remain where I am until he finishes dressing.

"Up you go," he says softly, reaching down to help me to my feet.

I wince as I stretch out my admittedly bony knees and I have to lean on him a little until the ache subsides. I didn't used to be this frail, but I've lost a lot of muscle tone and endurance since my cheerleading days, and not eating properly certainly hasn't helped.

"Easy," Mr. Thorne whispers, sitting down with me in his lap. Gently, he runs his hands across my legs. "Next time, we'll get you a pillow, hmm?" he says, massaging my knees.

"Thank you, Sir. That would be good."

"Are you all right?" he asks.

I nod my head, surprised by his question. I'm not sure if he's referring to my legs or the blow job. His concern is nice, though. His hands trail upward to my bare breasts, brushing over my stiff nipples. I bite back a moan as he gives them both a little tug before pulling the dress back in place, covering me up. When I dare to look up at him, he's wearing a smirk, obviously quite aware of the fact that he's aroused me.

"Are you able to stand now?" he asks.

"Yes, Sir."

"Good. I'd like for you to reheat the food and bring me a fresh plate and utensils."

I climb off his lap and do as I'm told. Once the food is hot again, I serve him another plate, only to have him pull me back onto his lap, where he settles me comfortably. I stare at him as he loads some mashed potatoes onto his fork and holds it up to my mouth.

"Open."

"Sir?"

"I want to feed you," he says, as though that's perfectly normal.

Um, okay. I accept the offering, and he smiles.

"Good girl. You need a bit more meat on your bones."

"I'm working on it," I whisper.

He nods, placing the fork on the plate as he reaches for the wine glass, bringing it to my lips. I don't like wine at all, but I take a sip anyway, not able to hide the way my lips pucker as the sour taste hits my tongue.

Mr. Thorne laughs, setting down the glass. "You don't drink wine?"

"No, Sir." I went to some parties in high school, but I haven't had a drink since becoming pregnant.

"I don't drink soda myself, but I believe there's some in the fridge for the cleaning staff and the gardeners," Mr. Thorne says.

"Not even at the movies?" I blurt out. "Er, soda, I mean."

"The movies?" He looks surprised. "I honestly can't remember the last time I went to a movie." He helps me off his lap. "Go get your soda. Then we can talk some more while you eat."

Two minutes later, I'm back on his lap, being fed dinner, a tall glass of Coke next to the plate.

"So, do you go to the movies a lot, Abigail?"

I shake my head, swallowing. "Too expensive," I elaborate. While I know Mr. Thorne is aware of my financial circumstances, it still makes me uncomfortable to discuss it.

"Of course," he murmurs. "That's a shame. A young woman like you should enjoy herself."

He seems genuinely regretful for me. Slowly, I move my hands from my lap and run them up his torso, holding him around his neck. "This is pretty enjoyable," I say.

He observes me for a moment, the fork paused mid-air between the plate and my mouth. Then, he smiles. "That it is."

I return the smile before taking another bite of food. "What's your favorite movie?" I ask after I've swallowed.

His eyebrows go up and his lips purse. "I don't know," he says, offering me a drink. "I don't have much time for movies anymore."

"You work a lot."

He nods.

"Well, if you did have the time, what would you watch?"

"Indiana Jones, probably."

My mouth drops open. That definitely wasn't the answer I was expecting. I thought he'd mention an old black-and-white film, not an action movie.

"Seriously? I mean, uh, really, Sir?"

"Hey, I'm a child of the eighties," he says with a grin.

"So, um, how old would that make you?"

"Thirty-nine."

I observe him more closely than I have before. I thought he was a little older, but maybe that's because of how he dresses and does his hair. I try to imagine him in a T-shirt and jeans with unstyled hair, but I can't. Besides, I like that he dresses nicely. He's quite ... sexy. I've always had a thing for older men in movies and on TV, though I never thought I'd ever actually be with one in real life.

I realize I'm staring at him and when I meet his eyes, my face heats. He tilts my head up, holding my chin.

"Not too old to make you blush, pretty girl?" he asks, his hazel eyes lit with amusement.

"No," I whisper, "not too old, Sir."

"Good to know." He offers me another bite, which I accept. I'm feeling more comfortable speaking with him now, and he seems very open at the moment. I don't want there to be any weirdness between us.

"I'm sorry about earlier. In your office ... I shouldn't have."

"Shouldn't have what?" he asks. "Sought comfort?"

I nod my head. "I'm here for you," I whisper. "Not the other way around. You said so."

"I remember," he drawls. "I'm also the one who held you when you were upset. Now, what does that tell you?"

"I don't know."

He pierces me with his gaze. "It means that I get what I want. If I want to hold you, I get to. If I want to comfort you, I get to. If I want to fuck your mouth, I get to. If I want to feed you dinner, I get to. Don't be mistaken, Abigail. Whenever I do something, it's of my own volition."

"Y-yes, Sir. I'm sorry."

I'm worried I've ruined the nice mood with my comment, and now I wish I hadn't said anything.

"Don't be sorry," he says. "Be mine."

"Yours?"

He nods. "Surrender to me. Trust me. Let me be in charge. All you have to do is obey. If I invite you into my arms, don't pull away like you did earlier. If I give you pleasure, don't deny yourself. I want your tears, your words, your thoughts, your orgasms. I want all of it. Understand?"

I understand what he's saying, but to give him everything is impossible. I'm a mom first. Always. Luke comes before anyone else. Mr. Thorne wants me to put him first and I can do that while I'm here, but he'll never get everything.

"All that, and worship too?" I ask, hoping to lighten the mood.

The corners of his lips twitch. "Definitely worship too."

"I can do that, Sir."

"I know," he says, lifting the fork to my lips again. "You won't regret it, sweet girl."

An hour later, I've cleaned up and I'm back in my own clothes. Mr. Thorne leads me to the door, his hand once again resting on my lower back.

"I want to see you again," he says, handing me another manila envelope.

"You do?" My heart beats faster. I can't deny the thrill of excitement I feel at the thought of spending another night in Mr. Thorne's company.

He nods and pulls out his phone, tapping the screen a few times. His mouth twists and his brows draw together. When he looks back at me, he's still frowning.

"I'm going out of town," he says, "so I won't have time to see you until this time next week."

"Oh. That's okay, Sir." I'm just happy there will be a next time at all.

"Will you be all right until then?"

His question startles me, but I recover quickly. "Um, yes, Mr. Thorne. I'll be fine."

"Good. That's good."

After a moment, he reaches into his pocket again and hands me another envelope, but this one is white and has writing on it—the name of a spa downtown.

"Sir?"

"It's for you," he says. "A gift card."

"What ... uh, what would you like me to get done, Sir?"

Please don't say waxing, please don't say waxing.

"That's entirely up to you," he answers. "Although," he

adds, looking at me again. "I'd prefer it if you didn't cut off your hair. And no long, fake nails. And keep your eyebrows natural-looking."

"I don't know what you want me to have done," I admit. "Is there something you want ... different next time?" I motion to my body.

He seems perplexed. "No, don't change a thing. You're perfect. Just enjoy yourself."

"Thank you, Sir," I say, still confused. *Did he just give me a gift?*

He takes a step closer and reaches out to take my hand in his. His thumb traces over my knuckles a few times before he lifts our joined hands to his mouth, pressing his lips against my skin for a moment.

"Thank you, Abigail," he says. "I've had a lovely evening." His eyes are large and sincere. Looking into them makes my chest feel funny.

"Me too, Sir."

"Same time next week, then?"

I nod wordlessly and he smiles. Outside, the taxi honks its horn and Mr. Thorne leads me through the doorway, still holding my hand. He pays the cabbie and holds the door open for me as I climb inside. Leaning down after closing the door, he motions for me to roll down the window.

"Yes ..." I glance at the driver in front, who's busy fiddling with his radio. "Sir?"

"I forgot to tell you," he whispers, leaning in closer. "Next week, I have every intention of fucking you, which means I *will* make you beg for my cock, Abigail. In fact, I look forward to it."

My mouth drops open. The driver is right there, for Christ's sake! Mr. Thorne sees my shocked expression and takes pity on me.

"Get home safely, sweet girl," he says softly.

I regain my wits. "Have a safe trip, Sir."

He straightens himself and taps the roof of the cab twice, which makes the cabbie start the car. I look back as we drive off. This time, Mr. Thorne is still standing there, his hands buried in his pockets, watching me leave. What will he do now? Go back to his work? I guess I shouldn't care, since I'm off the clock, so to speak, and yet ...

Is he lonely late at night, just like me?

He's such a strange man. Stern and cold one minute, playful the next, and definitely not without quirks. But there's also a kindness to him that I never would've expected. He cares for me in his own weird way, I think. Next week, he's going to make me beg for him to fuck me again, and if he does again what he did to me tonight, I'll probably do it—and mean it. I remember his fingers, how they felt inside me. His hand warming my backside, the rough sound of his voice, and the taste and feel of his cock in my mouth. The way his eyes fluttered closed right before he came and the sound of his moans, the feeling of knowing I was the one giving him pleasure.

I clench my thighs, embarrassed by the dull throbbing sensation between them. What the hell is wrong with me? This isn't normal. This shouldn't feel good.

Twenty minutes later, I knock softly on Jo's door. The moment I see her, looking so familiar and safe, I burst into tears.

"You w-were r-r-right," I hiccup. "I'm in w-way over my h-head!"

CHAPTER ELEVEN

Jo pulls me into a fierce hug. "Oh my God, Abbi," she whispers. "Did he hurt you? Should I call the police?"

I shake my head, trying to get my blubbering under control. "N-no, n-nothing like that. I'm not h-hurt."

My best friend holds me at arm's length, scanning my face. "Are you sure? You can tell me. He can't do bad stuff to you. I don't care how much he's paying."

I compose myself as best I can. "Yes, I swear."

"Then what's wrong?"

"I'm—" I stop and look around the quiet apartment. "Where's Luke? Did it go all right?"

"Yeah, he's just fine. Come see."

Relieved, I follow Jo to her bedroom, where she holds the door open. Luke and Jo's two girls, Piper and Pippa, are sprawled across the king-size bed, all three of them fast asleep. There are pillows and blankets everywhere and the room looks a complete mess. Jo shrugs.

"They went a little wild making a fort, and then fell asleep in the middle of it."

A wave of calm settles over me and I smile, happy they've had a good time.

"Now, will you please tell me what's going on with you? I'm kind of freaking out here."

"Yeah, I'm sorry."

Jo leads me into the kitchen where I sit down at her small table, resting my head in my hands.

"If this were a movie, I'd be pouring you a stiff drink right about now," Jo says. "But you know I don't have anything like that, so this will have to do." She places a pint of ice cream and two spoons on the table and joins me. I smile at her and watch as she opens it and hands me a spoon. "Start talking," she orders.

"Well, he doesn't have a dungeon or anything like that."

"That's something. So what's his deal?"

"I don't know," I sigh, dipping into the ice cream. "He has this 1950s housewife thing, I guess. He made me dress up with an apron and everything and cook dinner for him."

I keep talking. A lot. Before I know it, the ice cream is gone and Jo is staring at me, her mouth hanging open.

"I *liked* it, Jo. The spanking, the way he touched me, the things he said. I almost ... you know."

She clears her throat. "Wow."

"Is there something wrong with me?" I whisper. "I mean, I'm not supposed to like it, right?"

She's quiet for a little while. "Says who?"

I frown, confused.

"Who says you're not supposed to like it?" she elaborates. "You're a woman, Abbi. You have feelings too, including horniness."

"Horniness?" I can't help but laugh. "Is that even a word?"

Jo grins. "Whatever. It should be. Listen, if a good-looking man touches you like that, it's normal to have a reaction. I never thought I'd say this, but the way you described it, it sounded pretty hot."

"I guess," I mumble. "I haven't really felt like that before.

Never when I was with someone else." I blush, realizing what I've just told Jo.

"I think that's pretty normal," she says. "You've only been with the douche, and I'm guessing he didn't know much."

I nod my head, not willing to elaborate on Patrick's poor lovemaking skills.

"But your Sir, on the other hand," she says, rubbing her hands together, "he sounds like a *real* man."

I stare at her. "What? You're a fan of his now?"

"He doesn't sound so terrible, Abbi," she says seriously. "He wants you to get something out of it, too. And you did say that he's nice to you."

"Yeah, he is. I'm not sure why, though. He can still have me without being nice about it."

"Maybe he's just a nice guy?"

"Who likes spanking," I supply.

"What if I told you that I used to tie Thomas up and make him call me *Ma'am*?"

"You didn't." I'm sure she would've told me already.

She chuckles. "No, that's not really my thing. But would you stop being my friend if it were true?"

"Of course not."

"My point is," Jo says, "that you can't really judge someone by what they like in the bedroom. I was worried your guy was into some really scary stuff, but it doesn't sound like he is from what you've described. You should still be careful, of course ..."

"But?"

"But I don't think there's anything wrong with you enjoying it when you're together."

"So, 'surrender,' like he said?"

"Surrender?" Jo makes a face. "Why are you fighting this so hard, Abbi? I mean, what's the worst that could happen? You have good sex with a nice, handsome guy *and* you're able to support yourself and Luke by doing it?"

I sigh, tracing my spoon through the melted ice cream. "I

don't know. I never thought I'd be a sex worker, not in a million years, but I am. That's one thing. But to actually enjoy it too? Doesn't that make me a total slut? It's supposed to be a job, but tonight it didn't really feel like it at times. I don't know what to think, or who I even am anymore."

My best friend grabs my shoulders. "Listen to me," she says. "Luke needs food, clothing, and shelter. You're giving him that. Is it ideal? Fuck no. But what other choice did you have? You're doing what you have to. End of story." She draws a breath. "And as for slut-shaming yourself, you have to stop thinking like that. There's nothing wrong with enjoying sex if it's what you both want. I know your parents are super strict and you were raised a certain way, but you're out from under them and no one in your life is judging you but you."

I look up, seeing how sincere she is. "Thank you," I whisper. "I don't know what I'd do without you."

She waves her hand, dismissing me. Jo isn't exactly what you'd call touchy-feely.

"Can I just add one more thing?"

I nod.

"There are a lot of people who enjoy their jobs. I'm just saying."

"I hear you. I do."

She smiles at me. "So, can I ask how much he paid you this time?"

"Oh my God!" I groan, reaching for my purse. "I didn't even check. How messed up is that?"

Jo doesn't answer but waits patiently as I pull out the unmarked envelope and peer inside.

"Looks like another thousand dollars," I say, counting the crisp bills with the tips of my fingers.

"Jeez," Jo breathes. "He must really like you."

"He likes the way I make him feel: strong, powerful, in control ..."

She looks at me, eyebrows raised.

"But, yeah," I amend, "I think he does like me, in his own way." I pause. "He gave me a gift," I add, fishing out the marked envelope and handing it to her.

"Whoa, this is for five hundred dollars!"

I shake my head lightly. I can't imagine having that much money at my disposal to be able to use on something as frivolous as a spa.

"So, are you going to sell it?"

"It's tempting," I admit. "But probably not. It was meant as a gift. Besides, what if he asks what I had done? I've never been to one of those places before."

"Me neither."

"Hey, will you come with me?" I ask. "I'm sure we can both get something done for that kind of money."

Jo lights up. "Really? Oh my God, I'd love to! Next Saturday? My mom's staying the weekend and I'm sure she wouldn't mind watching Luke too."

I feel a tiny stab inside my chest, and Jo reaches for my hand. She knows how I'm feeling. Her mom didn't abandon her when she became pregnant. She wasn't forced to choose between her baby and her parents. Jo's mom, Cecile, wasn't thrilled when her only daughter got knocked up at seventeen, but she's been a part of her life all this time. She often drives here to spend time with her daughter and granddaughters, especially since Jo decided she'd had enough of Thomas' unfulfilled promises and pipe dreams of making it big as a musician.

"We can ask her about your parents," Jo says gently.

I breathe deeply through my nose, shaking my head. "No."

"Okay."

This is one of the things I love about Jo. She doesn't push. I give her hand a squeeze before releasing it. It's been a long day and I'm bone-tired.

"Do you mind if we crash here?" I ask. "I don't really want to haul Luke into a cab at this hour."

Jo smiles and nods, as I had anticipated, and helps me make up the couch. As I look at her, making room for me in her home, I realize I've been selfish lately. Every conversation has been about me and my problems.

"Hey, are things going all right with Thomas?" I ask.

Jo pauses for a moment and hands me a clean sheet. "They're okay. He still comes by to take the girls out and he's been better at paying child support on time."

"That's good, right? That he's getting his act together?"

She nods but doesn't say anything. I have a feeling she's still in love with Thomas, but she won't admit it. Jo is tough as nails. I don't want to push her, so I merely offer her a smile of support. I'll be here if she wants to talk.

Jo ends up taking Piper's bed, deciding to leave our kids in her bedroom, while I make myself comfortable in the living room. I can't fall asleep; my thoughts keep going back to Mr. Thorne, no matter how hard I try not to think of him. I wonder if he went to bed already, if he thinks of me when I'm not there, and what he does when I'm not around. Mostly, though, I think about what to do when I see him again in a week's time. I don't know if I'll be able to truly release all my inhibitions and give him everything he wants from me. Is Jo right? Is there really no downside to this arrangement if I'm able to let go of my reservations? I toss and turn for a long time, not coming up with an answer. Finally, around 2:00 a.m., I manage to drift off to sleep.

I wake early, feeling the presence of a small, warm body next to mine.

"Morning, hon," I mumble, holding Luke closer to me. "You sleep okay?"

"Pippa kicks," he grumbles.

"Aw, sorry," I tell him, stroking his hair. "She doesn't do it on purpose. But did you have fun last night?"

"Yeah."

"So you'd rather stay here than with Mrs. Watt?" I already

know the answer but smile when I feel him nodding against my shoulder.

"Mommy?"

"Mmm?"

"Where did you go?"

My eyes snap open and I draw a breath. "Well, Mommy got a job."

"Like Aunt Jo?"

Not exactly. "Yes."

"Why?"

"So I can get money and buy stuff for you, sweetie."

"Oh. Cool."

"It *is* pretty cool, isn't it?" I ask, kissing the top of his head. "In fact, how'd you like to go by the mall on our way home today? I want to get you a present."

He jumps up. "Really?"

"Really."

His brilliant smile makes everything worth it and reminds me why I decided to take this job in the first place. I don't ever want to be that close to being broke again. I have a job now that pays well, and I just have to keep treating it like a job, even though last night it was easy to forget. But just like Jo said, plenty of people enjoy their jobs.

I will be whatever Mr. Thorne wants me to be. I will do whatever he wants. I will obey. I will give in. And, I will do my very best to enjoy my time with him and not feel guilty about it.

CHAPTER TWELVE

The following Saturday, I'm in a cab headed across the bridge to Medina, nervously clutching my purse between my hands. I can feel a hard, square object inside the soft, worn leather—the *Indiana Jones* box set I bought while Luke and I were at the mall. It caught my eye and I immediately thought of Mr. Thorne. I haven't decided if I'll give it to him. He might think it's stupid of me, but I want to thank him for the spa somehow.

Running my fingers through my newly styled hair, I try to get my nerves under control. It's layered and only a little shorter than before—I hope Mr. Thorne will approve. Tonight, I'm wearing a black skirt and a white shirt, which he may not like, but it's necessary since I had to convince Jo's mom that I'm working as a server when I dropped Luke off this afternoon. Technically, it isn't a lie. I *will* be serving Mr. Thorne tonight, but not in the way she thinks.

My heart beats faster as we drive down the lane to his house. The moment the cab stops, the door opens, and Mr. Thorne comes outside, looking handsome in dark gray pants and a white button-down. I sit still while he pays the driver, and I watch as he walks around to open the door for me.

"Good evening, Abigail," he greets me, offering his hand to help me out of the taxi.

"Good evening, Sir," I whisper, taking it.

He escorts me inside, and I'm so nervous I can hardly breathe; my heart feels like it's going a mile a minute. Tonight, I'm going to allow myself to enjoy it.

Tonight, I'm crossing another line.

The moment the door closes behind me, I feel the air change around us, becoming somehow charged, making the hair on the back of my neck stand up and my skin prickle. I turn to face him, unsure what to expect.

"You look beautiful," he says, reaching out to touch a lock of my hair.

"Thanks," I whisper. "The spa was very nice."

He nods, giving me a small smile.

"Did, uh, did you have a good trip?" I ask.

"It was productive."

I run out of things to say and we simply stand there for a few moments, looking at each other. I'm not sure what he's waiting for. Usually, this is when he would order me to do something, but tonight he doesn't. The way he looks at me is unmistakable, so I know he hasn't changed his mind about having me here. He wants me and he knows he can have me. So why doesn't he command something of me?

I remember what he told me: that he doesn't just want me to obey, but for me to *want* to serve him. Drawing a deep breath, I drop my purse and slide my open jacket off to join it on the floor. Slowly, I undo the buttons of my shirt, revealing my naked skin to him. Usually, I don't bother with a bra, but I wore one tonight since my shirt is sheer. Both items join the others on the floor, and I drag the skirt down my hips, taking my underwear with it. I step out of the pile of clothes, toe off my Converse knockoffs, and stand completely naked in front of him.

Mr. Thorne is still, watching me impassively. I can tell he's pleased, though. His eyes sweep across my face and body, and he's breathing faster than before. Slowly, I walk to him, stopping right before I touch him.

"Are you all for me?" he asks.

I swallow my nerves. "Yes, Sir. I'm yours. Your good girl."

He leans in, his lips brushing against my cheek. "Are you?" he whispers. "Mine?"

"Y-yes, Sir."

"Prove it."

I start to kneel, but he pulls me back up, pressing my naked body against his.

"Prove it," he says again. "Prove that you're mine."

I don't know what else to do and look up at him, hoping he'll clue me in. The second his eyes dart to my lips, I understand. He wants me to kiss him. Of course. Kissing is intimate and, if Hollywood depictions are accurate, not something that belongs in prostitution. He wants to pretend this is real.

Drawing a deep breath, I stand up on my toes and softly press my lips against his. Our first kiss. The moment we touch, he exhales, and then his hands are on me everywhere. His mouth is demanding where mine is yielding. My body is supple where his is hard. He kisses me as if he's been waiting for it a long time and now wants to experience it all at once, overwhelming me with his forcefulness. We move and I feel the wall against my back.

"Touch me," he groans.

I scramble to comply, opening his pants with shaky fingers. His cock is in my hand and he's hard, so hard. I stroke him but stop when I feel his fingers wrapping themselves around my wrist. He lifts my hand up.

"Lick."

I wet my hand and he brings it back, helping me touch him. His other hand squeezes my breast before moving down to my ass.

"Fuck. Fuck," he chants, holding me to him, claiming my lips again.

I feel the heat between us and this time, I acknowledge it. This is lust. I want him. I want him inside me.

"Ohhh!" He groans against my lips and I feel him coming on our joined hands and my stomach. His head drops to my shoulder and he rests there, leaning on me and the wall.

"Oh, sweet girl," he breathes. "A week is too long. Much too long."

"Haven't you ..."

He lifts his head and looks at me, still winded, but with a serious expression on his slightly flushed face. "There's only you, Abigail."

Oh. I didn't even wonder if there was someone else. But, of course, there could have been. The fact that there isn't, though, pleases me more than it probably should. He lets go of my hand, fixes his clothes, and leaves me in the hall. A minute later, he returns with a soft rag and cleans off my stomach and fingers without a word. Then he hands me my clothes. I should be relieved, but I'm not. I'm disappointed.

"Was that all, Sir?" I whisper.

"Would you like for there to be more?"

Does *he* want there to be more? His expression is completely neutral, which is really frustrating. It's so hard to know what he's thinking or feeling.

"Yes," I admit, truthfully.

He takes the clothes from my hands and drops them on the floor before pulling me into his arms. I gasp softly as he reaches down to hitch my leg up. Never looking away from my face, he slides his free hand up my thigh until his fingers are gently probing between my legs.

"You're wet," he states.

My face heats up. "Yes, Sir," I moan, gripping his upper arms as his fingers rub tight little circles on my swollen, wet skin.

"Would you like to stay longer?" he asks.

"Oh, yes, Sir," I breathe.

His fingers trail downward and dip inside me, quickly moving in and out. "Do you want me to fuck you? Make you come?"

I nod my head. "Yes, Sir. Yes, please." *Oh, God. I really mean it.*

"Good girls don't mind waiting, do they?" His fingers leave my skin and I want to grit my teeth in frustration. He's watching me, looking amused.

"No, Sir," I manage. "I don't mind."

"There's my sweet girl." My jaw drops when he brings his fingers to his mouth and cleans them off. "Mmm." He grins. "Definitely sweet."

He just sucked ... and they were inside ...

"Run upstairs and change," he chuckles, releasing me and leaning down to pick up my stuff again. As he lifts my bag off the floor, something falls out, landing with a dull thud.

"What's this?" Mr. Thorne asks, picking up the gift-wrapped item. He looks serious all of a sudden.

"It's f-for you," I stammer, suddenly worried I've crossed a line.

"How did you know I just had a birthday?" he asks, narrowing his eyes. "Did you check up on me?"

"No, of course not."

He watches me, still frowning.

"I swear, the thought has never crossed my mind." *Until now.* "I just wanted to thank you for the spa. I didn't know you had a birthday. Well, of course you *have* a birthday, but ... you know what I mean. When was it?"

"Yesterday."

"Happy birthday," I say weakly. "Did you have fun?"

"I spent most of it on a plane, so no, not particularly."

"Oh. Wait—was it your 40th birthday?"

He nods.

"And you spent it on a plane, alone?"

He shrugs, and it makes me sad. He spent his 40th birthday all alone, traveling, and he's chosen to spend his celebration—or whatever—with me, the hired help. Before I realize what I'm doing, I've thrown my arms around him, holding him against me. He hesitates for a moment before sliding his large, warm hands around my naked back, returning the embrace.

"I'm baking you a cake," I murmur. "You should have a birthday cake."

He doesn't say anything, but he nods, holding me closer.

CHAPTER THIRTEEN

Tonight, in the kitchen, Mr. Thorne doesn't observe me at a distance. He's behind me, looking over my shoulder, distracting me with his wandering hands. I guess dressing me in only an apron is a fantasy of his, which is how I find myself in his beautiful kitchen, baking a chocolate cake, butt naked except for a few scraps of soft white fabric covering my front. Maybe I'm getting used to his quirks, because I didn't even bat an eyelash when he told me what I'd be wearing—or not wearing.

"Mmm, that smells good," he murmurs, brushing his lips against the side of my neck. "Why do you do it like that? Why not just put it in the pot?"

I look down at the chocolate chips I'm melting in a bowl over a pot of boiling water, and I draw a blank. "I actually don't know. I've always done it like this," I tell him, stirring slowly.

"Who taught you?"

My spine stiffens. That's not a question I want to answer.

"Abigail?"

"My, uh, my mother, I guess," I reply, shrugging my shoulders.

"Do you see her a lot?"

"Please, Sir. I'd *really* prefer not to talk about it," I implore, looking over my shoulder at him. "Please."

His eyes scan my face before he nods once. "I didn't realize it was painful for you. I apologize."

"It's not painful." *Yes, it is.* "I just ... we're not close anymore. At all."

"That's a shame," Mr. Thorne says. "I won't bring it up again."

I turn and quickly press a kiss onto his cheek. "Thank you, Sir," I whisper before facing the kitchen island again. Leaving the melted chocolate to cool off, I start measuring and mixing the rest of the ingredients carefully.

"How can you remember all this without a recipe?" he asks, sounding impressed.

I smile to myself. Chocolate cake is Luke's favorite. "I don't know," I lie, dipping a clean teaspoon into the chocolate. "I've always liked baking." That part is true.

I lick off the spoon, tasting the chocolate, and add more sugar to the other bowl. I need this cake to be perfect—not just because Mr. Thorne demands perfection, but because I want him to enjoy this. I don't have much money, and I don't live in a beautiful house like this, but I've never had to spend my birthday alone. No matter where I've been in my life, I've been with people who matter to me on that special day. For some reason, Mr. Thorne doesn't have that in his life, and while I'm a lousy substitute, I'll do my best to make sure he has a nice time tonight. Underneath all the weirdness, he's not so bad.

"Don't *I* get a taste?"

I look over my shoulder at him, nodding, before dipping the spoon back into the chocolate and turning to face him, holding it up. He looks at the spoon, chuckling softly before angling it toward my mouth instead. Then he kisses me, invading my mouth with his velvet-soft tongue, groaning as he tastes me. The sound makes my insides liquefy and I stand up on my toes, kissing him back and pushing my body into his.

"You are so fucking sweet," he murmurs, nipping at my lips.

"I-it's the chocolate," I stutter.

"No, it isn't."

I can't help it; I blush underneath his gaze and a secret thrill runs through me, knowing how pleased he is. Really, I should feel ridiculous standing here in just an apron that barely covers my breasts, but I don't. "Thank you, Sir."

"Thank *you*, Abigail."

I put the cake in the oven and clean up while he sits at the counter, alternating between watching me and typing on his phone. He doesn't offer to help, but that doesn't surprise me at all. He likes to watch.

"I'm done, Sir," I tell him when I've finished washing the bowls and utensils.

"Very good. Unfortunately, I have a few calls to make. You go upstairs and take a bath while I make them and order us some dinner."

"Really, Sir, I don't mind cooking," I begin, remembering how he said he enjoys a home-cooked meal. "I can easily—"

He's off his chair immediately, wrapping me up in his arms and cutting me off by pressing his lips against mine. His kiss is aggressive, his tongue demanding access to my mouth. I yield, pliant in his embrace, and let him kiss the hell out of me. When our lips part, he gives me a stern look, still holding me firmly against his chest.

"Who makes the decisions, Abigail?"

I draw a gasping breath. "Y-you do, Sir."

"Who?" he whispers, sliding his right hand underneath the apron to grab my breast, tweaking my nipple harder than normal.

I hiss, looking up into his eyes. "You, Mr. Thorne. *You* decide."

The stinging sensation on my chest fades, soothed by his wet tongue, as he quickly unties the knot and moves the apron to the side, leaning down to suck my nipple into his mouth. He pushes his right leg in between mine and grabs my ass, grinding me against the hard muscles of his thigh.

"Oh, oh," I whisper, holding on to him to keep my balance. His mouth is on mine again and I moan, melting into the kiss while my lower half ruts against him. I could come like this, I think.

Of course, he won't let me do that. He ends the kiss, running his thumb across my lips.

"That's right," he says. "*I* decide."

I nod, forcing myself not to grind against him anymore, even though I *really* want to.

"So when I tell you to relax and take a bath while I order us dinner, what do you say, Abigail?"

"Thank you, Sir?"

He smiles. "You're welcome, sweet girl." He releases me and tells me to set the timer on the oven. I do as I'm told, and with a playful swat to my behind, he sends me on my way.

"Abigail?"

I pause on my way up the stairs, turning to see that Mr. Thorne has followed me into the hall. "Yes, Sir?"

He climbs the stairs until he's just one step away and even then, he's still so much taller than me. "During your bath," he says, running the backs of his fingers up my naked thigh, "you may wash yourself, but don't make yourself come. Are we clear?"

Blood rushes to my cheeks. "Yes, Sir. We're clear. I ... I don't do *that*."

At least, I haven't in a long time.

"You will, for me," he says simply. "I like to watch."

I swallow hard. Of all the things he's asked of me, that one might be the most difficult to do. It's so private, and I suspect that's part of the appeal for him. He wants all of me.

"Yes, Sir."

"Go take your bath and then change," he says. "And don't wash your hair; it looks very pretty like this."

I nod my head and resist the urge to rush up the stairs. Knowing that he's most likely watching my ascent, I try to walk slowly, seductively, all the while acutely aware of the fact that I'm completely naked and on display. Mr. Thorne chuckles behind me, the sound sending shivers up my spine.

"Oh, sweet girl. The things I'd like to do to that ass of yours," he murmurs before I hear him walk back downstairs.

In the bathroom, I look at myself in the mirror, noticing my flushed cheeks and swollen lips. Running my hands over my skin, I shiver, remembering how we kissed when I arrived earlier tonight. The memory of his fingers caressing me makes me press my thighs together to quell the ache between them. It's been a very long time since I had an orgasm. Patrick never seemed to care and I was never brave enough to guide him, or take matters into my own hands during sex, so to speak. And after Luke was born, those urges seemed to have vanished.

I won't pretend that I don't still have mixed feelings about my arrangement with Mr. Thorne, but I made a decision when I came over here tonight and I'm sticking to it. I'll do my very best to please him, no matter what he asks of me, and I won't deny myself pleasure—if he gives it to me.

God, I hope he does.

I fill the tub, add bubbles, and pile my hair up with a hair tie Mr. Thorne left out for me next to the hairbrush. After a quick bath, I dry off and put on lotion, then turn to the dress I'll be wearing. It's *so* pretty: a short, black, sleeveless party dress with a small bow tied around the waist. It looks old; *vintage* is the right term. Forgoing underwear yet again, I slip it on, happy that it fits my slender frame. I can't zip it all the way up on my own, but I can't do too much about that. I gently brush my hair, restoring the stylist's work, and put on the kitten heels I wore last time. Turning, I admire myself in the mirror. I look like I'm going to a party, and I guess in a way I am.

Downstairs in the kitchen, I find Mr. Thorne on the phone. I pause by the door, seeking his approval before entering, listening to the foreign words coming out of his mouth. He turns and stops talking for a moment, smiles at the sight of me, and motions for me to come in before continuing his conversation. It sounds like it could be Russian, or something Eastern European—I'm definitely impressed. He ends the call after I've taken the cake out of the oven and comes over to me.

"Lovely," he says. "Turn."

I do a twirl for him and he helps zip up the dress, looking me over again.

"Perfect," he says, holding up his phone. "May I?"

"Take my picture?"

"Yes."

"Why?"

"Because you're beautiful."

"You won't show anyone, will you?"

"I won't be posting it on Facebook, if that's what you mean."

"You're on Facebook?"

He laughs like I'm being silly, and I guess I am. But I can't imagine Mr. Thorne updating his status or commenting on a friend's post.

If he even has any friends at all.

"It's just for me," he says. "Please?"

I can't see anything wrong with it. After all, I'm fully dressed and not doing anything incriminating, so I nod and smile.

Holding his phone up again, he snaps a picture of me and then puts it away. "No more work tonight," he says, brushing past me to open his wine fridge. He takes out two bottles and opens the white one with a pop. Pouring the fizzy liquid into a wine glass, he hands it to me.

"*Asti Spumante*," he says with a bit of an accent. "You'll like it."

I'm not so sure. I really don't care for wine at all. Mr. Thorne pours himself a glass from the other bottle and I lift mine up. "Happy birthday, Sir."

He gazes at me for a moment before touching his glass to mine. "Thank you, Abigail."

I take a small sip, surprised that the wine is sweet and fruity. I can hardly taste the alcohol.

"You like it?" he asks.

I nod my head.

"Good. I brought it back with you in mind."

I can't help but feel touched by his thoughtfulness and give him a big smile. "Is it from France?" I guess. I know that's where champagne comes from.

"Italy," he says. "Have you ever been?"

I shake my head and shrug. "I've never been outside the state."

He doesn't comment, but I can see that he's surprised. I decide to change the topic.

"Were you in Rome?"

"Yes, and a few days in London as well."

"Wow, must be nice," I say quietly.

Mr. Thorne shrugs, taking a sip of his wine. "Truth be told, it gets old after a while. Staying in hotel rooms, eating room service, spending most of my time in airports or on a plane."

"It sounds lonely," I whisper.

He looks at me but doesn't comment. Instead, he goes to the stereo on the wall and turns on music—something unfamiliar.

"Who is this?" I ask, taking another sip of wine.

"The Drifters. They're old like me," he says, grinning.

I smile at him. "You're not old, Sir."

"I've still got some moves." He holds out his hand to me, an almost hopeful expression on his face. I put my glass down and walk to him, placing my right hand in his and my left on his shoulder. "Just follow my lead," he murmurs, drawing me close.

I smile and follow his steps as we start dancing, moving effortlessly together. I feel his fingers gently caressing my back and close my eyes, listening to the song, surprised he's put on something so romantic. His lips brush against my forehead and I have to concentrate not to lose my rhythm as he twirls me across the floor.

"You can really dance," he says.

I look up at him, and his surprised grin makes my heart flutter. "I can, Sir." I took dancing lessons for many years growing up. It was my mom's idea of raising a proper lady, I suppose, but I quickly discovered how much I loved it. I also took a little ballet before I joined the cheerleading squad freshman year.

"I never would have guessed."

I suppose he wouldn't, given my current circumstances. I wonder where Mr. Thorne thinks I come from. I bet a comfortable childhood in a small town isn't his first thought when he looks at the girl who has to sell her body to keep herself fed.

"My life wasn't always like this," I confess. "I had plans, dreams for the future."

"Tell me."

"You know—college, seeing more of the world, a good job." *Giving my son a good life.*

"And now?" he asks.

"Make rent, pay my bills, and put food on the table." *Why am I telling him all this?* I shouldn't be saying this stuff to Mr. Thorne. This is *his* celebration and I'm ruining it, bringing my unfortunate reality into his fantasy. "I'm sorry," I whisper and stop moving, stepping out of his embrace and averting my eyes.

"Look at me."

I obey, drawing a stuttering breath. He doesn't look angry, but I can tell his previous levity has dimmed.

"I asked you," he says. "Don't apologize for telling me the truth."

"Yes, Sir."

He lowers the volume of the music and turns to me again. "Your financial trouble is the reason why you went to that sleazy club the night I picked you up?"

I nod my head. "I was looking for a job."

"You were upset," he says. "You were crying when you ran into me."

"I was a mess. Why'd you follow me outside?"

"I wanted you." His tone is factual, his stance unapologetic. "I thought maybe they'd rejected you because you were too young."

"No," I whisper, wrapping my arms around my waist. "Too thin. Not sexy enough."

He scoffs, leading me over to the kitchen island again and handing me my wine. "You *are* thin," he says, "but I'm guessing it's not your natural shape?"

I shake my head, chewing on my lower lip as he reaches out to touch a lock of my hair.

"I meant what I said last time. I'm going to take good care of you and you're going to get healthy again."

"Thank you." I like the idea of having him take care of me.

"I don't regret my decision to follow you outside that night," he says. "I hope you don't regret getting into my car?"

I shake my head again. "Can I ask you something, Sir?"

He nods.

"Why were you there? The club, I mean."

"I was looking."

"For what?"

His eyes burn with unexpected intensity. "You. Only I didn't know it at the time."

I don't know what to say. His words sound romantic, but he probably doesn't mean them that way.

"I'm very pleased with how this arrangement of ours has turned out," he adds, stepping forward to pull me back into his arms.

"You are?"

He leans in, brushing his lips against mine. "Yes. Aren't you?"

"Yes, Sir."

"Mmm," he hums, kissing me. "I think you like being my good girl, Abigail."

"I do, Sir." *When did my voice become so breathy?*

We're so close and all I want is to launch myself at him. I shiver as he strokes my naked arms and his lips and tongue caress my neck.

"You're so sweet," he whispers in my ear. "I can't wait to taste you everywhere."

Oh, God. Everywhere!

We're interrupted by the loud ring of the doorbell and Mr. Thorne lifts his head to smile at me. "To be continued," he says.

"Please, Sir."

"You already do. I'll get dinner; you set the table in the dining room."

"Yes, Sir."

"Oh, and Abigail?"

"Sir?"

"Would you prefer one or two place settings?"

He's asking me? I gape at him. This has to be a test, but instead of trying to figure out what he wants me to say, I search my own feelings. Do I want to sit next to him, eating at my own place, or sit in his lap? The first option doesn't feel right to me. It'll be normal, and my relationship with Mr. Thorne is anything but. I like sitting with him. I like his hands on me.

His arms make me feel safe and warm. I like the way he looks at me when he's pleased with me.

"One place setting, Sir," I tell him.

He smiles at me. "There's my good girl."

Yes, here I am.

CHAPTER FOURTEEN

After setting the table for one and lighting tapers, I join Mr. Thorne in the kitchen, where he tells me to put the food in serving bowls before he heads into the dining room, bringing our wine and glasses with him. I'm not sure what I expected when he said he'd order us dinner. Maybe pizza or Chinese food. It turns out that Mr. Thorne's idea of take-out is something very different. I open the Styrofoam boxes to find a meal from what must be a fancy restaurant: an orange, creamy soup to start and a rice dish with mushrooms, sautéed vegetables, some kind of meat surrounded by puff pastry, and a dark red sauce. I have no idea what any of this stuff is called, but the smell is mouthwatering. Carefully transferring the soup to a bowl, I grab a ladle, a soup plate, and a spoon, and carry them to Mr. Thorne, who's already seated at the head of the table and smiling at me. I notice he's drawn the curtains and put on music, creating a cozy setting in the large room. The gift I brought him is sitting next to him on the table.

"May I serve you, Sir?" I ask.

"You may."

After placing the plate in front of him, I'm surprised that he doesn't eat; instead, he pulls me onto his lap, making sure

I'm situated comfortably before offering me the first taste. I close my eyes, savoring the flavor—it's delicious.

"Mmm."

"I love watching you eat."

"I love eating, so you're in luck, Sir."

He grins at me, taking a spoonful for himself. "It *is* good," he agrees.

"I didn't know upscale restaurants deliver," I say, accepting the spoon again.

"They don't, usually, but I'm a very good customer."

"You go there a lot?"

"All the time. I can't cook and a man's gotta eat. It's a very nice place."

I nod my head.

"Maybe I'll take you there sometime," he says, lifting my wine glass to my lips.

Wide-eyed, I drink the bubbly wine, staring at him. "You want to take me out ... in public?"

"Why not?"

"Well, you're *you* and I'm ... me. I won't fit in over there, in such a fancy place. I'd embarrass you."

He shakes his head disapprovingly. "What you are, Abigail, is a sweet, beautiful young woman. You're not used to the finer things in life, obviously, but I don't see how you'd ever embarrass me. In fact, I'd be the envy of most men if I had you at my side."

"Thank you, Sir," I whisper. "Aren't you worried what people might think, though? About us, I mean."

"Well, I assume they'd think you were my lover, which is true," he says, shrugging as he eats some more soup.

My stupid heart flutters in my chest. I'm his lover? That sounds a lot better than what I've been calling myself. Does he really think so highly of me? And why can't I do the same thing? I don't think any less of Mr. Thorne for paying me, so shouldn't I give myself a break?

"You *are* my lover, aren't you, sweet girl?" he asks, reaching up to caress my cheek.

"I'm whatever you want me to be," I whisper, leaning in until our noses are touching. "I'm here for you, Mr. Thorne, to worship you."

His lips mold themselves to mine as he kisses me slowly, tightening his arms around me. When I moan, I feel him smiling before he pulls away.

"Are you ready for the main course?" he asks, running his hand up my naked thigh. I'm not sure if his double entendre is intentional or not.

"Whatever you'd like, Sir."

He grins in response, lifts me off his lap, and tells me to heat up the entrée. I carry the dirty dishes out with me and quickly warm up the rest of the food before carrying it to the table along with clean silverware and a new plate. I have to make two trips and, again, Mr. Thorne doesn't offer to help. Instead, he watches with a look of satisfaction on his handsome face.

We eat in silence, but it's not uncomfortable. The food is amazing, and I can see that Mr. Thorne really does love watching me eat, because he feeds me the biggest share of the portions.

"I can't wait for dessert," he tells me afterward. We're in the kitchen while I'm frosting the cake.

"I'm not sure it'll do the rest of the menu justice," I tell him honestly. He bought us a gourmet meal and I've made him a simple chocolate cake.

"You made it for me," he says, embracing me from behind, "to please me."

"Yes," I admit.

"Then it'll be perfect," he whispers, placing soft kisses on the side of my neck. "You may serve coffee in the living room when you're done. Bring a cup and plate for yourself."

"Yes, Sir."

"Good girl," he tells me before he leaves.

Thankfully, Mr. Thorne's coffee maker is pretty standard and I'm able to brew a pot without difficulty. I put everything on a tray and walk slowly out of the kitchen, realizing I have no idea where the living room is located.

"Mr. Thorne?" I call out. "Where are you?"

"Marco!"

I can't help but grin as I follow the sound down the hall. He's such a weirdo. I never know what to expect from him, but I realize that's actually one of the things I like about him. None of his many personality quirks are unpleasant. I like all of them.

"Polo," I say softly, entering the living room.

"Over here," he says, motioning for me to place the tray on the coffee table.

This room is just as beautiful as the rest of the house, furnished impeccably to fit Mr. Thorne's masculine taste with dark wood and a large couch. There's a huge flat-screen TV mounted on the wall, throw carpets on the hardwood floors, and, next to the present he's brought with him, a few newspapers and magazines on the table. Finally, a room that actually looks somewhat lived in.

"Join me," he says, sitting down on the couch.

"I need one more thing."

He nods once, and I hurry into the dining room, bringing one of the lit tapers with me. "You didn't have any birthday candles," I tell him as I join him on the couch. "But still," I clear my throat. "Happy birthday to you, happy birthday to you, happy birthday, dear Si-ir," I sing, drawing out the word. He smiles in response, eyes lit up as he looks at me.

"Happy birthday to you," I finish, holding the candle out to him. "You wanna make a wish?"

He shakes his head. "Wishes don't work for me. Never have."

I stare at him. That's how I've felt for years, that my wishes never come true. I never thought I'd have anything in common with him, but the more I get to know him, the more I'm starting to realize we're not as different as it seems. Has he been hurt too? Does he long for more than the life he has, just as I do? Retracting the candle, I bring it up to my mouth.

"Wait." He draws a deep breath, rubbing his palms against the tops of his thighs. "Why don't you make one," he finally says.

"All right."

I wish ... I wish Mr. Thorne will find happiness.

Blowing out the flame, I hope this wish will come true. There's definitely sadness within the man next to me, but I don't know what caused it. I think he might be all alone in the world.

"Thank you, Abigail," he says, taking the candle from my hand. "I haven't celebrated my birthday in years."

And there's the sadness. "Do you have family, Sir?" I whisper.

"I don't want to talk about it," he responds curtly, looking straight at me. "That's not what you're here for."

His clipped words shouldn't hurt my feelings. After all, who is he to me, and who am I to him? But they do.

"Excuse me." He stands and walks out of the room, leaving me on the couch.

Why couldn't I keep my mouth shut? I'm not his girl-friend. He doesn't owe me any part of himself besides what he chooses to share. I need to get my head on straight. Wine, romantic music, and candles don't change why I'm here, and I feel like an idiot for getting lost in the fantasy.

He comes back a few minutes later and sits down next to me.

"Sorry," I whisper.

He shrugs a shoulder at me. "Forget it. Let's not let it ruin our evening. You have your issues about family and I have mine."

"What a pair we make."

He smiles at me, but it doesn't reach his eyes. Impulsively, I lean over and kiss him, hoping to chase away his dark thoughts. He responds, pulling me into his arms, and I feel his tension melt away with each deep kiss until the grin he gives me is genuine.

"Would you like your dessert now?" I ask.

"Yes." His eyes sweep over me. "But I'll take some cake first."

I laugh, cutting him a big piece and serving him a cup of coffee with it. He digs in and hums in approval.

"It's wonderful," he says. "Have some for yourself."

We eat in silence and I notice his eyes drifting to the gift-wrapped item more than a few times.

Might as well get it over with.

"You can open it, if you'd like," I say, pushing it closer to him.

"I think I will," he says calmly. I can see a spark of excitement in his eyes, though, which he can't hide.

"It's really nothing much," I warn him, wringing my hands. "If I'd known it was your birthday, I would've gotten something bet—"

He holds up his hand and I stop talking. Like a child, he lifts up the square box and shakes it to guess what's inside. Of course, it doesn't make a sound, so he proceeds to unwrap it while I hold my breath.

"Oh," he exhales, pushing the wrapping paper away. He runs the tips of his fingers across the front. "This is really something, Abigail. Thank you."

"You're welcome. I didn't know if you already had them?"

"No. I did, once, but I never got around to replacing them. I can't believe you bought this for me."

"You said they were your favorites. It's not a big deal."

"It is to me," he says, smiling faintly. He looks at the box set again. "The fourth movie is on here. I never got around to watching it. Have you seen it?"

I shake my head. "I think I saw some of the older ones when I was a kid, but definitely not the newest one."

"Well, in that case," he says, smiling widely, "I would like you to join me for a movie, Abigail."

"I'd like that, Sir," I tell him honestly. "May I use the bathroom first?"

He shoots me a wicked grin. "What would you do if I said no?"

"I'd hold it, Sir."

He gazes at me for a moment, appearing almost more excited about this than watching the movie. "Yes, you would," he concludes.

I nod my head, maintaining eye contact.

"Of course you may use the bathroom," he says, smiling. "You don't have to ask again."

His excitement doesn't have anything to do with the bathroom thing, I realize. It's the fact that I'd do what he says, even if the request is odd.

After a quick bathroom break, I'm back on the couch, watching the opening credits with Mr. Thorne by my side. He's eating his second piece of cake, eyes glued to the screen. After a few minutes, he puts the plate on the coffee table and pours both of us more wine.

"Cheers," he says, clinking his glass to mine. "Thank you for all this, Abigail."

"My pleasure, Sir," I whisper.

"Your pleasure? Yes, we'll definitely get to that later."

I move closer, taking a big sip of wine before putting it on the table. Mr. Thorne looks me over, wetting his lips with the tip of his tongue.

"You need it badly, don't you?" he murmurs, his free hand slipping underneath the hem of my dress to caress my thighs. "How long has it been for you, pretty girl?"

"S-since what?" I gasp as his fingers easily locate the place where I feel the most.

"Since you came on a cock," he says roughly, pulling my legs apart to push a single finger inside me. "Since you were fucked until you came, screaming."

"N-never," I moan, leaning into him, spreading my legs wide open for him. "I've never done that, Sir."

"Fuck," he mumbles, lowering his head down to gently bite my naked shoulder. "I'm going to enjoy this so much."

"Enjoy what?" I ask, moving around to get him to touch me more.

"Enjoy showing you what it's like. You'll be insatiable once you get a taste, I know it. You'll be begging me to fuck you." He pushes another finger inside, causing my back to arch.

"Won't you?" he whispers, kissing up my neck, making me groan with pleasure.

"Yes, Sir!"

Abruptly, he stops touching me, and I want to scream in frustration. But instead of going back to the movie, he turns off the TV and stands up, grabbing me by the hand.

"C'mon," he says, practically dragging me from the living room.

"Where are we going?" I finally manage to ask as we reach the third floor, where I know his office is located.

"To bed," he answers. "I need more room to do all the things I wanna do to you."

"W-what do you mean?" I stutter, nervous once more. "What are you going to do to me?"

He stops and turns, right outside the door to the room where he's headed, and looks me up and down, the heat in his eyes making me shiver.

"Whatever I want."

Just like that, we're back to the first night I met him and the giant leap of faith I took getting into his car. He watches me closely, gauging my reaction to his words while his hand around my wrist loosens slightly. I draw a deep breath and remember that this is the same man who thoughtfully fed me dinner, who brought wine all the way back from Italy just for me, and who, most of the time, looks at me and treats me as if I'm precious to him, even calling me his lover.

"Whatever you want, Sir."

He doesn't reply, but smiles at me before pulling me inside the room. I look around, breathing out in relief that it is, in fact, a regular bedroom and not a place with whips and chains. Well, *regular* is probably the wrong word considering the opulence before me: a huge bed, a plush carpet, heavy drapes. There's one thing missing, though—missing all over the house. There are no pictures anywhere. Sure, there's art on the walls, but nothing of a personal nature. I think of his pristine kitchen, the sleek surfaces. People say that a kitchen is the heart of a home, and by that estimation, there is no heart here at all. The thought makes me sad.

"Abigail?" Mr. Thorne is watching me closely, his thumb stroking across my wrist. "I won't hurt you," he says softly, misinterpreting my hesitation.

"Yes, Sir."

"Undress," he orders after a few seconds.

I step out of the heels, enjoying the sensation of the soft carpet beneath my bare feet for a moment before turning my back to him. "Will you unzip me, please, Sir?"

He helps me remove the dress and I place it carefully on the bedside table, now standing naked in front of Mr. Thorne.

"Lie down on the bed," he directs, "on your back, legs spread."

I do as I'm told, breathing rapidly from both nerves and excitement. Mr. Thorne opens the drawer in the bedside table, pulling out what looks like one of those sleeping masks I've seen people wear in movies.

"Put this on."

"Why?" I whisper.

"You'll feel more," he says, "and tonight, I want you to feel everything I do to you."

I slip it on and close my eyes.

"Hold on here," Mr. Thorne says, lifting up my arms and wrapping my fingers around the edges of the pillow underneath my head. "Don't let go, no matter what happens."

"Yes, Sir." I'm restrained by his words only, but vow not to lower my arms, giving him the control he wants. The bed dips beside me as he climbs in next to me.

"It's beautiful," he whispers. "Your submission."

I don't know what to say about that so I keep quiet. His hands trail down the length of my body and I arch up in response.

"You're such a good girl, Abigail. Anything I ask, you do. You've been so patient tonight, letting me delay your pleasure." I gasp as his fingers part me, sliding into me without resistance.

"You're so fucking wet," he growls, "so needy."

"Please, Sir," I breathe, letting my legs fall completely out to the sides. I feel his breath against my neck before he trails lingering kisses down my torso, pausing to suck on my nipples for a moment. All the while, his fingers fuck me deeply and his thumb moves over my clit, making my hips lift off the bed to gain more of the delicious friction.

"You have no idea, do you?" he asks from somewhere above me.

"About what?" I pant.

"How fucking desirable you are," he tells me. "I've been hard all day, knowing you were coming over tonight—knowing I'd get to do anything I want with you."

"Yes, please, you can," I moan, practically incoherent at this point.

"You're going to come for me, Abigail. First, on my fingers ..." He curls them inside me, touching a place that makes me gasp loudly. "Then, on my mouth," he continues, covering my lips with his in a searing kiss. "And, finally, you're going to come on my cock," he says, pressing his still-covered erection against my hip. "You're going to come so hard for me, sweet girl. Is that clear?"

"T-three times, oh!" I pant, bucking up my lower half, so very close. "That's impossible, Sir."

"We'll see about that." I feel his mouth on my chest again, his tongue flicking over my nipples while his thumb rubs my clit with purpose. Moments later, I come. And it's nothing like I remember; it's better—*so* much better. My body curves upward; I moan loudly as I clench around his fingers and then relax down onto the mattress again.

"Thank you, Sir," I exhale, trying to catch my breath.

"Don't thank me yet," he mumbles, kissing his way down my upper body. "You can do better than that. You can come much harder."

I don't know that I can, but I'm afraid to disappoint him by telling him that what he just did was pretty much the most fulfilling sexual experience of my life. I doubt it gets much better than that.

"Have you ever had a man taste you, Abigail?"

"No," I admit, suddenly happy about the sleep mask I'm wearing so I don't have to look at him while I answer.

"Fuck," he groans, nipping at my belly. "You're practically a virgin."

When I start to protest, he stops me. "You haven't been fucked properly. You haven't even had real foreplay. Whoever he was, he neglected you, so he doesn't count. I'm your first."

I inhale sharply as he spreads my legs and kisses his way up my inner thigh, his lips and tongue soft and gentle in their exploration.

"Say it." His hands snake up my body and grab my breasts none too gently before pulling my nipples.

"You're my first," I groan out. His hands return to their place underneath me and he holds me up slightly, keeping me open wide for him. Knowing that he's inspecting me so closely makes me want to cringe and pull away, but after a few seconds his mouth is on me again, and I forget those thoughts.

The sensation is somehow deeper than when he used his fingers, more acute. I'm so sensitive and I squirm around, trying to get away from his very insistent stimulation. "Please, Sir," I protest weakly.

"Lay still!" he snaps at me. "And don't you dare move those hands."

I hadn't noticed I'd let go of the pillow and quickly grab it again, my heart racing at the sound of him being so harsh, so commanding. It excites me more than I'd ever admit out loud.

"You can come again," he says, softer now. "I know you can."

I draw a breath, nodding.

"I love the way you taste. Let me be in charge."

I nod again, doing my best to relax. Seconds later, his mouth is back: licking, sucking, and tasting me as though he's ravenous. His hands knead my ass roughly, adding to all the sensations I'm already experiencing. I have no idea how much time passes, but after a while the near-painful sensitivity turns into something else entirely and I find myself pressing up against his mouth, gasping wildly.

Suddenly, I feel something brushing against a place no one has ever touched before. I realize Mr. Thorne's right hand has moved ever so slightly, his fingers now busy spreading my wetness around between my cheeks.

"What—"

The pressure increases, and as I open my mouth to protest the intrusion, the tip of his finger slips inside and he sucks down on my clit, hurtling me into a powerful orgasm. Everything clenches and I nearly lose my breath as he continues lapping at me, drawing out every last ounce of pleasure. The moment he lets go, my legs flop out to the side, but I can't seem to care at all. Faintly, I hear Mr. Thorne moving around and then the sleep mask is dragged up and off my face. I blink a few times to focus and soon my attention is drawn to Mr. Thorne, who has opened his pants and pushed them down, working quickly to put on a condom.

Resolutely, he lifts up my legs and with a swift thrust, pushes his cock inside me, making me yelp.

"Fuck," he groans, grinding against me to get even farther inside. "You feel good."

All I want is to sleep, or at least rest for a little while, but the way he looks at me lets me know that's not an option. Surrendering to his will, I draw a stuttering breath, trying to adjust to his size and the feeling of being completely filled.

"That's it," he says, leaning over me and staring straight at me while he begins to thrust. "Let me fuck you."

When he lets go of my legs, I wrap them around his waist; he uses his hands to caress my breasts, my belly, and my hips.

"You're so beautiful," he moans, thrusting harder.

"T-thank you, Sir." I feel beautiful right now, sexy and desirable.

His fingers slip between my thighs. "And so wet," he continues. "I knew you'd love a good fucking." His dirty words have the opposite effect than I would've expected. Rather than repel me, they arouse me.

"Don't you?" he whispers roughly, reaching up to grab my hair, forcing my head back and exposing my neck.

"Yes, yes, Sir!" I cry.

Satisfied with my answer, he starts massaging my clit and I whimper in response. I'm so tender, but he feels good inside me, so I attempt to focus on the delicious sensation of him stretching and filling me to perfection.

"Oh," I moan, clenching as he pushes inside again. "Oh, God!"

"That's it," he encourages, thrusting harder. "Take it like a good girl. Let me feel you come."

"Please!" I gasp. "More."

"Yeah?" he pants. "You need more? More cock?"

He fucks me relentlessly while I writhe beneath him, completely naked and at his mercy, and yet I somehow know he won't harm me. I hear myself babbling but I don't know what I'm saying anymore. I need for him to never stop what he's doing. I tremble under his hands as he runs them up my body, cupping my breasts before framing my face. He covers my body completely, and at the end of each thrust, rotates his hips so that he presses against me. His face is inches from mine, and I can't look away.

"Come," he orders softly. "Let me feel it. You're so fucking sweet. Give me this too."

He moves his hands to my wrists, pinning me down, fucking me into the mattress. I can't move. I'm trapped. I'm his. I'm his. I'm ...

I come, screaming, but I don't think I make a sound. He takes my body and gives me this feeling in return. And in that moment, it's so worth it. I never want it to end. Of course it does, as all good things do, and I feel him sitting up between my legs. I watch, still breathing harshly, as he pulls out, peels the condom off, and jerks his cock twice before he comes on me, gasping my name.

"You're mine now," he groans, spilling himself on my over-heated skin. "You're mine."

"Yes," I agree, sighing as he practically collapses, half his body on top of me. He kisses me with surprising tenderness before exhaling deeply and resting his head on my chest. Acting on instinct, I run my fingers through his hair and realize my mistake too late.

"I'm sorry, Sir," I whisper, lifting my arms back up.

"No, don't stop," he says. "It feels good."

Smiling to myself, I stroke his head, messing up his neatly styled hair. I know I should probably contemplate what transpired here: my discovery that sex can be utterly mind-blowing and the fact that I want to do it again—very soon—but I'm just so tired. I drift a little and I think Mr. Thorne does, as well. It's peaceful and quiet.

Suddenly, his whole body jerks, startling me out of my near slumber. With a soft curse he climbs off the bed, saying something about the bathroom. I stretch my body, smiling lazily at the ceiling. I can't remember the last time I felt this relaxed. Mr. Thorne returns after a few minutes, holding a wet rag and a small towel. Obligingly, I spread my legs and let him wash between them, which he does very gently.

"You're still so swollen," he comments, tracing his thumb over my clit before circling my entrance with his index finger. "And wet," he adds.

I feel embarrassed that his simple touches are making my heart beat faster and causing my body to awaken once more.

"Oh, to be young again," Mr. Thorne says teasingly. "I knew you wouldn't be able to get enough, once you were properly fucked."

I blush, feeling like a hussy, but I can't help it; he's right.

"Would you like to be fucked again, sweet girl?"

"Yes," I admit, ignoring the feeling of shame that automatically creeps up on me when I voice my desire.

"You'll have to wait a little while," he says unapologetically. I understand. He's forty years old, after all. But while I don't mind waiting, time is an issue for me tonight.

"What time is it, Sir?" I ask.

"Why?"

"I have to be home by midnight."

He smiles. "Or you'll turn into a pumpkin?"

"Not exactly," I say, returning the smile. "It's just ... my friend is expecting me."

Mr. Thorne's eyes leave my body and snap up to meet mine, the severity in his gaze making me nervous. "And what is this friend's name?" he demands.

"Jo," I whisper.

His nostrils flare and his eyes darken even further. He's upset. Why?

"Who is he to you?" he asks.

He? Oh, shit.

"Jo's a girl," I explain quickly. "Her full name is Joanne, but I've only ever known her as Jo."

The moment I say it his expression turns soft, and he strokes my thigh. *Was he jealous?*

"Oh. I see," he says. "Why is she expecting you so late?"

I squirm a bit, this time not from horniness, as Jo would call it. "Well, she's not, really," I lie. "But I thought it might be safest if someone knew where I was, who could call ... someone, if something happened to me."

Mr. Thorne stares at me, his eyebrows drawn together as he frowns. "I won't hurt you," he finally says. "I'd never do that."

"I know," I whisper. "It just seemed safest for someone to know where I am."

He nods. "I understand. And I'm glad you're being careful, Abigail. The world can be a dangerous place." He runs his hand down my upper body, tickling my belly until I smile. "This Jo, does she know about our arrangement?"

"Yes."

"And?" he asks, looking into my eyes.

"She's cool. She won't tell anyone else, I promise."

"She's a good friend?"

"The best," I answer immediately.

He smiles at me. "I'm glad you have someone in your life you can trust. Come on, let's go downstairs again. You can call your Jo and tell her you're spending the night." He stands and holds his hand out to me, an expectant look on his face.

"Spending the night?" I ask, sitting up slowly. "The *whole* night?"

"Yes. That's not a problem, is it?"

Actually, it is. If it were just a matter of telling Jo, it would be fine, but her mother is there, as well, and she thinks I'm out working as a server. Do servers really stay out the whole night?

"No, it's fine," I lie, taking his hand and getting up off the bed.

Mr. Thorne purses his lips, giving me a look. "Abigail, I don't want to force you to do anything. If you'd rather not stay the night—"

"Really, it's okay," I say, but even I can hear how weak it comes out.

"If you're worried about spending the night with me, don't. I have a guest bedroom for you to sleep in."

"Oh. I wouldn't stay in here with you?" I ask, motioning to his bed.

"No. I sleep alone," he says curtly. "Always."

Weird. "Well ... if we're not sleeping together, would it be all right if I go home when you go to bed?" I ask, holding my breath.

"Yes, I suppose that does make sense," he agrees. "But until then, you're mine, and I like to stay up late on my days off."

I beam at him. "Yes, Sir!"

He chuckles at my happy expression. "I guess you like sleeping in your own bed as much as I do, sweet girl."

That's not it at all. Of course, I don't say that. I merely keep smiling as he helps me put the black dress and heels back on and leads me downstairs to call Jo, while I pray she'll be able to convince her mom that it's perfectly normal for a server to stay out until the middle of the night.

CHAPTER FIFTEEN

After ending the call with Jo, I return to the living room and sit down next to Mr. Thorne, who has turned the TV back on.

"Everything all right?" he asks.

"Yeah. I'm yours for the rest of the night."

"I like the sound of that."

"I do too, Sir." And I really mean it.

"Here, I brought you a Coke," he says, handing me a tall glass, the sides damp with condensation. "Almost like being at the movies, huh?"

I take the drink, gaping at him. It's such a small gesture, but there's so much meaning behind it. He remembers our talk last time about how I can't afford to go to the movies, so he's giving me the experience at home. It's one of the sweetest things I've ever experienced. I take a sip and place it back on the table.

"Thank you, Sir. Can I get you anything?" I ask. "I can make popcorn."

He smiles at me. "It does go well with a movie, but I couldn't eat another bite. Besides, I have no idea if there's popcorn in the house."

"You don't do your own shopping?"

"No, I have an assistant who takes care of a lot of things, including the grocery shopping. I don't know half of what's in the cupboards, I'll admit."

"An assistant? Is she pretty?" *Where did that come from?*

Mr. Thorne laughs. "Andrew is quite attractive, if that's your type."

"Oh."

"Yes, *oh*," he says, smirking. "Nothing for you to be jealous of, sweet girl. I already told you: There's only you." My cheeks flame from embarrassment as Mr. Thorne pulls me closer. "Only you, Abigail," he murmurs softly, stroking my hair. The look in his eyes is hypnotic and all I can do is stare up at him.

"And what about you?" he continues.

"What about me?" I whisper.

"Are you seeing anyone else?"

Immediately, I start to shake my head, but he holds me by my chin, stopping me.

"I realize I don't have a say in what you do when you leave here, so I want you to be honest with me."

"There's no one, Sir. Only you. I'm yours completely."

He closes his eyes for a moment, as though he's savoring my words. "I'd like for you to keep it that way," he says, gently running his fingers across my throat, making me shiver. "Is that too much to ask?"

I shake my head. It's not as though I have guys lined up around the block. Making this promise to Mr. Thorne is easy.

"Only you," I say, "Sir."

His lips are on mine in the next moment, kissing me with so much heat that I feel it all over. I let him push me onto my back and slide my dress up. Moaning wantonly, I wrap my legs around him, unable to stop myself from rocking my hips. What is it about this man that makes me lose all inhibitions? His dark chuckle reaches my ear before he bites on my neck, probably marking me, but I just don't care.

"More, please."

"So eager," he says, lifting me up to reach for the zipper in the back. I feel no shame at the moment and as he unzips my dress, I pull up his shirt, wanting him naked. My hands slip underneath the fabric, and what I feel against my fingers isn't smooth skin but rather something bumpy and uneven. As I flatten my palm against his hard abdomen, trying to figure out what I'm touching, I realize Mr. Thorne has stopped moving entirely. For a second, we're both frozen in position, but then he pushes himself off me and I catch a glimpse of a white criss-cross pattern of scars where my hand touched his skin. There are so many of them, and just thinking of how they got there makes my stomach turn.

Mr. Thorne doesn't say anything, his expression stony. With slow, deliberate movements, he tucks his shirt back in and sits quietly next to me, staring into space. I sit up slowly.

"Did someone do that to you?" I whisper.

He doesn't respond.

"I'm sorry." I move a little closer, tentatively placing my hand on his shoulder.

He gives me a curt nod, clenching his jaw several times. His posture is rigid. "You can go put your own clothes on now. We're done for the night."

His dismissal stings, but I'm not sure he actually means it. It's obvious he didn't want me to see what I've seen. He's never really taken any of his clothes off in front of me, which I always thought was one of his weird quirks, but now it makes sense.

"I'd like to stay," I tell him, moving my hand up to caress his hair. "Watch the movie with you, Sir. Or whatever else you'd like to do."

"Why?" He looks at me. "I'll pay you the same amount, if that's what you're worried about."

I have no idea how to respond to that. Realistically, that *should* be my only concern. But it isn't. The money he pays me is my main motivation for being here, but I didn't *have* to offer to bake him a cake, I didn't *have* to sing "Happy Birthday" to him, and I certainly didn't *have* to buy him a present. I did those things because I wanted to, of my own volition.

"I don't want our night together to be over yet," I say. "It's still your birthday, sort of. I'd like to spend it with you."

He examines me closely. "You really are such a sweet girl, aren't you, Abigail?"

He's asked me that before, and I know my answer. "Yes. *Your* sweet girl, Mr. Thorne."

I lean in, kissing him on the lips. A spark of tenderness rushes through me as he responds, reaching up to gently cup my cheek. "Do you want to, uh, continue?" I ask.

He shakes his head. "The moment's passed, wouldn't you say?"

I don't know what to tell him. If I hadn't put my hands up his shirt, he'd probably be fucking me on this couch right now, and I know it's my fault the mood is ruined. Feeling disappointed, I can't hold back a small sigh.

"Let's watch the movie," he says, touching me under my chin before zipping up my dress again. "It's all right. There'll be other nights."

"Yes, Sir."

He pours more wine for both of us and starts the movie. While he seems perfectly at ease, I can't help but feel awkward just sitting here. We've never done this before and I'm not sure how to act around him.

"What is it?" he asks. "You're fidgeting. Are you cold?"

"Oh, uh, maybe a little."

"C'mere," he says, lifting his arm in invitation. I move into the corner of the couch with him and curl my legs underneath me, relaxing as he drapes his arm around me. "Better?"

"Much, Sir. Thank you."

"Thank *you*, Abigail," he says, giving me a small squeeze.

We watch the movie like that. I can't remember the last

time someone held me for a long period of time. It's really nice. But at the same time, I can't stop myself from wondering about the man who's embracing me. How did he get those scars? Even from my brief glimpse I could tell it had to have been a serious injury. What if it wasn't an accident and someone hurt him on purpose? The thought makes me shiver.

"Still cold?" he asks, rubbing my arm.

"I'm okay." I lean into him and close my eyes, soaking up his warmth and affection as he slowly caresses my skin from my fingertips to my elbow, over and over again. At some point, I must nod off, because suddenly I'm being awakened by Mr. Thorne saying my name and stroking my cheek. I pry my eyes open, looking into his warm hazel gaze. I'm still in his arms, heavy and sleepy.

"Is the movie over?" I mumble.

"Mmhm."

"I'm sorry I missed it. Was it good?"

"Not really," Mr. Thorne chuckles. "There were aliens for some inexplicable reason."

"Oh, that's too bad," I say, frowning.

"Perhaps my expectations were too high."

"You were right. You don't always get what you wish for—not even on your birthday."

Mr. Thorne brushes my hair off my forehead, stroking the length of it down my back.

"Not always," he murmurs, leaning down to kiss me, "but sometimes."

CHAPTER SIXTEEN

"Hon, start finding the toys you want to bring to Aunt Jo's, okay? We have to leave soon."

"Okay!"

I smile at my reflection as I finish putting on my makeup. Not too much, though—Mr. Thorne likes me looking natural.

The weeks have flown by. I've spent my days with Luke, exploring the city in new ways. Now that we have money, we have new opportunities. We've gone to the good parts of town to visit parks and playgrounds where I don't have to worry about needles in the sandbox. We've bought a new couch to replace our old, lumpy one, and gotten some pretty knick-knacks for our apartment, which is looking more like a well-kept home. We've had Jo's girls over for a slumber party and it felt fantastic being able to reciprocate and give her a much-needed night off. We've baked, we've had movie nights, and we've hung out at the mall. I've even gone on two job interviews, but my lack of experience is holding me back. I still look for work, but not nearly as much as before, and I know it's because I enjoy being with Mr. Thorne so much. After the night of his birthday, I was worried things would become awkward or he'd stop asking me to come over, but thankfully that didn't happen.

I can't say that we've developed a routine, because I never know what to expect when I go to his house. Some nights I cook; others, he orders in and I only make a dessert for us to enjoy after dinner. Sometimes he ravishes me the moment I step through the door, and other times he saves it for the end of the night. We've had sex in his bed, on the couch, on the kitchen table, in the hallway, and on the stairs. One night, I spent twenty minutes on my hands and knees, scrubbing his already immaculate floors while he watched. Then he pushed up my dress and fucked me from behind, warning me that I'd better keep on scrubbing unless I wanted a spanking. Smiling to myself, I slid the brush across the wet floor and out of reach, delighting in his reaction as he called me a naughty girl and thrust even harder while bringing his hand down on my ass again and again until I came so hard, I could hardly see straight.

The memory makes my face heat up. The truth is that visiting Mr. Thorne doesn't feel like a job anymore.

I'm putting on my shoes when there's a knock at the door. I'm not expecting anyone, so I stand up on my tiptoes to peer through the peephole. What I see is enough to make me lose my balance and stumble backward.

"Abigail, I know you're in there."

The voice is muffled, but I'd recognize it anywhere. It's a voice from my childhood, stirring up memories both good and bad. I don't want to open the door, but I do it anyway. Just a few inches.

"What do you want?" I blurt out.

"Well, that's certainly a nice greeting. Are you going to let me in?"

"No, Mom. What are you doing here? How'd you know where I was?"

Her lips pucker with displeasure as she pulls her coat

tighter around herself. "I've always known where you were, Abigail."

"Five years?" I whisper, the pang of hurt I feel surprising me. "You've known for five years and you never came by?"

She doesn't say anything, but her strong gaze wavers and she looks down.

"What do you want?"

"I want you to come home."

I've heard the expression *jaw-dropping*, but it's never happened to me before this moment. I recover quickly. "No. Absolutely not."

"I know what's going on," she says.

My gut twists in anxiety. She knows about Mr. Thorne? That I'm a rich man's ... whatever it is I am?

"I know Patrick is gone and you're alone now," she continues.

"I'm *not* alone," I hiss, relieved that she doesn't know about my job and angry once more. "I have my son. Or did you forget about him?"

"Of course not."

"How'd you even find out about Patrick?"

"Cecile Simpson."

"You're lying. When have you ever talked to Jo's mom?"

"She talked to *me*. Yelled at me. In the middle of the super-market, no less! She says her daughter is always watching your child until all hours of the night. Is this true, Abigail?"

"I have to work," I grit out. "Now, if you'll excuse me, Mother. I have to go."

"I'm not leaving," she says with an edge to her voice. "This has gone on long enough. It's time for you to come home."

I feel a tug on my shirt.

"Mommy, is it time to go to Aunt Jo's? Who's that lady?"

"It's no one, baby. Can you start putting your shoes and jacket on, please?" I say, blocking my mother's view of Luke.

"I can watch him for you," she says. "If you're going out."

I gape at her. "I'm not leaving him with you! You're a stranger to him."

"I know," she admits, regret lacing her voice.

"And that's your own fault," I can't help but add. "Goodbye."

She's still out there when we leave. Her eyes are glued to Luke as I tug on his hand and hurry down the hall toward the stairs.

"Abigail!" she calls, her voice cracking. "Your father ... he's very ill. Please come home."

I don't stop and I don't reply. Moving on autopilot, I hold my son's hand and navigate us through the streets until we reach Jo's, only half-listening to Luke's happy, untroubled chatter. All this time I've held out hope that someday my parents might contact me, realizing they made a mistake, and ask to see me. Having my mom show up and practically order me to come home isn't something I was prepared for, and it's not something I'm willing to do. She didn't even apologize or ask what I wanted. Just like when I lived at home.

Inside Jo's apartment, Luke leaves my side, excited to show off his new toys.

"Abbi, are you okay?" Jo asks as we watch the three kids play. "You look ... off."

"Tell me the truth, please," I mumble, turning to her. "You'd tell me if you didn't want to babysit Luke for me anymore, right?"

"What are you talking about? You know I love having him here. The girls never fight with him around."

"My mom came by today."

Her eyes nearly pop out of her head. "Are you serious?"

I nod my head.

"What'd she want?"

I scoff. "For me to come home. I guess your mom verbally attacked her at the store or something, saying that Luke is always here at night because Patrick left us."

"Oh my God," Jo groans. "I *told* her not to say anything."

"It's okay. I know your mom means well." I run my fingers through my hair. "I don't think I've seen the last of mine, though. If she ever finds out what I do for a living—"

"She won't," Jo says, putting her arm around me.

"If *anyone* ever finds out, I could lose Luke," I tell her, biting the inside of my cheek to force my eyes not to well up.

"No one will find out. I won't tell and you know Mr. Thorne won't, either."

Drawing a deep breath through my nose, I do my best to be Zen. "I have to get over there," I say. "How do I look?"

"Pretty," Jo says with a sad smile.

I say goodbye to Luke, giving him a big hug before heading out to find a cab to take me to Medina.

Three hours later, I'm still holding it together. I play my part to perfection, wearing a beautiful dress, heels, and even a string of pearls as I clean up after the—if I do say so myself—delicious meal I cooked and served. I've sent Mr. Thorne demure smiles and batted my eyelashes at him, asked to sit on his lap, and called him Sir in a breathy voice. Everything he loves. I haven't been thinking of my mother showing up. I haven't been thinking of my father's illness, whatever it might be. I'm focused solely on the man next to me, on pleasing him.

"Abigail, is something wrong?" he suddenly asks.

I don't stop loading the dishwasher. "No, everything's fine, Sir."

"Are you certain?"

"Absolutely."

I feel him watching me and I force myself to smile as I start the program and stand up to face him. "All done," I say cheerfully.

"You're very domestic," he observes. "I like that."

"You don't say," I remark dryly.

He flashes me a grin and pulls me close, trapping me against the counter as he towers above me. "Not so timid around me anymore, are you?"

I hold his gaze. "No, Sir."

"That's good," he says, running a large hand down one side of my body, outlining my slight curves.

"Is it?" Suddenly I'm worried I'm being too bold. He said he likes submissive women, and that's what I've been trying to portray all night.

He cocks his head to the side, giving me an inquisitive look.

"I mean, you like me acting submissively," I explain.

He takes a small step forward, pressing me against the counter while both his hands roam freely across my body. "Spread your legs," he whispers in my ear, nipping lightly at the lobe.

I moan as he massages my breast and slides one hand up my inner thigh to caress me with the certainty of an experienced lover.

"You like this, Abigail?"

"Yes," I breathe, reaching up to hold on to his broad shoulders.

"The things I want to do to you," he murmurs softly, dipping his fingers inside me, "to use your sweet body for my pleasure. Would you like that?"

I nod my head, closing my eyes as I rest my forehead against his chest, my fingers clawing at the fabric of his shirt while he moves his fingers faster and faster.

"Should I let you come?" he asks, sweeping his thumb across my clit. "Or should I deny you? Have you been a good girl?"

His words make me whimper, they feel so good to me, causing me to spasm around his fingers. "P-please," I beg, lifting my left leg up, opening myself to him. "Fuck me, Sir."

The next thing I know, Mr. Thorne has tossed me onto the kitchen island, stuff flying everywhere. He reaches behind me to yank down the zipper of my dress and I quickly push it down around my waist while he opens his pants with hurried movements and puts on a condom. He doesn't speak. He lifts my lower half, pulls the dress off me, and holds my legs open, thrusting his cock inside me with a low groan. He doesn't pause. Immediately, he pulls back and then pushes inside again. Again and again. He takes me with a savagery I've only read about in romance novels, where the ruggedly handsome pirate ravishes the barmaid because he simply can't contain his manly desires. This is like that, but real. Better. I writhe on the hard surface, lifting my hands up above my head, surrendering to him, letting him do whatever he wants. It feels incredible.

"Fuck," Mr. Thorne pants. "There you are. Look at you. Look at you."

His right hand lets go of my hip and glides up my body with a firm touch, pausing to grab a jiggling breast and pinch my nipple. I shiver as he leans over me, his hand moving upward to grasp my throat in a sign of complete domination as he takes my body without apology. I open my mouth to speak, not sure what I'm going to say, but he silences me with his eyes.

"You *love* this," he says, emphasizing his point with a sharp thrust. Involuntarily, I arch my back, reveling in the feeling of his thick cock inside me, his hand on my throat, his eyes on my face.

"Y-y-yes!" I croak as he continues to pound into me, and I come with an unprecedented intensity that makes me lose my breath and screw my eyes shut.

Once I'm able to breathe again, I draw deep gulps of air, willing my heart to slow down its furious pace. Mr. Thorne is slumped on top of me, heaving for air as well. I bring my limp arms down in a half-hearted attempt to stroke his hair, even though I'm completely worn out. After a little while, he raises himself up on his elbows and looks at me.

"Did you enjoy that, Abigail?"

I nod my head, giving him a tired smile.

"And you still think you're only *acting* submissively?"

"What?" I whisper.

"I don't know what's going on with you tonight, why you were putting on a show earlier. But you and I both know that's not what I want. I don't want you acting, which is what you've been doing all night. I want the *real* you: the girl I just fucked. No pretending, no posing, just a love of being dominated. You *crave* it. You come so fucking hard when I hold you down, when I take control. That's who I want. Be that girl all the time, the natural submissive you truly are."

He leans down, kissing me gently, before moving off of me. I listen as he fixes his clothes and moves around, feeling as though I've had a bucket of ice water thrown in my face. Why would he say something like that? I sit up on the edge of the island, looking down to avoid Mr. Thorne's gaze as I gingerly lower myself down, unsure what to do now. Should I get dressed again? Start cleaning up the mess we made? I wrap my arms around myself, both uncomfortable and chilled, shaking as I feel my own wetness on the insides of my thighs—a harsh reminder of what we just did.

"Come here, Abigail."

Mr. Thorne's voice is soft and soothing, as though he's speaking to a skittish animal, which isn't that far off, I suppose. His outstretched hand beckons me and part of me wants to run to him and fling myself into his arms.

"You're wrong," I say. "About me."

"Am I?"

Yes. No. I don't know.

"Come here," he says again, even softer this time. "You know it's the truth, deep down."

I *don't* know that. What I do know is that he just fucked

me to prove a point. So what has he proven? That he'll be able do rougher stuff with me now, since he's convinced I crave it? What does it say about me, about the kind of woman I am? That I can't take care of myself or my son? That I need a man to take charge of me? That I'm weak? Helpless? Is that how Mr. Thorne sees me?

"No." I shake my head minutely.

"No?"

"No," I say again, bending down to grab the dress and cover myself with it.

"Abigail—"

"I'd like to call it an early night. Please, Sir?"

I need time to think. Intellectually, I know his claims are accurate: I react positively to him being dominant; it turns me on. Emotionally, however, I'm more confused than ever. I'm scared about what this means for me. Will I ever be able to have normal sex again and enjoy it? Or will I keep going down this dark path, losing all control of what happens to me? The thought terrifies me.

"Very well," Mr. Thorne says, although he doesn't look happy.

"Thank you, Sir."

I run upstairs as quickly as my legs can carry me, cleaning up and changing back into my own clothes. I have to get out of here. Too much has happened today and I feel my control slipping.

"The cab should be here shortly," he tells me as he hands me the manila envelope by the door.

I nod my head, not sure what else to say. The silence is deafening and for once I wish I'd familiarized myself with the bus schedule so I could just leave now, instead of having to stand here and wait. Mr. Thorne sighs softly, scrubbing his face with his hands.

"Look, Abigail," he starts, "I think I owe you an apology."

I don't know how to respond, so he continues.

"It's taken me a long time to figure out what sort of person I am, and what I like. I shouldn't have said the things I said, knowing how young and inexperienced you are. But the truth is, I'm frustrated."

"Frustrated?" I whisper. "With me?"

"No." He shakes his head. "You're everything I want. In fact, I'd like to make you an offer." He draws a deep breath. "I'm tired of always sending you home at the end of the night, not knowing where you go or if you're going to be okay. It's not enough, what we have now. I want more."

My head starts spinning.

"Abigail, I want you to move in here with me, and make our arrangement permanent. The money I'll pay will ensure you won't ever want for anything. You'll have your own room, of course, and I won't ask too much of you, I promise. But after getting to know you, I'm convinced we want the same things, both in regard to sex and getting along in general. I think— no, I *know*—having you here will make me a happy man, because I'm—"

A car horn honking right outside interrupts him and the sound snaps me out of the state I'm in, forcing me to really look at the man in front of me, who's offering me a very good deal: a chance to be a part of his world, his affluent lifestyle, and to never worry about money again. His expression is open, hopeful even, as he gazes down at me.

I feel as though I've been punched in the gut. Move in with him? To be his live-in fantasy? Impossible. I live in the real world. Outside this lovely house, outside this rich neighborhood, far away from this beautiful man is a small boy who needs me more. And I will always put him first. He's the reason I'm doing this in the first place, and he can never know how I earn my money, how his mom likes to crawl around on the floor in front of a rich man. I'd die if he ever saw me like that. The person I am when I'm with my son can never fit into Mr. Thorne's life, and the fact that he asked me to live here proves just how little he really knows about me. The invitation is for me, not for me and my son.

"Say something," Mr. Thorne murmurs.

"I can't do this."

"Abigail—"

"I can't, Mr. Thorne! I've lied to you. I'm not who you think I am at all. And this," I wave my hand around, hyperventilating. "I can't do this. I'm so, so sorry."

Watching his open expression change to one of disbelief and disappointment is heartbreaking. Fighting back tears, I scramble to open the door and exit the house on unsteady legs.

"I don't understand," he says, following me outside as I reach the waiting cab.

I look up at him again. I instilled false hope in myself thinking this could ever work out. I made him believe I could make him happy, and in another life, maybe I could have. But in this life, it's impossible.

"Everything I've made you do," he asks, his voice low and gritty. "Did you hate it? Was it all an act?"

I don't want to be a liar anymore. I don't want to hurt him any more than I already have. I don't want him to believe he's forced me to do anything I didn't want, when the truth is, I've loved every moment of our time together.

"No," I sob, as my voice cracks. "N-no, Mr. Thorne."

I jump into the cab. "Please, just go!" I cry to the puzzled driver.

"Abigail, please wait!"

I watch as Mr. Thorne reaches for the door handle just as the taxi starts to move. His usual composed exterior crumbles as he chases us halfway down the driveway before stopping and putting his hands on his knees, lowering his head.

"Are you okay?" the driver asks. "Should I call the cops?"

I shake my head, feeling hysterical. I'm not okay at all. None of this is okay. But after a few minutes, I've calmed down enough to give the driver my address. I can't have Luke seeing me like this right now. Digging out my new pre-owned cell phone I bought last week, I send Jo a text, telling her I'm not feeling well, but that I'll pick Luke up in the morning and not to worry.

I watch the dark waters as we drive across the bridge, knowing I won't be making this trip again. The thought brings a fresh batch of tears and I cry silently until the driver pulls up in front of my building.

Feeling numb, I climb the stairs, wanting nothing but a hot shower and to lie in my own bed. I have to figure out where I go from here, but right now, my head is fuzzy and I'm so very tired.

Abruptly, I stop dead in my tracks. The door to my apartment is partly open, but I know I locked it behind me when Luke and I left. With a shaking hand, I push it open, listening carefully for sounds. There's nothing. I step into my hallway, already seeing the devastation in the living room: The coffee table has been knocked over and there are books scattered everywhere. The DVD rack is empty.

Luke's movies.

There's sudden movement in my peripheral vision and I gasp when a man comes barging out of my bedroom, a duffle bag over his shoulder. He's wearing a ski mask. My heart slams against my rib cage as we stare at each other.

"Please don't hurt me," I manage to croak, my throat constricting with fear. "I have a child."

"You got money?" His voice is gruff.

"Y-yes, yes!" I cry, pulling out the envelope and throwing it in his general direction. "It's a thousand dollars."

He picks it up slowly, glancing into it before stuffing it into his bag, only taking his eyes off me for a moment. Without warning, he jumps forward and slams into me, knocking me down before I can react. Thankfully, he doesn't stop, running out the door and then down the hall.

Stunned, I sit up before jumping to my feet and slamming

the door shut. The lock's broken, so I can only use the chain. Feeling safer, I quickly walk through the apartment with one goal in mind.

Please be there, please be there.

The moment I turn on the lights in the bathroom, I start to cry. On the floor is the now-empty Tupperware container I'd taped to the back of the toilet, which once stored all the money I'd saved. There's nothing left.

I walk back into the living room and sink down on the floor, looking around at the ruins of my life. I'm right back where I started. Nothing has changed for me, after all. I promised Luke we'd be okay. I promised him and I've failed him once again.

At that moment, I'm beyond relieved that I didn't go by Jo's to bring Luke home. My son is safe, but for how long? I can't bring him back here. We've been lucky up until tonight, but this is such a bad neighborhood and break-ins, muggings, and robberies happen all the time. Just a few weeks ago Mrs. Watt chased a prowler off her fire escape. This will probably happen again, and then what? What if it's someone violent or on drugs who breaks in next time? Someone who isn't content with stealing money and DVDs, who will see a young woman and her child as easy victims?

I look down at my hands. They're shaking. Wrapping my arms around my body, I rock back and forth as hot tears stream down my face.

"Please," I sob into the quiet of the night. "I can't do this anymore. I need help. I need help."

By the time it starts to get light outside, I've made a plan. I clean myself up, straighten up the mess, and pack a bag, knowing I won't spend another night here ever again. First, I'll go to Jo's to pick up Luke, and then we'll go to Pinewood, back to my parents. It's not what I want, but it's what I have to do. I have to go home.

I have to cross another line.

CHAPTER SEVENTEEN

"Abbi, no! You can't!" Jo exclaims, then quickly lowers her voice to a whisper. "Sorry."

We're sitting at her kitchen table, both of us sipping strong coffee, and I've just finished telling her everything that happened tonight. The kids are still asleep, thankfully.

"What choice do I have?" I say. "I can't go back to my place."

"No, I agree. But going to your parents', after everything that's happened? They don't deserve you or Luke back in their lives."

"I don't know what else to do. All the money's gone. I should've hidden it better."

"Why did you keep it all at home?" Jo asks. "You have a bank account, right?"

Sighing, I nod my head. "I don't know. It seemed safer, I guess? It sounds ridiculous, considering what happened, but Patrick still has access to the account and it's not like I had paychecks to show where I got the money. What if someone started asking questions? How does an unemployed woman suddenly have thousands of dollars each month?"

"Yeah, I see your point." She draws a deep breath, bringing

her hands together. "Okay, here's what's going to happen. You and Luke will move in here with us."

"Jo—"

"No, Abbi. I know what you're going to say: that you don't want to impose, that I can't afford it, that this place is too small, and probably a million other reasons why this isn't a good idea, but I just don't care." She grabs my hand, squeezing it tightly. "You are *not* going back to Pinewood to have your mom shame you for the choices you've made. We'll work it out somehow."

"Oh, Jo."

"Don't you 'Oh, Jo' me, Abigail Winters," she says sternly. "You'd do the same for me, and you know it. You're my best friend, you're staying here, and that's final."

I'm completely overwhelmed with gratitude, but knowing Jo, a grand speech about how she's the most amazing friend in the world will only make her uncomfortable. So instead, I nod my head. "Okay."

Jo smiles, standing up to clear the table. "Now, I want you to go lie down for a while in my bed. I'll keep the kids quiet when they wake up so you can get some sleep and then we'll figure everything out, all right?"

I nod again, and as I pass by her on my way to bed, I reach out and hug her from behind. Jo doesn't stop rinsing off the mugs we've used, but she leans her head back against mine as I cling to her. "Thank you," I whisper.

After what feels like only five minutes of sleep, I'm woken by Luke jumping on the bed.

"Mommy, you're back!"

"Shhh, baby. Not so loud," I scold gently, wrapping my arms around him.

"Come and play," he begs.

"Why don't we play the sleeping game?" I suggest, only half-serious. "Both of us close our eyes and see who can pretend to sleep the longest?"

"That's boooring," he complains, tugging my hand. *Well, it was worth a shot.* Reluctantly, I sit up.

"There's donuts," Luke tells me. "Pippa and Piper's daddy brought them. I had three!"

Thomas is here? "That sounds good, baby," I say, stifling a yawn as I follow him out.

In the kitchen, the girls are eating and chattering away, their faces sticky from donut glaze. Jo is at the sink, and on a chair sits an awkward-looking Thomas, stiff postured, with a shirt and tie and strangely groomed hair. He looks nothing like the red-eyed, lazy guy I remember from Pinewood, who always wore ratty band T-shirts and wild blond curls.

"Hey, Thomas," I mumble, clearing my hoarse voice.

"Abbi, hi, hey. You, uh, nice to see you ... you," he says, wiping his hands on his pants.

Okay, weird.

The girls ask to put on a movie and disappear with Luke in tow, leaving me alone with their parents. Jo is still fake-cleaning the mugs she already washed this morning and Thomas just sort of sits there, wide-eyed and jittery.

"Is there any coffee?" I ask. *Or did Thomas drink it all?*

"Oh, sure," Jo replies, practically pushing me into a chair as she starts serving me with hurried movements.

Finally, she acknowledges her ex-boyfriend's presence. "Thank you for the donuts," she says. "Abbi and I have a lot to do today, so ..."

"Right. Right," Thomas says, standing up, fiddling with his tie. He starts to walk out of the kitchen, but then he stops, turning to look at my best friend. "Jo. I know ... I know I haven't been perfect, and I've made a lot of mistakes, but I—I love you. I've never stopped loving you."

Oh, boy. "I'll just ..." I say, pushing my chair away from the table.

"No, stay, please," Thomas says. "I want you to hear this too, Abbi, so Jo knows how serious I am." He turns to her again. "I've made you a lot of promises in the past, I know that, but I swear I've changed. I have a steady job now. I can take care of you and the girls. And, more importantly, I want to. You're all I've ever wanted."

Hesitantly, he slides a small box in front of her. "Will you marry me?"

Jo's stance doesn't change and I feel as though I can't breathe, waiting for her reply. But after a minute, when Jo still hasn't thrown herself into his arms saying, "Yes, yes, a thousand times, yes!" I realize I shouldn't be listening to this. As stealthily as I possibly can, I stand up and tiptoe out of the kitchen, leaving the two of them. The kids are watching a Disney movie; I can't remember the name, but going by Luke's mesmerized expression, I'm sure I'll learn it soon enough. The minutes tick by without any news from the kitchen. I'm dying to know Jo's reply, my own problems momentarily forgotten.

"Look, Mommy, she can do snow magic!" Luke's exclamation penetrates my thoughts and I smile at his excitement. Glancing at the screen, I see two girls skating inside a large room, having a great time.

"I see it, baby," I reply.

"Abbi?"

I look up, seeing Thomas in the doorway.

"Jo wants to talk to you."

In the kitchen, Jo is now sitting at the table, looking red-eyed and happy. It's like she's been lit up from the inside.

"I said yes," she tells me unnecessarily.

"Of course you did," I say, choking up as tears well in my eyes. "B-best wishes."

"Oh, Abbi!" Jo exclaims, rushing to embrace me. "Please don't cry. You're still staying here with us. We'd never ask you to leave."

"T-that's not, I'm not ..." I blubber, still hugging her.

"Of course you're staying," I hear Thomas say. "Oh, shit, Abbi, don't cry. We'll figure everything out."

129

"I'm just s-so happy for you guys," I manage to get out. "I'm sorry. I'm a mess. When's the big day?" I ask, eager to change the topic.

"No idea," Jo says. "There's no rush or anything."

"Right. I'm just happy to be home." Thomas' voice is soft as he gazes at Jo. I feel like an intruder in their happy moment.

"I'll take Luke to the apartment for a little while. You should tell the girls and celebrate in private."

Both of them start protesting, but I cut them off. It's almost noon now and the safest time to go. This morning, I only managed to throw a few things in a bag before leaving. I know Luke will want his toys and I need to pack up some more clothes.

"Take a cab," Thomas finally says, handing me some money. "I insist." His words remind me of Mr. Thorne, making my heart feel heavy.

Half an hour later, driving toward our old neighborhood with my son next to me, I'm happy to be able to give my new roommates some privacy. With the two of us moving in, they won't have much of that from now on.

"Are we going home now?" Luke asks after a few blocks.

"Yes. We're just getting a few things, though. We're gonna stay with Aunt Jo for a while."

"Why?"

"Because ..." I don't know if I should tell him the truth. I don't want him to be scared.

"Is it like a slumber party? That'd be awesome!"

Relieved, I smile, giving his hand a small squeeze. "That's exactly what it is, hon. You're going to have so much fun with Pippa and Piper."

He grins up at me. "Can I bring all my toys?"

"We'll see how much we can fit in the trunk," I laugh. Exiting the cab, I ask the driver to please keep the meter running for us. This won't take long.

"C'mon," I say, helping Luke out onto the sidewalk. "Let's go pack, buddy!"

But we don't go pack. Instead, I freeze on the spot, my heart jumping into my throat at the impossible sight of *him* standing there, right in front of my building, only ten feet away. His back is half-turned to me, but I know it's him. Mr. Thorne. Here, in my neighborhood, looking completely out of place in his expensive suit and coat.

My instinct tells me to run, to hide, but I can't move. I watch, terrified, as he turns and the anguished look on his face melts into relief as our eyes meet.

"Mommy! Let's go!" Luke complains, tugging on my hand.

Mr. Thorne's gaze flickers and settles on my son, who's trying unsuccessfully to pull me forward. His lips part, his eyes widen, and he takes an unsure step back just as Luke manages to free himself, rushing for the door of the building and tripping right in front of Mr. Thorne.

"Luke!" I run to him, reaching out to help him up, but another pair of hands is faster than mine. I look up into Mr. Thorne's face as he lifts my son to his feet and then immediately recoils as though he's been burned.

I get it. I do. But it still hurts seeing him so repelled by my son.

"You okay, hon?" I ask, looking Luke over.

"Fine," he replies, before glancing at Mr. Thorne. "Thanks!"

"You're ... welcome." His voice is hoarse, faint, as he stares at Luke.

All of us stand up and Luke grabs my hand again, tugging it impatiently.

"Abigail, I ..." Mr. Thorne's face is ashen at this point and he looks as though he'd rather be anywhere but here.

"Please," I whisper hurriedly. "Just go. It's okay." I allow myself to get lost in his eyes one last time, knowing this is it. Somehow, I hope he'll understand what I can't say out loud.

I'm sorry I lied. I didn't mean to hurt you. Thank you for everything. Goodbye.

"Come on," I tell my son, ushering him inside.

The door slams behind us and we walk up the stairs. I make it to the apartment door before the prickling sensation starts at the corners of my eyes. Ignoring it, I hold Luke behind me and look inside to make sure it's safe before letting him in. He runs to his room while I shut the door, putting on the chain while I suppress the urge to start sobbing. I can't do that right now. We have about five minutes to pack and then we have to leave again.

Pushing myself away from the wall, I stop midstep at the firm knock on the door. Time seems to stand still.

It can't be.

My hand trembles as I take the chain off and open the door.

"M-Mr. Thorne, Sir?" My voice cracks and I absolutely hate how it highlights my emotions. But not as much as I despise the tears that now refuse to stay put, and instead trickle down my face for him to see. "What are you doing here?" I demand.

"May I come in?" he asks.

"Why?"

"I have a proposition for you."

CHAPTER EIGHTEEN

M r. Thorne takes a step forward, examining me closer. It's fairly dark in the hallway since most of the light bulbs need changing and the windows haven't been cleaned in forever.

"Why are you crying?" he asks with a hint of alarm in his voice, reaching out to brush his fingertips against the apple of my cheek. "Sweet girl?"

"Please don't call me that," I whisper, closing my eyes.

He sighs, tilting my face upward. "Abigail, look at me."

I do as I'm told. He looks tired and worn, just like me.

"Let me in. There are things to discuss."

I feel like Molly Ringwald in *Pretty in Pink*. I do *not* want Mr. Thorne to see where I live, especially not with the state the apartment is in at the moment.

"What things?" I ask. "What proposition?"

Mr. Thorne glances around. "I'd really rather talk about that in a less public place. I'm sure you can appreciate why."

"But ... my son."

"I can be discreet."

"How did you even find me?"

"I tracked down the taxi driver this morning. Told him it was very important that I talk to you."

"And?"

"And when that didn't work, I paid him." He's unapologetic. "I *had* to see you again, Abigail," he elaborates. "The way you left—I was worried."

I draw a deep breath, stepping aside to hold the door open. "All right, we can go into the kitchen, I guess."

Mr. Thorne walks past me and I close the door, putting the chain on it again.

"What happened?" He touches the busted lock, frowning.

"Break-in. Last night," I respond.

His lips purse and his brows draw together. He's angry but doesn't say anything as he follows me into the kitchen.

"You can," I motion to the kitchen table, "sit down, if you'd like. You want ... coffee?" I have no idea how to act.

"Coffee would be lovely," he answers, taking a seat.

I put the kettle on to boil and take out the jar of instant coffee, spooning some into two mugs, while he watches in silence. It's an eerily familiar scenario for the two of us.

"Can you just start talking, please?" I ask over my shoulder, before bringing the coffees to the table.

"Very well," he says, giving my chipped mismatched mugs a long look before pulling one of them toward him. "I'd like to discuss the offer I made you last night. It still stands."

"You can't be serious."

"I am. This changes nothing."

"Of course it does," I protest. "It changes everything!"

"Not for me," he says firmly.

"I'm a mom," I say, wringing my hands.

He takes a sip of the coffee, not even making a face at the bitter taste of the cheap instant brand, even though I know he's used to high-quality French roast. "I guess it's not a complete surprise to me."

I stare at him, wide-eyed, shocked by his statement. "It's not?"

"You're very nurturing, very caring." His gaze travels down my body. "And you have little white stretch marks around your belly button and hips. I just thought maybe you'd been heavier at one point."

"I was. When I was pregnant."

He looks up at me. "You must have been a child yourself."

"It wasn't planned," I admit, taking a seat across from him. "I was in high school. Luke was born after I graduated."

"Luke," he says, almost to himself. "He's a good-looking boy."

"He is."

"Where is his father?"

I sigh, pressing the heel of my hand against my forehead where a headache is starting to build. "I don't know. He's gone."

"Gone?"

I nod.

"He left you?" Mr. Thorne exclaims. "With a small child to care for?" His eyes flicker and he exhales before looking at me again, realization dawning. "You said you needed the money. That's why you got into my car in the first place. Why you agreed to do anything I wanted."

"*Everything* I do is for my son," I say. "But ..." *No more lies.* "I did like it, being with you," I continue. "You weren't wrong about me, about what you said last night."

He leans forward, resting his elbows on the table. His eyes are trained on mine. "Why did you run away?"

I feel more tears pressing behind my eyes and inhale deeply through my nose. "I was scared," I croak. "I can't ever be what you want. Don't you see that?"

"No," he says, so very softly. "No, I don't see that at all, sweet girl."

"*Mommy!* My movies!" Luke wails from the living room.

Before I can get up, he comes running into the kitchen, red-faced and teary-eyed. "My movies. They're gone!"

I put him on my lap, stroking his hair. "I know, baby. I'm so sorry."

"Where'd they go?" he asks.

I have no idea how to explain this to him, but I have to try. "Someone borrowed them," I say. "Without asking."

"Who?"

"I don't know."

"But you're not supposed to do that!" he protests.

"That's right. It wasn't very nice at all."

"Will I get them back?"

"I'll get you new ones," I promise. *I just don't know when.*

"This sucks," he mumbles, sniffing loudly. "I was gonna watch them with Pippa and Piper for the sleepover."

"I know." I sigh. "But you can watch their movies. You liked the one with the snow magic, right?"

"Yeah," he admits. "But I like Lightning McQueen better."

"I do too," I whisper. "We'll get him back."

"Okay." He sniffs. "I finished packing."

"Oh, God. The taxi!" The meter must've been running for a good ten minutes by now.

"I sent him off, the driver."

I narrow my eyes at Mr. Thorne. "Why?"

"I'm happy to drive you anywhere. And I needed time with you."

I turn to Luke again. "Can you go play for a little while, hon?"

"Who's he?" my son asks, now staring unabashedly at Mr. Thorne as he climbs off my lap and walks right over to him. "Who are you?"

Mr. Thorne stands, hesitantly reaching out his hand. "I'm Mr. Thorne," he says. "How do you do?"

Luke giggles. "Do what?"

"It means *hi*," I explain.

"Oh, hi!" He grabs Mr. Thorne's hand. "I'm Luke. Do you know my mommy?"

Mr. Thorne glances at me, wide-eyed, and eases his hand back from Luke's grip. He's obviously not used to being around kids and if the situation were different, I would probably find their interaction funny.

"Luke, I need to talk to Mr. Thorne. Can you please go play for a while?"

"But I already put my toys in the bag," he complains. "I wanna watch a movie!"

"You can't, honey."

Luke makes a face that I know all too well; a tantrum is coming unless I do something quickly.

"Here," Mr. Thorne says, holding out his phone. "YouTube?"

Thank God. I pull up a *Cars* playlist, showing Luke how to press play. "Go watch in your room, okay? We won't be long."

Tantrum forgotten, Luke beams at Mr. Thorne, holding the phone like it's a treasure. "Thanks!"

He scampers off, leaving the two of us alone.

"His movies?" Mr. Thorne asks, sitting back down.

"The burglar I saw took them," I say. "I guess to sell them."

"You . . . you saw him?" He gives me an incredulous look.

"He was here when I got home last night. Some creep in a ski mask," I say, shivering at the memory of the stranger from last night.

"You could've been hurt!" Mr. Thorne throws up his hands, agitated. "Fuck, you could've been killed! You can't stay here anymore, Abigail. This place—" He looks around, scrunching up his nose like he smells something rotten.

I see red. "I know that! I'm not stupid," I hiss. "I did the best I could. In case you didn't notice, I'm fucking broke. My boyfriend left us high and dry and I couldn't find a job. I *starved* myself to feed my son. I did the best I could!"

I'm practically yelling now. "How dare you come into my

home and judge me? You have no idea what it's like to go hungry, to care for a child and feel so desperate you'll do *anything* to make sure he doesn't end up on the street or in the goddamned system! I know this place is a dump, I know that. But it was our home. It's the only home Luke has ever known, and now we have to leave. And I'm so fucking scared!"

I draw a shaky breath, choking back a sob. Mr. Thorne stares at me in stunned silence. I've never talked to him like that before. I wonder if anyone has.

"I'm so sorry," I whisper, realizing all of what I just yelled at him was really directed at my mother.

I start crying, burying my face in my hands to muffle the sound. Luke can't see me like this. I'm so scared of everything: of staying here, of leaving here, of Mr. Thorne realizing what a huge mess I am, of the future for me and Luke.

I feel his hands on me, lifting me up as though I weigh nothing at all, and then the warmth of his body against mine as he sits down with me on his lap, wrapping me up in his arms.

"Shhh, sweet girl," he soothes. "It's all right. It's all right now. I'll take care of you. Let me take care of you."

I get lost in the feeling of being cared for, of being held, for just a few minutes. I know there are lots of things we need to talk about, but I need this so desperately.

"Tighter, please," I hiccup.

He squeezes me gently and it feels like heaven being cocooned in his embrace, breathing in his familiar scent, my cheek pressed against the soft wool of his coat. After I've calmed down, he wipes away my tears and offers me a hand-kerchief from his pocket for my runny nose. Finally, I'm able to open up my eyes and look at him.

"Hi," I whisper, because I don't know what else to say. The side of his mouth twitches and the tiny wrinkles in the corners of his eyes appear.

"Hi."

I know what's coming as he leans down and I welcome it,

letting him kiss me with so much tenderness that it almost takes my breath away. Then the mood switches and his lips become demanding. I moan as he takes control, burying his hand in my hair to tilt my head and gain better access to my mouth. It only lasts for a few moments but it's enough to leave me panting and flushed with my heart pounding wildly.

"Don't you see," he mumbles against my lips, "how good we are together?" He kisses me again. "I want you," he breathes.

I feel a twinge of panic. *Not here! Not now!*

"We should ... talk," I manage.

"We should," he agrees, brushing my hair away from my forehead. "Are you all right now?"

"Yes. Will you let me up, please?" I mumble. "I can't concentrate with you this close." My admission makes me blush, which amuses him.

"Good to know I've still got it," he jokes.

"I don't think there was ever any question of that," I reply as he slowly helps me to my feet.

Taking a seat across from him, I fold up the used handkerchief and draw a deep breath, trying to center myself.

"So," I say.

"So," he says. "There was the matter of my proposition."

"Right." I sit up straighter, folding my hands on the table. It looks like we're getting down to business.

"I want you and Luke to come live with me," he says. "Clearly, you're not safe here and that's unacceptable."

"But—"

"Please, let me finish," he says, holding up his hand.

Reluctantly, I nod my head.

"You'll have your own rooms downstairs and I'll take the top floor. I'll pay you handsomely, Abigail, and I mean it when I say you won't have to worry about money anymore." He gives me an expectant look.

That's it? I'm not ungrateful for Mr. Thorne's offer, far

from it. But it's clear that he hasn't thought this through, which I can't blame him for. After all, he had all of thirty seconds from the time he saw me and Luke downstairs to the moment he knocked on my door.

"It's a very good offer," I tell him. "But I just don't see how it would ever work."

"What do you mean?"

"My son can't ever know what happens between you and me. No one can. Ever."

"Agreed."

"But with Luke around, I wouldn't be able to do the things I did for you before," I clarify. "The, um, dressing up and having ... sex ... everywhere."

"When is his bedtime?" Mr. Thorne asks.

"Seven-thirty, sometimes eight."

He nods. "All right. How about we say our time will be from nine 'til midnight, then? Provided I'm at home, of course. On the nights I'm out of town, you're free to do whatever you like. Before nine, I won't intrude on your time with your son."

"That ... might work," I say, a bit stunned to actually be considering this.

"And there are always the days," he continues. "I can work from home a few days a week, if I'd like more time with you on your own. We'll see how it goes."

"During the day? What about Luke?"

"You don't want him in school? Or is it preschool at his age?"

"Pre-K," I whisper. "I haven't been able to afford it."

"Oh, I'll take care of that," Mr. Thorne says, like it's no big deal. "There are some good places around. My neighbor's son goes to preschool just down the street. You could probably enroll him there if you want. It's up to you."

Just like that, as though he has no idea what this means to me, how huge this is. To him, it's just a phone call and a check in the mail, but to me, this is a dream come true: a nice place to live; a chance for Luke to make friends, to have what other kids have, and to learn from actual teachers. It's everything.

"M-Mr. Thorne," I sob, clutching his handkerchief. "I ... I—"

"Please, no more of that," he scolds gently.

"I'm s-sorry," I cry. "This is really overwhelming."

He gets up and I watch as he finds a glass in the cupboard, pours me some water, and places it in front of me, telling me to drink. I drain it, wiping my eyes afterward.

"Look," he says. "Why don't you and your son come spend the weekend at my house? See what it's like. No strings, no expectations."

"Like a trial run?"

He smiles. "Exactly. I'll be working quite a bit, so you'll pretty much have the place to yourself. Then, on Sunday, you can tell me what you want to do."

"There's just one more thing," I say, remembering why I ran from him last night. It feels like ages ago.

He nods.

"What you said about me being naturally submissive ... it might be true, I don't know. But you can't order me around in front of Luke, or say anything sexual in nature. I don't *ever* want him to see me like that. It has to be completely professional between us when he's around." I lean forward. "Promise me."

He leans forward too, a severe expression on his face.

"Abigail, I wouldn't do that. I promise."

"Why are you doing all of this for me, for us?"

"Because I want you," he says simply. "And I want you happy."

He holds my gaze, not wavering at all.

"O-okay," I stutter, although I'm not at all clear how this fits into our relationship being strictly professional. I want to make him happy too, though.

"Now, where am I driving the two of you today?"

"My friend Jo's, if you don't mind? I just need a few minutes to pack some stuff."

"Take your time," he says, reaching for his coffee. "And see if you can get my phone back for me." He flashes me a smile that makes the inside of my chest flutter.

"Yes, Sir," I murmur, noticing how my choice of words changes his expression from playful to something else entirely.

"Good girl," he whispers, straightening himself in the chair.

The look in his eyes makes my fatigued body come alive; my heartbeat increases and a secret thrill rushes through me. He wants me. He really does want me in his life, this beautiful man. Even after he saw where I come from, even knowing that I'm a mother, he still wants to continue our arrangement.

I find Luke in his room and tell him we're leaving in a few minutes. "Mr. Thorne needs his phone back," I add, holding out my hand.

"Aww," he grumbles. "Okay."

I take the phone and close down the browser, staring in surprise at the background picture. It's me, in a beautiful black party dress. The picture he took of me the night of his birthday.

He didn't just keep it; he made sure he'd see it all the time.

My chest flutters again.

"Hon, how would you like to go on a little vacation with me this weekend?" I ask Luke.

"What's a vacation, Mommy?" he asks. "Something good?"

"I think it could be," I answer, feeling cautiously hopeful. "I think it could be good."

CHAPTER NINETEEN

I t's a strange realization that my whole life can fit into two bags, one for me and one for Luke. I look around the apartment and realize I don't need to take anything else. It's just stuff. What matters is that Luke and I are going to a safe place.

"We're all packed," I tell Mr. Thorne, who's still in the kitchen. He smiles and takes the heavy bags from me, hoisting them over his shoulder with ease.

"After you," he says like a perfect gentleman, following me out.

Leaving the apartment unlocked isn't ideal, but I don't have much choice in the matter. I shut the door tightly, hoping nobody will realize they can walk right in. As we walk down the hallway, I pause in front of Mrs. Watt's apartment, slipping the note I've written underneath her door. I probably should knock, knowing she's always home, but I can't explain Mr. Thorne to her. In the note, I tell her about the break-in, urging her to be careful and also asking her to notify the building manager. I also give her Jo's address in case the manager needs to reach me to change the lock, although I won't be holding my breath on that one.

Once outside, we follow Mr. Thorne down the street to where his car is parked. It's really nice—a BMW, I think. Black and sleek. Definitely expensive. I remember the only time I've been in it, the first night we met, and marvel at how different everything is now.

"Nice ride," I comment, for lack of anything better to say.

"Thank you," Mr. Thorne says, putting our bags in the trunk. He looks at Luke. "Do you like cars?" he asks, a bit hesitantly.

"Uh-huh." Luke nods. "Too bad yours isn't red. *That* would've been cool." He climbs into the backseat, leaving Mr. Thorne speechless.

"Sorry," I say. "He, uh, tells it like it is."

Mr. Thorne doesn't say anything, but I swear his eyes light up with humor for a second. I join Luke in the backseat and make sure he's safely buckled up before putting on my own seatbelt. I give Mr. Thorne the address, which he puts into his GPS, and we're off.

It's a short ride to Jo and Thomas' place, and the only one talking in the car is Luke. He tells Mr. Thorne about Piper and Pippa, as though he's supposed to know who they are. To his credit, Mr. Thorne smiles and nods along with Luke's prattling like he's totally interested in why Piper is cooler than Pippa because she likes Lego better than Barbie, but Pippa is fine with watching *Mater's Tall Tales* so she's okay too, even though she kicked him in her sleep that one time.

Mr. Thorne is lucky and finds a spot right outside. Before I've unbuckled Luke, he's holding the door open for us, even offering me a hand as I step out into the cold autumn air.

"Thank you," I whisper, holding on to him for a second longer than necessary.

He unloads our bags as I help Luke out, but I'm surprised to see him still carrying them when I turn around.

"Lead the way," he says, motioning to the apartment building.

"You ... want to meet my friends?"

"If that's all right?" he asks.

"Um, sure. It's just ... Jo's boyfriend, he doesn't know about you."

"He'll find out this weekend anyway, won't he?"

I nod my head, still feeling uneasy.

"You work for me," Mr. Thorne says calmly. "That's all he needs to know."

"You're my mommy's boss?" Luke pipes up. "Thanks for the toys!"

"I didn't—"

"I told him I got a job so I could buy stuff for him," I explain.

"Oh." Mr. Thorne looks at Luke. "You should thank your mother. She bought them, not me."

"I did already," he says. "Right, Mommy?"

"You sure did," I say, giving him a smile. "Let's go see what Pippa and Piper are doing, okay?"

Outside their door, I decide to knock rather than enter like I normally would. It doesn't feel right to barge in when I have someone with me that they don't know.

"Here comes the bride!" Jo exclaims, flushed and laughing as she opens the door. On her head is what looks like a veil made out of toilet paper. "Come on in, Abbi, we're ..."

She trails off as she looks behind me. Her eyes widen and her mouth opens and closes a few times.

"Celebrating," she finishes, looking at me again. "Is that—"

"I'm Mr. Thorne," he says, stepping up next to me and holding out his hand. "How do you do?"

"That just means *hi*," Luke helpfully supplies, before slipping past her with his toy-stuffed backpack.

"Um, hi?" she says, taking his hand.

"I see best wishes are in order," he responds, giving her a charming smile.

145

"Oh my God," she whispers, using her free hand to yank off the makeshift veil. "Thank you."

"Babe, what's the holdup?" Thomas calls over the music playing in the living room. He dances out to join us, wearing a toilet-paper bowtie around his neck.

"Oh," he says, wrapping his arm around Jo. "Who's this?"

"This is my boss, Mr. Thorne," I say.

"Hey, man." Thomas reaches out to shake his hand, friendly as always. "You wanna join us for a drink? We're having a bit of a celebration here."

"Thank you, no. I don't want to intrude on your happy occasion. But congratulations." He turns to me.

"We should ..." Jo says, already pushing Thomas inside, "let them say goodbye. It was nice to meet you!"

"Nice to meet you, too," Mr. Thorne says to the door as it slams shut.

"They, uh, just got engaged," I needlessly explain.

"I gathered."

"It's usually a lot quieter around here," I say, not sure why I feel the need to tell him that. "Just Jo and the kids."

"Oh? Is he stationed somewhere usually?"

"Uh, no. They've been apart. Thomas had some ... problems."

Mr. Thorne's expression turns serious. "Legal problems?"

"No, no!" I protest. "Nothing like that. I mean, he was a bit of a stoner after high school, but he's a really good guy."

Shit! Why did I say that? Instantly, I feel horrible for blurting out intimate details about Thomas to a man he doesn't even know. Mr. Thorne looks anything but placated. In fact, he looks frighteningly upset.

"Drugs," he practically sneers, "are unacceptable to me, Abigail. Is he still using?"

"No!" I assure him. "Do you really think I'd stay with my son in a place with drugs? Thomas stopped all that when he found out Jo was pregnant. I swear."

He holds my gaze for a very long time; I see the anger slowly seeping out of him before his shoulders drop suddenly, like a deflated balloon, and he puts my bags on the floor with a dull thump.

"I don't like drugs," he says quietly.

"Neither do I." I stare at him, wondering what the hell just happened. Why did he react so strongly? I didn't say Thomas did hard drugs or was violent. Marijuana is legal here in Washington, so even if he did still use it, it wouldn't be a crime.

Mr. Thorne nods once before straightening up to his full height. "Friday?" he asks.

"Yeah," I say, still a bit stunned by his reaction. "We'll come."

"Good," he says, shocking me even further as he reaches out for me and pulls me into his embrace.

"I shouldn't have said that," he murmurs, caressing my face. "You wouldn't put your child in danger. I apologize."

"It's okay."

He tightens his arms around me and I can't resist the urge to snuggle against him, closing my eyes. My body is so tired, but my spirit is elated. I smile as he rests his chin on top of my head, exhaling deeply, relaxing against me. When he holds me like this it's easy to forget he's just my boss. Too easy.

Slowly, he pulls away. His face is neutral again, but his eyes are still warm as he gazes down on me. He reaches into his pocket, retrieving his wallet.

"Here," he says, pulling out some bills and handing them to me.

"No," I protest. "I haven't earned that."

He takes my hands, holding them and the money.

"You will *not* starve yourself again," he says sternly. "Those days are over."

I nod my head, trying to control my emotions.

"Just ... buy something nice to eat for you and your friends

147

for dinner tonight," he adds. "And take care of yourself and Luke."

"Okay," I whisper, taking the bills from him. "Thank you."

"Friday at four? And take a cab."

"Okay," I say again.

He kisses me softly, sweetly at first. Then he reaches around me, crushing my body against his as he lifts me up. I feel my feet dangling in the air as his tongue touches mine, making me whimper. I cling to his shoulders, responding eagerly to the kiss, wanting more and more.

"Fuck," he groans against my lips. "Sweet girl, what are you doing to me?"

"Don't ... know," I pant. Whatever this is, it's powerful. It's so unlike the only other relationship I've had. Mr. Thorne isn't going to pick me up at my parents' house and introduce himself. He isn't going to take me to the school dance. He isn't going to bring me to the movies for a date and then spend the whole time trying to cop a feel. He and I aren't going to argue about unpaid bills or lack of responsibility. We won't spend our nights with our backs turned. In fact, we won't spend our nights together at all. But we'll have three hours together each night before bed. Patrick never set aside so much time for me. By the end, I was lucky if I saw him three hours total in a whole week.

This is a job, but I don't know if that's necessarily a bad thing. Whatever this is, I know I want it. I want *him*.

Gently, he lets me down. I fist my hands in the lapels of his coat to steady myself.

"I have to go," he breathes, obviously as affected as I am. "See you Friday."

"See you," I sigh as he walks down the stairs. I press my hand against my chest, feeling my heart thundering away. Definitely powerful.

Inside the apartment, Jo gives me a long look. I can tell she's bursting at the seams, wanting to know what happened, but for now she focuses on her family. I do the same, making sure Luke's space is set up in the girls' room, a sleeping bag on a small mattress on the floor. He's beyond excited to sleep there tonight. Afterward, we join the celebration in the living room and the day passes quickly in a blur of laughter, cake, Disney, and dancing.

"Be sure to thank your boss for this," Thomas says, patting his stomach. It's late and we've just finished the last of the Chinese takeout. The kids passed out a while ago after eating their fill.

"Yes, that was really nice of him," Jo agrees, grinning at me. She turns to Thomas. "Why don't you go relax on the couch, baby? Abbi and I will clean up."

"No." He shakes his head, making a few of his previously combed-down curls stick out. "I'll do it. You two take a load off." He leans over to kiss Jo before he starts clearing the table. She gives me a look of surprise, but doesn't hesitate to drag me into the living room.

"Okay, tell me absolutely everything!" she exclaims, throwing her hands up in excitement. "What happened? How did he find you? No, wait. First, can we just talk about how freaking gorgeous he is?"

I chuckle a little, nodding my head.

"I mean, you said he was handsome, but Abbi, holy shit!"

"I know. He's hot."

She laughs at me. "Tell me everything!"

Half an hour later, Jo is still listening intently as I finish recounting the day.

"So we're going over there at four on Friday, and then we'll see how it goes," I finish. She's quiet for a few beats, shifting around a little.

"Well, it's a really great offer," she finally says, looking down at her hands instead of me.

"It is," I agree, watching her closely. She was excited for

149

me before, but now I get the feeling she isn't being honest. "But?" I prompt.

Her eyes flicker up to mine and she takes a deep breath. "You know he's just talking about hiring you, right? It's still a job. Just like it was before."

I try to ignore the spark of irritation I feel. "I know that."

"Okay." She hesitates. "It's just the way you described it just now, and the way you looked when you came over here..."

"What?"

"I thought maybe you and he were in a real relationship now. You know, dating."

"That's crazy. I know what he's offering and it's amazing. I mean, school for Luke? A nice neighborhood, no more worries about money. How can I say no to that?"

Jo reaches out to touch my hand. "Hey, I'm not saying you should say no. It really is an amazing offer. I just don't want you to get hurt."

"I won't. I can handle it."

I can. I have to. It's a job. It's just a really good job.

"Just remember it's temporary, okay? Eventually DSHS will launch an investigation, realize that Patrick isn't paying Luke's child support, and then you'll get some real help. This isn't forever."

I nod. "Of course. Besides, we're just going over there for a trial weekend. Nothing's set in stone."

Jo still looks unsure. "That guy, Abbi, he's gorgeous and smooth as hell. I wouldn't blame you if you started feeling something for him."

"I won't!" I snap, instantly regretting it. I sigh. "I'm sorry. Please just be happy for me, okay?"

"I am. You know I am."

"Thank you."

Thomas comes into the living room, smiling at both of us. "You ladies wanna watch some TV?" he asks, plopping down between us.

He puts his arm around Jo, who hands him the remote. We watch a sitcom together, but I can't enjoy it completely. I feel Jo's eyes on me throughout the evening, the wary expression she wears whenever I catch her looking.

Everything's okay. I'm just happy to have this job, one that will give Luke a good place to live. That's all it is.

CHAPTER TWENTY

I'm committed to treating the coming weekend at Mr.
Thorne's house as the trial we agreed to and nothing more.
If there's one thing I've learned, it's not to get your hopes up
too soon, because if something looks too good to be true, it
probably is. So I try my best to prepare myself for the very real
possibility that Mr. Thorne's proposition won't work out, for a
number of reasons. What if Luke doesn't like it there? What if
Mr. Thorne realizes he's not really interested in bringing a
child into his house after all, and calls the whole thing off?
What if he doesn't respect my time with Luke and gets
annoyed about not being my first priority?

Still, I can't help but fantasize about what it will be like,
living with him, seeing him every day if we get to that point.
Up until now I've only been at his house one or two nights a
week, and it was always in a particular setting. This weekend
we'll be seeing each other during the day too, interacting with
Luke around. How long does he see this arrangement of ours
lasting? There's so much I don't know about him, about his
past and his present. It's scary, but not as scary as not giving
this arrangement a chance. I know an opportunity like this

won't come around again, and I owe it to both Luke and myself to go into it with an open mind.

"When we get to Mr. Thorne's house, I want you to be on your best behavior, okay?" I tell Luke. We've just crossed the bridge to Medina and we're almost there.

"What does that mean?" he asks.

I have to smile at my own foolishness. Luke is a great kid and there's really no point in my telling him this. "Nothing, hon," I say, reaching out to take his hand. "You just be yourself."

"Who else am I gonna be?" he says. "You're silly, Mommy."

"Yeah, I know."

We arrive at the house at 3:58, and I draw a deep breath, trying to calm my nerves. We're not even out of the taxi before Mr. Thorne comes out of the house.

How does he do that? Is he always waiting by the window?

He smiles as he pays the driver, smiles as he unloads our bags, and smiles as he says hello to Luke.

"Hi," I whisper, feeling shy.

"Hi," he says back, gazing down upon me.

"Who lives here?" Luke asks.

"I do," Mr. Thorne says, walking us to the door.

"Just you?"

He looks at me again. "Yes," he says. "For now."

"It sure is a big house. Are you rich?"

"Luke," I scold gently. "You don't ask people that."

"Why not?" He stares up at me with wide, innocent eyes.

"You just don't ask someone how much money they have. They might not like it."

"Oh." He turns to Mr. Thorne, tilting his head back to look up at him. "I'm sorry. I have fifteen dollars and seventy-five cents. It's in my money jar."

Mr. Thorne glances at me and I nod my head. Thankfully, the burglar didn't get to Luke's room before I interrupted him.

He took the movies from the living room, but everything else of Luke's was untouched.

"That's a lot of money you've saved," he says as we walk inside. "Good job!"

I wonder if he notices how Luke beams at him.

We remove our coats and shoes, and, standing on the polished hardwood floor in my socked feet with Luke's old, muddy boots in my hand, the reality of the situation finally dawns on me. I'm bringing a child into this pristine house.

"Where should I put these?" I ask, holding up the boots. "Do you have a shoe rack or something?"

Mr. Thorne looks at the boots, frowning. Obviously, he doesn't want them on his clean floors any more than I do. Shit, I hope he doesn't change his mind about this. Kids mean mess, that's just a fact, and Mr. Thorne is more than neat.

"Uh, no. Wait here." He walks to the kitchen and returns with a dishtowel, which he places on the floor next to the door.

"This will have to do for now," he says. "The coats go in the closet over there."

Luke's hand in mine, Mr. Thorne leads us down the hall, turning left to a part of the house I've never seen before. He pauses outside the last door, opening it slowly.

"Cool!" Luke exclaims.

The room is big, with light blue walls and large windows overlooking the lake. But that's not what has my son enthralled. Absolutely everything is covered in *Cars* merchandise: There's a Lightning McQueen race-car bed with sheets to match, red curtains with the same motif, movie posters on the wall, and a throw rug that looks like a racetrack with little toy cars on top. There's a dresser and a nightstand in dark wood and a small flat-screen TV on the wall. On a low shelf, there are more toys and a few books. I can't believe he did this —that he remembered, and that he'd do so much for a boy he's only met once.

"Do you like it?" Mr. Thorne asks Luke.

"This is for *me*?" Luke's eyes are wide in disbelief.

"Just for you."

My son walks into the room, slowly and unsurely at first. Then he turns to look at me. I blink back the tears in my eyes and nod my head.

"Oh my gosh!" he yells. "This is so cool! This is so cool!"

I watch as he runs around the room and jumps on the bed to roll around in it.

"It's red!" he exclaims. "A red car!" Rolling off the bed again, he runs to us, barreling into Mr. Thorne.

"Thank you, thank you!" he pants, throwing his arms around Mr. Thorne's leg. Before Mr. Thorne can say anything, Luke runs across the room to look at the toys.

"So I take it that he likes it," Mr. Thorne says, giving me a smirk.

"It's perfect," I whisper. It's the kind of room I would have made for Luke, if I'd been able to afford it. The fact that I couldn't do it on my own fills me with regret, which I know is a useless emotion.

"There's even a red car," I say.

"I'm nothing if not observant."

"He's never going to want to leave," I chuckle.

Mr. Thorne raises his eyebrows, nodding in a knowing way.

"You don't play fair," I tell him.

"Never said I would," he replies. "Do you want to see *your* room? It's right next to his."

Honestly, I wouldn't care if I had to sleep in the linen closet or on the floor next to Luke's bed. This place is safe, and that's all I want.

"Yes, please," I tell him, anyway. "Luke, I'll be in the next room, okay?"

"Uh-huh," he answers, not looking up from his new books and toys. I shake my head, smiling. Mr. Thorne opens the door next to Luke's room, motioning for me to go inside.

The room is beautiful, but I expected it to be. Mr. Thorne's house is exquisitely decorated, after all, and this is no exception. It's nothing like I imagined, though. I'm a little stunned by what I see.

"Don't you like it?"

I look up at him. There's an edge to his voice; it's laced with anxiousness.

"I love it. It's so pretty."

He doesn't look satisfied. "But?" he asks.

"Nothing," I promise. "It's perfect. But it doesn't look like you, really."

He tilts his head to the side.

"You're, well, sort of old-fashioned. I guess I thought you'd put me in a room with, like, heavy curtains, and a canopy bed, and maybe even a vanity or something. I don't know, like that would be your idea of what a woman's bedroom should look like."

"Oh." Finally, he smiles. "Your observation about me isn't wrong." He leads me inside, his hand resting on the small of my back. "But this is *your* room, Abigail. Yours alone." He turns me to face him. "Do you really like it? I want you to like it here."

"I do. I love it." I look around again and take in the cream-colored walls, the white bed with its lavender bedspread, the reading nook in the window surrounded by light floral curtains, the comfy-looking armchair, the dresser, the flat-screen TV on the wall. It's feminine and romantic, yet still young. Like me, I guess.

"Thank you," I whisper. "For all of this. You don't know what it means to me. Luke is so happy." I meet his eyes. "I'm so happy," I add.

"Mission accomplished, then," Mr. Thorne says.

"What should I do now?" I ask. "Make you dinner?"

"No, I have drinks and a dinner meeting in the city tonight."

"Oh." For some reason, I thought he would be home with us tonight. Then I realize how ridiculous the thought is. Mr. Thorne is my boss, not my boyfriend. And he's already promised not to interfere with my time with Luke.

"Is there anything you need?" he asks. "There should be plenty to choose from in the kitchen for your dinner and you're welcome to use the living room tonight to watch TV and so on. All I ask is that you don't go upstairs to my floor. My office is up there and that's my domain."

"Of course," I say immediately. "We'll stay downstairs, I promise."

"Good. It's for the best. To establish some boundaries."

"Absolutely," I say, nodding.

He reaches into his pocket and hands me a key, as well as a piece of paper. "To the house, in case you decide to go out, and the code to the security system."

"Thank you."

"Anything else you need?"

"I don't think so." Honestly, I have no idea. I need a few minutes to collect myself.

"All right. You two have a good night." He walks to the door before pausing, turning to look at me. "I'm very happy you're here," he says.

He gives me a long look before he leaves, and I wonder if it means he's reluctant to go. I'd like to think so, because I'm a bit sad he won't be here tonight. I'm not sure what I expected, though. That he'd want to hang out with Luke and me? He's a busy man, obviously, and that's not what this is about. It's an arrangement in which he pays me for my company and sex, and I get much-needed security for myself and my son in exchange. It's enough. It *has* to be enough, and I won't ruin this because of some fluttery feeling in my chest.

Luke and I stay in for the night. After a quick text to Jo, I set him up at the kitchen table with coloring books while I cook us a simple dinner of spaghetti and meatballs with carrot sticks.

After our usual nighttime routine I let Luke pick out a movie for us. In the kitchen, I look out the window at the streetlights and the neighbor's house, with its friendly-looking lit windows. The only sound is the low hum of the microwave oven behind me as it makes popcorn for our movie—it turns out Mr. Thorne did have some in the house. It's peaceful here. Quiet. Secure.

It could be like this for Luke every night: a healthy meal, a warm bath, cuddle time on the couch, and then a good night's sleep in a race-car bed.

And for me: no worries about money, no yelling, no sirens outside my window, no crying myself to sleep. Instead, spending time with Luke at the beginning of the night, and Mr. Thorne at the end of the night.

The best of both worlds, I suppose— my two lives finally co-existing in a way I never expected.

Smiling to myself, I shake the popcorn into a bowl and join my son for a movie.

At five minutes to nine, I'm in my room, drying my hair. Luke is fast asleep in his new room and I'm almost ready for Mr. Thorne. I've put on my nicest pajamas since I don't own any lingerie and I hope that's okay. I really want to make him happy tonight. With my hair done, I open the door to my room, and sit down on the bed, ready.

Half an hour later, I'm still ready, but there's no sign of Mr. Thorne. I check on Luke, who's still out cold, and tiptoe through the house, which is dark and quiet. He must not be back from his dinner. How long do things like that last anyway? Mr. Thorne said he was going to the city for drinks and dinner, so does that mean he has drinks first or last? He could be only on appetizers at this point.

Feeling dejected, I head into the kitchen, where I make myself some more popcorn and grab a soda before going back to my room. My TV has Netflix, as it turns out, and I can't help but smile again at Mr. Thorne's thoughtfulness.

Slipping underneath the covers, I sigh with pleasure as I get comfortable. The bed is amazing and the sheets are unbelievably soft. Looking around the beautiful room, I still can't believe that I'm really here, that this is where I'll be sleeping tonight, and maybe many nights to come. Turning to the TV again, I choose a romantic comedy I haven't seen before and nibble at the popcorn, but soon my eyelids grow heavy. I sit up straighter, forcing myself to pay attention to the movie, but it's impossible. Spending the last couple of nights on Jo and Thomas' lumpy couch means I haven't slept through the night and now I'm tired. So very tired.

"Sweet girl ..."

I feel something brush against my forehead and struggle to open my eyes.

"Shh, sleep."

"But ... Sir."

"It's okay. I didn't know I'd be this late. Sleep, Abigail."

"Wanted to be with you," I mumble.

He caresses my cheek so briefly I barely register it before the covers are pulled up around my shoulders. Warm and tired, I go back under.

The next thing I know, it's morning and Luke is worming his way underneath the covers to snuggle with me. I blink against the brightness of my room and look around. The TV is off and there's not a trace of my snacks from last night. Which means it wasn't a dream. Mr. Thorne came for me last night, but I'd fallen asleep. I sit up with a start.

What a disappointment it must have been for him, coming home to find me snoring away with popcorn grease on my face. I'm not off to a great start.

"Let's go make some breakfast," I say, giving Luke a hurried cuddle.

After a quick trip to the bathroom, we head into the kitchen and I find everything I need. Sitting on a chair by the kitchen island, Luke helps me whisk eggs and make pancake batter. I have no idea if Mr. Thorne likes pancakes, or even eats breakfast for that matter, but I have to do something to make up for not keeping my end of the bargain last night. I turn my attention to Luke and teach him how to flip the pancakes using a spatula.

"Good job, baby," I praise as he carefully lifts one onto the plate next to the pan.

"It's okay, Mommy?"

"Perfect," I tell him.

He grins proudly.

"You wanna make another one?"

"Uh-huh!"

I help him distribute the batter and hand him the spatula again, glancing up to check the time. I startle, seeing Mr. Thorne by the door to the kitchen, watching us. He's wearing an undecipherable expression, a faraway look in his eyes.

"Good morning, Mr. Thorne," I say.

His features become neutral in an instant. "Good morning, Abigail."

"Would you like to join us?" I motion to the set table. He looks at it and then back to us. For a split-second, I think he'll say yes. Then he takes a small step back, shaking his head.

"Thank you, no," he says. "I take my breakfast in the dining room. Would you mind bringing in the paper?"

"Of course." *Is he unhappy with me?*

"Good morning, Luke," he says.

"Morning, Mr. Thorne!" Luke says. "I'm making pancakes!"

Mr. Thorne smiles and nods before retreating. Hurrying, I run outside to get the paper before I assemble a tray for him, and while the coffee is brewing, I set Luke up with his own plate at the table.

In the dining room, Mr. Thorne is already seated at the head of the table, dressed impeccably in another suit.

Is he working on a Saturday?

"Thank you," he says, giving me a smile as I set the tray down and pour him a cup of coffee. "This is just lovely."

"You're not upset with me, then?" I ask, folding my hands to keep myself from wringing them.

"Not at all."

"I, uh, I didn't mean to fall asleep last night," I mumble.

"You were tired," he says simply. "And I was late, unable to reach you. Which reminds me, I should have your phone number and you mine."

I nod in agreement.

"We'll work it all out as we proceed," he says with confidence.

"So you do want to proceed?"

"Of course," he says immediately. "I'm very happy you're here. Both of you."

He takes a sip of coffee.

"What are your plans for today?" he asks, digging into his food.

"I'm not sure," I admit.

"You should go shopping," he suggests. "I noticed that Luke needs new boots. It'll be cold out soon. Get whatever the two of you need." He reaches into his pocket and takes out his wallet.

"Mr. Thorne, I don't feel comfortable—"

161

He silences me with a stern look. "I thought we already went over this. Let me take care of you. I *want* to."

"I know, but you've already given us so much."

"Is it going to be an argument every time I want to spend money on you?"

"No, Sir," I mumble. "I'm just not used to it."

His expression softens. "That's fair. But you're under my roof now, and I told you I'd take care of you, didn't I?"

I nod.

"Good." He hands me a black debit card. "I can drop you off at the mall on my way to work. Get anything you want: clothes, shoes, toys."

"Thank you," I say again, reminding myself that this is part of the agreement we made. "Will you be working all day?"

He sighs. "Probably."

"But you'll be home for dinner?"

"Yes, absolutely."

I beam at him and he smiles before he turns serious again.

"In the future, I'd like you to dress before starting breakfast."

"You don't like my pajamas?"

"I like them very much," he replies. "You look soft ... and warm. It makes me want to ..." He shakes his head lightly. "Well, no matter. We agreed to keep everything professional during the day, so a less casual atmosphere is better."

"Oh. Luke too?" I ask.

"No, he's fine. It's *you*," he replies, looking me up and down. "Between nine and midnight, you have my full permission to wear something like this."

"All right. I'll go get dressed," I tell him.

"Make sure you have some breakfast first. This is delicious."

I flush with pleasure. "Thank you, Sir."

I leave him to his food and his paper and join Luke in the kitchen. He's excited about our trip to the mall, and so am I.

Inspired by our conversation just now, I'm going to buy an outfit for tonight to make up for the fact that I fell asleep last night. I want Mr. Thorne to be pleased with me and show him we can make this arrangement work under these conditions. Tonight has to be perfect.

CHAPTER TWENTY-ONE

"Shit, shit, shit!"

I check myself in the bathroom mirror, dismayed by my frazzled appearance. So much for a perfect night. It's already past 9:00 p.m. and I'm supposed to be upstairs with Mr. Thorne, showing off my purchase. Instead, I'm still in my regular clothes with dried bathwater stains on the front of my shirt, my hair pulled back into a messy ponytail. I look like what I am: a tired mom.

Making the transformation into Mr. Thorne's fantasy is not an easy one, but I do my best, taking the world's fastest shower and running a brush through my hair. By the time I'm standing outside his office door it's after 9:30 and I know I'm in trouble. This might not seem like a big deal, but I know Mr. Thorne. He doesn't do tardy.

I swallow down my nerves along with a few deep lungfuls of air before knocking lightly on the door.

"Come in."

Mr. Thorne sits at his desk, typing on his laptop, not acknowledging my presence at all. The room is warm thanks to the lit fireplace, but it does little to relax me. Finally, Mr. Thorne looks up at me, his eyes scanning me from head to toe.

I feel naked underneath his gaze, which is actually not that far off. I'm wearing pale blue cotton and lace—a nightie I picked up today, hoping he would approve. Judging by the way his eyes have darkened, I'd say I've succeeded in that feat, but that doesn't mean he's going to let this go. It means that he wants me, though, so that's something.

"I asked you to be here at nine," he says. "That's not an unreasonable request, is it?"

"No, Sir, but—"

"And it's now," he continues, glancing at his watch, "almost a quarter to ten."

"I know."

"And you know how I feel about punctuality."

"It couldn't be helped. I'm sorry, okay?"

"No, not okay. Why are you late? We agreed that our time together is nine to midnight."

"I couldn't get Luke into bed," I admit. "Look, maybe ... maybe this can't work."

Admitting this to both myself and him isn't easy, but now it's the second night in a row something has disrupted our agreement. Maybe the universe is trying to tell me something. Having a child means keeping a perfect schedule is impossible. And I should have known that before ever agreeing to this.

I wait for Mr. Thorne to say something, but he just sits there quietly observing me. It irritates me that he's so calm and collected all the time, which only highlights how emotional I feel around him, not in control of my feelings at all.

"This was so stupid," I say. "I-I told you I can't be what you want. I told you, but you wouldn't listen. I can't keep to your ridiculous, perfect schedule and take care of my son at the same time. It doesn't work that way. This isn't working!"

The moment I turn to leave I hear him get up, and he's behind me before I can even get the door unlocked, whirling me around to face him again.

"You're angry with me," he says, surprise evident in his

voice. "I didn't think a sweet little thing like you had it in her."

His words fuel my anger, and I clench my fists. "Excuse me?"

He grins. "It's ... cute."

My mouth drops. "Cute?!"

"And very sexy," he adds, gathering me into his arms.

I push on his chest, but it's like trying to move a brick wall. Tightening his left arm to keep me in place, he lifts his right hand to pull down the strap of my nightgown, palming my breast. His lips caress the shell of my ear.

"Are you still angry with me, hmm? You wanna yell at me some more?"

Trying and failing miserably to hold on to my anger, I moan as he kisses my neck and plays with my nipple.

"You can leave, but you're not going to. You know why?"

"Why?"

Grabbing my hips, he lifts me up and carries me to his desk, spinning me around and bending me over it. With a firm grip on my neck, he lifts up the hem of my nightgown, exposing me to him.

"You're not going to leave," he tells me, tapping my inner thigh to make me spread my legs farther. "Because you love submitting to me far too much."

I can't help but groan as he sinks two fingers inside me, curling them to hit the right spot. He moves his fingers slowly, each pass making me want him more until I'm squirming.

"See what I mean? You want me to fuck you, Abigail? Make you come? Even though you disobeyed me?"

I nod eagerly, startling as he stops touching me and instead grabs my shoulders, spinning me around to face him. With rough hands, he pulls the nightgown off my body and winds my hair around his left hand so I'm forced to look up at him.

"You didn't say *please*," he tells me, his eyes glinting with something dark and a bit dangerous.

I shiver as he cups my naked breast again, massaging it

none too gently before pulling my nipple. I'm trapped between his large body and the desk, completely naked and at his mercy. Somehow, it only makes me want him more.

"Please, S-sir," I manage, my breath catching in my throat. "Will you?"

He smiles. "Will I what?"

I frown. He knows what.

"C'mon," he coaxes, making his voice soft, "beg me for it, pretty girl. You can do it. Beg for my cock."

I feel another spark of irritation at his demand and it surprises me. I'm not usually like this with him.

"Hmm, defiance," he muses, his lips quirking upward. "Am I pissing you off again, Abigail?"

I raise my chin, staring right back at him.

"Well? I'm waiting."

"Fuc—" I don't get to finish the swear. It happens so quickly, I barely have time to register it before his mouth is on mine, kissing the hell out of me. It's aggressive and wild, and I don't hold back, tearing at his clothes as his hands roam over my body, grabbing and groping.

"You little brat," he growls at me, biting my lip. "I'm going to fuck the defiance right out of you."

He lifts me up and practically tosses me back onto the desk, face down. I gasp as he enters me with a rough thrust. He fucks me hard, grabbing my hips to keep me in place as I cry out each time his hips slap against my ass.

"Good girl." He slides his hand to my front, caressing my slick skin with firm touches until I'm panting, teetering on the edge. "You ready to beg me?"

"Never!" I yell, all the while arching my back and pushing back against him. The sound of his dark laughter sends pleasant chills up my spine, as does his hand making impact with the fleshiest part of my ass. I love it all and I never want him to stop.

"Please, please, make me come, Sir!" The words spill from

my mouth suddenly, with no hesitation. I can't seem to remember why I wouldn't beg him before. I cry out as he fucks me through my orgasm, my body tightening and then relaxing down onto the desk, my limbs limp in the aftermath.

He's not done with me yet. I've only just managed to catch my breath when he starts again, pulling me back onto his cock in slow, deep repetitions, enjoying my surrender and how I'm freely letting him move me for his pleasure. He leans over me then, cradling my jaw and brushing his thumb against my lips.

"Suck. Make it nice and wet."

I do as he tells me, moaning around his thumb as his strong hips keep up a steady rhythm. He removes it from my mouth and the next thing I know it's back *there*, stroking gently. I tense up and he stops moving.

"Let me. I won't hurt you."

"Are—are you going to . . ?" I can't even say the words out loud.

"Not tonight," he murmurs, pressing the digit lightly against me. I gasp softly, clenching my fists as he slowly presses on and my muscles give way.

"I-I can't ever do *that*, Sir. You're too ... big."

"Shh," he soothes, his free hand stroking my back. "Of course you can, beautiful. And what's more, you'll like it, I promise. I'll never do anything you don't want me to."

I groan as he starts fucking me again, his palm making gentle passes over my skin until I feel myself relaxing into his touch, but still tensing slightly as he penetrates me completely with his thumb.

"Here you go," he coos, reaching his other hand around to my front to touch me. Moaning, I unclench as I focus on the other sensations.

"There's my sweet girl," he praises, taking me with slow, deep thrusts. "Just enjoy this. Fuck, you're so wet right now. I knew you'd love this."

"Oh, please," I groan, gripping the edge of his desk.

"Tell me you love it," he commands.

"I do, Sir."

He presses against my front and starts moving his finger in and out of me, timing it with the thrusts of his hips. I never would have thought I'd like this, something so lewd, but I do. God help me, I do.

"Ahh, feels good. Sir, I, please," I babble. "So good!"

It doesn't take long before I come again, the feeling of his stroking fingers and his thick cock making me cry out in abandon. He follows immediately after, nearly collapsing on top of me as both of us gasp for breath. I had no idea it could be this good.

"Mmm." He sighs, inhaling deeply against my skin before giving my shoulder a gentle bite. "Perfect. You were perfect."

After he's recovered, Mr. Thorne lifts himself off me, telling me not to move. I hear him leaving the room, and a few minutes later he returns, cleaning me with a warm, wet towel. I stay where I am until he comes back again, still completely exposed, but it doesn't bother me anymore. Gently, he helps me off his desk and puts my nightgown back on. I can't help but avoid his eyes, feeling shy after what just happened.

"Darling girl," he whispers, tilting my head up to examine my face. He must like what he sees, because he smiles at me. "We will make it work with Luke's schedule. We can talk about it later, all right?"

Relieved, I return the smile.

"Fancy heading downstairs for a movie?" he asks. "It's still early."

I'm surprised that he's asking me; this is his time. I'm not complaining, though.

"Sure. Would it be all right if I put something else on? I'd rather not have Luke see me like this if he wakes up."

Mr. Thorne nods. "Of course."

"Can I get you anything?"

He tells me to get the bottle of red already open from

dinner, and to get myself a drink too. I go to the bathroom before changing into my pajamas and checking in on Luke, who is thankfully still asleep, before getting the wine, and I make some popcorn while I'm at it. Mr. Thorne isn't in the living room, so I sit down and wait for him. He comes in after a few minutes and I do a double take, seeing him dressed in a pair of plaid pajama pants and a gray T-shirt. His hair, which is usually severely styled, is now tousled and damp from the shower. He looks ... *young.*

"So what types of movies do you like?" he asks, handing me the remote. "Pick one."

He wants me to decide?

"Not horror or tragedy. I like happy endings."

"Don't we all," he murmurs, picking up his wineglass and swirling the ruby liquid.

"Well, yeah," I say awkwardly.

He glances at me. "You were different tonight. Upstairs."

"Good different or bad different?" I ask apprehensively. I can't always be sweet and accommodating now that we're together 24/7 and I wonder if he's realized that too.

He chuckles. "You really have to ask after what we did?" He raises his eyebrows. "After how I fucked you?"

I blush, looking down to hide my smile. "I guess not."

"Maybe I should make you mad at me more often, if that's what happens." He reaches out to touch my cheek. "If it gets that fire in your eyes again."

"I thought you didn't like that sort of thing," I admit.

He shakes his head. "Just because you're sexually submissive doesn't mean you're a doormat, Abigail, far from it. It takes a strong person to let someone else be in charge."

"I never really thought of it like that." I take a few seconds to consider what he's saying. "So you liked that I was, uh, a brat?"

He laughs softly. "In everyday situations, I expect you to do as I say, but there's that and then there's sex. Your subsequent submission was all the sweeter because I had to work for it a little. I had to fuck the defiance out of you, manhandle you a little. And you liked it."

I more than liked it. It was incredibly hot having him take charge of me like that. It makes perfect sense that he'd like that too, because I did submit in the end and happily so. But I thought he wanted to be in control of everything all the time, so why does he want me to do things like pick out what movie we watch? He's so confusing.

"It really was amazing." I blush again.

"Agreed. So will you tell me what made you angry?" he asks, handing me my wine.

"Luke wouldn't get out of his bath, and he didn't want to go to sleep. I'm used to that happening sometimes and it's usually not a big deal. But I knew I had to be with you by nine and I was stressing about being late. When you mentioned it, I couldn't help but feel like this will never work and that Luke was in the way of you getting what you want."

"That's not how I felt," he says.

"My parents and even Luke's own father, they all saw him as an inconvenience."

Mr. Thorne blows out a breath. "I know the feeling."

"You do? How?"

"Let's just say my father was of the belief that children should be seen and not heard. Or, actually, not seen either."

"Will you tell me about it?" I ask carefully. I haven't forgotten how he reacted the last time I asked about his family, telling me in no uncertain terms to mind my own business, but he seems very open tonight. And maybe things have changed between us since then?

"I grew up in an all-boys boarding school," he says after a beat of silence. "It was very strict and everything was on schedule. It's second nature to me now, I suppose. I didn't see my father a lot growing up, and when I did it was best to stay out of his way."

"I'm so sorry," I whisper.

He leans a little closer, running the backs of his fingers down the length of my hair. "You aren't like that with your child, and based on experience, I'd say that's a good thing. I can be more lenient about when our time together starts at night."

"Really?"

"Yes. But that doesn't mean you shouldn't aim for nine o'clock. I want those three hours a night with you when I'm home," he says in a firm voice.

I nod eagerly. "Thank you, Sir."

"Good, now find a movie for us to watch."

"Yes, Sir."

He frowns a little, taking a sip of his wine before looking at me again.

"Is something wrong?" I ask.

"Come here," he orders softly.

I tuck myself into his side, amazed at how right it feels when he puts his arm around me. I start scrolling through the movies, smiling as I feel him smelling my hair.

"Abigail?"

"Yes, Sir?"

"When we're like this," he says softly, "and I tell you it's all right, you may call me by my first name, Simon."

My heart skips a beat and I tilt back my head to look up at him, but I don't get a chance to speak before his lips are on mine, kissing me tenderly.

This feels nothing like a business arrangement.

A little stunned, I go back to the movie selection.

"*Back to the Future?*" I ask. "I've heard it's good, for an *old* movie."

"Brat," he laughs, tickling my side.

I grin up at him before pressing PLAY and settling in with his arm still around me, a huge smile on my face.

CHAPTER TWENTY-TWO

The next morning, I wake early. It's Sunday, the end of our trial weekend, and I'm worried what might come out of our talk today.

As per our agreement, I change out of my sleepwear and into a pair of jeans and a sweater before leaving my room and checking on Luke. He's still asleep, tangled up in his Lightning McQueen bedding, and I tiptoe out of his room again, deciding to let him sleep in. Tonight, he's back to sharing a room with Jo's girls, and I'm sure they'll keep each other up way past their bedtime. The arrangement isn't ideal, but I don't have anywhere else to take him if Mr. Thorne doesn't ask us to come back here. I'm not completely sure if he will. This was a trial, and I know Luke has had a great "vacation" here, but things haven't been completely smooth between Mr. Thorne and myself. I know he enjoyed last night and I did too, but that was less than three hours out of a whole day, and I still have no idea how he feels about having us around the rest of the time, especially since he was out all day yesterday.

Half an hour later, Luke joins me in the kitchen as I'm cooking breakfast and helps me set the table for two. I know

Mr. Thorne won't be joining us, but I've made enough so that I can serve him in the dining room when he wakes up.

"This tastes good, Mommy!" Luke exclaims with his mouth full, eating his maple syrup and berry oatmeal with gusto.

"Thanks, baby," I reply, taking a sip of coffee. "When we've cleaned up, I think we should go for a walk. What do you say?"

Luke groans, but nods anyway. He's not big on the cold, and neither am I, but we've been inside the whole weekend and a little fresh air will do us some good.

"Good morning."

I look up, seeing Mr. Thorne at the door, dressed very casually in a sweatshirt and jeans. His hair is unstyled and he looks relaxed.

"Morning, Mr. Thorne!" Luke waves his spoon excitedly, sending a spray of oatmeal across the table. Immediately, he slinks down in his chair, eyes averted. "I'm ... I'm sorry," he hiccups.

"It's okay, hon," I soothe, pulling him into my lap. "It's just a little mess, no big deal."

As I cradle him, I glance up at Mr. Thorne, who's wearing a startled expression. Is it there because of the mess or Luke's reaction? He walks to the kitchen sink and returns with a rag, cleaning up the oatmeal.

"See?" he says. "All gone."

Luke lifts his head and Mr. Thorne smiles at him. My heart flutters in my chest.

"All gone," Luke echoes, jumping back into his seat and continuing to eat as if nothing has happened.

I walk to the counter and watch as Mr. Thorne rinses out the rag. I want to jump into his arms and kiss him. I want to thank him so much for not yelling, which is what Luke expected him to do, because that's what his father would have done. I tried my best to shield my son from Patrick's outbursts, but sometimes it was impossible.

"I'm off to the gym," Mr. Thorne announces.

"Oh, no breakfast?"

"Save me some for when I get back? I'll be a couple hours." He lowers his voice a little. "And then perhaps we can have our talk?"

My stomach flips. "Of course."

"I'd better get going. With all this delicious food I'll be eating from now on, I can't skip the gym."

From now on? That must mean he wants us to move in, right?

"I'm sure you can find ways of working it off between nine and midnight," I whisper, feeling my face flame.

Mr. Thorne lets out a surprised laugh, brushing my fingers with his in a hidden caress. "I'm sure I can."

Luke and I finish our breakfast and after cleaning up the kitchen, we head out. It's getting cold outside, and I'm thankful for our new coats and boots as we walk down the long driveway, hand in hand. There are lots of people out and about today, and we pass several couples walking their dogs and families who have also ventured out into the cool autumn morning. We find a playground about half a mile from Mr. Thorne's house and Luke asks if he can go play.

After a few minutes, we're joined by a couple and their little boy. The woman is a gorgeous blonde with piercing blue eyes and the man is tall and broad with a well-trimmed beard. They could be movie stars with their impeccable clothing and hair, and I feel a little self-conscious.

"Mama, can I play with him?" their son asks, pointing to Luke.

The woman turns and looks at me, wearing an open, friendly expression.

"Yes, of course," I manage.

"Go ahead," she tells her son.

The boy runs straight up to Luke and asks if he wants to play. He has a little wagon with him which is filled with toys, and soon we parents are completely forgotten as they run around the monkey bars, waving little plastic swords, their shouts and laughter echoing through the air. I smile at the sight of Luke playing with another boy, something he hardly gets to do.

"So, are you new to the neighborhood?" the woman asks me.

"Oh, uh, yes," I stammer. "It's very nice."

"We love it here," she says, and the man nods in agreement. "Is your son in school?"

"Not yet. He's been home with me until now. But maybe soon?" *Why am I asking her?* "Um, what about yours?"

"J.R. is in Pre-K just down the road at Oak Street. It's fantastic. He only goes part time right now, but we'll see what happens when the new one arrives. I'm pregnant, by the way. Already starting to show and I'm still nauseated 24/7. Isn't motherhood awesome?" Her eyes light up with humor.

I nod my head, not sure how to respond.

"Honey, you're doing that thing again," her husband says, sending me an apologetic smile.

"Oh, hush. I'm just being friendly," she says to him before turning back to me. "Just tell me if I'm being too much, okay?"

"Oh, no. You're, uh, fine."

Her smile is blinding. "So you're a stay-at-home too? What does your husband do?" She points her thumb at the man. "He's a director. You know, like a movie director, but with music videos and stuff. That's how we met."

"You're a singer?"

"Pff, hardly." She laughs. "I used to model. Can you believe that?"

I can definitely believe it, although she's just shattered the stereotype about models being aloof.

"I'm sorry, I'm not letting you get a word in," she says. "You're at home too?"

I draw a breath, trying to figure out what to say. "Er, no. Not exactly. I just started working in the neighborhood. I'm a ... a housekeeper." I look over to where Luke and their son are playing and smile at the sight of them chasing each other around. Both of the parents smile too.

"We should do a play date sometime, if you're going to be around," the woman suggests. "I know J.R. would love that."

"And you'd love having someone to gossip with," her husband supplies, sticking his hand out to me. "I'm Dave McLean and this nosey creature is my wife, Lila. She's really quite nice, I promise."

I shake his hand, laughing a little as she elbows him in the ribs. "Abigail Winters," I say. "And that's Luke," I continue, pointing to him. "I'm sure a play date would be fun. I just have to check with Mr. Thorne—I mean, my boss, first, about his schedule."

Lila's eyes widen. "Wait, not Simon Thorne, right?" she asks.

I look at her nervously. "You, uh, you know him?"

The two of them share a look. "We're just next door," the man, Dave, says. "His neighbors."

"O-oh. That's nice."

Lila is still staring at me like I just grew a second head. "I had no idea Simon had hired someone," she says. "That's so weird."

"Lila." Her husband sends her a chastising look.

"Oh, shit. I'm sorry," she tells me. "It's just that I suggested the very same thing to him last year, and he rejected the idea completely, like I was ridiculous for even suggesting it. Said he didn't want or need a housekeeper."

Fuck. "Oh." I pretend to be clueless. "I don't know anything about that."

"No, of course not. I'm sorry. I was just surprised. Simon is pretty private. Hey, are you with an agency?" she asks, smiling. "We've been talking about getting some help around the house, so if you could recommend someone?"

I stare between the two of them, struggling to come up with a good answer. Thankfully, the kids decide to come running over at that moment, distracting both of us. Luke's face is flushed with excitement and J.R. is panting.

"Can I go over to Luke's house?" he asks, jumping up and down. "It's really close. His mom's boss got him a really cool room! He's got a race-car bed too, and a TV! Please?"

Lila's eyes meet mine, and I feel like withering beneath her blue stare. "You're living with Simon?"

I can't very well lie about it and give her a weak nod. My neck feels hot as she assesses me, a frown on her face.

"I've seen you before ..." she trails off, looking pensive.

Oh, God. I grab Luke's hand, doing my best to fight the panic I'm feeling. "We should get going," I manage. "It was nice to meet you."

"Nice to meet you too," Dave says with a friendly smile. "Tell your boss to call me about a game sometime soon, all right?"

I say yes, although I have no idea if he's referring to watching a game or playing one. Mustering up all my courage, I look at Lila again. After a few seconds, her expression warms, and she gives me small smile.

"We have to go too. I'm sure I'll see you around," she says, holding my gaze.

I manage to nod. I watch as they collect the toys they brought and walk off in the same direction from where we came. Luke plays a little more afterward, but it's not as fun with me as it was with a boy his own age, so we head home soon, my head still swimming with thoughts of what just transpired.

About an hour after we've gotten back, Mr. Thorne catches me in the kitchen as I'm finishing making his breakfast.

He looks refreshed and handsome in slacks and a pullover, his hair still slightly damp.

"Luke?" he inquires as he enters.

"In his room. Where would you like to eat?"

"Here's fine," he says, motioning to the kitchen table.

I serve him breakfast and coffee, and clean up while he eats. I smile as I retrieve his empty plate, happy that he liked the food I prepared for him.

"Thank you. Please join me when you're ready."

I nod mutely, clearing away his plate before bringing my own mug to the table and refilling his at the same time.

"Thank you," he says again. "You're very thoughtful, Abigail."

"I try."

His eyes are warm as he gazes at me. "You succeed, sweet girl."

I don't know what to say, so I end up simply smiling at him.

"So," he begins, straightening in his seat. "I'd like to thank you for coming over this weekend. I've had a lovely time."

"Me, too. I'm sorry it didn't go exactly as planned."

He waves his hand, taking a sip of his coffee. "It went just fine. How has it been for you?" he asks, regarding me over the rim of his mug.

"Good," I reply. "You've made us feel really welcome here."

"Because you are," he says simply.

"Thank you, Sir."

"I'd like the two of you to move in here permanently so we can continue our arrangement. Have you thought beyond this weekend?" he inquires, cupping the mug between his hands. He appears casual, but there's something about the look in his eyes as he watches me. Uncertainty, maybe?

I have thought about it. A lot. If I reject his offer, what would the future look like? Luke and I would go back to Jo and Thomas', mooching off them for God knows how long until the state concludes Patrick isn't in our lives, financially or otherwise. And then what? I get another cheap apartment in a bad neighborhood and look for low-paying work. Even if I were able to someday get a scholarship to go to school, I'd still have to cover our living expenses. I'd always be scraping by, living hand-to-mouth, afraid to shut my eyes at night and unable to breathe easily. Here, I have a chance, a real chance for a better life. To save up and one day make something of myself. It's not the route I would have chosen, but now that I'm here I can't bring myself to regret it. I would miss the man sitting across from me. Desperately. I want to be with him, and at the same time create opportunities for me and my son, and it seems like this is the only way to do that.

"Yes, I have," I whisper. "And I accept your offer."

Mr. Thorne's shoulders drop and he exhales slowly as a smile spreads across his handsome face. "You'll come and live here?"

"Yes. There's, uh, just one thing, though."

"What is it?"

"I ... I need a contract."

Mr. Thorne's mouth opens as he inhales, sitting up a little straighter again. "A contract?" he asks, frowning a little. "Abigail, I'm not asking you to stay here as my submissive. That's not what I want from you. If that's—"

"No!" I gasp.

"No?"

"That's not what I meant at all. I didn't even know ... they have contracts for *that*?"

"Yes," he answers calmly.

"Oh. I just meant like a work contract. If people ask."

"People?"

"We met your neighbors at the playground today. I was talking to the woman, Lila, and your name slipped out. They know we're staying here, me and Luke."

He watches me impassively.

"Aren't you worried what they'll think? What everyone will think?" I ask. "I mean, if they suspect something is going on?"

Lila suspects. I'm sure of it.

He shrugs, taking a sip of his coffee. "No."

"No?"

"One of the perks of becoming older, Abigail, is that you care a lot less about what other people think of you. But," he adds, giving me a smile, "if it will make you feel better, we can certainly make a contract for your employment here. Did you have something specific in mind?"

"I told them I was your housekeeper," I admit. The more I think about it, the more I like the idea of a contract. I have to think of this as a real job, which it is, so making everything official makes a lot of sense.

"That's fine. What about the salary?"

"Just what you'd pay a regular housekeeper." I can see that he's about to protest, so I continue, "There's going to be an official investigation at some point, to prove that I'm not receiving child support from Luke's father, so they're probably going to be looking into my finances. Everything has to be completely by the book: the salary, taxes, and so on."

He nods, thankfully agreeing. "All right. Hiring you as a housekeeper works. On paper, at least."

"Only on paper?"

"Well, I already have a cleaning service and a laundry service, so I don't need you to do any of that. Cooking will be plenty." He gives me an expectant look, and I realize we're now negotiating the terms of my position here. It's not like I'm dying to clean this huge house on my own, so it's sort of nice he has other people for that.

"I'd like to do your laundry," I tell him.

"My suits go to the dry cleaner."

"Your underwear and socks, then, and your casual clothes, like jeans and T-shirts."

"You want to wash my underwear?" he asks with a grin. "Fold my socks?"

"Yes, Sir."

He leans forward, resting his elbows on the table. All humor has vanished from his features. "Why do I find that so fucking hot?" he whispers.

He reaches out and takes my right hand, tracing a circle in my palm. Even this slight contact makes my heart jump and my breathing speed up.

"I ... I don't know."

"You feel it too, don't you? When I touch you?"

"Yes, Sir," I breathe. "I'm not sure I understand it."

"Attraction, desire, longing," he murmurs, running his finger up the inside of my forearm, making my skin contract underneath his touch. "You want my hands on you. You like how it makes you feel when I take control over you. When I dominate you."

"But . . ." I close my eyes for a moment, trying to regain my wits. "You don't want a submissive."

"I don't want you to act according to the rules of a contract," he says softly. "I don't want to control every aspect of your life and punish you when you fail to meet those rules. You don't need a list of written rules to be what I want."

"What *do* you want, then?" I manage.

"Just you, being yourself. You're naturally submissive, Abigail."

I begin to pull my arm back, about to protest.

"That's *not* a bad thing," he says in a firm voice, holding my hand in his. "I can tell it upsets you, but I don't know why."

"It scares me," I admit. "I don't know what it means for me in the bigger picture."

"Nothing necessarily. It doesn't define every aspect of who you are," he explains. "It just means you like it when your partner takes control during sex, and you naturally put the needs of others before your own."

"Only with you," I whisper. "My ex—I didn't like it when he tried telling me what to do."

Mr. Thorne makes a face, curling his lips in obvious disgust. "He didn't treat you well, did he?"

I shake my head.

"He didn't deserve you. You have to respect someone to let them take charge, but it works the other way around too. I respect you, Abigail. I don't see you in any way inferior to me. I know from someone on the outside, someone who doesn't understand the dynamics of this arrangement of ours, it might not seem that way, but it's the truth. I'm very happy you've chosen to share that part of yourself with me."

"I am too, but I'm still not sure how we do this. You'll hire me as a housekeeper, but what about the, uh, rest? What do you expect of me?"

"I expect that you'll try to make it upstairs by nine o'clock every night I'm home, and that you'll cater to my needs, as long as they don't interfere with the needs of your son."

I exhale, feeling my shoulders drop. Knowing that I'll be able to always put Luke's needs first is a huge relief and my main concern, though not my only one.

"What about the ... actual sex?" I whisper. "Your expectations?"

"I expect for you to trust me," he says seriously. "I know you're inexperienced, and I'll remember that. Tell me, is there anything we've done that you haven't enjoyed?"

I shake my head. I've more than enjoyed it all.

"Even last night?" he asks, raising his eyebrows. "You enjoyed *everything*?"

I blush furiously, knowing exactly what he's referring to. "Y-yes," I stutter, looking anywhere but at him.

"No need to be embarrassed," he says, taking my hand

again. "Nothing between us is off-limits if it makes us both feel good, all right?"

I look back up, drawing a breath before nodding.

"If I ever want to go beyond what we've done, I'll check in with you first. I won't ever do anything more without your strict permission. How does that sound?"

"Good, Sir," I say, relieved. I truly *have* enjoyed everything, but going beyond some of what we've done so far is a daunting thought.

"Do you trust me, Abigail?"

"I ... *really* want to, Sir," I say honestly.

The corners of his mouth turn down ever so slightly. He's displeased. I can't help that, though. He wants the truth from me.

"I've been taking care of myself and Luke for a really long time. Even before I got pregnant, I felt like I only had myself to rely on," I explain. "I don't trust people easily." I motion around his beautiful kitchen. "You offer me all of this, and it just seems way too good to be true. I guess I'm still waiting for the other shoe to drop, for you to do something awful or demand something outrageous of me."

"Thank you for being honest," he says, giving my hand a squeeze. "That's the most important thing. Everything else we'll figure out along the way, as long as we're open with each other."

"You make it sound so simple."

"It is. I want this to work out." He draws a deep breath. "The truth is, Abigail, that I'm tired of coming home to an empty house at the end of the day."

I can definitely relate to that. I've always had Luke with me but I've been lonely a lot of nights, wishing there was someone there I could talk to, or just share the couch with. Sometimes I'd turn the TV on just to create the illusion of company, and even wished Luke would wake up so he could fall asleep again in my arms. So yes, I definitely understand what he's saying. But what I don't understand is why he wants to pay someone to fill that void.

"I understand. But why this sort of, er, arrangement?" I dare to ask. "I mean, why not just get a girlfriend?"

"I don't think I'd have much to offer in a romantic relationship," he says matter-of-factly.

His words make me frown. Not much to offer? He's generous and kind, sexy and rich. From where I'm sitting, Mr. Thorne is the whole package.

"You don't agree?"

"No, Sir. I don't understand why you'd say that. I think you'd make a great boyfriend."

He purses his lips, taking a long pause. "I work all the time. I'm sure you must have noticed that."

I nod.

"I'm at the office fifty to sixty hours a week, and that's just when I'm in the city. I travel a lot too. I don't have time to date. And even if I did, I'd have a hard time finding a woman who's willing to put up with my schedule, as well as ..." He folds his hands on the table, hesitating. "I like things a certain way, and I know my preferences aren't conventional. I want a woman who will cater to my needs, sexual and otherwise, without complaint. More so, I want a woman who *wants* to do that, who enjoys my kind of sex and wants to take care of me. And she'd have to be okay with my schedule. The last thing I need is to feel guilty for not being around when I'm working."

He takes a sip of his coffee, which must be pretty cold by now. "Maybe that makes me selfish. But that's what I want. I've worked very hard to get where I am today, and I don't want to compromise." He looks straight at me. "With you, I believe I can have exactly what I've always wanted."

Taking my hand in his again, he continues, "You'll be here for me when I come home, you'll cook for me, serve me, dress up for me if I tell you to. When I take control, you'll love it. When I fuck you the way I want, you'll beg for more." His words are harsh, but his expression is open and unguarded, and the way his thumb caresses my hand is gentle. He's so contradictory.

"Are you trying to scare me away?" I whisper. He's not telling me anything I don't already know, so I don't understand why he feels the need to say this.

"No." He sighs softly. "But I do want you to understand what you're saying yes to. You said this was too good to be true, making it sound almost like a fairytale. I assure you it's not. I'll be away a lot working, but when I'm here, I expect you to be available to me between nine and midnight, as well as during the day when your son isn't around. This will be your home too, but also where you work."

I nod silently.

"Do you *really* want to do this?" he asks.

"Yes, Sir."

"Even though it means no dating or relationships?"

I snort indelicately. "Who'd wanna date me? I'm a penni-less single mother on the verge of homelessness."

Mr. Thorne gives me a chastising look.

"All I care about is my son's well-being. I'm grateful you've accepted him so easily."

"I'll admit it will take some getting used to having a child in the house, but I doubt our paths will cross all that much with me mostly upstairs and you two down here. He's a nice boy, Abigail. You've done a good job with him."

His praise surprises me just as much as it pleases me. "Thank you. I'll have to talk to Luke first. If he doesn't want to live here—"

"Of course," Mr. Thorne says without hesitation.

"I think he'd probably like to stay here, though."

"So if he wants to live here, you will?"

I nod my head and he gives me a big smile, then pulls out his phone and types for a few seconds. I realize he's making notes.

"Now, is there anything from your apartment that you need here?" he asks.

I shake my head. I took everything of importance when Mr. Thorne drove us to Jo's apartment earlier this week.

"Good. I'll find storage and hire movers. Did you pay a deposit when you moved in?"

"I think so."

"Write down the name of your landlord before I leave for work tomorrow, and I'll see about getting it back when you're moving out."

Wow. "Just like that? You really think that's possible?"

Mr. Thorne nods. "Despite the ... condition of the building, you kept it up nicely as far as I could tell. If he wants to keep the deposit, he'll have to prove that you've damaged what he intends to repair."

"Thank you, Sir. That's ... thank you so much."

He waves me off, returning his attention to his phone. After a few seconds of swiping his finger back and forth across the screen, he focuses on me again. "I hope you don't mind, but I took the liberty of making an appointment for you and Luke at the school down the street."

"I don't mind at all," I say, beaming at him. "When?"

"Tomorrow at noon."

"Wow, that's soon."

Mr. Thorne gives me a wry smile. "I don't play fair, remember?"

I grin back at him, loving how lighthearted he can be at times. My heart is lighter than it's been in a long time. Luke is going to go to school, just like any other kid.

"Do you know how much the tuition is?" I ask.

"I'll take care of it."

"Sir, I—"

He holds up his hand, leveling me with his eyes. "Don't fight me on this, Abigail. The school is expensive. There's no way you'd be able to afford it on a regular housekeeper's salary.

I want you and your son taken care of. It's as simple as that. So let me."

Is it really that simple, though? It's not something a regular boss would say. Does it mean he cares about us, even just a little?

"I was just going to say thank you," I whisper.

He quirks an eyebrow at me.

"Okay," I admit. "I was going to ask if my salary would cover it. I'm more than happy to pay for at least part of the tuition myself, but ..." He wants to take care of us. For some reason, he seems to enjoy doing that. "Thank you, Sir," I continue. "You have no idea what this means to me, to us. I'll do anything you ask of me."

He regards me closely, a gleam in his eyes. "Be careful about making promises like that, Abigail."

"You won't hurt me," I state with confidence.

"No," he agrees. "But I will push your limits and I'll use you as I see fit. For my pleasure." He reaches out to take my hand. "And yours," he adds.

"I know." The thought of him using me for his pleasure, like he did last night, makes my skin tingle and my thighs clench.

"Speaking of which," he says, leaning forward to rest his elbows on the table. "I'd like to retain the babysitting services of your friend, Jo. Once a week, your son will spend the evening at her place." He pauses for a moment. "That is, if it's agreeable to you and Luke."

I can't help but feel touched by his added comment, him considering the feelings of both me and Luke and ultimately making it my decision. "Okay. He likes spending time over there and I'm sure Jo won't mind."

"I will, of course, compensate her," Mr. Thorne says, sounding very businesslike.

I shake my head, smiling at him. "You can try, but I think she'd feel weird taking money to watch Luke. Just like I'd feel

188

weird getting paid to watch her girls. We're best friends. We help each other out."

He considers that for a moment before nodding. I'm not sure he really gets it, though. Does he have any friends at all? Someone who would help him without getting paid for it? He seems so used to simply throwing money around to get what he wants: the fancy restaurant in the city that sent dinner here even though they don't deliver, the movers for my apartment, Jo, even me.

"You'll make the arrangements, then?" he asks.

"Of course. Can I ask why, though?"

"I want you for myself," he says. "One night a week when I can do anything I want to, when I don't have to wait until nine o'clock to have you, and we won't have to stay upstairs."

"O-oh," I stutter. "Yes, Sir."

"Do you like that idea, Abigail?" He lifts our joined hands up, pressing a kiss onto the back of mine. "You dressing up for me and serving me? Letting me fuck you right here on this table before dinner just because I feel like it? Or maybe having you naked on your knees next to me as I eat, waiting for me to finish so you can be my dessert?"

Oh my God. Blood rushes to my face.

"Yes, you'd like that, wouldn't you?" he teases.

I would, but what does that say about me? "Does that ..."

"What?" he asks.

"Do you think it makes me a ... a bad mother, for wanting that?"

He lowers my hand, but keeps it in his. "No," he says in a firm voice. "If your friend Jo wanted a night a week to herself for any reason, would you think that about her?"

"No," I say immediately.

"Then it's non-negotiable," he states. "One night a week, just the two of us. End of story."

"Yes, Sir." My reply comes easily after hearing his reasoning and his order. It feels good having him make the decision so I won't feel guilty. Is this what he meant about me being naturally submissive? It wasn't scary at all. He listened to my concern and made me see it was unfounded.

He smiles at me. "There's my sweet girl."

I smile back, elated.

After that, the negotiations are done, and Mr. Thorne goes up to his study, asking to be served dinner at seven o'clock as usual.

I go into Luke's room and join him on the bed, where he's watching a movie. He snuggles up in my arms and for a while, neither of us says anything. Soaking up his affection and warmth, I feel strong. I know this is the right decision. Luke has a chance for a real life here: friends, school, and a mother who makes a steady income.

"Hon," I murmur, pausing the cartoon. "Do you like it here at Mr. Thorne's?"

"Mmhm."

"How would you like for us to live here all the time?"

Luke tilts his head back, looking up at me.

"Mr. Thorne has asked us to move in here so Mommy can be his housekeeper."

"What's a housekeeper?"

"Well, I'll cook and do laundry. Stuff like that."

"Like a Mommy."

I smile at him. "Yes, like a Mommy, I suppose."

"What about Daddy?" Luke asks quietly. "Is he gonna live here too?"

Oh, God. I hold him tighter to me, tucking his head underneath my chin. "No, honey. Daddy isn't going to live with us. Not anymore."

"Never again?" His voice is so small.

"No, baby."

"Good."

I suck in a breath in surprise. Luke sits up and turns to face me.

"I don't *like* Daddy. He's mean and he yells, and he makes you cry. I hate him! I hope he never comes back! Never, ever!"

I stare at my son, from his clenched little fists to the fierce look in his eyes, and I suddenly see the past ten months in a different light. Every time Luke asked about Patrick, it wasn't because he missed him, as I'd thought. It was because he was worried he'd come back.

"Is that bad of me?" he asks. "Do you want him to come back, Mommy?"

"No," I whisper, answering both of his questions before pulling him back into my arms. "It's just you and me now," I tell him.

"And Mr. Thorne."

"And Mr. Thorne."

CHAPTER TWENTY-THREE

Later that afternoon, while I'm prepping dinner, I call Jo.

"Hey, it's me."

"Hey. How's it going over there?"

"Good. I wanted to tell you, we're staying here."

She's quiet for a moment. "Abbi, this isn't because of what I said, is it? Because you're always welcome here. And I'm sorry if I was negative."

"No," I say immediately. "I know you're just worried about me, and you were right. It is a job."

"But you like him," she says.

"I do. He's been really great. I mean, you should see the rooms he's made for me and Luke. The whole weekend's been wonderful. And it's not just the sex, even though that's amazing too. I like talking with him, and he actually listens to what I have to say. And he's generous and so nice to Luke. He makes me feel beautiful and wanted and ..."

"Wow," she says quietly.

"What?" I ask.

"You *really* like him, don't you?"

"Yes," I whisper. I could spend hours denying it, listing all the reasons why that's absurd and ridiculous to assume, but what's the point? I know the truth and so does Jo. I'm falling for Mr. Thorne. "But he can't know that." I sigh. "That's not what he wants at all."

"Are you sure? Because it kind of sounds like he does."

"I'm not sure about anything, to be honest. Sometimes it really seems like he does, because he cares so much about making us happy, but then other times he's all business, sticking to the rules we've set out. It's confusing the hell out of me."

"Is it enough, what you have now?"

I pause. "Life isn't a fairytale. He's so good, Jo. We have a real chance here. Luke is happy."

"But what about you?" she asks gently.

"I'm happy too. Really, I am. I feel safe with him. Plus, I thought Patrick loved me and that we'd live happily ever after, and look how that turned out."

"Yeah. I see what you're saying. And you know I'm one hundred percent supportive of you. Just remember that you can always come stay with us—if it doesn't work out."

"Thank you. How did your alone weekend with Thom go, by the way? Your mom had the kids, right?"

Jo laughs. "I'm exhausted!"

I grin into the receiver, reminding myself to offer to take the girls off her hands the next time Mr. Thorne goes out of town. I like hearing her this happy.

The night passes easily. We have a nice dinner—Luke and me in the kitchen, and Mr. Thorne in the dining room. Then it's Luke's bath time, storytime, and bedtime, and before I know it, it's nine o'clock and I'm ready to head up to Mr. Thorne's part of the house—on time. Tonight, I'm wearing a simple cotton robe and underneath a soft, pale pink nightgown with lace trim. My heart pounds with excitement as I knock on the door to his office and wait for him to allow me entry.

"Come in."

As usual, he's sitting at his desk, engrossed in something on his computer screen as I enter and walk toward him. Without hesitation, I slide the robe off and kneel next to his office chair, keeping my eyes on the floor. I don't know much about submission, but I do know that he mentioned something like this when we talked earlier. For a few minutes, I listen to the sounds of the keys tapping on his laptop mixed in with the music softly playing in the background, doing my best to breathe calmly and steadily. I like this, I realize. Kneeling and waiting for him to acknowledge me. The anticipation, the excitement that I don't know what he'll ask of me or when. It's turning me on.

"Good evening, Abigail."

I look up. "Good evening, Sir."

He swivels the chair around to face me before leaning down, gently pressing his lips against mine. When he pulls back, I raise up on my knees and attempt to deepen the kiss. He chuckles softly, reaching up his hand to cup my cheek as he sits back in his chair, out of reach. I'm disappointed, but I lean into his touch as he caresses my face, smiling at me.

"Please put your robe back on," he says, "and make some tea."

He wants tea? Here I am, showered, shaved, and dressed for sex, and he wants tea?

"Now, Abigail."

I stand, suppressing a sigh.

"No pouting," he admonishes. "Unless you want a spanking?"

My stomach does a little flip, but I remain unmoving.

"Well? Do you?" he asks, looking amused.

Well, yeah, kind of. It seems he's right about me, because the thought of being across his lap with my ass in the air, the heavy thud of his hand slapping against my skin is ... not unpleasant.

"Maybe, Sir," I whisper.

He chuckles. "Be a good girl and make that tea."

"Yes, Sir."

He reaches into his desk drawer, handing me a black monitor. "I got this earlier today when I was out. Put it in your son's room. We'll be able to hear if he wakes up."

I smile. Relaxing and enjoying our time up here will be so much easier if I don't have to worry about Luke waking up and looking for me, and the fact that Mr. Thorne thought about it makes my heart beat faster. He's just shown me that he's able to put Luke's needs ahead of his own.

"Thank you, Sir."

I put my robe back on and head back downstairs to the kitchen, where I put water on to boil before going to Luke's room to place the monitor.

I put the pot, a mug, milk and sugar, and some cookies on a tray and carefully carry everything back upstairs, wondering what we're doing tonight. Was he serious about having me kneeling next to him while he eats? Maybe that's what we're doing now with the tea. The thought of it gives me a twinge of excitement.

"Just put it on the coffee table, please," Mr. Thorne says as I re-enter his study.

I do as I'm told, noticing that he lit a fire while I was gone. The room is even more inviting and warm now.

Mr. Thorne comes over to me, motioning to the couch. "Have a seat, Abigail."

I sit down on the edge and look up at him, wondering if we're going to talk about something. Leaning down, he lifts up my legs, turning me sideways so I'm reclined against the side of the couch, and then grabs a pillow, which he places behind my back so I'm even more comfortable. I watch in stunned silence as he pours tea into the mug and turns to me.

"You take sugar, right?"

He's serving me? I nod, confused about the sudden switch of our roles. It's so thoughtful of him, though. I can't help but like it. He smiles and adds sugar before placing it on the table within my reach. Then he goes to his desk again, takes something out of a drawer, and comes back to me. All the while, I stare at him like a moron.

"This is for you."

He places a tablet in my lap. An iPad. I've never had one, but I know how they work, sort of, since Jo's girls have one.

"For me?"

"I got one for Luke too," he says with a shrug. "You decide when he should have it."

"I-I, Mr. Thorne—" I'm completely overwhelmed. "T-thank you," I manage after several stuttering breaths.

"You're welcome."

"What, uh, what do you want me to use it for?"

"Whatever you like. Games, books. I have some headphones if you want to watch something. Just enjoy yourself."

He hands me the tea, grinning at my stunned expression.

"I don't understand. This is *your* time. Don't you want me to ... you know, do something for you?"

"This *is* what I want you to do for me," he says.

He's said that before, that he only does something if it's what he wants. But why would he want to spend his night like this?

Because he likes me and wants me to enjoy myself. The thought is intoxicating, making my heart race.

"Thank you, Sir," I say softly.

He nods once and the corners of his mouth lift up. "Enjoy your tea," he says before he returns to his desk.

I stare down at the treasure in my hands. Games and movies don't interest me that much. Books, however—I've always loved reading. It's one of the few things I've always been able to afford, thanks to public libraries. I quickly open the internet browser and go to Amazon.

"Mr. Thorne?"

He looks up.

"Can I ... can I buy a book, please?"

"You can buy all the books you want, sweet girl. Just add your card to your account."

I beam at him and catch the sound of him laughing softly as I jump off the couch and sprint downstairs to find the card he gave me.

Five minutes later, I'm scrolling through Amazon, ready to buy something, but I have absolutely no clue what to get. I take a sip of the tea and as I place it back on the table, I glance over at Mr. Thorne, who's still working with a small smile on his handsome face. The sight of him sends a rush of warmth through my chest.

He likes having me here.

Even when I'm just sitting here, doing nothing much of anything, it gives him enjoyment. Is it the certainty that he can command me to do sexual things at the literal snap of his fingers? Or is it knowing that he provided me with this enjoyment and relaxation? I don't really get it. The sex is one thing; I understand that. And even when he dresses me up, I get that too—him wanting something pretty to look at. But this? I don't even know if we're "on the clock," so to speak, or if this is like a night off.

I reach for the mug again and as I take another sip, I realize this is exactly what I wished for the first night I came up here and saw his study: to curl up by the fire with a cup of tea and a book on a cold night. Back then, I never thought it would happen, and almost ruined our evening by crying because Luke would never know what it was like to live in a house like this, to feel safe and protected. All of that has come true, thanks to Mr. Thorne. Tonight is a cold night and here I am, enjoying the warmth of the fire. Downstairs, Luke is sleeping peacefully in a quiet neighborhood, with a full stomach, about to start at a very good school. I owe everything to Mr. Thorne. He has literally made my dreams come true. Now, I want to make his come true. I will be the best ... whatever the heck I am, and do everything in my power to please him.

Turning my attention back to Amazon, I sneak a glance at him again, and then type in the word "submissive."

Holy shit. There are so many titles, and some of the covers are verging on pornographic. I meant to find a textbook or something, but the highly suggestive covers call out to me, and soon I find myself engrossed in a novel, my eyes and fingers flying across the screen as I lose myself in the sordid tale.

"Abigail? What *are* you reading, you naughty girl?"

Oh, fuck. My heart feels as though it's trying to pound its way through my chest as I turn my head toward his voice. Mr. Thorne's still at his desk, but now his attention is on me. How long has he been watching me? How long have I been reading?

"Sir, I-I ... um, what do you mean?" He can't possibly see what I'm reading from across the room. Discreetly, I click the button on the front of the iPad to close down the Kindle app.

He shoots me a roguish grin and comes over to me. Slowly, he moves to sit on the other end of the couch, reaching for my ankles. I uncurl my legs, letting him put his hands on my feet, which he starts to caress with a gentle touch.

"You don't have to hide what you're reading from me," he says.

"I'm sorry. My father once caught me with a, er, mature book. He got really angry with me, and he punished me, not that I think you'd do that."

"Did he hit you?" There's a sharp edge to the tone of his voice.

"No, nothing like that. He never even spanked me, thank God. That would make what you and I do really awkward."

Mr. Thorne chuckles, nodding his head before turning serious again. He runs his thumbs across the soles of my feet. It feels incredible.

"He took away all my books," I tell him. "My dad was really strict."

"Mine hit me," Mr. Thorne says, staring into space. "He was a mean son of a bitch."

"What about your mom?" I whisper, a stab of pain making my chest ache.

He shakes his head, his eyes still unfocused. "She died giving birth to me, and he remarried pretty soon after. My stepmom wasn't interested in raising someone else's kid."

"Is that why you went to boarding school?"

"Maybe. It's not so uncommon in England. Did I tell you I grew up over there?" He finally looks at me and I shake my head, amazed at how much he's suddenly sharing with me. That must be why his accent doesn't sound completely American.

"How long were you there?"

"From seven to eighteen. It was better than being at home."

I watch him in silence, waves of pity and compassion washing over me. The more I learn about him, the more I feel for him. What a horrible childhood it must have been to prefer a strict boarding school to home. With an abusive father, a deceased mother, and the violence that his scars reveal, the kindness he shows me and my son is all the more amazing.

"I'm so sorry," I whisper, placing my hands on top of his.

"It's okay. It was a long time ago. I don't miss them."

"I miss mine sometimes," I confess. "Even though I shouldn't."

Mr. Thorne gives me a sad smile. He continues massaging my feet, and I practically melt into the softness of the couch, closing my eyes.

"So, will you tell me what you were reading?" he asks after a while.

I suppress a smile, grateful for the change of topic. "It was a ... a dirty story," I admit.

"I gathered as much. I know what you look like when you're turned on."

I open my eyes to look at him, reveling in the warm smile he gives me.

"It's okay," he says. "What was it about?"

"Um, a Master and his submissive. Some of it was very … descriptive."

He laughs. "I can imagine. I don't have to ask if you liked it."

I shake my head, feeling a little embarrassed. "I was trying to learn more about this sort of thing. There's so much I don't know."

"You can always ask me. I'd enjoy talking with you about that particular topic." He grins at me, lifting my foot and placing a kiss on top of it. Then his mouth moves lower and he delivers a gentle bite to my big toe. The sensation sends a jolt of electricity through my body.

"You have a thing for feet?" I ask, all the while wondering if there's anything he could introduce me to that I wouldn't like. It seems like he knows my body better than I do.

"I have a thing for you," he replies, lowering my foot.

Jo said he was smooth and she's right. But I don't think it's just a line. I think he really does have a thing for me, and not just sexually, even if he doesn't realize it yet. There are just too many aspects of our relationship that feel real.

His hands slide up my naked legs, but he stops as he reaches the hem of my robe, giving my legs a gentle squeeze before returning his attention to my feet.

"Why'd you stop? Don't you want to?"

The hungry look he sends me answers my question and sends tingles up my spine. "I always want you," he says, his voice husky. "But if I start, it'll be past midnight before I'm done with you, and that isn't what we agreed upon."

Boldly, I untie my robe and slide onto the floor, kneeling between his legs. "I don't care. I want you too."

"Come here, then."

He surprises by lifting me up, undressing me, and placing me on my back so I'm spread out before him. Instead of me worshipping him, he kisses his way down my body, his hands gently stroking me.

"This is what I want," he says just before dipping between my legs.

His kisses and caresses are slow and sweet, making me shiver with pleasure. He moans against me, mumbling something about how good I taste before diving back in, teasing me with gentle little flicks of his tongue until I hear myself begging him for more, burying my hands in his hair as he gives me what I want. Flushed and panting, I feel him move up my body until his mouth is on mine and I taste myself on his tongue.

"Fuck me," I moan. "Please."

He pulls back, a sexy grin playing on his lips. I watch, breathless, as he reaches down to unzip his pants. But then he stops, looking pensive and holding himself still above me. His eyes search mine and he holds my gaze as he reaches for the top button of his shirt, unbuttons it, and then continues until it's hanging open.

I hold my breath, scared that even the slightest movement will make him change his mind about this, about taking this huge step forward with me. I want this so badly with him.

Hesitantly, yet with a determined look on his face, he shrugs the shirt off and tosses it on the floor. He stands, toes his shoes off, and removes his pants and socks, standing naked in front of me for the first time.

The healed wounds on his stomach don't bother me at all. His body is perfect. It's strong, lean, and powerful with well-defined muscles and long limbs. He's showing me all of him, including something I wasn't expecting—a tattoo of a scraggly matchstick figure on his right arm near his shoulder, the word *Alive* written underneath.

"Album logo," he says, touching it briefly. "Misspent youth and all that."

"You're beautiful," I say, meaning every word.

His gaze softens as he leans over me, spreading my legs to

drape them around his waist. "You're the beautiful one. Come here."

He wraps his arms around me and lifts me up, setting me on his lap. He smiles at my stunned expression, palming the back of my neck and pulling me down until his lips are on mine. As he positions himself, I break the kiss.

"You're not wearing a condom."

"I've been tested." He draws a quick breath. "And I can't get you pregnant. Vasectomy."

"Oh." I have no idea how to respond to that. Why would he be this vigilant about not having kids? "I've only been with one person, but I've been tested too."

"Good." His eyes seek mine. "I don't fuck around, Abigail. It's you and me, and no one else."

I nod, relaxing into his touch as he cups my breasts and seeks my mouth again. I love kissing him. He lifts me up, sliding against my wetness.

"I haven't ever, Sir," I mumble in between kisses.

He pauses, the corners of his mouth lifting up. "Simon," he whispers, applying gentle pressure on my hips until I lower myself onto him slowly, inch by inch. We both moan in unison as my inner muscles clench around him.

"It feels ..." I shake my head, not able to describe it, the exquisite feeling of fullness, of having him inside me with nothing between us.

"It feels fucking perfect," he says gruffly before his lips smash against mine and his tongue invades my mouth.

I've never been on top before, and I'm not sure what to do. Tentatively, I start to rock back and forth on him, loving how he can't seem to stop touching me everywhere, how he gasps when I tighten my fingers in his hair and kiss his neck. His big hands settle on my ass, helping me move, faster and faster. Feeling my orgasm approaching, I throw my head back, my body taking over instinctually as mind-numbing pleasure sweeps over me, making me cry out.

"Simon, oh, Simon."

I hear myself still chanting his name as I resurface. He's reclined, watching me with an intensity that's almost too much to take, his fast breaths making his lips part. Surprisingly gently, he cups my cheek and pulls me down for a hungry kiss, wrapping his arms around me. I shift on him, stopping abruptly at the sound of the hiss he lets out against my lips.

"Did you?" I wonder out loud.

He chuckles, running his hands up and down my back. "You didn't notice?"

"No," I admit, feeling myself blush, hiding my face in the crook of his neck.

"You were a bit preoccupied." He laughs softly. "It was so fucking hot seeing you like that."

"Really? Even though I was on top?"

"Mmhm." He pulls my hair back, kissing up my neck and nipping at my earlobe with his teeth. "You did what I told you to do," he says, tightening his hold on my hair. "I like that. A lot." He taps my hip. "Up you go."

Disappointed I don't get to keep enjoying his embrace, I lift myself off him, my body already feeling cold without his touch. I'm barely on my feet before he pulls me down and turns me onto my side, facing the fireplace. He squeezes in behind me, draping his right arm around my waist to keep me from falling off the couch as I rest my head on his left one.

"Did I say you could go anywhere?" he whispers, molding his front to my back.

"I'm sorry ... Simon."

"Good girl."

"I really should clean up, though. I mean, without the condom ..."

He tightens his hold on me. "Fuck it. It's worth a little mess."

I can't help but smile. It seems he likes the closeness as much as I do.

For a while, I enjoy the quiet, closing my eyes and listening to Simon's breathing and the crackling noises of the fireplace. His hand makes lazy passes over my body and finally settles on my breast, where he circles my nipple until it hardens.

"Tell me more about the story you read," he whispers. "What did the Master do to his submissive?"

I'm glad he can't see my face, the way my cheeks fill with color. "He ... he spanked her."

"Mmm. You like it when I do that to you." His fingers walk down my stomach and settle between my legs, making me gasp softly as he caresses me. "Did he fuck her?"

I nod, unable to hold back a moan. "He used a, um, a vibrator on her first."

Simon laughs through his nose, delivering a gentle bite to my shoulder. "Maybe I should do that to you, sweet girl. Tie you up and tease you. You'd love that, wouldn't you?"

"Yes," I admit, my heart already racing at the thought. "Being tied up by you, it's not scary anymore."

He turns me over to face him and I see that he's smiling. I start to lift my hand to touch his face, as he often does to me, but hesitate, unsure if he'll like it.

"You don't have to be afraid to touch me," he whispers. "I've noticed you rarely do."

"You want my hands on you?"

"Among other things. Kiss me. Show me how much you want me."

His eyes are intense and demanding, but his lips are soft as I lean in, his kisses deep and tender. Before I know it, he's between my legs, pushing inside me with a muffled groan. My hands slide over his skin, truly touching him for the first time, and it's heavenly. I feel drunk on him: the sensation of having his naked body against mine, the taste of his lips, the faint smell of his cologne, the sound of his moans, and the pleasure-hazed look in his eyes as he moves in me, slowly and gently.

This is making love. This is how it feels.

I bury my face in his neck as tears pool in my eyes, my heart so full my emotions threaten to spill over. Thankfully, he doesn't notice, too busy working me toward another toe-curling orgasm, which I yell out, clutching him to me in a silent promise to never let him go.

I love you, Simon.

Later that night, way past midnight, he walks me to my room downstairs, lifting my hand to his lips to press a kiss there. Impulsively, I stand up on my tiptoes to kiss him. He reciprocates immediately, moaning softly as I caress his tongue with mine.

"I could get used to this," he murmurs. "Having every night be like this."

Pulling back, he regards me cautiously, a line worrying the space between his eyebrows as though he's scared he's said too much. Doesn't he know? I'm so his.

I kiss him again. "Sleep well, Simon," I say, his parting smile making my heart stutter.

I know he felt it too.

CHAPTER TWENTY-FOUR

The following morning, I can't stop smiling or thinking about everything that happened the night before. It's different now—not from the realization that I love him, because I think I've known that for a while. The acknowledgement of my feelings, however, changes everything. I'm just not sure if it's for the better or the worse. I've been repressing my feelings, telling myself to simply enjoy this job for what it is, but now I know I want more, and for the first time it seems like Simon—after last night it feels right to call him that in my head—does too. If I let this play out, will it turn into a real relationship? My biggest wish is that one day soon he'll simply ask me to be his girlfriend. Nothing much would have to change. I wouldn't mind his work hours. I'd still take care of him just the same, because I love doing it. He and Luke could get closer, and we'd be a real family. Last night Simon shared more of himself with me than he ever has before, and it gives me hope. A fool's hope, perhaps, but hope nonetheless.

I bring the paper in and put it on the tray with the rest of Simon's breakfast before carrying it into the dining room. He's seated at the head of the table as usual, watching me as I enter.

"You look lovely today," he comments, looking me up and down.

I've dressed up for Luke's school interview, wearing a pretty white top with some lace on the collar and fitted dark jeans. I also put on makeup and styled my hair. "Thank you, Sir."

He tugs on the hem of the apron I have on over my clothes as I start serving him. "Nice touch."

I can't contain my smile, knowing how much he likes seeing me looking domestic.

"Where's Luke this morning?" he inquires.

"I let him sleep in since we don't have to be at the school until noon."

"Good." He reaches for me, pulling me into his lap, and before I can protest, his lips are on mine, his large hands cupping my face. I surrender to the kiss, but I don't relax completely, my ears straining as I listen for any indication that Luke might be up and around.

Simon pulls back. "What's wrong?"

"Nothing. It's just ... you know." I nod my head in the direction of the hall.

He frowns, letting go of me. "I apologize. Our agreement was nine to midnight. It won't happen again."

"No!" I exclaim, much too loudly. "I mean, that's not it. I liked kissing you 'good morning.' I was just nervous about Luke walking in."

Appeased, he smiles.

Feeling bold, I lower my voice. "Tomorrow morning I could set my alarm early and sneak into your room."

As quickly as it appeared, the smile washes off his face. He pierces me with his gaze. "You're not to come into my room when I'm asleep, Abigail. Not for any reason."

"Okay," I whisper. "I'm sorry, it was just ... never mind." I climb off his lap, quickly unloading the tray as I avoid his eyes. His rejection makes my throat constrict, but I do my best to breathe through it. Last night felt like a huge leap forward for us, but this is a step backward.

"Abigail."

I force myself to look at him, startled at how tired he suddenly appears. Slowly, he reaches out his hand, placing it on the table, palm up. An offering. I don't have to think about it; I place my hand in his.

"It was a very sweet suggestion," he says softly, "but I don't share a bed with anyone for a good reason." Breathing deeply, he continues. "You've seen that mess on my stomach. I was attacked. In my sleep." His voice is monotone, his eyes fixed on our joined hands.

"I'm ... I'm so sorry," I whisper, feeling tears well up in my eyes. When I first met him, I thought he was a weirdo. Then I accepted his sometimes-strange demands, his need for control, thinking it was a quirk of his. But now I realize it's much more than that. He's damaged. Someone damaged him —badly.

"I'm so sorry," I repeat, not knowing what else to say. One of my tears lands on our joined hands, and he startles, looking up at me. Quickly, I wipe my wet cheeks with my other hand, trying to get myself under control.

"We can't ever share a bed," he rasps. "Please, don't bring it up again."

"I hog the covers anyway," I say, trying for a smile as I shrug my shoulders. "And I have perpetually cold feet."

His tension disappears, the line between his eyes easing away as his face relaxes. "I'll get you a heated blanket."

"Thank you, Sir."

"Thank *you*, sweet girl," he says, tightening his hand around mine for a second before letting go.

After his revelation, it's difficult to leave him to his solitude in the dining room, but I know that's how he wants it to be. Is this the real reason he wants an arrangement like ours rather than a traditional relationship? Am I hoping for too much?

Luke joins me for breakfast about half an hour later, excited for the visit at school. Then Simon appears at the door.

"Good morning, Luke."

My son grins, giving him a wave. "Hi, Mr. Thorne! Guess what? Me and Mommy are going to live here. Like, all the time!"

I stifle a laugh at my son's innocence and his belief that this is news.

"I know." Simon chuckles, smiling at my son. "Your mother told me."

"And I'm going to school today," Luke continues, bouncing up and down in his seat.

Mr. Thorne remains passive; his eyes dart to mine for a second before he looks at Luke again. "Really?" he asks, sounding surprised. "Are you big enough for that?"

"Uh-huh!" Luke nods eagerly. "I'm almost five. It's my birthday soon, right, Mommy?"

"That's right," I chime in. "In two weeks."

"See," he says, "I'll be five in two weeks."

Simon nods. "Are you going to have a big party?"

Luke's face falls a little. "I ... I don't know."

"Of course you'll have a party, honey," I tell him. "We can go to Aunt Jo's."

"You can have it here if you want."

I look at Simon. "Really?"

"Of course. Whatever you want. Use your card; invite your friends."

"Would you like that?" I ask Luke. "A party here? You can even get a Lightning McQueen cake if you want."

"Cool." Luke breathes out the word. "You'll come too, right, Mr. Thorne? To my party?" He stares up at Simon with bright, excited eyes.

Oh, shit.

"I, uh ..." Simon looks taken aback. "Don't you want it to be just for your friends?"

"You're my friend," Luke says, like that's obvious even though they just met a few days ago.

"All right. Thank you. I'll come," Simon finally answers, sounding very formal.

Luke just smiles and digs into his food again. I'm not sure how I feel about this. On one hand, I'm happy that Luke likes Simon enough to want him there for his birthday. On the other, I'm not sure it's a good thing if my son becomes attached. It's one thing for me to fall for Simon, but it's quite another if Luke does. If this doesn't work out ...

"Abigail, will you come with me for a moment?"

I try to gauge his emotions, but come up empty. His face is completely neutral.

"Of course. I'll be right back," I tell Luke as I follow Simon out of the kitchen and into the hallway. There, he opens a door I haven't noticed before and leads me into the garage. He must want to talk in private about what just transpired in the kitchen.

"You don't have to come," I murmur. "I mean, it's not ... you know." I have no idea what I'm trying to say. He turns to look at me, wearing a slight frown.

"You'd rather I didn't." It's not a question.

"No, it's not about me."

"Do you think Luke invited me out of obligation, then?"

I can't help it. I snort out a laugh, immediately covering my mouth with my hands. "I'm sorry, I didn't mean to laugh at you."

Thankfully, he doesn't look upset. "I said something funny?"

"Well, yes. Luke is *four*. He doesn't understand the concept of obligation. He only does what he wants."

"Oh." Simon ponders this for a bit. "So it would hurt his feelings if I didn't show up?"

"Yes," I admit.

"All right, then. I'll come," he says resolutely. "What does he want?"

"You can give him the iPad you mentioned last night."

He shakes his head. "That's yours to give."

"Are you sure? It's a great gift. He'll love it."

"Which is exactly why you should give it to him, Abigail." He smiles at me, hesitating for a moment before reaching out to tuck a lock of my hair behind my ear. The tips of his fingers linger against my skin as they trail down my neck, making me shiver. When he touches me like this it feels like so much more than a sexual arrangement. It's no wonder I'm confused, but I can't help but think he's confused too, about his own feelings.

"Thank you," I manage. "I'll think of something, okay?"

"Okay." He reaches into his pocket and hands me a set of car keys, sweeping his arm toward a very nice-looking gray car next to his black one.

Holy shit. "You didn't buy me a car ..." I exhale, trying to get my bearings.

Simon chuckles. "No, sweet girl. This is my second car. I only use it when the BMW is in the shop. You may borrow it until you can afford your own."

"My own car?" I whisper.

"You do have a license, don't you?"

"Oh, yes. I haven't used it in a while, but I'm a good driver."

"Wonderful. Once you've saved enough for your own, I'll be happy to help you pick one out. Until then, you can use this one for driving Luke to and from school and running errands like grocery shopping."

"Thank you," I say, overwhelmed. "Wow, my own car."

He watches me, looking pleased. "It would mean a lot to you, wouldn't it? Buying it yourself, rather than having me simply give you one."

I nod my head.

"I respect that. Despite my preferences in bed, I do like

211

your independence very much, sweet girl. At least some of the time." He gives me a wink, telling me he's only half-serious.

"I like being yours," I tell him truthfully, gazing up at him. "I like it very much, Sir."

"As do I," he murmurs, stepping closer to me. "I like knowing that you belong to me. That you're mine."

He backs me up against the wall, leaning in to whisper in my ear. "But even more than that, the fact that you want this as much as I do, Abigail, that you get wet at the sound of my voice when I tell you to kneel, to worship me, and that you bend to my will, gladly, that you enjoy it when I take charge of you. It's ..."

"It-it's what?" I stutter, feeling my heart hammering in chest.

"It's *everything*." His lips trace the column of my neck, breathing warm air against my skin. My eyes flutter closed. Suddenly, I can't wait for tonight.

"I'm off to work soon, but we'll continue this later."

I open my eyes, blinking as I look up at him.

He smirks at me. "Have a good day, Abigail."

"You too, Sir," I tell him, willing my body to calm down.

He reaches out to caress my face, his thumb tracing across my lips before he turns and walks away, seemingly unaffected. I wonder if he's just good at hiding it, if his heart is perhaps beating as fast as mine underneath his polished surface.

Drawing a deep breath, I follow him out of the garage and watch as he heads upstairs, his long legs taking two steps at a time with ease, while I stumble into the kitchen and sit down with Luke. A few minutes later, Simon comes back and hands me a note with the school's information.

"Thank you," I tell him. "What would you like for dinner tonight?"

He smiles. "Whatever you feel like cooking."

"I want hot dogs!" Luke volunteers.

Simon chuckles. "Hot dogs for him, whatever you feel like making for me."

I nod my head, returning the smile.

"Have a good day at school, Luke. Learn a lot," he says.

"I'm going to a meeting," Luke says, sounding awfully precocious.

Simon grins, holding up his hands. "My mistake. Have a good meeting, young Mister Winters."

My son turns to me. "What does that mean, Mommy?"

"It's like your grown-up name," I explain.

Luke looks very happy hearing that, grinning around his toast as he takes another bite. I stand and indicate with a subtle head tilt that Simon should follow me to the kitchen island.

"His name is actually Jones," I admit, "after his father."

Simon purses his lips. "Would you like to change that?"

I chose to give Luke Patrick's last name at the hospital. At the time it seemed like the natural thing to do, but looking back with the clarity of hindsight, I can see that it was to get Patrick more interested in his infant son since he'd done his best to ignore my pregnancy, never coming with me to ultrasounds and doctor's appointments. Obviously, it didn't work, and Patrick was never a good father.

"Yes, very much," I tell Simon.

He nods slowly. "And custody?"

"I, uh, I don't know, actually. We were never married. I don't know how it works."

"He just left?"

"Yeah," I whisper. "It's been almost a year now. I don't know where he is."

Simon takes a deep breath, angling his body toward mine. "Do you miss him?"

"Not even a little bit," I say without hesitation.

He looks relieved. "What about Luke?"

I shake my head. "He really wasn't ... well, I guess some people just shouldn't have kids."

"That's very true," he responds, his voice grave. "Some people."

I wait for him to continue, but instead he draws a breath and steps away from me.

"Have a good day," he says. "You have my number if you need anything, and I'll see you tonight."

"Tonight," I echo as he leaves the kitchen.

I look down at the piece of paper in my hand. There's something I have to do before Luke can start school.

Half an hour later, I shake out my shoulders and ring the bell next door. Lila appears, her eyes widening at the sight of me and Luke on her doorstep.

"Hi!" my son says eagerly. "Can J.R. play?"

"Oh, uh, now?"

"No, I'm sorry, that's not why we're here," I interject. "I know it's early."

She laughs, tightening the tie of her robe. "It's not that early. We're off to a late start. But please come in." She calls for her son and as soon as Luke's boots are off the two of them run off, talking over each other excitedly.

"Do you want coffee?" Lila asks, showing me into the kitchen. "There's some already made."

"We won't stay long. I know it's a school day. But yes, please." I take a seat and look around the space, admiring how lovely it is, and how lived-in compared to Simon's house. Lila brings a cup for each of us and joins me at the table.

"So, this is a surprise," she says.

"Uh, yeah." I take a quick gulp, burning my tongue in the process. "I wanted to clear up some things. Our kids are going to be attending the same school and we live next door to each other. We're going to be seeing each other all the time and I just—"

"It's okay. You and Simon are involved, right?"

I stare at her, blinking. "No! I-I just work for him. Why would you think that?"

"I've seen you visiting him at night," she says. "I didn't recognize you at the park at first, but when you said you were living over there, I put two and two together. You've been coming for months, usually around dinnertime."

Panic makes my heart pound. My hands feel clammy.

"We eat early because of J.R.," she continues. "I usually take a walk after dinner and saw the taxis. Please don't think I spend my nights spying on my neighbors. It's just that Simon never has any visitors, so I couldn't help but notice when a cute brunette started showing up. I figured he'd finally gotten a girlfriend." She takes a sip of her coffee. "But you said you were his housekeeper. Even though I've seen him escort you inside, like you were a guest."

Escort. Did she use that word on purpose?

She looks at me again. I swallow nervously, trying to read her, trying to figure out if I can lie my way out of this. I can't. She knows something is going on, but doesn't seem unfriendly. I remember her husband joking that she likes to gossip. The last thing I need is her spreading rumors about me and Simon. Maybe I can make her see my side of things.

"I take care of him," I hear myself whisper, clutching my cup between my hands.

She nods slowly. "That's good. He needs taking care of."

I relax a little. "And he takes care of me."

"Like the school for your son?" she asks. "I know how expensive it is."

I nod, taking a quick sip.

"I take it the two of you have ... an agreement of sorts?"

"Yes. It works for both of us."

At least, it's been working. Now I know I want more, but I'm not about to push the subject before I sense Simon is ready for it.

215

"That's what I figured," Lila says.

"I know what you must think of me," I whisper.

"No, you don't."

I look up, surprised by the friendly tone of her voice.

"I used to model, Abigail. And it's a dirty business, especially for young girls. I've done a lot of things I wish I hadn't. I'm the last person to judge someone." She scoffs. "And I did them to get ahead, to get more shoots, to attend parties. It seems so ridiculous now."

"I'm sorry," I offer.

"I really appreciate you being honest with me, and you don't have to worry. I'd never say anything about you—or Simon. I like to talk, but despite what my husband says I don't run with gossip. Not that kind, anyway." She stirs her coffee.

"I always wondered about him," she says thoughtfully. "He's handsome, obviously, but I've never seen him with a woman, or a man for that matter—not even at social functions."

"You socialize with him?"

"We're at the same club," she explains. "He's very courteous, but a complete mystery. We've been neighbors for years, you know, but we've never moved beyond small talk. The same with my husband. He's always asking Simon to go golfing with him or play racquetball at the club, but it rarely happens. He mostly keeps to himself."

I nod. That was my impression of him too—at first.

"That's why I was so surprised when I realized you'd moved in over there. And with a kid!"

"Oh?"

"I always got the impression he doesn't like children at all."

I'm not sure he does, either. A vasectomy doesn't exactly scream *kid person*.

"I remember when J.R. was born, and we were out walking with him in the stroller," she tells me. "Well, we met Simon, and J.R. started fussing, so Dave picked him up. Simon was nice enough, congratulating us and stuff, but when Dave asked if he wanted to hold the baby, it was like he'd asked him to hold a live grenade with how quickly Simon declined. I think he even backed away."

Wow. He really doesn't like children.

But he does seem to like Luke. Maybe he's changed since then. I hope he has.

"Still, there's something about him, isn't there?" she muses. "I always felt a bit sorry for him, but I'm not sure why. I've tried to set him up with friends of mine, but he declined every time. And I know most of the single women and even a few married ones at the club have hit on him with no luck. So in the end I just figured he liked being a recluse." She gazes at me. "I was wrong, it seems."

"I don't know about that. He's really private, but he's also very kind. Both to me and my son. I was in a really bad situation and he, well, he sort of saved me. I don't want you to think I'm just using him for his money, or that he's taking advantage of me. We both want this. I've never done anything like this before, and I wouldn't if I didn't feel that—" I stop myself, realizing I'm sharing way too much. "Does your husband know?" I ask carefully.

"No. But even if he did, I don't think he'd be bothered by it. He knows about my past. I won't tell him anything if that's what you'd prefer."

"Thank you. Luke would be sad if he couldn't come over and play with J.R. again, and maybe ..."

"I'd love to hang out again," Lila says, sending me one of her blinding smiles. "More coffee? Then I can tell you all about the school, *and* which mom cliques to avoid over there, especially the no-sugar, all-organic ones. Suburbia, man. It's tough out here."

I laugh, holding out my cup. Coming over here was definitely the right move, and I think I just made my first friend in the neighborhood.

CHAPTER TWENTY-FIVE

The next two weeks are without a doubt the happiest of my whole life. The school that Luke attends is amazing and he loves going. I was worried he might be behind the other kids, but so far he hasn't struggled too much with the curriculum, which involves both music and arts besides more academic subjects.

We've quickly fallen into a routine. In the mornings, I pack an afternoon snack for Luke since lunch is included in the program, and then we have breakfast together in the kitchen. After Simon leaves for work, I drop Luke off at school, my heart nearly bursting with happiness as I watch him being greeted by his new classmates. Then I have the whole morning and most of the afternoon to myself, which feels strange, but I keep busy. I handle all of the grocery shopping and meal planning, do the laundry, and make sure the house is kept in order. My afternoons and early evenings are spent with Luke and my nights are spent with Simon. It's the best of both worlds.

Simon drew up a contract of employment for me and I signed without hesitation. My salary is good and I don't pay rent. He insists that I buy all of the food for me and Luke using the card he gave me, so all I really need to pay for myself is stuff like clothes and shoes. I have more than enough to start saving up—and Simon handled that too, in his own efficient way. All it took was a signature from me, and he closed my old account and opened a new one at his bank in my name. My paycheck is deposited there automatically, and I'm the only one who can access it. The days of worrying about Patrick taking my money are gone.

We haven't been officially moved in for long, but already it feels like home. Our names are on the mailbox, and I've received my first letter: the state of Washington has finally started its investigation of Patrick's abandonment. I'm not sure what this means exactly, but I hope it will lead to my getting full custody of Luke if they can't track Patrick down. And even if they do find him, I doubt he'd put up much of a fight. We're doing just fine on our own, thanks to Simon and his generosity.

Truthfully, he's spoiling us. Hardly a day has gone by without him bringing home gifts both big and small, from coloring books and crayons for Luke all the way to a beautiful pair of earrings for me. Whenever I've tried to thank him, he's waved it off, usually silencing my words with sweet kisses. It's no wonder I'm smiling nonstop lately. Most of the time I don't even think about the fact that I'm here doing a job, and Simon doesn't feel like my boss. He's the man I've fallen in love with, the one who makes my heart pound faster and my body sing with pleasure every night. He said he doesn't have much to offer a romantic relationship, but it's clear to me that he's wrong about that. I love what we have, what we do together, and every day I feel us growing closer. He sends me texts throughout the day, asking what I'm doing, encouraging me to spend time with Lila and enjoy myself, telling me he can't wait to come home to me. I stay up with him way past midnight every night, sometimes making sweet love, other times fucking like animals, and sometimes simply cuddling on the couch watching movies. I love all of it. I love him. And I think he might love me too.

The day before Luke's birthday is a Friday, and I pick him up early, excited for the weekend. Simon has a dinner thing in the city, so it's just the two of us this afternoon. After a light snack, we end up watching a movie in his room. As it's playing, my eyelids grow heavier and heavier. I sink back into the pillows as I hug my son, happy and content.

I sit up with a start, realizing that I'm alone on the bed. There's now a blanket covering me and the TV's off. Luke is nowhere to be seen. I must have fallen asleep.

"Luke?" I get off the bed and start walking through the house, knowing Luke will be somewhere inside. If he tried to leave, the alarm on the door would've gone off. In the empty kitchen, I glance at the clock, wincing as I see that it's nearly 6:00 p.m. I've slept for more than two hours and am now way behind schedule. In the hallway, I pause when I notice Simon's coat on the hanger. He's home early and my heart leaps with excitement before I remember I still haven't found Luke. There's only one place he could be.

I hurry up the stairs to Simon's part of the house, a place I'm only supposed to go on invitation. Luke knows he's not allowed up there and that he shouldn't disturb Simon. But sure enough, I hear voices through the partially opened door to his office.

"... like going to school?"

"Oh, sure," Simon says.

"Really?" Luke sounds like he doesn't believe him. "Even math?"

"Well, maybe *like* is too strong a word," he chuckles. "I'm good with numbers now, though. You'll be too, I'm sure."

"Is this right?" Luke asks.

"Let me see. Hmm, hang on. Okay, I have two paper clips here, right?"

"Uh-huh."

"And here's three more. If I put them together, two plus these three, how many do I have?"

"Five."

"That's it. So two plus three equals ..."

"Five!"

"Exactly. Good job! Write that on your worksheet."

"Mr. Thorne?"

"Hmm?"

"I think I like math."

"Good."

I tiptoe a few steps forward, peering inside. Simon is seated at his desk, typing on his computer. On the other side of the desk, Luke is kneeling on a chair, bent over his schoolbooks. The scene before me is completely unremarkable—a grown-up helping a child with his homework—yet it brings tears to my eyes, seeing the two of them together like this. Luke picks up some paper clips, hesitating for a moment before putting four in one pile and then adding three.

"Four plus three is ... seven," he says, looking at Simon for confirmation.

"That's exactly right."

Luke's smile is as bright as the sun as he scribbles down the answer, but what makes my heart gallop is the warmth in Simon's gaze as he watches my son before returning to his own work.

I retreat, barely holding it together. He might not like kids in general, but he clearly likes Luke. *Don't make a big deal of this. Don't. Act normal.*

But it *is* a big deal. Simon has always been nice to my son, and generous too. This, however, is the first time they've spent any real time together and I don't want to freak Simon out by showing him just how excited this makes me, seeing them enjoying each other's company.

I head downstairs to my bedroom and find my phone. There's a text from Simon from over an hour ago, telling me that his dinner was canceled and that he's coming home after all.

Drawing a deep breath, I head into the kitchen and start looking through the freezer for something to make for dinner. I start defrosting a steak and putting together Luke's and my dinner as well, knowing my son is probably starving by now. Simon usually takes his dinner at seven o'clock, so at least I can make that happen almost on time.

I can't get the image out of my mind of the two of them together, of how sweet Simon was with him, how interested in helping him. It's the complete opposite of how Patrick used to be around Luke. I know I should march up there and get Luke. I know that. But I don't want to. I want the two of them together; I want all three of us together. I have a fantasy of the three of us going out together on a Saturday, maybe to the zoo, Simon's arm around me and his other hand holding Luke's. I can see it so clearly in my mind, my dream for the future.

"Hi, Mommy!"

I look up, smiling at my son as he runs into the kitchen, taking a seat at the table.

Simon follows a few seconds later. "Hello."

"Hello, Sir."

"We were just upstairs," he says, walking over to me. "I hope that's all right?"

It's so much more than all right. "Of course. I'm so sorry. I didn't mean to fall asleep."

He waves it off, leaning a bit closer to me. "I kept you up late last night."

"I remember, Sir." My cheeks heat up, and he gives me a knowing smile.

"I didn't want to disturb you," he whispers. "You're very pretty when you sleep."

The shyness I feel hearing his compliment makes no sense. This man has seen every inch of my naked body, done unspeakably delicious things to it, and yet knowing that he covered me up and took care of my son to let me sleep feels a lot more intimate than anything we've done in his bedroom. It shows how much he cares.

"Thank you. It was a nice nap. I'm a bit behind now, though," I admit. "But your dinner shouldn't be much later than you like." I motion to the food that's almost done. "This is for Luke and me."

"I'm hungry. What's for dinner?" Luke asks from his seat.

"Tomato soup and grilled cheese."

"Oh, yum! That's the best! Don't you think so, Mr. Thorne?"

"Well, it's been a while," he says, smiling at Luke.

"I'm making steak for you," I interject, knowing he likes that.

"Don't you like grilled cheese?" Luke asks, disbelieving. "Mommy makes the best ever."

Simon looks at me. "Does she now?"

Luke jumps off his chair, and the next thing I know, he's pulling Simon by the hand toward the kitchen table. "Eat with us."

"Luke, I'm sure Mr. Thorne would rather –"

"Is there enough?"

I stare at him for a second, sure I must've misheard him, my pulse pounding in my ears. Simon takes a seat next to Luke, looking a bit uncertain and out of place in his fine suit.

"Of-of course," I manage. "Luke, help me set the table."

My son jumps to the task, and soon everything's ready. There's an awkward moment when I don't know if I should stand and serve Simon like I usually do, but he grabs Luke's bowl and ladles the piping hot soup into it before reaching for mine. As I take my seat, he glances at me, smiling.

"Thank you," I say softly.

His fingers brush against mine as he hands me my bowl, and it makes my insides flutter so much I can hardly concentrate on the task of eating.

"You have to dunk the sandwich," Luke instructs Simon. "That's the best part."

"Just using my fingers?"

I can't tell if he's being serious, but Luke laughs at him, dunking his own grilled cheese into the soup before shoving half of it into his mouth.

"All right; here goes."

I stifle a chuckle seeing how gingerly Simon holds his sandwich compared to Luke as he too dips it before taking a bite.

"Mmm, it *is* good."

"See? I told you." Luke grins at both of us.

"Not how you usually eat soup?" I ask, smiling.

"Ah, no. But it really is good," he assures me before taking another bite.

We eat in comfortable silence. It's peaceful and perfect. The kitchen's warm and cozy, and Simon refills our bowls and drinking glasses as though we've done this a hundred times before. If someone were to look in through the window, they'd think we were ...

A family.

The pang of longing I feel is so palpable that it takes my breath away for a second, and I do my best to hide my emotions by taking a drink of water.

"So, are you excited about your birthday tomorrow?" Simon asks.

"Uh-huh! J.R. from school is coming, and Piper and Pippa! And there's gonna be balloons and presents and everything!"

"Their parents will be here too," I add. "I hope you don't mind."

"It's fine. Do you need help with anything?"

"No, thank you. They won't be here until two, so there's plenty of time to get everything together. We won't bother you if you need to work before the party."

"I'm going into the city for a little while tomorrow morning anyway."

"Work?"

"Just some things to do at my office, but I can pick that cake up on my way back. I insist."

"What cake?" Luke asks. "Am I really getting a Lightning McQueen cake?"

"You'll have to wait and see," I say, giving him a wink. "Now, eat up."

As we continue the meal and I see the two of them talking and laughing, a warm glow of contentment settles over me, and I hope every night will be like this. It isn't my imagination; things really have changed between us. My dream for the future doesn't seem unattainable at all.

CHAPTER TWENTY-SIX

The next day we celebrate Luke's birthday. He and I set everything up in the kitchen, which is big enough for this small gathering. Using the dining room felt too formal, and that's the last thing I wanted for today. This isn't Luke's first birthday party—I've always made sure to throw him one, no matter how small—but it's the first one where I don't have to fake smiles and ignore Patrick's lack of enthusiasm, the first one where I have a big present for Luke, and the first one where I've had someone to help me. Simon kept his promise and picked up the cake I ordered, which might not seem like a big deal, but to me it is. Having someone that I can depend on besides Jo is definitely still a novelty, and I can't stop smiling as I watch all the guests gathered at the table to celebrate my son, eating the snacks I've put out. There's one seat left, next to Simon, and he smiles at me as I take it.

"This is delicious," Lila says, reaching for another mini pizza. "Did you really make all of this yourself, Abbi?"

I smile at her compliment. "I did. Luke helped."

"Abigail's a great cook," Simon says.

"We should get a cook too," Dave chimes in, nudging Lila.

"Hey, I cook," she protests with a grin. "Sometimes. Well, I try."

"I can teach you," I volunteer. "I mean, if you'd like."

"Really? That would be awesome!" Her smile is genuine. We've become good friends already, and she's helped me settle into the neighborhood, even introducing me to some of the other moms at the school.

"Just let me know," I say, putting some food on my own plate. Everyone digs in and I look around the table again, my smile becoming even wider as Simon rests his arm on the back of my chair. He's not touching me, but he may as well be. Whether consciously or unconsciously, he's mimicking the poses of the two other men. There are three couples here. Three families.

"So, do you want cake or presents first?" I ask Luke after a little while.

"Presents!" he answers predictably.

While he opens everything, I take a lot of pictures of both him and everyone around the table, feeling dizzy with happiness. This is what a birthday is supposed to be like—friends, good food, and my son's dazzling smile as he tears into his gifts with unbridled enthusiasm. When he gets to my gift and sees the iPad, he stares at me for a second before running around the table to throw his arms around me.

"Happy birthday, honey," I whisper as I scoop him up to sit on my lap.

"I love you, Mommy," he whispers back, burrowing his little face into the crook of my neck. Of course it's impossible to hold back tears then, and I laugh and apologize at the same time, gratefully accepting a handkerchief from Simon to dab my eyes.

"Can we go play with it now?" Luke asks eagerly after a few seconds of cuddling. The other kids are already on their feet.

"After we've had cake."

"I have something for you too," Simon says, reaching into his inner pocket. He hands a thick envelope to Luke. I wonder what it could be. I gave Simon a few suggestions for a present, but none of them would fit in an envelope. Carefully, I help Luke open it, watching as he pulls out a bunch of papers.

"Fireworks! And a castle! And there's Mickey Mouse," Luke says, pointing at the cover of the colorful brochure in his hand. "Where is this?"

I can't believe this is happening. "It's, uh, it's ..." I'm completely at a loss for words.

"It's a trip to Disneyland in California," Simon says. "Have you ever been there?"

"Disneyland?" Luke sounds breathless. "No."

"We're going to Disneyland?" I finally find my voice.

"Disneyland is awesome!" J.R. exclaims. "We've been there two whole times!"

I find the plane tickets. Why are there so many of them? I scan the names on them, one at a time. There are ones for Luke and me, but also Jo, Thomas, Pippa, and Piper.

I stare at Simon. "All of us?" I whisper. "We're all going?"

He merely nods, smiling. I look at Jo and Thomas.

"What?" Jo asks from across the table.

"You're coming too. It's for all of us. You, me, Thomas, and the kids."

"What?" The table erupts in chatter and excited shrieks as everyone seems to catch on simultaneously. It's complete mayhem. All three kids yell and scream, jumping up and down, and J.R. joins them for the hell of it. Jo and Thomas are on their feet, flabbergasted and laughing, while J.R.'s parents try to calm their son to no avail.

"Thanks, man!" Thomas is flustered as he comes over to shake Simon's hand. "I don't even know what to say. I can't believe this!"

"Thank you so much!" Jo exclaims, grabbing his other

hand. "You have no idea how much this means to us, to the kids."

Simon clears his throat, taking a step back, obviously out of his element. "Well, call it an early wedding present." He nods once before taking his seat again, glancing in my direction.

"Thank you," I mouth. *I love you.*

The corners of his eyes crinkle as he smiles at me, and in the next moment, they widen as Luke barrels into him, nearly knocking him off his seat.

"Thank you, thank you, thank you!" Luke chants, throwing his arms around Simon's neck before hugging him. Simon hesitates for a moment, his eyes meeting mine, before he gently pats Luke on the back, lowering his gaze.

After a few seconds, Simon lifts Luke off him and places him on the floor, handling him delicately, as though he might break. I pull him into my lap, giving him a cuddle as I look over the tickets again. There are six of them. Simon isn't coming with us. I'm not surprised, but I wish he were, just the same. Could I tell him that once we're alone? Maybe he'd like to come with us and doesn't know how welcome he is.

"It's for Thanksgiving weekend," Simon says, fixing his tie. "I hope that won't interfere with anyone's plans."

"My mom will understand," Jo says immediately.

"You won't need me for the holidays?" I ask Simon quietly.

"I'll be traveling," he says. "No Thanksgiving in Europe."

"Business again?" Dave asks.

"As always. I'll be away for a couple of weeks this time, unfortunately." He glances in my direction.

A couple of weeks? My heart sinks. I don't want him to go away that long, especially now that everything is going so well, when we're finally moving in the right direction.

"But you'll be back for the Christmas event at the club, right?" Lila asks. "It's for charity."

Simon gives her a tight smile. "Thank you, but I'll settle for writing you a check. Holiday parties aren't really my thing."

"You know that," Dave says to his wife. "Simon's house is the only one on the block without decorations come Christmas. He's our resident Scrooge." His tone is light and teasing, and I get the feeling they've talked about this before. "Maybe you can bring a little holiday cheer to the house," he says, directed at me.

I simply smile and shrug. It's not a bad idea, though. I could ask Simon to spend Christmas together here at the house, letting him know we want to be with him during the holidays. That would show him I don't think of him as my boss anymore.

"Can we have cake now?" Luke asks.

I get the cake from the fridge, hoping it tastes as good as it looks. They really made it look like Lightning McQueen, and I know Luke will love it. Lighting the five little candles, I carry it to the table, feeling a bit in the spotlight as I start to sing "Happy Birthday." Thankfully, everyone joins in—even Luke, his eyes alight with excitement as I place the car-shaped cake in front of him. I smile at Jo, who's already aimed her phone at Luke, ready to snap a picture.

"Okay, make a wish, hon."

He closes his eyes, draws a deep breath, and blows out all the candles in one go. Everyone applauds.

"What'd you wish for?" Pippa asks.

"If you tell us, it won't come t—" I start, but Luke interrupts me.

"I wished Mr. Thorne would be my daddy!"

Oh, no. My gaze darts from Luke's happy grin to Jo's wide eyes. Yes, he really just said that. I didn't imagine it. *Fuck.*

The kitchen is completely quiet. I can see Simon out of the corner of my eye sitting stock-still, but I don't dare look in his direction.

"That's dumb!" Piper's outburst echoes off the walls. "You can only have one daddy!"

"Nuh-uh!" J.R. protests. "Jeremy at school has two daddies! Right, Mom?"

"Oh, uh, that's right," Lila confirms.

"See!" JR is triumphant. "*And* you can have two mommies too."

The kids all start talking about two daddies and mommies, but the adults are silent. Dead silent. I'm dying inside.

"Lila, how far along are you?" Jo asks, referring to the visible baby bump she's sporting in her tight shirt.

"Six months," she replies, placing her hand on her stomach. "I'm getting so big already compared to the first time."

Dave puts his hand on top of hers, giving her a loving look.

"I think you look great," Jo says. "God, I was such a whale when I was expecting."

"You were not," Thomas protests. "More like a really cute manatee."

All of them laugh as Jo pretends to choke Thomas, and the tension evaporates, the talk flowing easily around the subject of babies and pregnancy. I put on a brave face, cutting the cake and handing everyone a slice. Except the seat next to me is now empty. No one mentions it, but we've all noticed Simon's departure.

After cake and coffee I step outside, drawing deep breaths. *Everything is okay. It didn't ruin anything. He's not upset, just surprised. Everything is okay.*

"Hey, Abbi."

I look over to see Thomas lighting a cigarette.

"My only vice now, I swear," he says with a grimace.

I wave my hand.

"So, good party," he says, watching me closely.

"Disaster is more like it," I mumble.

"He's not just your boss, is he?"

I sigh softly. I could use the answer to that myself.

"Hey, I'm not judging. He seems like a great guy."

"But?"

Thomas takes a drag, shrugging. "Nothing. I just don't really get it. Why are you working for him? Why aren't you just, you know, his girlfriend?"

I look at him, taking in his open expression. No, he isn't judging me. I can tell.

"I don't know." I shake my head. "It's complicated. I don't think he's ready for that."

Thomas nods his head, pensive. "It took me a long time," he says, "getting to where I am now. I didn't appreciate what I had, and it kills me to think of how much I missed out on." He stubs out his cigarette and bends down to collect the butt. "By the way, I think you're great," he says. "You were there for Jo when she needed a friend the most, and God knows you've been through enough shit already."

"Yeah."

"I guess what you have to figure out is if he's worth it. If he's good enough for you and Luke to wait around for. I mean, I'm pretty much the luckiest bastard in the world that Jo decided to wait for me to get my head out of my ass."

"I'm glad you did. Get your head out of your ass, I mean."

He grins at me, smoothing back his wild curls. "I meant what I said, Abbi. You're great. And you should be with someone who appreciates you, who wants to give you everything. And I don't mean this fancy house and all the stuff that comes with it."

I nod my head. "Thanks, Thom."

He pats my shoulder. "Let's get back and make sure the kids haven't trashed the place."

"There's a good chance," I reply, smiling.

Hours later, all evidence of the party has been cleared away, and everything is back to normal. At least on the outside. It's a little before nine o'clock, and Luke is fast asleep. It's time for me to start my time with Simon. Only tonight, I'm trembling with nerves. I haven't seen or heard from him since he left the party, but I know he's home. His car is in the garage. I go through the routine of making myself ready, but I don't know what to expect when I reach the top of the steps and knock on his office door. Will he pretend it never happened? Or will he acknowledge that things have changed between us?

As I approach his office, I can hear music coming from inside, louder than usual. I don't know the song, but it's definitely rock—guitars, heavy drumbeats, a man singing slurred words.

I knock, wait, then knock again. "Simon?"

Finally, the volume of the music is lowered, and I watch as the door opens slowly. He looks the same as always, except not really. His eyes are red-rimmed, his eyelids hooded; his face is ashen, and he smells like alcohol.

"Yes?" he asks.

"It's, uh, nine o'clock."

"Is it?"

"You missed dinner." I hold out the tray I've brought with me.

"Thank you, but I'm not hungry."

"Please, you should eat something."

"Don't tell me what to do," he snaps, the severity in his voice forcing me to take a step back. Palming his forehead, he exhales slowly, closing his eyes. "I'm sorry. I don't need anything. Please, leave me." He looks at me, his eyes sweeping over my face, my body, and the tray I'm holding. Then he shakes his head again.

"If this is about what Luke said, I'll talk to him." I had planned on doing that anyway tomorrow.

"Kids say the darndest things. Heh, I used to watch that show." He laughs, holding on to the door.

"Show?"

"You're s-so young," he slurs, frowning. "I forget sometimes. But you're so fucking *young*. You don't know ... Just leave me, I don't want anything."

233

"I want to be with you," I whisper, unable to stop myself. "Simon, please."

"Don't call me that. I didn't say you could."

"I'm sorry, I-I thought things had changed."

"They haven't." He looks straight at me, a cold, distant look in his eyes. "I don't want to fuck you tonight. You come to me when I say so. Not the other way around. Got it?"

I'm too stunned to speak. Wordlessly, he closes the door, locking it with a soft click before the music starts blaring again. I place the tray outside his door before I walk back downstairs, fighting tears.

CHAPTER TWENTY-SEVEN

Sunday morning is cold and gray—a fitting setting for my mood. I'm dreading having to face Simon. He's never dismissed me before, never rejected me. I knew what happened yesterday was too fast for him, but I didn't think he'd react this strongly, telling me to leave him alone and talking about our time together being just about him fucking me. It's been about more than that since we moved in here. I know it has. What will this mean for our staying here? Will he rethink moving us in? I also have to talk to Luke about his birthday wish, and I'm not looking forward to the conversation.

Luke and I make breakfast, but there's no sign of Simon, so we sit down at the table without him. It's nearly noon by the time he comes downstairs. I'm in the kitchen trying out a new dinner recipe when he enters, holding the tray I left for him last night. It's untouched.

"Good, er, morning," he murmurs, glancing at the clock.

"Hello, Sir."

He looks like he always does, freshly showered and dressed impeccably, as though last night never happened. "I'll just put this here," he says, placing the tray next to the sink.

"All right." I don't know what to say to him, if I should pretend everything is normal. "Would you like something to eat?" I finally ask.

"Thank you, that would be nice. Anything's fine. I'd like some coffee too."

He's being formal with me. Too formal. It's making me nervous. I nod, turning the burners off before heading to the fridge to get some lunch meats for a sandwich. When I turn back around, he's watching me, still standing there with his hands buried in his pockets.

"Sir?"

He takes a step back and then another. "I'll be in the dining room."

I watch as he retreats, letting out a shuddering sigh. So this is how it is now? He's back to eating in the dining room. After assembling a new tray for him, I carry it into the dining room where he's seated at the table. I quickly serve him, pouring some cold water before giving the little serving bowl containing two painkillers a small push toward him.

"Thank you," he says, fishing them out and swallowing them. He groans, moving his head from side to side a few times before reaching for his coffee. I turn to leave, disappointed at his formality, but at least he's not angry like he was yesterday.

"I'm sorry about last night," he says.

I face him again, surprised he's bringing it up. "You are?"

"I shouldn't have talked to you the way I did. It was disrespectful of me." He hesitates for a second. "You're a good employee, Abigail."

"Thank you." My response is automatic, but I can't breathe. An *employee*. After everything, that's all I am to him?

"Thank you for this," he says, motioning to his plate. "Would you please bring in the mail if you're not too busy? I forgot about it yesterday."

"Of course. Do you need anything else?" I ask, wondering if my voice sounds as dull to his ears as it does to mine.

"No. I'm going out for dinner tonight, and I won't be home until late. No need for you to wait up for me."

I waited up the other times he had to work late, setting up a snack for him on the coffee table. We cuddled on the couch and he told me how happy he was to be home with me finally. Those nights were wonderful, but now he's shut that down. It hurts more than I care to admit to myself.

"Have a good day, Sir," I say before leaving the dining room.

I feel his eyes on me as I exit, and I don't know if the sigh I hear is just a figment of my imagination. On my way to collect the mail, I see Lila, Dave, and J.R. in their driveway, getting out of their car, all of them laughing and talking. The three of them are a family. The three of us are not. Lila waves at me, and I wave back, faking a smile as I head to the mailbox. Among all of Simon's mail, there's a letter addressed to me, and for a moment my heart stops as I recognize the familiar handwriting listing my old address. It's from my mother, and it's been forwarded here. She doesn't know we've moved.

Back in the kitchen, I open it with trembling hands. Inside the blue envelope, there's a letter and a card. "Happy 5th Birthday," it reads above a picture of a cartoon boy on a bike. I'm stunned—they've never sent anything for Luke's birthday before.

I open the card. Inside it simply says, "Happy birthday, Luke. Grandma and Grandpa." There's a crisp fifty-dollar bill too. It's a completely appropriate but also indistinct gift and card, highlighting that they know absolutely nothing about my son.

That was their choice, I remind myself, glancing over my shoulder to make sure I'm still alone before opening the letter.

Dear Abigail,
I don't know how to begin this letter. I realize saying how

sorry I am will sound hollow and most likely dishonest to you, but it's still important that I say it. I miss you. I've been missing you. You're my little girl. Abigail, we made a mistake, a horrible mistake. Please, I hope you'll let me apologize to you. Things have been very difficult for you because of us. I realize that now, and we didn't do right by you. Your father misses you too. He's not well.

I hope you'll go with Luke and buy him a present with the money I've included. You don't have to tell him it's from us. If you need anything, please let me know. I'm so sorry.

Love,
Mom.

My eyes are dry, but I feel as though my heart is being squeezed in a vise. They want to help? Well, too little, too late. What does she expect from me—that I'll just forgive and forget? She's been missing me? She's got some fucked up way of showing it, practically kicking me out when I was pregnant and scared to death and then completely abandoning me and my newborn baby, leaving us to fend for ourselves with an asshole for a breadwinner. Fuck her. Fuck them. Fuck it all! I finally lose the battle against the tears, and they start pouring out of me as I cover my mouth to avoid making any noise.

I force myself to stop, not wanting Luke to see me like this, drawing a ragged breath as I wipe my eyes, my chest still contracting painfully with the need to sob. I stare at the letter and the card in my hand. What do I do? Can I ever contemplate talking to them again, let alone letting them back into my life, into Luke's life? I just don't know. Even with everything that's happened, they're my parents. My only family. Could they really have changed? I glance out toward the hallway, which leads up to Simon's part of the house. Do people ever change?

Well, I have. I'm not in denial about my feelings anymore.

Falling for Simon wasn't something I planned, but now it's happened, and it's made me careless. I've made a mistake by not discouraging his relationship with Luke. It's one thing to have my feelings hurt, but it's not fair to my son.

Later that morning, after Simon has gone back upstairs, Luke and I have a talk about his birthday wish. He's confused, and I once again blame myself for not keeping the two of them apart. In the end, I explain the difference between sharing a house with someone and being a family, promising Luke that he's the most important thing in my life and that the two of us will always be our own little family, and that we have lots of friends.

I suggest we go next door for a visit. I can't sit around here, hoping Simon will throw a few scraps of affection my way whenever he feels like it. His words from last night resonated clearly with me. I won't come to him anymore unless he asks me to. All I can do now is the job I was hired for and continue to save up to build a life for me and my son.

For the next week, I do everything according to my employee contract. I take care of the grocery shopping. I do laundry and light cleaning, and I cook Simon's breakfast as well as serve him dinner promptly at seven o'clock on the nights when he's home. But that's it.

I don't go up to his part of the house anymore. I hold out hope that he'll come for me at nine o'clock, but he doesn't. I spend my nights in my room, either reading or watching TV, and he mostly stays upstairs doing God knows what. At least he doesn't drink heavily again—as far as I know that was a one-time thing—but he remains just as distant. He's not mean to Luke or me. He doesn't raise his voice or make outrageous demands. He's courteous, polite, and professional. And I can't stand it.

I'm acting like the perfect employee, but it's all for show. We both know I'm not here to just do the laundry and cook. I told myself I would stop hoping, but I can't—I want things to go back to the way they were before the party, when we ate in the kitchen together, all three of us. What Luke said freaked Simon out, and I don't blame him at all. Anyone would be freaked out in that situation. But I thought he'd get over it after a few days, that he'd come back to me, and he hasn't—and it hurts like hell seeing him every day but never being able to touch him. So that weekend, I drop Luke off at Jo and Thom's, determined to take matters into my own hands.

"Thank you so much," I say to Jo after we've set up a makeshift bed for Luke in her girls' room.

"Still the same, huh?" she asks, giving me a sympathetic smile as we sit down at her kitchen table.

I sigh, nodding my head.

"So what's the plan for tonight?" Jo inquires, pouring both of us a cup of tea.

"Cook dinner for him, dress up, try to ... I guess try to recreate a typical night for us, the way it was before we moved in."

Jo nods. "Going back to square one?"

"Pretty much. We can't go on like this. I refuse to believe he's happy with the way things are going now. He didn't hire me because he actually needed a housekeeper. He did it because he wanted me, but—" I have to pause to take a deep breath, getting my emotions under control. "But what if he doesn't want me anymore?" It comes out sounding just as pitiful as I feel.

"Impossible," Jo says. "I saw how he was looking at you at Luke's party. I can't say anything about how he feels, but there's no doubt he wants to bang you like a Salvation Army drum."

I snort out a laugh, nearly choking on my tea. "Jo!"

"Well, he does," she says with a shrug.

"I just don't know anymore. He never touches me. What Luke said at the party, it spooked him."

"Well, I guess I can't blame him for that."

"Yeah, I know. Everything was going so well before that, but it's my fault that it happened. I did nothing to stop Luke from becoming attached."

"How's he doing now?"

"He's okay. I've explained it to him as best I can, and we're not even home that much anymore. We've been spending a lot of time next door, so he hasn't had a lot of opportunities to see Simon anyway."

"*Simon*, huh?" Jo's smile is sympathetic.

"Yeah. I can't pretend he's just my boss. You were right to be worried."

"I didn't want to be. I want you to be happy."

"Good thing we're going to the happiest place on Earth soon," I say, hoping to lighten the mood by mentioning Disneyland.

Jo grins. "I can't wait. Did you know there's a kids' club with supervision so we can actually go out one night, just the three of us?"

"That does sound amazing."

"Right? I'm bringing a dress. I can't remember the last time I went to a restaurant that didn't have crayons and placemats you can draw on!"

I laugh at her enthusiasm. It's going to be a great trip, and it's just two days away. Simon is leaving for Europe tomorrow, and tonight is the last night we'll be in the house together before his trip, which is why I arranged for Jo to babysit. He has no idea, but I know he'll be home. I'm hoping ... I don't know. Maybe if he remembers how it was between us before Luke's birthday party, we can start over somehow. I know he felt something for me then. I couldn't have imagined it.

"Are you nervous about tonight?" Jo asks, and I realize I've drifted off.

"A little," I admit. "I want him to want me—the way he used to. I miss him touching me, kissing me ..."

"Fucking you?" Jo whispers, wagging her eyebrows.

I grin. "Yeah, that too. I think we both need this night."

"Go get him, then. I'll watch Luke and everything will be great."

"I hope so."

Back home, I prep dinner before going into my room. I don't reemerge until nearly two hours later, bathed, shaved, and groomed. I'm wearing the green polka dot dress Simon put me in the first night I cooked him dinner. My hair is curled and styled. There are kitten heels on my feet, and I have on a pearl necklace to complete the outfit. I know he'll like this—and I like it too, looking like this for him. I remember that night very well, how he bent me over the dining room table and touched me, spanked me, and asked me if I wanted him to fuck me. Back then I was still too shy, too unsure of myself and what I liked to say yes. I'm not anymore. I want him—badly.

I start making a pie crust, remembering to put on a white apron first, not only to keep my dress clean but also because I know Simon likes seeing me like this. As I'm slicing the apples, I sense him behind me and look over my shoulder. He's leaning against the doorframe, his gaze traveling up my body slowly until his eyes reach mine. I don't even have to act—his piercing look makes me lower mine, recognizing his authority over me in this scenario.

"Good evening, Sir," I murmur.

"What's all this?" he asks.

"I'm making you dinner ... and dessert." I return to the apples, shivering lightly as I feel him approach me.

"Where's Luke?"

"At Jo and Thomas'. Per your request, I've asked her to babysit. Luke is spending the night over there."

He lets out his breath, and it tickles the back of my neck, making me hyper-aware of his proximity.

"So it's j-just the two of us," I stutter as I feel him gently tugging on a lock of my hair to watch the curl spring back into place.

"All right," he says softly. "You can set up two place settings in the dining room, and I expect to eat at seven."

"Yes, Sir." I close my eyes, drawing deep breaths after he leaves. Two place settings mean I won't be sitting in his lap or eating off his plate, but it's better than nothing. He could have said no completely and had me eat in the kitchen, after all.

At seven o'clock sharp, I serve Simon before taking my seat to his right, and we start eating—in complete silence. I feel him glancing at me several times, and I struggle to come up with anything to say.

"Delicious, as always," he comments after a while, taking a sip of wine.

"Thank you." *God, this is so awkward.*

I barely touch my food, the torturous silence making me lose my appetite entirely. Simon doesn't eat much either, and the meal is over quickly. He stays seated as I carry the dirty dishes into the kitchen.

"Dessert?" I ask, trying for a smile when I return. "I baked a pie."

He looks up at me, shaking his head, and my heart plummets. This was so stupid of me. I feel ridiculous in my dress and apron and have to swallow hard to keep from bursting into tears. *What the hell was I thinking?*

"If that'll be all then, Sir," I whisper, reaching across the table for his wine glass, willing my hand to stop shaking. I gasp softly as his hand shoots out, grabbing my wrist. He tugs it, forcing me to place my other elbow on the tablecloth to keep my balance. He's on his feet and behind me before I can react, his hand that held my wrist now on my shoulder, pushing me down so I'm bent over the table completely.

"Is this what you want?" he whispers, placing his other

hand on my hip before pushing his very prominent erection against me.

I'm still too stunned to speak, overwhelmed by the show of possession, the way he's holding me down, slowly rutting against me.

"Hmm?" He skims the side of my body, giving my breast a firm squeeze. "Is this what you want, Abigail? Is this what you need?"

"Yes, Sir."

"Lift up your skirt."

It's just like the first time, when he asked me to present myself to him after dinner. I reach down and pull it up, fisting the material as I lean on the table again. Simon sighs behind me, the tips of his fingers caressing my naked skin.

"Close your eyes."

I exhale, doing as I'm told and trying my best to relax.

"So pretty," he murmurs, stroking my hair and turning my head to the side. "Suck."

His thumb pushes past my parted lips at the same time his other hand delivers a firm smack on my backside. He does it again, harder this time. My face heats up as I hear myself moan, long and low, sucking eagerly on his thumb.

"Yes, you like that," he says. His fingers part me, finding me wet and ready even though he's barely touched me, and he penetrates me with two long fingers, making me moan again.

"There's a good girl," he croons, moving his thumb in and out slowly. "You like to have me in your mouth, don't you?"

I can't answer him, but it's evident that I do from how easily his fingers are gliding. It feels so good having him touch me, and I know I'll come if he continues.

"Do you want this?" he asks, pressing himself against my hip as he removes his thumb from my mouth.

"Yes," I gasp as he spanks me again.

"Where do you want it, pretty girl?"

"Anywhere," I moan, clenching around his fingers. "Anywhere you want, Sir. Please, make me—"

His fingers are gone, and he pulls my upper body up, holding me against him from behind, his mouth at my ear. "My bedroom. Now."

I nearly trip over my own feet running upstairs, him hot on my heels. Once inside, he's all over me, overwhelming me with unrestrained kisses. He attacks my neck as he starts tugging at my dress.

"I've missed you," I moan. "God, I've missed this. I thought you didn't want me anymore."

He stops, slowly lifting his head. "I always want you," he says.

I don't get a chance to say anything else. He lifts my chin, capturing my lips in a searing kiss that makes my knees go weak.

"Do you want this?" he asks.

"Yes. I just want things to go back to the way they were," I tell him.

He gazes down at me. "The way things were?"

I nod.

"Being my sweet girl?" he asks slowly. "Like before ... everything else?"

Relieved, I smile. I want nothing more than to go back to the way things were before Luke's party. "Yes, Sir."

He frowns for a second and exhales through his nose before nodding and taking me in his arms. He leans in, pressing his lips against mine, but before I can deepen the kiss he pulls back, and I watch as his expression changes into something else—something a lot sterner that commands obedience. I recognize that look, and feeling my body react to it startles me—the rush of heat underneath my skin, the way I lower my eyes immediately. God, he really does own me.

Wordlessly, he undresses me and leads me to the bed, holding on to my hand as I crawl on top of the mattress, lying down on my back. Slowly, he holds up the apron I was wearing.

"Remember what I said I wanted to do to you, using this?"

"You wanted to tie me to your bed," I whisper.

"That's right."

He doesn't do it, though. Instead, he waits for me to lift my arms above my head, and I do, silently giving him permission.

"Do you trust me?" he asks, tying my right wrist.

He asked me that once before, and I said that I wanted to. Now, my answer is different. "Yes, Sir, I do."

"Good girl."

I feel him tying my other wrist, and as I tug on my bindings, I realize I can't lower my arms. I'm trapped now. His.

"How does it make you feel?" he asks. "Knowing that I'm in control, that I can do anything I want to you, and you're powerless to stop me?" He runs his hands down my torso, palming my bare breasts as I arch up into his touch. "I get to use this sweet body any way I want," he adds, pinching my nipples.

"It's a little scary," I admit, barely holding back a moan as he tugs on them, forcing my back to arch even further.

"But?" he prompts.

"It excites me too. So much."

"I can tell. And you don't have to worry. If I do anything you don't like tonight, just say the word, and I'll stop."

"You mean a safeword?" I whisper.

The sound of his deep chuckle makes me blush as he gently massages my breasts. "Have you been reading more dirty stories, sweet girl?"

"Sometimes. Is that okay?"

"Of course." His hands glide over my naked skin. "But you don't need a safeword. Just tell me to stop, and I will."

"I don't think I'd ever tell you to stop."

"No, I don't imagine you would," he chuckles. "But you have to if I do something you don't enjoy. Promise me."

"I promise."

"Good. Because I plan on pushing your limits tonight."

"You do?"

Gently, he spreads my legs. "Yes, Abigail, I do. Tonight, I'm going to play with you." His fingers tickle my inner thighs before moving upward, making me gasp. "I'm going to make you come so many times, you'll beg me for mercy." His voice is low and gravelly as he pushes two fingers inside me, testing my readiness.

"Please, Sir." I'm already panting for breath.

"Let's begin. Remember our conversation about vibrators?"

Hours later, I'm a hot, sweaty, sticky mess. My skin is covered in massage oil, my ass is sore from repeated spankings, and I'm practically delirious from more orgasms than I've been able to count. I'm on my front, struggling to stay up on my knees as my legs shake from fatigue. My hands are still tied, and I'm spread open for Mr. Thorne, who's behind me, taking me with slow, unhurried thrusts. Each time he pushes in, his pelvis bumps the toy he gently coaxed into me, sending jolts of pleasure up my spine. I moan loudly as he grinds against me, gripping my hips.

"You like that? How about this?"

I gasp as he starts pulling the toy out, only to push it back inside me, timing it with his thrusts as he does it again and again. Groaning, I can't stop my hips from moving with him, silently encouraging him.

"Yeah, you love this, don't you? You love when I fuck you like this." His free hand caresses me, lifting my hair to blow cool air across my damp skin, his tender action a stark contrast to his dirty words. The truth is, I *do* love it. By the time Mr. Thorne brought out this particular toy, I was half-delirious from his teasing of my body, and I heard myself begging for it, for him to work it inside me.

"Dirty, pretty, perfect girl," he moans, taking me harder. "Fuck, so good."

I revel in the decadence, the sheer overpowering lust I feel. Simon never makes me feel ashamed when we're together like this. Somehow, even now, doing this, he makes me feel cherished.

"I want you to come again," he tells me, his hand slipping down between my legs. "Come on my cock."

I bury my face in the pillow, letting out a low whine as he starts rubbing me. I'm so sensitive, I'm not sure I can. Of course, he doesn't accept that.

"Do it," he commands, "or I'll spank your ass and flip you over to use your mouth, and then it's the vibrator again."

I can't take any more orgasms from that thing. They're too intense, and then I really *will* be begging for mercy.

"Yes, Sir," I pant.

"You're my sweet girl." He grunts, fucking me harder, his fingers sliding across my slick skin with ease. "You look so good tied to my bed. Maybe I'll ... keep you like this ... so I can fuck you whenever I want."

"Oh, God."

"Would you like that? Being my little sex slave?"

I nod my head, feeling that familiar tightening in my belly, gasping for breath as he pummels me, causing me to scream out until I come. For a few moments, it's as though I've lost consciousness, and I'm only barely aware of Simon grunting and groaning as he pushes me into the mattress, finishing inside me. He rolls off me, giving me room to breathe, but his hands continue caressing me, gently stroking my tired body.

"You were perfect," he whispers in my ear. "Thank you."

I mumble my own thanks, slowly coming back to the surface as he unties my hands and pulls out the toy before leaving the bed. I drift, completely blissed out.

"C'mon," he murmurs, turning me over onto my back. "Let's get you taken care of."

I'm as weak as a newborn kitten as he carries me into his bathroom, lowering me into the filled tub, and I sigh as the warm, fragrant water envelops me. Kneeling next to the tub, he gently bathes me and cares for me, placing a rolled-up towel behind my head.

"Stay," he orders, leaning down to kiss my lips before he leaves.

My body feels boneless and completely satisfied, and I can't stop smiling. All of that worry was for nothing. After a while, Simon comes back, dressed in a pair of pajama pants and a T-shirt, his wet hair slicked back, some of my clothes in his hands. He must have used one of the other bathrooms.

"Up you go," he says, helping me out of the tub before rubbing me down.

I stand still, letting him fuss over me, moaning softly as he rubs lotion on my sore backside before covering the rest of my body in it and dressing me in one of my nightgowns. He even combs out my hair, being careful with the tangles, a look of concentration on his handsome face. I've never felt so cared for in my whole life.

"Sleep now?" he asks, wrapping his arms around me and kissing me.

"Whatever you want, Sir."

He grins, stroking my cheek. "Perhaps a movie, then?"

I nod, giving him a smile, knowing he won't mind if I fall asleep in his arms as I have before. "Let me clean up in there first," I offer, nodding my head toward his bedroom.

"I'll do it," he says. "The toys need sterilizing, and I know how."

"Oh." My face heats up. "Of course."

"You really were perfect." He leans in, brushing my lips with his. "I'd like some new sheets for the bed, though."

I nod, drawing a deep breath as he leaves. It doesn't take more than a few minutes to clean up the bathroom, but Simon is already gone by the time I go back into his bedroom. Smiling, I notice that he's stripped the bed of the dirty sheets so it's easy for me to remake it. I grab the apron off the floor and lift it toward the bedside table, my arm stopping abruptly as I see it, my blood running cold.

On the table, leaning against the lamp, is an all-too-familiar-looking manila envelope. I'm sure it wasn't there when Simon helped me out of the bed because I looked over, my curiosity getting the best of me, wanting to sneak a peek at the toys he'd used. But it's there now, waiting for me. I take a step back and then another, unable to take my eyes off of it.

No. No, he wouldn't do this. My stomach rolls, and I have to lean on the wall for a few seconds. *It has to be a mistake.*

I find him in the kitchen by the sink with his back turned to me, but he hears me enter and turns to smile at me. It washes clean off his face in seconds.

"Abigail? Is everything all right?"

"The envelope," I manage, holding it out to him.

He approaches slowly, taking it from my hands. "Is it not enough?"

I stare at him. *Not a mistake, then.* "Enough?" My voice has a hint of hysteria to it, even to my ears. "Enough? I didn't look inside!"

His eyebrows draw together, creating a deep crease between his eyes—I recognize it as his worry line. "Please ..." He holds it out. "Take it."

It's as though my right arm works independently from the rest of me, and I watch as it slaps the envelope out of his hand, causing it to skate across the well-waxed floor. Simon looks stunned.

"I. Don't. Want. Your. Money." The tone of my voice is startling to my ears. I never knew I could sound like that. I never knew I could feel like this. He made me feel like this. "You'll never see me as anything but a whore," I whisper, turning on my heel and sprinting toward my room.

I slam the door shut and lock it, standing in the deafening

silence that follows, unable to move as everything crashes down around me. His sweet kisses, his thoughtful gifts, his texts, his arms around me, eating dinner with Luke and me, and every conversation we've ever had—has it all been a lie? Have I been lying to myself, reading meaning into everything he's said and done?

"Abigail." There's a light knock at the door. "Abigail, please open up."

I finally find my voice. "No!"

"Please?" He sounds so solemn, so sad. Unable to help myself, I unlock the door, opening it to him. He looks tired, anguished. Did I do that to him?

"Why?" I whisper.

"I thought it was what you wanted."

I stare at him. "How could you think that?"

"You said you wanted things to go back to the way they were before."

"That's not what I—"

"It's better this way." He interrupts me, running his right hand through his hair. In his left, he's holding the envelope. "Less complicated." He nods. "Everything you let me do to you tonight, you should be compensated for that."

Now I don't want to slap the envelope out of his hand. I want to slap *him*.

"Excuse me, but I didn't *let* you do anything to me!" I half-yell. "I did all of that stuff *with* you because I wanted to, because it felt fucking good. The only thing you've done to me that I didn't love was when you handed me that goddamn envelope!"

We stare at each other, me breathing heavily, him as calm as ever.

"Don't you get it?" I whisper. "Don't you understand *anything*?"

He sighs softly, taking a step back before lowering his eyes. "I'll see you when I get back from my trip." He takes another step back, his gaze on the floor. "I hope you and Luke have a good time in California. Use your card as much as you'd like."

With that, he turns and starts walking away.

"I regret it now," I tell him, unable to keep the venom out of my voice.

He stops, keeping his back to me. "What?"

"Trusting you. You said I wouldn't regret it—but I do."

His broad shoulders move up and down as he draws a deep breath and lets it out. Then he buries his hands in his pockets and slowly walks away.

CHAPTER TWENTY-EIGHT

The trip to Disneyland is bittersweet. Everyone is excited and I do my best to hide the fact that my emotions are in turmoil. At the hotel, we're shown to one of the deluxe suites and given the royal treatment with free passes to everything, with a full Thanksgiving dinner already set up for the following day. It only serves to confuse me all the more about the man who's responsible for all this, for giving my son and my friends this experience. Why would he go through all this trouble and money if he doesn't see me as more than an employee? It makes no sense to me at all.

For the rest of the day, I try to push away my thoughts and simply enjoy the vacation, but it's impossible. I have no idea what will happen when this trip is over. Simon said he'd see me when he gets back from Europe in a few weeks, so I don't believe I'm fired. But I don't think I can keep working for him under these circumstances. Part of me thinks it might be better to simply move out and cut my losses, but that's a scary thought. We can stay with Jo and Thomas, but for how long? I know they'd say we can stay as long as we need, but it'll be crowded, and we'd be an economic burden. I can't risk jeopardizing my friendship with them. There's also the fact that I don't want to leave. We were happy before Luke's birthday. I know we were. If we could only get back to that place some-how, I think we could make it work.

The next day, we have a fantastic turkey dinner around the large dining-room table in our suite, and I realize just how lucky I am to have not only my son but also the best friends I could ask for. I can't help but think of Simon, all alone and halfway around the world in Europe somewhere, no one to celebrate with. It must be such a lonely time of year for him, and it's no wonder he never decorates his house for Christmas. Maybe I should take Dave's advice and bring some holiday cheer to the house, show Simon that he doesn't have to be alone. I remember how he said to me that he was tired of coming home to an empty house at the end of the day, and even though he did hurt my feelings, I want to believe he didn't do it to be cruel. After every-thing he's done for me and Luke, all of the kindness and generosity he's bestowed on us, should I give him the benefit of the doubt? I want to. More than anything, I want to be with him, to love him, and have him love me and my son in return. I want to show him what it's like to have people waiting for him when he gets home from his trip. I need one last chance to make things right between us, to show him we can have a real relationship.

Feeling inspired, I give Lila a call, wishing her and her family a happy Thanksgiving before asking if she'd like to go shopping for Christmas decorations when we get back from our trip. We make a plan, and once again I dare to feel cautiously hopeful.

That night, in the privacy of my room while the others are watching a movie, I find the strength to make the call I've been dreading. I pull up my mother's number, drawing deep breaths to calm my nerves. We haven't spoken since the night she came to my old apartment, demanding that I come home. We didn't exactly leave things on good terms, but she reached out to me again through the letter and the birthday card to Luke.

The truth is I miss her and my dad. I miss having a big family, and it's not something I want my son to miss out on if it's possible to reconnect with mine.

I wonder what my parents are doing right now, if they have their friends from church over as well as our extended family for Thanksgiving—just as we always did when I still lived at home. I dial and clutch the phone in my sweaty palm, listening to it ring and ring for a long time. My heart jumps when there's finally an answer.

"Hello?"

"Hi, Mom." Silence.

"Abigail." She breathes out my name as though she's relieved to hear from me.

"Yes, it's me."

There's a strange squeaking noise on her end along with heavy breaths. "I'm so glad you called," she says in a garbled voice. *Is she crying?* "How's Luke doing? Did you get our card?"

"I did. Thank you. We went and bought Legos for him the next day." I hesitate for a second. "I have a picture of him playing with them here on my phone. I can send it to you, if you'd like?"

"Really? Oh, that would be wonderful. Your father will want to see that." She's quiet again for a few seconds, sniffing softly.

"Mom? How's Dad?" I whisper.

"He's not well," she whimpers, clearing her voice. "But he's strong."

"I remember," I murmur. My feelings about my father, about both my parents, are more than a little complicated. I'm angry with both of them for how they reacted when I became pregnant, and for how they raised me. But none of that is something I want to get into now. I'm choosing to view the letter and birthday card as an olive branch, and this is me showing them I'm willing to accept it and maybe start over with them.

"Would you and Luke ..."

"Would we what?" I ask.

"Consider coming home? For a visit," she adds quickly.

"We can't right now." I steel myself, preparing for the worst. I expect a scathing remark or a reprimand, but it never comes.

"All right. I—I understand."

"It's just that I got a job, Mom. A really good job."

"That's wonderful." It sounds like she actually means it.

"And I don't know how much my boss will need me. He travels a lot," I explain. "But maybe between Christmas and New Year's?"

"Really?" Her voice is so filled with hope, I can hardly stand it. What happened to her to evoke this change? She didn't want anything to do with us for so long. I desperately want to believe it's genuine.

"Really," I say. "I'll check with him and get back to you."

"Thank you," she whispers. "I'm so sorry for everything. I wasn't a good mother, and I don't expect you to forgive me for how I treated you."

I draw a deep breath. I'm not ready to forgive and forget, but hearing those words means a lot to me. "Thank you for saying that." I hear Luke calling me in the distance. "I have to go now, Mom. Luke needs me."

"Of course. I have to get back too."

"Do you have people over?" I ask.

"No, not this year. Happy Thanksgiving, Abigail."

"Happy Thanksgiving."

She hangs up, and I take a few seconds before joining Luke and the others again. I send her the picture of Luke before putting my phone on mute. I'm happy I made the call—it feels like I made the right decision, but now I'm even more nervous about what's really going on. No guests on Thanksgiving? My father must be worse off than she let on.

The rest of the holiday goes by smoothly, and everyone has a great time, but I'm looking forward to getting back. I don't like the way I left things with Simon, so up in the air. I consider calling him, but decide against it. I can't imagine having an honest talk about our future over the phone. It'll have to wait until he gets home from his trip, which gives me more than a week to prepare myself.

After Thanksgiving weekend, Luke goes back to school, and I resume my routine of taking care of the house, visiting with Lila next door almost daily. She's become a good friend in such a short time and I've started giving her cooking lessons—something both she and her husband are happy about. I'm grateful for their help too, as all of us go out shopping and Dave helps me decorate Simon's house on the outside, putting up twinkling lights around the windows and even in the bushes. It looks beautiful at night, and I hope he'll like the surprise when he gets home sometime this weekend. Luke and I buy a small Christmas tree that we set up outside the front door—it'll shed all of its needles if we bring it inside. We put lights on it, so it's looking festive. Inside, I place red poinsettias in the kitchen window, and we hang up a few decorations around the house and arrange red votive candles on the kitchen and living-room tables. I don't want it to be too over the top, but enough to feel like Christmas. I don't know if it'll make a difference to Simon, but for the first time this place actually looks like a home.

The following Friday night, Luke and I are baking cookies when I notice him coughing. I feel his forehead, frowning. "You okay, hon?"

"Uh-huh." He looks up at me with glazed eyes, his cheeks flushed.

"Oh, sweetie, I think you're getting sick," I say, picking him up. "Let's get you to bed."

"But the cookies," he protests weakly, resting his head on my shoulder as I carry him off.

"We'll make them later. Christmas is weeks away. There's lots of time."

As the night passes, Luke's fever climbs steadily until it reaches 101.5 degrees. It's not alarming, but I don't leave his side for more than a few minutes as I get him juice and cold cloths for his forehead. He's been sick before, but it's always awful to see him like this, and I can't help but fuss over him—especially since his cough only gets worse. He drifts off into an uneasy sleep around eleven, and I head into the kitchen, rummaging through the cabinets, hoping to find something for his cough and possibly a painkiller that's safe for kids. I come up empty and curse myself for not being prepared. I really don't want to have to drive to a 24-hour pharmacy with my son at this time of night, but if he gets worse, I won't have a choice.

I'm making myself some coffee when I suddenly hear the front door slam, making my heart jump into my throat. He's home, and I feel both nervous and excited to see him again. Seconds later, I'm face to face with Simon—jaw clenched, face flushed, a murderous glare in his eyes. He's livid.

"What the fuck did you do to my house?" he demands, throwing out his right arm.

Oh, shit. I try to quell the panic I feel, but my throat constricts painfully, making words impossible.

"You had no right. No right!" he exclaims.

"I'm—I'm sorry," I gasp, gripping the kitchen counter behind me.

"I want it gone. All of it. It's bad enough I can't go anywhere without seeing all of that *shit* everywhere," he continues, pacing back and forth, still pinning me with his gaze. "Do you hear me, Abigail?"

I nod quickly, fighting tears.

"Stop looking at me like that!" he yells, making me jump.

I lower my head, sniffing loudly. "I'm sorry. I thought—"

"I don't pay you to fucking think," he snaps.

I inhale sharply, raising my head again as anger surges through me. My gaze meets his, and I hold it. After a few seconds his shoulders drop, and the hard look in his eyes fades somewhat.

"I'll take it all down tomorrow," I say as calmly as I can.

"Now." His voice is softer than before, but it's still a command.

"No." My voice, on the other hand, is cold as ice. "All we did was try to make a nice homecoming for you. You don't like it. Message received. But right now I have to take care of Luke. He's sick."

Simon's eyes widen, and his posture tenses even further. "What's wrong with him? Where is he?"

Before I can answer, he turns on his heel, heading out of the kitchen in long strides. I catch up to him as he stops abruptly just inside Luke's room, staring at him in the bed. Luke coughs, letting out a low whine, and I brush past Simon to attend to my son. I help him sit up, and he drinks a little before his eyes flutter closed. I press my lips against his forehead, relieved that his fever doesn't appear higher than the last time I checked. I'll take his temperature again in half an hour, though, to be on the safe side. Stroking his damp hair, I ease him back against the pillows before grabbing the cloth from his bedside table, which needs cooling down again. Simon is still by the door, rooted to the spot as I walk past him on my way to the bathroom. I wring out the cloth and go back to Luke, placing it on his forehead. He whimpers but stays asleep. I turn my head. Simon's still standing there, his hand curled tightly around the door handle. As Luke coughs behind me, I see him grimace before making his face neutral again.

"He needs to go to the hospital," he says.

I shake my head slowly, but he's already approaching the bed. He leans down and gently scoops Luke up into his arms.

"Wait!" I whisper-yell, putting my hand on his arm. "What do you think you're doing?"

"We're going to the hospital. Now."

"No! Are you crazy?" I exclaim. "It's only a light fever and a cough. They'll just send me home and tell me he needs rest and fluids. And they'll still charge me."

"We'll see about that," he mutters, walking around me with Luke still sleeping in his embrace.

I jog next to them out into the garage, trying to reason with Simon, but it falls on deaf ears. He places Luke in the booster seat and tells me to strap him in. He returns after a minute, holding Luke's duvet, which he hands to me.

"Let's go." He turns for the driver-side door.

"Stop!"

He looks back at me.

"This isn't necessary," I insist.

"Yes, it is," he says, getting into the car without another word.

I strap myself in next to my son, tucking the duvet around him. I don't want to sit up front with Simon. I watch him silently as he opens the garage door and backs out. This is so not necessary. Why is he reacting like this?

We drive in silence. Simon's shoulders are tense, his movements choppy as he steers the car through nearly empty streets. We reach the hospital, and I barely have time to get out of the car before he's unstrapped Luke, whom he eases into my arms before marching us into the emergency room, his hand firm on my lower back.

What happens next is mortifying. Simon makes what can only be described as a scene, barking out orders to the befuddled staff, demanding a doctor attend to my son at once. They ask him to sit down, to be calm, but it has the opposite effect. I send apologetic looks to the staff, clutching Luke to me. He's awake now, but just barely, and lets out a cough.

"Can't you hear that?" Simon yells at the nurses, motioning to Luke. "He's sick! Fix him!"

Finally, a doctor arrives, an older man with a calm demeanor. He takes one look at Simon and orders him to settle down at once, or he'll call security.

"Try it," Simon growls.

Everyone around us looks tense, on alert. Holding Luke with one arm, I place my free hand on Simon's arm, feeling him flinch.

"Stop," I say firmly. "Sit down."

His gaze instantly meets mine.

"You're not helping," I continue. "They'll kick us out. Let the doctor look at Luke. *Please.*"

His jaw ticks several times before he backs away, taking a seat near the wall. I turn to the doctor, explaining Luke's symptoms. He nods and leads us to a room where he examines my son and concludes what I already suspected: Luke has the flu. I'm to watch his temperature, give him cough syrup and fluids, and make sure he rests. I can also give him children's painkillers to lower his fever so he can get some uninterrupted sleep. The doctor hands me a note to take to the pharmacy, giving me a look of concern.

"Is it safe for you to go home?" he asks, his eyes shifting to the door for a moment.

I gape at him before his meaning resonates with me. "Yes." I nod my head. "Yes. Absolutely. He'd never ... He was just concerned about Luke."

My words soften my heart. He really was concerned about Luke, much more so than Patrick's ever been. It doesn't excuse his overbearing, controlling behavior, though. I'm Luke's mother and he didn't even listen to me.

"If you're sure."

"I'm sure. I can handle him."

The doctor chuckles, leading us back out. Simon jumps to his feet, his face a picture of anxiety.

"Don't worry," the doctor says immediately, "your son is going to be just fine. I've given your wife instructions on how to take care of him." He gives me a smile before leaving.

I hardly dare look at Simon. After a few seconds he goes to the front desk, and I see him talking to the receptionist before coming back to us. His face is stony.

"I have to go to the pharmacy," I tell him, shifting Luke in my arms.

Simon takes him from me, and we get the things on the doctor's list. The car ride home is silent and tense, and Simon goes upstairs without saying a word to me. After I've given Luke some cough syrup and painkillers, I put on my pajamas and curl up in a chair at the end of his bed, exhausted and emotionally raw. I have no idea what is going to happen tomorrow, but I know it'll be impossible to go back to the way things were after tonight.

I don't want that, anyway. I want more—but I don't think I'll ever get it. I just wish I knew why. He hasn't given me any indication he doesn't want me, and it's obvious he cares about Luke. Even after getting angry about the Christmas decorations, he didn't ask us to leave. He wanted them gone, not us. I don't understand him at all.

I startle awake at some point, confused as I stretch my body. I'm lying down. Lifting my head, I look around and find myself on the floor next to Luke's bed, my mattress underneath me and my duvet covering me.

I sit up and immediately notice him. He's in the chair now, asleep, still in his suit from last night. I glance at my son, who's sleeping peacefully, before getting up. Simon's neck is bent at a weird angle, and I know he'll be sore from it tomorrow.

"Mr. Thorne?" I whisper, approaching him.

He doesn't move at all except for the rise and fall of his chest. I watch his face, so open and unguarded, and my heart clenches. He stayed up to watch over us.

"Simon?" I murmur softly. Unable to stop myself, I brush

my fingers across his cheek, the slight stubble tickling me. A second later, he's on his feet, turning the chair over and pushing me away. Hard. I land on my ass, my lack of breath the only thing stopping me from crying out. I gasp, staring up at him. He's against the wall, breathing hard, his eyes wide. They dart to mine for a second, and I can see the anguish in them before he pushes himself forward and storms out of Luke's room. I get my bearings and climb to my feet, wincing at the pain in my tailbone. Luke is still asleep and thankfully didn't see what happened. I feel his forehead, which is a little warm, but nothing compared to last night.

I find Simon in the kitchen. He's at the sink, clutching the edges of the countertop, still breathing heavily. At my approach, he whirls around, wiping his mouth with the back of his hand. His face is ashen and glistening with perspiration.

"I'm sorry," I croak.

He shakes his head, squeezing his eyes shut. "Are you hurt?" he asks.

"No. Not really, I mean."

He opens his eyes again but doesn't look at me. Silence stretches between us, uncomfortable and charged.

"Luke is a little better," I say.

"I can't do this," he whispers, clenching his fists at his sides.

"Do what?" I ask, even though I know.

"This!" he whisper-yells, making a sweeping motion with his arm. "I can't do this again!"

Again? "D-do what again?" I stutter.

Instead of acknowledging me, he grabs the poinsettia in the window, crushing its petals in his fist before tossing it on the floor.

"I don't want this. I can't have this. This isn't what I wanted," he sneers, finally looking at me. His eyes are cold. "This playing house bullshit!" He gazes at me like he's silently daring me to disagree.

"You're a liar!" I blurt out, taking the bait. "This is exactly what you wanted from day one. You wanted to play house at first. To pretend. Then you wanted us to move in here with you." I walk over to him and look up into his face. "Everything you've wanted from me—someone who takes care of you, someone you can care for and spoil, someone who enjoys the same kind of sex as you, someone to come home to at the end of the day—you know what that is?"

He doesn't answer.

"It's a relationship, Simon. That's what you've wanted all along. You never wanted a submissive. You wanted a girlfriend who's submissive in bed. You want me. You want Luke too. I know you care about him. Whatever's making you say this, please tell me. Because I don't believe you don't want this, that you don't want a real relationship with me!"

"My son is dead!" he shouts, squeezing his eyes shut before turning away.

I freeze in place, shocked.

"My son is dead. There. Now you know." He turns to me again, his eyebrows drawn together and his lips curled. It's a look of derision. He opens his mouth to speak several times, but nothing comes out.

I'm having trouble breathing. He had a son. A son who died. "Simon—"

Startling me, he grabs ahold of me and crushes me against his chest, holding on for dear life. But it doesn't last. He pulls back slowly, running the back of his fingers across my cheek—a familiar touch that only brings me pain. Because deep down, I know what it means.

"Simon, I'm sorry. I'm so sorry. I can't imagine—"

"No, you can't. And I hope to God you never will."

"But that doesn't mean you and I can't—"

"Yes, it does. This is too much. I thought I could ... but no." He takes a quick breath, avoiding my eyes. "We need to go back to how it was before."

"What?"

"I'll still take care of you and Luke. Get you a nice place to live. You can come and see me. Like we did in the beginning."

I take a step back, feeling stricken. Back to calling him Mr. Thorne, back to getting those manila envelopes. Having his body but not his heart. There's no way. I could do it before I fell in love with him, but now the thought makes me feel sick. I'd end up losing myself. My heart would break every time I saw him, having him so close yet so completely far away, and ultimately I'd end up hating him. And myself.

"No." My voice is a lot stronger than I thought it would be.

"I still want you," he says, his voice raw. "I'll always want you, Abigail."

My lips tremble, and I blink to hold back tears. I resist the urge to clutch my chest to make sure my heart is still there, that it's still beating.

"I know you do. You just don't want all of me." I wait for him to object, knowing in my heart he won't.

"I'm sorry," he says brokenly. "I never meant—it's my fault. This is all my fault."

I want to disagree with him, to tell him I've acted just as irresponsibly as he to enter into this sort of arrangement, that I've been a fool to fall in love with him, to think I could ever change him, but I can't get it past my lips.

"We'll leave as soon as Luke is better," I say.

"There's no rush."

I give him one last look, seeing the hurt on his face plain as day. I know he didn't mean for this to happen and I believe he's sorry. But it doesn't change anything, and I can't stay here a minute longer than I have to.

"Yes there is," I whisper, brushing past him.

He doesn't follow me.

CHAPTER TWENTY-NINE

What do you do when everything you hoped for turns out to have been an impossible dream all along? When you can't see a happy ending for yourself anymore? When you realize that you've fallen in love with a man who isn't only unwilling love you back, but actually unable to?

I see Simon three times during the two days it takes Luke to recover. The first time, I find him with an anxious look on his face outside Luke's room, watching him sleep. He excuses himself quickly when he notices me. The second time is in the kitchen the following morning. He stops abruptly inside the door, staring at me for a long moment before backing away. I leave him a plate of food, knowing he must be hungry and that he doesn't cook at all. The last time is right before we move out. Everything is packed up in Thomas' car outside, and Luke is already strapped in. I head into the room that used to be mine, placing every gift I received on the bed. A part of me wants to keep it all—the books, earrings, perfumes, iPad, and clothes, every token of his generosity and affection. But I need a clean break.

Simon stands behind me in the door as I turn around,

hands in his pockets, hair uncombed, a lost look in his eyes and dark shadows beneath them.

Who will take care of him now?

I approach slowly, feeling no anger, only sorrow for both him and myself. Maybe I should hate him, but I don't. I just feel sorry, for both of us.

"Where will you go?" he asks, his voice hollow-sounding.

"Thomas and Jo's."

He nods. "Will you be all right?"

I look up into his face, swallowing back tears. "Will *you?*" I whisper.

He doesn't answer. Instead, he reaches for my hand, lifting it up as he strokes my knuckles with his thumb before pressing his lips against my skin for just a second.

"Goodbye," he mumbles, hesitating before continuing. "I left something for you on the kitchen table. Please don't argue. Just take it ... and take care of yourself and Luke." He lets go of my hand and turns around, walking away with fast steps.

"Goodbye," I whisper, pressing my lips together to keep from crying.

This is how it ends. Not with a bang, but a whimper.

On the kitchen table I find an envelope, similar to the one that started all of this, similar to the one that ended all of this. I fold it and put it into my jacket pocket.

Later that night, in Jo's kitchen, I open it to find that Luke's tuition has been paid for the next six months so he can finish Pre-K, and a bus service has been arranged to get him there and back again every day. There is also a severance package for me: three month's salary and medical insurance for the next year. I finally break down and cry in Jo's arms, allowing myself to feel the full extent of what I've lost—though it was never really mine to begin with.

I honor Simon's last request and accept the contents of the envelope. I don't want to be a burden on Jo and Thomas, and this, along with the amount of my salary I've been able to save, gives me at least a little time to figure out what to do next.

If there's one thing I've learned, it's that life can be relentless. A week after leaving Simon's house, I find myself on a bus to Pinewood after receiving a frantic phone call from my mother.

"Are we there yet?" Luke asks, shifting in his seat.

"Soon," I tell him, feeling a twinge of anxiety in the pit of my stomach. "Pippa and Piper's grandma is picking us up at the station, and then you're going to stay at her house for a little bit this afternoon."

"Okay."

I gaze down at him and smile. Half a year ago, separating from me would've made him scared. Everything that's happened—staying at Simon's house, making friends at school, and knowing Patrick isn't going to be a part of our lives anymore—has turned my son into a confident, happy kid, ready to take on the world. At least one good thing has come out of all of this. Turning my face toward the window again, I see the "Welcome to Pinewood" sign on the side of the road and draw a deep breath that does nothing to slow down the frantic beating of my heart.

Jo's mother, Cecile, is already there when we arrive, giving both of us warm smiles. Luke knows her from his sleepovers with Pippa and Piper, and I'm so grateful she's willing to look after him for a few hours. I have to do this alone. We drive to her house, and I watch with gratitude as she starts fixing Luke a snack and finds some of the toys and books that her grandkids usually play with on their visits.

"You can borrow my car if you want," she offers. "Or would you like something to eat first?"

"Thanks, I'm not really hungry." I try for a smile even though my face feels oddly numb. "I think I'll just walk over there."

She nods, pouring Luke a glass of chocolate milk before turning to me again, a look of concern on her face.

"It's bad, isn't it?" I whisper. "My mom was vague."

"Yes, I'm afraid so," she says. "I'm so sorry, sweetheart."

I welcome her arms around me as she embraces me, patting my back, her warm, soft body the closest thing to maternal affection I've felt in years. It's enough to bring tears to my eyes. I do my best to blink them away as she releases me, rubbing my arms.

"Take as long as you need," she says. "You and Luke can sleep here if you'd like."

"Thank you." I sniff, pulling myself together. "Hon, I'm going now," I call to Luke, who's engrossed in a huge pile of toys. "I'll be back before dinnertime."

"Uh-huh. Bye!" I can't help but laugh as he dismisses me.

Cecile walks me to the door, her hand on my shoulder. "You remember the way there?"

"I don't think I'll ever forget," I murmur, pulling up the hood on my raincoat as I step into the light drizzle. "I'll be back later."

"We'll be here."

Walking through the once-familiar streets, I keep my head down. I don't want to face anyone else. Seeing my mother and father is just about all I can handle, and I'm not even sure I *can* handle that. But I have to. My mom made it pretty clear on the phone that time was of the essence. In my mind, my father is a tall, strong, and intimidating figure. It's difficult to imagine him sick at all.

Growing up, I knew my parents were different from those of my friends from school. They had me late in life, having been unable to conceive for years and desperately wanting a son to carry on the family name. Instead they got me, and they pushed me toward academic, athletic, and social accomplishments with the highest expectations. I never felt good enough for them. When

I became pregnant, it threw a huge wrench in their plans. They wanted me to attend an Ivy League university, join a fancy sorority to form connections with daughters of upper-class families, and marry an eligible young man with a bright future. My father was a small-town mayor with big political aspirations. An unwed pregnant teenage daughter didn't fit into that scheme, and my parents gave me the choice of quietly terminating the pregnancy or hiding it and then giving the baby up for adoption. I chose neither. I was done being a pawn in my father's game. I thought they'd accept things after Luke was born, their love for a grandchild overshadowing their disappointment, but I was wrong. I've been wrong about so many things in my short life, but having Luke is the best thing I ever did. And I won't let my parents near him unless I'm sure they've changed, illness or no illness.

The house looks exactly as I remember, but the woman who spots me through the kitchen window and rushes to the door as I walk up the pathway doesn't. I stare at my mother. She looks disheveled and frazzled, her hair unstyled with gray roots showing near her scalp. She's wearing a housecoat; I didn't even know she owned one. She was always impeccably dressed when I lived at home, the perfect politician's wife. It's been less than two months since she showed up at my door, but she looks older. Much older.

"Abigail!" she exclaims, her hand fluttering to her hair. "I didn't think—I'm so happy to see you."

"Hey, Mom," I say softly, approaching her with caution.

She reaches for me but pulls her arms back immediately, holding out her hand instead, her eyes questioning. I take her hand in mine, and we stand there on the porch for a few seconds, just staring at each other. It's nothing like the warmth I felt when Cecile hugged me, but it's a start.

"I didn't think you'd come until tomorrow," she says. "Your boss didn't mind you leaving?"

I know she isn't aware of the double meaning of her words, but they still make my chest tight.

"No, he didn't mind," I mumble, even though it's a lie.

"Come inside," my mom urges, letting go of my hand. "Luke isn't with you?"

"He's at Jo's mom's," I tell her. She looks disappointed, the corners of her mouth turning down. "He's never seen a sick person before," I continue. "I didn't know what to expect ... here." *What to expect from you.*

"How long are you staying?" she asks as I remove my jacket and boots.

"I don't know," I tell her honestly. "Where's Dad?"

"Upstairs. The nurse is with him right now. I was making coffee. Do you drink coffee?"

I nod. "I started when Luke kept me up all night screaming from colic for three months straight, and I was so exhausted I thought I'd lose my mind, and no one was there to help me." My words are harsh. I didn't intend to say that much, but now it's out there, floating in the air between us. The accusation. The anger I feel.

My mom's eyes dart around the room, focusing on anything but me. The awkwardness is palpable. "You, uh, were the same," she finally says. "The colic, I mean." She looks at me. "I wish I would have acted differently—helped you."

I give her a nod. "So do I."

More silence follows. I'm not sorry about what I said. I don't want her to think I've forgiven or forgotten anything just because I showed up. They let me down so completely, and being a mother myself, I can't imagine ever doing that to Luke.

"I'd like that coffee, please," I say. "We were up early."

My mom smiles, obviously relieved to change the subject, and leads me into the kitchen, where I take a seat at the table. The place looks the same—except for one thing.

"No Christmas decorations?" I ask, watching my mom pour coffee for both of us.

"No," is all she says, bringing over the cups before sitting down across from me.

We sip our coffee in silence, both of us stealing glances at each other, unable to think of anything to say. Thankfully, we're interrupted a few minutes later when a woman in a nurse's uniform comes into the kitchen, informing my mother that my father is done. Done with what, I don't know.

"Would you like to see him?" my mom asks me.

"All right," I say, sounding more confident than I feel.

She leads me upstairs to their bedroom, pausing outside the door. I glance down the hall to my childhood room, overwhelmed by the onslaught of memories.

"He's changed a lot," she says to me, a wary look in her eyes.

I nod, trying to prepare myself as she opens the door. The first thing I notice is the smell: disinfectant and sickness rolled into one. It's dim in the room, the curtains only open part of the way. My parents' old bed is gone, replaced by a twin bed and a hospital bed next to it. The man in the latter bed is unfamiliar to my eyes, and I barely hold back a gasp. His hair is patchy and mostly gray, his cheeks hollow. His eyes are closed and his thin lips parted. He's so gaunt and his skin is sallow. The bedside table is littered with medical supplies—tape, gauze, and various pill bottles. I approach slowly, taking a seat on the edge of the chair next to his bed.

"George," my mom says, walking to the other side. She raises the head of the bed with the press of a button and arranges the pillow behind his head. His eyes flutter open, looking at my mom.

"Abigail's here," she whispers, turning his face toward me.

He blinks, his eyes focusing on me, and we stare at each other. I don't know what I expected to feel when I finally saw him again after all these years, but it wasn't this—overwhelming sadness and pity.

"Hi, Daddy," I say softly.

He closes his eyes and his face scrunches up into a pained grimace, his lips trembling slightly as a sob escapes. When he looks at me again, his eyes are wet, the hand closest to me moving toward me. I don't think about it; I reach out and take it into mine, feeling the papery skin and fragile bones underneath.

"A ... Abbi," he rasps, tightening his hold on my hand, his eyes pleading with me.

"I'm here," I whisper, leaning forward.

"Sorr ..." he starts, drawing out the word along with a ragged breath. "I'm sorr—" A weak cough stops him from continuing, and after it's over, he looks exhausted, fighting to keep his gaze on me.

He's dying. Unexpected grief sweeps over me, and I can't hold back my tears. I feel no anger or resentment toward this shell of a man. It's simply not there.

"I forgive you, Daddy," I blurt out. His eyes flicker and well up again before he closes them. "Sleep," I whisper, stroking his hand with my thumb. "I'll be here when you wake up."

I watch his face as his features relax and become peaceful, the sound of his breathing the only indication that he's still alive. When I finally tear my eyes away, I notice that my mom has left the room.

I sit with him while he sleeps, never letting go of his hand. After a while, my mom comes back in, carrying coffee and a plate of cookies that she sets down on the table next to me.

"Can he have that?" I ask.

"No, it's for you," she replies. "I thought you might need a pick-me-up."

I look up at her, surprised at her thoughtfulness. "Thank you."

"That was a wonderful thing you did, forgiving him," she murmurs.

I don't know what to say in response, so I take the cup and blow on the hot liquid. I didn't think it would be so easy to let go of all the negative feelings I've harbored. I haven't forgotten the past, but I also know I won't gain anything from denying him this last wish. I want him to go in peace.

"How long does he have?" I whisper, taking a sip.

"Days. Maybe a week or two according to the doctors."

I glance up at my mom, seeing her blinking back tears. "There's nothing they can do?" I ask even though I already know the answer.

She shakes her head. "They offered us a bed in a hospice, but I brought him home. He—he should die in his own home." Her voice cracks, and she walks out of the room. I set down the coffee cup and let go of my father's hand. He's still fast asleep, clearly heavily medicated. My mom is downstairs in the kitchen, cooking up a storm, bowls, pots, and cutting boards everywhere. She looks up when I come in, quickly wiping underneath her eyes as she plasters on a fake smile.

"I hope Luke likes meatloaf," she says.

"He does. Mom—"

"I'm making chocolate chip cookies for dessert. He's not allergic to anything, is he?"

"No." I walk over to her, stilling her frantic movements by placing my hands on top of hers. "Mom, are you all right?"

"Yes, yes, I'm fine. You will bring him over for dinner, won't you?" she asks, obviously deflecting. "Your father would love to see him."

"Okay," I say, sighing softly.

My mother keeps cooking, and I go upstairs to watch over my father. Half an hour later the nurse from before comes back, and I leave her to do whatever it is that she does.

"I'm going over to Cecile's," I tell my mom, who's still busy in the kitchen. She nods. "Can I invite her over for dinner?" I ask hesitantly.

My mom's head snaps up.

"She's been watching Luke all afternoon. I'm not sure if she's even had time to cook for herself."

"I ... I don't know." Her hand goes straight to her hair, trying to smooth it.

"She's not going to care how you look, Mom. She's really nice."

"I've never really spoken with her—except that time in the grocery store."

"She cares about me," I say, by way of explanation.

"I know. She was there for you when I wasn't. I know that." She draws a breath. "Yes, she can come if she wants."

"Thank you," I say softly. "She really is nice. And Jo—I don't know what I would've done without her. I'm going to be her maid of honor, you know."

My mom gives me a small smile.

"I won't be long."

I walk back toward Cecile's house, trying to sort out my conflicting emotions. I'm relieved that my mom really does seem to have changed—she's so much softer and kinder now—but at the same time heartbroken that it had to come to this, for my father to be on his deathbed for it to happen. I'm also nervous about bringing Luke over there, of how he might react to seeing his grandfather like that. We've never talked about death, and I'm not even sure Luke understands the concept. I never imagined I'd have to have this talk with my son so soon, and I don't feel ready for it at all. I could keep Luke away—my father and mother have done nothing in the past to deserve having him in their lives—but they've both apologized now, which is huge. I've never once heard either of them admit they've been wrong about anything. And I'm exhausted from holding on to my feelings of anger toward them. It feels good to let it all go and I'm hoping we can start over somehow.

I wonder how Simon would react if he knew where I was right now. From the way he talked about his father, I'm sure he never let go of his feelings of anger, but he seemed genuinely regretful for me when I told him I wasn't close with my mom anymore.

But of course he would be. He lost his mother before he ever got a chance to know her. The thought brings tears to my eyes. I can imagine him as a little boy, lonely and sad, longing for something he'll never know. He never got to be a loved son, and he never got to watch his own son grow up. My throat constricts and I have to stop walking. Impulsively, I fish my phone out of my pocket and pull up Simon's number, staring at it. I want to call him, to hear his voice. I never felt happier than when I was with him, never felt more at peace. Without him I feel lost, at sea. I look down at his number again. Have I *ever* called him? No, I realize. I haven't. And he's never called me. We've never really been out together in public or gone on a date. I don't know what happened to his son or where he got his scars, or even why he hates Christmas. I don't really know him at all.

I still love him just the same. But he won't let me.

I sniff loudly, putting my phone away. Calling him would only make everything worse. I have to learn to be happy without him. I start walking again, putting one foot in front of the other. That's all I can do: Keep moving forward.

If Cecile is surprised by the dinner invitation, she doesn't show it. We drive over there with Luke safely strapped into his car seat, and I'm grateful she's with me, knowing she's completely on my side in all of this. My mom greets us at the door as we enter.

"Thank you for the invitation, Maude," Cecile says, giving her a firm handshake. "I've had my hands full with this guy."

She smiles at Luke, who's fumbling with his zipper. I kneel down and help him with it.

"Hon, this is my mom," I say. "Remember I told you about her and my dad?"

Luke looks up at my mom.

"Hi, Luke." My mom's voice sounds scratchy. "I'm your grandmother. You can call me Nana, if you want."

He reaches out his little hand, and my mom takes it in hers. "How do you do?" he asks. "That means hi."

Cecile and my mom laugh, but I can't join in their merriment.

"That's what Mr. Thorne said," he continues, much to my regret.

"Who's Mr. Thorne?" my mother asks.

Oh, God. "My boss," I say, standing up as I usher Luke into the kitchen, hoping to distract him.

I don't want my mom to know I don't have a job anymore, and I don't want her to know how desperate my circumstances will be if I'm not able to find a job within the next couple months. We may have started over, but not showing any sign of weakness in front of her is second nature to me, and I wonder if I'll ever be able to let go of that.

We sit down to dinner, and I'm once again grateful for Cecile's presence. She effortlessly comes up with neutral topics of conversation like what's going on around town and, of course, her excitement that her daughter is getting married. It's actually a nice dinner, which I didn't expect at all. Luke attacks the meatloaf with his usual healthy appetite, making my mother smile from across the table.

"How come you don't have a Christmas tree?" he asks her suddenly. "You need one so you can get presents."

"Oh." My mom's smile turns sad. "I don't think I'll be celebrating Christmas this year."

"No Christmas?" Luke is shocked.

"Remember how I told you my dad, your grandfather, is sick, hon?" I ask him. "That's why. They usually have Christmas together, but this year they can't really."

I glance at my mom. Her eyes are wet, and Cecile reaches over to place her hand on top of hers.

Luke suddenly lights up. "You can have Christmas with us, Nana!" he exclaims. "Mommy makes the best dinner. And there's presents and candy, and we sing songs and watch

Muppet Christmas Carol!" He turns to me. "Right, Mommy? Nana can have Christmas with us, right?"

My son has such a good heart. I can't possibly say no.

"Of course she can," I say, looking over at my mom. "We'll have Christmas here this year."

"Yay!" Luke goes back to his dinner, unaware of my mom holding back tears across the table, now clutching Cecile's hand.

"Excuse me," she says, getting up. "I'd better check on George." I breathe out once she's left the kitchen.

Cecile gives me a reassuring smile. "I think it's a wonderful idea. Jo, Thomas, and the kids are coming up for the holidays, so we'll be close by, all of us."

That makes me feel a lot better, but I'm still a bit wary.

"Will you stay here tonight?" she asks.

"I'd like to stay at your place, if that's okay. This is all a little overwhelming."

"I can imagine. You stay as long as you need to."

"Thank you, not just for that, but for coming over here with me. I'm worried about her."

"I am too. We should talk later," Cecile says, glancing at Luke.

I nod. He doesn't look like he's paying attention to us, but I've been wrong before. Mom comes back after a few minutes, appearing composed again, and we finish dinner with more small talk. Afterward, I take Luke into the living room for a little talk.

"Now, hon, I don't want you to be scared, okay?"

He nods.

"Your grandfather is very sick, so he'll be in bed the whole time we're here. And he probably won't be able to talk a lot."

"Can't you make him better, Mommy?" he asks. "Like when I was sick?"

My chest constricts painfully. "I'm so sorry, baby, I wish I could. But he isn't going to get better." *Don't cry, don't cry, don't cry.*

"But what will happen then?" Luke asks.

I sigh softly, pulling him into my lap. I don't want to lie to him. "One day soon he'll just ... fall asleep. And he won't wake up again."

"Will he still dream?"

"You could say that. A lot of people think that you go to a place called Heaven. And it's beautiful there and peaceful. Your Nana believes that."

"But why is she so sad, then," he asks, pouting his lips, "if he's going to that place?"

"Because she'll miss him," I whisper. "Even though he's going to such a nice place, she has to stay here without him. Understand?"

He nods, looking thoughtful. "I think I should give Nana a hug, then."

I smile through tears. "I think she'd like that a lot, sweetheart." I follow him into the kitchen where he runs right up to my mom, tugging on her shirt until she kneels down, a puzzled look on her face. He throws his arms around her neck.

"Don't be sad, Nana," he says. "Don't be sad."

I watch as my mom's walls crumble, finally, and she starts crying openly, hugging Luke to her. My legs move as if on their own, and I find myself kneeling next to them, feeling my mom embrace me too, sobbing against my shoulder.

"I'm so sorry," she says, over and over again. "I'm so sorry for everything."

Cecile extracts Luke and picks him up, carrying him out of the room while I too start to cry, the last remnants of animosity I've harbored toward her escaping through my tears.

"I forgive you, Mom," I tell her. "I didn't get pregnant on purpose, but it was the best thing I ever did, bringing Luke into the world."

"It is. It is," she agrees, pulling back to look at me. "I'm so proud of you, Abigail, of the woman you've become. I can't take any credit for it. It was all you."

I stare at her, warmth washing over me. "Thank you," I whisper.

We hug again before helping each other off the floor, wiping our eyes. I look at her as she collects herself. We'll never be able to go back and change our past relationship, but for the first time, I dare to believe we might have a future one. And Luke could have a grandparent in his life.

"Will you really stay for Christmas?" she asks quietly.

I nod.

"Then we have to get a tree," she says, giving me a smile, "so I have a place to put your presents."

I smile back. "That sounds great."

The next few weeks fly by as we help my mom get the house ready for Christmas. We spend the first night at Cecile's house before unofficially moving into my old room, which is just as I left it more than five years ago. The bed is big enough for both me and my son, and it feels good being here, watching him interact with my mom, who seems determined to make up for lost time by spoiling him rotten with attention and treats. I let her, loving every second of it, although this newfound happiness can't erase my longing for Simon. Being here with my parents feels right for now, but I know it's not where Luke and I truly belong.

Luke also meets my father, who unfortunately grows weaker every day, losing his ability to speak a few days after we arrive. Luke doesn't seem to mind, though. He seems comforted by the thought of his grandfather going to Heaven, and more than once I find him sitting next to my father's bed, telling him about his school, his friends, and things he has seen on TV. My father watches my son for as long as he can keep his eyes open, falling asleep with a small smile on his face. I often sit with him at night, giving my mom a break. I hold his hand and read to him to fill the silence or sing hymns I still remember from church services as a child. He squeezes my hand as I tell him goodnight, every day with less strength, and I know he doesn't have long. It's more than a week until Christmas, and although the doctor has said most dying people usually hold on until after the holidays, I don't think he'll be able to make it that long.

"I love you, Daddy," I whisper, leaning in to press my lips to his forehead.

Pulling back, I gaze into his eyes, seeing his love for me there. It's not something I remember ever having seen before, but now it's there, strong and unwavering. He grimaces in pain suddenly. Even the morphine drip next to the bed can't take it away anymore. Watching him in so much agony and being helpless to ease his suffering is devastating.

"It's okay to let go," I croak as tears fill my eyes. "We'll see each other again. And in the meantime, me, Luke, and Mom, we'll take care of each other. I promise."

He gives me the slightest of nods. It's barely visible, but it's there. He understands.

"I'll go get Mom, okay? I'll be right back."

My father falls asleep that night, never to open his eyes again. His one hand is in mine, the other one in my mother's. It's peaceful and quiet and how it should be. He dies surrounded by his loved ones, forever dreaming, according to my son.

CHAPTER THIRTY

My father is cremated three days later. I make the decision to wait to bury his ashes until after Christmas. I'm hoping it'll give my mom a little time to recover. She's not doing well at all, staying in bed most days and declining all visitors as well as most of the meals I bring her. I now find myself having to face parents of former classmates, distant and not so distant relatives, and townspeople I haven't seen in years, receiving condolences, flowers, and casseroles in abundance. While all of it is appreciated, it also leaves me exhausted. I've only just rejoined this family, and having this huge responsibility thrust upon me is more than a little overwhelming.

Thankfully, Cecile and Jo visit frequently, and between the three of us, we manage to hold off visitors. I wonder if I should be sadder—devastated like my mom—and I feel guilty for being able to go on, all the while knowing it's important that I do so. Luke needs me, and while he was sad that his grandfather passed away, he's now wrapped up in the excitement of Christmas. We decorate the house, and I do my best not to think of the last time Luke and I decorated and the disastrous results that followed. In fact, I try not to think of the past at all, focusing on the present and the future. We can't stay here forever, and I need to make sure my mom will be all right once we go back to Seattle.

"Mom? Can I talk to you?" I approach her bed slowly. Dad's hospital bed has been removed, so now it's just hers left in the bedroom.

She shifts, cracking open her eyes to look at me before pulling the covers up around her shoulders. "What is it?" she asks, not unkindly.

I take a seat on the edge of her bed. "We made hot chocolate and cookies. And we're about to watch *A Christmas Carol*. It's a tradition. We always do it on the night of the 24th."

"That's nice."

"Will you please come down and watch with us?"

"I'm tired."

"I know you are." I take a breath. "But it's Christmas, and your grandson wants to spend it with you."

She stares into space.

"Mom, please. There are things that need taking care of, things I can't do on my own, like Dad's memorial service. And Luke and I have to go home at some point."

"I know," she whispers, her lips trembling.

"Talk to me," I beg.

"I'm scared," she finally admits, moving up into a sitting position. "I'm not like you, Abigail."

"What do you mean?"

"You're so strong, so capable. I've never been on my own before." She looks at me. "I went from my parents' house to college, where I lived in a sorority house, and then your father and I were married right after graduation. I don't know how to be on my own."

I draw a deep breath. I know my mother is grieving, so I choose not to tell her that the only reason I'm so *strong and capable* is because I had no choice in the matter, and at times it was hard as hell. I can't help but think about Simon, how safe I felt letting go with him, how wonderful and freeing it was having him making some of the decisions. Will I ever feel that way again?

"I know it's hard," I whisper, "but you can do this. And you're not alone, Mom. You have me and Cecile and all of your friends around town. You should see how many flowers and cards you've received. Please come downstairs with us and celebrate Christmas." I hold out my hand to her and pull out the big guns. "Luke will think you're getting sick too if you don't get out of this bed. You don't want that, do you?" It's a cheap shot, but I can't let her lie up here, wasting away.

"All right," she says, throwing the covers off, "but I'm not changing out of my pajamas."

"Perfect," I respond, trying not to sound smug. "Slumber party it is. I'll go put on mine."

My mom mumbles something behind me as I leave, and I grin. If making her mad is what it takes to get her going again, so be it.

She joins us in the living room, and Luke sends her one of his megawatt smiles. "Come sit with me, Nana!"

She takes a seat on the couch next to him, and I hand her a hot chocolate with extra whipped cream on top, giving her what I hope is a warning look not to reject it. She needs to start taking care of herself, or she'll make herself sick. Thankfully, she takes it and sips slowly, looking around the room.

"The tree looks beautiful," she says quietly.

"It does," I agree.

"Do you need help with anything for tomorrow?"

"Everything's bought and prepped," I reply. "But I'd love some help with the actual cooking."

She gives me a small smile.

"C'mon, start the movie," Luke says, bouncing up and down. "Don't you think it's great, Nana?"

"I've never seen it," she tells him, earning a shocked look.

Luke is all over the place as we watch the movie, laughing loudly, hiding his face when the Ghost of Christmas Yet to Come appears, all the while assuring my mom that ghosts aren't real and not to be scared and singing along, completely off-key. It's perfect. My mom livens up at his antics, and actually laughs along a few times. She finishes her hot chocolate and eats some cookies, complimenting me on them in between bites.

After the movie is over, I flip through the channels, stopping on *It's a Wonderful Life* at her request. Luke quickly falls asleep, bored with the black-and-white images and the lack of Muppets, his head in my mom's lap. She gently strokes his hair with one hand and reaches for mine with the other. We sit quietly and watch like that, the room illuminated by the TV, the twinkle lights on the tree, and the candles I lit earlier. I look at my son's relaxed features and the small smile on my mother's face as she continues to caress his hair, and for the first time since leaving Simon, I feel something akin to peace. I lean my head on my mom's shoulder, and she gives my hand a squeeze. Tomorrow, we'll celebrate Christmas as a family. We'll open presents and go visit at Cecile's, attend church, and eat dinner together. My son and I will spend the day surrounded by family and friends for the first time ever, and the thought fills me with happiness. But even in the midst of the joy I feel, my thoughts stray again, and I imagine Simon sitting in his big, empty house, completely alone for the holidays, and have to blink back tears.

I would have loved to spend Christmas with him—but the fact that I thought it would happen only highlights how little I really know about him. He doesn't do Christmas, for some reason. It wouldn't have been a deal breaker for me, though. Neither would not sleeping together in the same bed. I would've accepted all of his quirks happily in exchange for his love. He's a weirdo, but he's my weirdo. No—he *was* my weirdo.

I turn my attention back to the movie and force myself not to think of him anymore. I don't think of him being all alone as we celebrate the holidays. I don't think of the anguished look on his face when he told me his son is dead as my mom and I plan my father's interment at the cemetery and the memorial service afterward. And I definitely don't think about him every night at nine o'clock, and wonder if he's found another sweet girl who knows how to bake apple pie.

We bury my father on a gray and rainy Wednesday between Christmas and New Year's. To shield us from the rain, the funeral home sets up a white tent around the plot, but it's nowhere near big enough to hold the large number of people who show up to pay their respects, and I know we'll have a full house afterward at the wake. My mom and I throw dirt on the urn and as we step backward and turn to take our seats again, my gaze drifts over the faces of the many people standing outside the tent, most of them holding black umbrellas. For a second, I think I catch a glimpse of a familiar face in the back and stop in my tracks, my heart skipping a beat. My mother tugs gently on my arm, and I look toward her for a second. When I turn back, frantically scanning the crowd, all I see are townspeople looking back at me. A trick of the light, maybe? Because I'm not thinking of him.

Feeling numb, I take my seat and watch as the vault is lowered into the ground. The priest speaks again, throwing dirt into the hole before it's covered completely. Next to me, my mom starts to sob, and I put my arm around her, sharing in her grief.

I'm in a sea of people, shaking more hands than I can keep track of. We're outside the tent, the sound of the rain hitting the umbrellas, almost drowning out the murmurs of condolences that I receive as we slowly make our way across the cemetery. I mumble my thanks again and again as one hand after another takes my outstretched one.

"Abigail, I'm so sorry."

I startle, staring at the large hand holding mine so gently, stroking the back of it in a way that brings back an avalanche of memories and a longing so strong I lose my breath. I raise my head, only to see him already turning, shouldering his way through the crowd as his hand slips from mine. He's gone from my sight seconds later, breaking my heart all over again.

I want to scream, run after him, throw myself at his feet, beg him to stay—to love me—but I don't. Stone-faced, I walk through the throngs of mourners with my mother at my side until we reach the car. I help her inside and go to the driver side, looking up again. There he is, about ten yards down the street, next to his car, facing me. His suit and coat are pristine, but his face is worn, his eyes tired. He looks like he's the one who buried someone today, not me. We stare at each other for a long moment before he slowly raises his hand. I mimic him, feeling the rain running into my sleeve and down my arm, chilling me to the bone. Then he turns and gets into his car, driving down the street and turning right, heading out of town.

I swallow my urge to break down in the street and instead get into the car, giving my mom a glance. Her eyes are closed, head leaned back in exhaustion. She didn't see what just happened, thankfully.

How did he know? Lila—that has to be it. I called her briefly on Christmas, telling her that I had to quit, and that I'm in Pinewood because of my father's death. I'll miss her and our newfound friendship. I'll miss a lot of things from my time with Mr. Thorne.

"Ready to head home?" I ask quietly.

"No," my mom whispers.

"Neither am I."

She turns her head and looks at me, giving me a tired smile. "I'm glad you're here."

"So am I, Mom."

~

It's late and the house is mostly quiet. My mom went to bed hours ago, but I've stayed up with Jo and Thom cleaning and tidying even though I'm dead on my feet, exhaustion making my movements slow and lethargic. I feel close to my breaking point. All day I've been keeping it together for my mom and Luke, making sure everything ran smoothly with the catering and guests, and now all I want is to curl up next to Luke and let sleep take me. Thom finds me in the kitchen; he's wearing his jacket and smells like fresh air and faint cigarette smoke.

"Abbi, there's, uh, someone waiting for you, I think."

"What?"

Thom fidgets, shifting his weight. "His car is parked just a few yards down the street. I guess he never left."

My insides twist with nerves. "Simon?"

"I don't know anyone else around here who drives a BMW like that. It's just sitting there."

"Oh. I guess I'll ..."

"Yeah, I'll finish up in here for you," Thom says, giving me a small smile.

My body moves on autopilot as I put on my coat and boots, stepping out into the cold night and walking to the edge of my parents' property. I spot his car parked underneath a street-lamp, and then I see him, leaning against the side of it. My stupid heart leaps and I have to take a few deep breaths as I approach him. I know the moment he senses me, his body angling in my direction. What's he still doing here? Why did he come here at all?

"Hi," I say, unable to come up with anything more eloquent.

"Abigail." His voice is hoarse as he moves off the car, stepping into my personal space. There's an unexpected intensity in the way he looks at me, a near-manic expression in his eyes. If he were a stranger, I'd be scared of the way he looms over me, the way he clenches his fists, but fear is the last thing I feel. "Come back to me."

I inhale sharply, looking up to see the surprise on his face, as though he hadn't meant to say the words. Out of nowhere, his hands settle on my shoulders and he pulls me into his body, pressing my face against the soft wool of his coat. I'm overwhelmed by his closeness, the smell of his cologne, and draw a shuddering breath, greedily inhaling his scent. God, I've missed him.

"Please," he breathes into my hair, his hands moving to my back, clutching me to him. "Reconsider my offer. Come back. I'll give you anything you want. A house. Tuition for Luke. More money than you can spend. Anything."

Anything but love.

I want so badly to say yes, to accept. It would be so easy. He'd take care of everything. Six months ago, I would have said yes.

"I miss you," he whispers, brushing his lips against my temple.

Listening to his plea is painful, but not as painful as pulling out of his embrace, my senses protesting the loss of his body against mine.

"I can't be your employee." I take another step back. "I *can't*, Mr. Thorne."

He stares at me, blinking several times, his expression open and heartbreakingly vulnerable. The look in his eyes hits me straight in the chest. It confirms what he already told me: he still wants me and he misses me. I know what longing looks like, loneliness too. Still, the situation hasn't changed. His offer stands, but no money in the world can give me what I really want.

"So it's all or nothing?" he mumbles.

"It's no more than what we both deserve," I tell him, sounding a lot calmer than I feel. For a split second I dare to hope, but then I see him shutting down, pulling away even though he's still standing right in front of me. The inches between us feel like miles.

"Goodbye," I whisper, turning on my heel. I hope the pounding of my steps as I run away will mask the sobs that rip through me as I leave him for the second time, a feat of strength I didn't think I possessed.

~

We celebrate New Year's with Cecile, Jo, Thomas, and the kids. My mom hasn't mentioned anything about my leaving or the fact that I've been here for weeks now without returning to my supposed job. Maybe it hasn't occurred to her to wonder, or maybe she knows the truth. At this point I don't really care. If she asks, I'll be honest and tell her I'm looking for a new one, that the old one simply didn't work out.

We have to go back to Seattle soon if I want Luke to stay in school. Jo and her family left already, but I've lingered, helping my mom get her new life started, all the while postponing my own. We sort through all of my father's things, deciding what to keep and what to throw away, and order her a new bedroom set since she got rid of their old double bed when he got sick. I also go with her to hear about my father's will. The lawyer is a severe-looking, middle-aged man, and it's obvious my mom is intimidated by him from the way she rounds her shoulders and lets him take charge of the conversation. I remember that feeling from when I first met Simon, the urge to shrink back. I don't feel that way now, though. I'm submissive in bed, but not a doormat, and I hold the lawyer's gaze each time I meet it. I think Simon would be proud of me.

As expected, the lawyer tells us the house and the cars will go to my mother, as well as the life insurance my father had taken out. It's a lot of money, which means she'll be taken care of in the future—a huge relief since she's never actually had a job outside of her home.

When the lawyer's done talking, my mom clears her throat, speaking in a soft voice. "I want Abigail to have my husband's car."

The lawyer nods while I gape at her.

"You need a car," she says to me. "And I don't need two. Please, take it."

"Thank you," I whisper. "I'll take good care of it, I promise."

"I know you will." She turns to the lawyer again. "I also wanted to, uh … is it possible to give Abigail some of the insurance money?"

My mouth actually drops open, but before I can respond, the lawyer does.

"This is besides the college fund?" he asks. "Because we're already talking about a considerable amount of money."

"What college fund?" both my mother and I ask at the same time.

The lawyer looks between the two of us, shuffling his papers. "Mrs. Winters, you are aware that your late husband set up a college fund for Abigail, aren't you?"

I stare at my mom, who looks just as shocked as I feel. "But that was so long ago."

"Yes," the lawyer says, glancing though his papers. "It was set up right after Abigail was born."

"And it's still valid?" I ask, barely able to get the words out.

"Yes. All I need is a signature."

I feel faint.

"Just remember your father saved this money for tuition, books, and housing." He looks at me over the rim of his glasses, giving me a stern look. "Not to go partying or shopping."

I snort out a laugh before I can contain myself.

"Abigail wouldn't do that," my mom says firmly. "She had a 3.8 grade point average, but more importantly, she's a responsible young woman and a wonderful mother to her son." She gives me a look filled with pride that warms me all over. "I'm so happy George kept the fund. It was always meant for you—if you want it."

I'm speechless for a few seconds. The ramifications of this are life changing, to say the least. I draw a deep breath.

"I know you wanted me to go to an Ivy League university," I say, "but I don't think that's for me. I'd never see Luke."

"I understand," my mom says. "I just want you to be happy."

"You know what would make me really happy? To share this with Jo. I want her to go to school with me. I don't think I would've made it without her, Mom. She saved me."

My mother's eyes well up, and she nods her approval. I feel like dancing around the room. I've wanted for so long to do something for Jo, and now I can. I know she wants to go to college, but I also know that she'd never prioritize herself over her family, having already chosen to start saving for her daughters to study. But now she can go too. We both can.

"How much money are we talking about?" I ask carefully.

"I don't know," my mom admits. "Some months he'd put a thousand dollars in, some a little less. But he always did it, every month."

The lawyer clears his throat. "With the added interest since you graduated high school, it comes to"— he glances at the papers again—"$192,400."

I gasp so hard that I almost choke, my mother patting me on the back as I cough loudly, tearing up, and not just from the lack of air.

"This is ... I can't even—" I start crying—sobbing actually. This changes everything. With my mom at my side, stroking my back as I cry, I feel safe and loved. There are no strings attached to this money. I'm in control of my own life for the first time ever, and it's both exhilarating and terrifying.

"Thank you. Thank you." I hiccup, trying to compose myself, remembering that we're in a stranger's office.

After I've calmed down, we sign the paperwork and head back to Pinewood, silent most of the way. In the kitchen at home, my mom makes us coffee, and we sit quietly, each of us contemplating what has transpired on this day.

"I suppose you'll go back to Seattle, then?" my mom asks quietly. There's no anger or resentment in her eyes, but rather a wistful sadness. "I understand," she continues. "But I will miss you both terribly when you go."

"I'll miss you too, and so will Luke. But we won't be far away, and with Dad's car, we can come and visit all the time. Maybe you can come and visit us too?"

"Of course I will," she says immediately. "And when you start school again, I could help you with Luke. Maybe he could spend a weekend up here every once in a while?"

"I think he'd love that. No, I know he would."

My mom smiles, reaching across the table to take my hand. "What are you going to study, then?" she asks.

I let out a happy laugh. "I don't know. It's ... I never thought I'd be able to go to school at all. But maybe ... I don't know, maybe culinary school?"

She nods for me to continue.

"I love cooking, especially baking. When I think back on you and me here in this kitchen, those were the happiest times for me, and Dad always made such a fuss over it when I made something, remember?"

She smiles through tears.

"I'll have to look into it more before I decide, of course. The work hours are probably brutal if you work in a bakery, but maybe someday I could work as a caterer or something. I'd really like that—making people happy with my cooking and baking. And I should take some classes in marketing and finance too, if I'm going to run my own business one day." I cup my cheeks, shaking my head. "Wow. This is really incredible. Thank you, Mom."

"No matter what you do, I'll be proud of you, Abigail. But I would really feel a lot better about sending you back to the big city if you'd consider getting a new apartment in a better neighborhood. With your part of your father's life insurance and the college fund, you could get a really nice place."

I don't tell her that we've already moved out and are currently living with Jo and Thomas. I simply promise her that I will get on that first thing. A new apartment for a new life.

Luke and I drive home to Seattle the next day, a visit with my mom set up for two weeks away, which makes me feel less guilty about leaving—that and the fact that Cecile has promised to look in on her often. The drive back is drastically different from the one that brought us here. I'm in my own car —an old, reliable Mercedes that my father took excellent care of, which means it runs like a dream—and I can see Luke in the mirror, grinning happily in his excitement to get back home to Pippa and Piper as well as his friends at school. I'm grinning too, because in just a few hours, I get to tell my best friend that we're both going to start looking at college classes this spring. And then I can look for a nice place to live, a real home for me and my son. I can't wait to get everything set up and have my own place again with my own furniture.

My furniture.

"Oh, shit," I whisper.

"What'd you say, Mommy?"

"Er, nothing. Do you want to listen to some music? I'll find something you like."

While I turn on the radio, I draw a deep breath to settle the rush of nerves. Simon put all of my belongings into storage when I moved in with him. Every single piece of furniture and kitchenware I own, not to mention my appliances, are somewhere only he knows, and I'll need them back when I move into my own place. Which means I'll have to contact him sooner or later.

For now, I choose later. I know Jo and Thomas won't mind if we stay there for a few more weeks while everything settles down. Besides, with how my heart still flutters at the very thought of Simon, I think it's definitely better to wait awhile until my feelings aren't so raw and exposed.

CHAPTER THIRTY-ONE

"Oh my God," Jo says, her whole face lit up with a huge grin. "Abbi!"

Both of us stand, throwing our arms around each other.

"Thank you!" she says, squeezing me tightly. "I can't believe it!"

"I couldn't either, but it's the real deal."

"College!" She laughs. "Fucking college!"

I pull back, nodding eagerly. "College. For both of us." We take our seats again, both of us still grinning like loons. "What do you want to study?"

"Nursing," she says without hesitation. "I've been dreaming about that for a while now. I just never imagined I'd be able to do it until the kids were much older."

"That's perfect. You're a natural caretaker."

"Thanks," she says softly. "What about you?"

"Something with food, I think. I'd love to become a caterer or maybe open up my own bakery one day, once I've saved enough."

"I could see that," she says with a nod. "You're great in the kitchen. You could also teach, you know? Like you did with Lila, right?"

"Yeah. I really loved doing that. I'm going to miss it."

"You're not seeing her anymore?"

I shrug. "I mean, I want to, but she lives ..."

"Next to *him*." Jo supplies the obvious conclusion. "I get it, but she's still your friend. That doesn't have to change, does it?"

"No, I guess not," I mumble. "Besides, I'll have to see him again eventually."

Jo raises her eyebrows, giving me a look.

"He has all of my belongings in storage somewhere," I explain. "Once I get a new apartment, I'll need them, won't I?"

"Yeah," she says. "Or not. You could just buy new stuff."

"I could," I admit, "but that seems really wasteful."

"Well, I could contact him. Ask him for you."

I nod slowly, pressing my lips together.

"But you don't want me to," she says with a knowing smile. "C'mon, Abbi. You're an open book. You don't actually *have* to see him again. You want to. Am I right?"

"No," I mutter.

Jo snorts.

"Fine. Yes. You're right. Does that make me pathetic?"

"No!" she says immediately. "I get it. You love him."

"I do," I whisper. "I really do, Jo." Blowing out a breath, I continue. "He looked so awful when he came to my dad's funeral. Like he'd been through hell and back. I'm worried about him."

"It must've been really hard on him. I mean, after what you told me about his son. I can't even imagine. I think I'd die if I lost Pippa and Piper. How do you keep going after something like that?"

I sigh, absentmindedly rubbing my hand across my chest as if to ease the constricting feeling within. "You close yourself off emotionally, and instead of a relationship, you hire a girl to sleep with you and tend to your needs, only to have her fall in love with you even though that's not something you can ever return?"

Jo gives me a sad smile. "Do you really believe that?" she asks. "That he can't ever return your feelings?"

"He won't let himself try, so there's no way to ever know. I can't change who he is, and I know I deserve more than he's willing to give me. I want someone who can love me back."

"Maybe I should be the one to contact him, after all," she suggests.

"No. I want to see him, make sure he's okay." I laugh a little, shaking my head. "I guess I really am a masochist."

Jo snorts, a smile tugging at the corners of her mouth.

"But maybe you could go with me?" I ask. "In case I need you?"

"Of course. Just say when."

"Right now, I want to focus on me, on getting my life back together."

Jo smiles. "So what's the plan?"

I smile back. "We start looking at classes."

The next couple of weeks are filled with a strange mixture of both hectic excitement and melancholy. Jo applies for the Certified Nurse Assistant program part time since she still needs a job to make the household budget work. I offer to help her, but she refuses, insisting that I need a much larger portion of the fund as a sole provider.

I decide to enroll in business school first, wanting to know more about the financial aspects of running a business before deciding on a career for the future. I know I like to cook and bake, and I'm pretty good at it, but that hardly seems like enough to start a business of my own. I have to be smart about it. An added perk of business school over culinary school is that Jo and I will be close to each other on campus, so neither of us will be completely on our own when we venture into the world of higher education years after high school.

In contrast to all of these positive developments is the grief I feel for my father and worry for my mother, combined with sheer longing for Simon. I miss him, and some nights I can't stop myself from crying when I know everyone else is asleep. I think of how he gazed tenderly into my eyes, how he smiled at me, how safe and cared for I felt in his warm embrace, how sweet he was with my son. And then I get angry, because he's the one who did all those things and a million others that made me fall in love with him. He did so little to discourage my feelings, even telling me not to fake anything with him, to give him everything. Only in the end, he didn't want everything. He didn't want my love.

On February 1st, I sign a lease for an apartment located in the eastern part of Seattle, a neighborhood called Madrona. At eight hundred square feet, it's on the small side with just one bedroom, which means I'll be sleeping in the living room on a pullout couch. I don't mind, though. It's clean and comfortable with a dining space in the kitchen and built-in closets, plus hardwood floors. Compared to our old place, it's a palace. Instead of a noisy, broken-down apartment building in the middle of the city, we're now the proud renters of the top floor of a quaint townhouse. The owners, Maxwell and Garrett, seem friendly and down-to-earth. They live downstairs and didn't mind renting to someone with a kid. They've been married since it was made legal in this state, and they're about to celebrate their anniversary on Valentine's Day. We should be moved in by then.

All I need is my furniture.

"I don't know if I can do this, Jo." I blow out a breath, staring at my reflection in the mirror, Jo standing behind me.

"You can." Her words reassure me as she moves a few of my curls around my shoulders. "I'll be with you. And you look great."

"I look like an idiot." I frown at the conservative dress and jacket I'm wearing. It's not my style at all, but I didn't feel right showing up at his office in jeans and a sweater. Last night, we sat down at the computer to find out where he works and discovered that Simon has his own company located downtown. The fact that I never knew highlights how naïve and stupid I was to pack up and move into his place—with my son —without knowing anything about him. He's an auditor and, apparently, a really, really good one, working all over the world for big companies. All of his travel now makes sense, as well as his endless stacks of paperwork. It all makes sense. Checking other companies for errors in their financial paperwork wouldn't exactly make you popular on arrival and would be a good way of avoiding emotional connections in your work life. If only he'd been this diligent about his home life.

"You look like a beautiful idiot, then," Jo says, bringing me out of my thoughts as she pinches my ass.

"Hey!" I grin at her in the mirror.

She grins back, ushering me toward the door, where I put on a new pair of low heels. Thirty minutes later, we're downtown in the financial district, parking my car outside a huge office building. Inside the lobby, we go to the desk and ask for Thorne Consulting Services. It's on the seventh floor, and I draw several calming breaths as we enter the elevator.

"You know what you're going to say?" Jo asks.

I nod. I've already rehearsed the words in my head—a calm explanation that I no longer need the storage and would like to get my belongings immediately. Beyond that, I don't think there's much else to say. I really just want to look him in the eyes, to make sure that he's all right, and so he can see that I'm all right too. Then I think I'll be able to move on. God, I hope so.

There's a young man sitting behind the desk in the waiting area, talking on the phone. He gives me a brief smile and looks me up and down as he holds up his finger, indicating that he's almost done. This must be Simon's assistant, but I don't remember his name. It was so long ago he told me, the night we celebrated his birthday. The memory is bittersweet.

"How can I help you?" the assistant asks, looking between Jo and me before settling his gaze on my face.

"Is Mr. Thorne available?" I ask.

"He's in a meeting right now, but he should be done soon. If I can just take your names, please?"

"Abigail Winters," I say, watching as he scribbles it down before glancing at Jo.

"It's just me," I add. "She's, uh ..." *Here for moral support.* "My ride."

"All right, *Miss* Winters?"

I nod.

"Miss Winters and 'my ride,' may I take your coats?" He smiles at his own teasing. "You can wait right over there." He motions to the chairs.

Jo and I sit down, me on the edge of my seat. I'm so nervous, I might vomit. Jo sends me a warm smile, and I inhale deeply through my nose, trying to center myself. Five minutes pass with me staring at the door to his office, which is located behind the assistant's desk. Whenever I glance in his direction, he smiles at me, and I feel forced to return it, acting as though everything is fine. I nearly jump out of my seat as the door opens, but it's not Simon who comes out. It's a woman. A beautiful forty-something woman in a blouse, skirt, and heels, carrying a briefcase. She turns in the door, her profile to me, and says something I can't hear, smiling.

She's smiling at him. Who is she?

I turn my head to look at Jo. She's also watching the woman closely.

"Who's that?" she whispers. "A client?"

"I don't know," I mumble, jealousy flaring inside me.

She's not his type at all, but maybe he's decided to move on to someone like her—an older, more confident woman who wouldn't fall head over heels, who could have a sexual relationship without feelings.

The woman closes the door to his office behind her. The assistant is already on his feet, helping her into her coat. As she turns our way, she sends me a polite smile before talking to the young man.

"Same time next week," I hear her say to him.

He enters it into his computer, and then she walks past us on clicking heels as my stomach churns.

CHAPTER THIRTY-TWO

"Abbi?"

I turn to Jo, realizing that I'm clutching the edge of my seat as though I'm scared of falling off.

"You all right?" she asks softly, a look of concern on her face.

"I'm really not," I say. "But I have to do this. I have to get it over with."

"Okay. I call ice cream and *Pitch Perfect* tonight."

"How about booze and *Thelma & Louise*?" I whisper, only half-kidding.

Jo laughs and I can't help but join her, drawing the attention of the assistant who gives us a curious look.

"Sorry," I mumble. My nerves are frayed, making me feel pretty unhinged.

"Never apologize for that beautiful laugh," he replies, giving me a wink before turning to his phone.

"Wow, flirty," Jo whispers, nudging me.

The assistant presses a few buttons, clearing his throat. "Mr. Thorne—" He pauses, listening. "Yes, sir, I do remember, and I cancelled them all, but you have a walk-in, a Miss Winters here to see you." He sits up a bit straighter. "Miss

Abigail Winters, yes." He glances at me. "She's here now, should I—yes, sir!"

He hangs up, quickly rolling his neck while I watch with bated breath. I guess I'm not the only one who finds Simon intimidating. "Miss Winters? He'll see you now."

"Thank you," I whisper, taking a few seconds to find my balance in the heels after sitting for a while.

"You want me to come in with you?" Jo asks.

"No, thanks." I send her a smile. "Just knowing you're out here is enough."

I square my shoulders and walk toward Simon's office, careful not to brush up against the young man who opens the door as I approach. I take a step inside, my eyes sweeping across the room, but I can't focus on anything besides the man behind the desk. It's been weeks since I've seen him, but now that I'm facing him, it's as if no time has passed at all, my stupid heart still fluttering at the sight of him.

Will it ever stop doing that in his presence? And then I realize it won't matter. I won't see him again after today. The thought is sobering and unwelcome.

"Would you like anything to drink?" the assistant asks behind me.

"No, thanks. I'm not staying long."

I hear the door closing behind me, and my nerves make me flinch at the sound, knowing we're alone.

"Abigail," he says.

I draw a quick breath as he stands up to approach me. He looks better than he did at the funeral, but there are still shadows underneath his eyes, and I'm pretty sure he's lost weight too, his jawline and cheekbones appearing even sharper than before.

"Please don't get up. I won't take much of your time." My gaze meets his, and for a few seconds, we just stare at each other.

"You look beautiful," he says.

"Oh, uh, thank you," I say, not expecting the compliment. "And thank you for coming to the funeral. I didn't get to tell you that."

He nods once, moving slowly around the desk toward me. The closer he gets, the harder it is to think.

"I just came by because ... because I need ..."

"What do you need?" he whispers, stepping right into my personal space, which forces me to tilt my head back to look up at him. He's so close, and he smells so good. I should've brought Jo in with me.

"What do you need?" he asks again, brushing his fingertips across the apple of my cheek, letting them linger on my chin.

I stare up into his eyes, helplessly drawn to him, unconsciously wetting my lips as my heart thunders away. I shiver as he brushes his thumb over my lower lip, his gaze leaving mine to follow the movement.

"F-furniture," I sputter, stepping around him and backing out of his immediate presence.

"Pardon?" He turns, looking at me with raised eyebrows.

"I didn't come here to ... to do whatever you just tried to do!" I exclaim, feeling my anger building. "You can't ... what are you doing? We aren't together anymore. I won't change my mind."

He buries his hands in his pockets and at least has the decency to look guilty. "I know."

"Right. So we're not ... touching like that. That's not why I came."

He sighs softly, nodding his head. "What is it you need, Abigail?"

"My furniture, please. I don't need the storage anymore."

"Oh." He frowns. "You're not at your friends' anymore?"

"No."

He gives me an expectant look, but I don't want to tell him anything else. I need to get out of here before I start either crying, yelling, or kissing him. Quite possibly all three.

"So if you'll just tell me where everything is, I'll have it picked up as soon as possible," I say, sounding a lot calmer than I feel.

"Do you need any help moving?"

"No, thanks. Just the info, please."

He watches me for a few seconds before he retreats behind his desk and sits down, motioning to the chair on the other side. I take a seat, clutching my hands in my lap while he rummages through his top drawer. He pulls out an envelope and hands it to me. It has my name written on the front in his elegant cursive.

"The lease is paid out for the rest of the year, so if you don't want to take it all now, you don't have to."

"Thanks. That won't be necessary, though," I tell him, standing up.

"You don't have to leave just yet. Would you like coffee?" he asks. "Or lunch? I can have Andrew—"

I shake my head, backing away. "Thank you. I'm fine." I'm not fine at all. What is he doing? Why is he doing this?

"Jo is waiting for me," I add as I reach the door. "Goodbye, Mr. Thorne." I turn with my hand on the doorknob, hesitating. "I hope you'll ... be happy. I really do," I say, opening the door and stepping out.

The assistant, Andrew, jumps out of his chair to fetch our coats, and Jo approaches, her eyes scanning me. I give her a quick smile and turn when the assistant holds my coat open for me to slip my arms in.

"Thank you," I tell him.

"No problem," he replies with a smile. "So I thought I'd ask ... would you like to go to dinner sometime?"

"That's really nice of you. But I can't. I'm sorry."

His face falls a little. "Oh, you're already seeing someone?"

"Uh, yeah, I am." It's easier to lie than to explain that I'm in love with his boss.

"Should've guessed," he says. "But nothing ventured, right?"

"Right." I give him a smile, which I guess he takes as encouragement.

"Do you want my number any—"

"Andrew! I don't pay you to socialize," Simon barks from behind me. I startle, my heart jumping into my throat.

"Yes, sir," Andrew says. "Of course." He helps Jo into her coat and slinks back behind his desk. I can feel Simon's eyes on me, but I don't dare turn around to face him. Jo's gaze flickers to the space behind me, and she nods to him before taking my hand. I follow her as we walk out of the office, my heart still in my throat.

"Holy fuck," she whispers as we step into the elevator. "Talk about tense."

I let my chin drop to my chest, blowing out a deep breath. "You don't know the half of it," I murmur. We get out to the car and I hand Jo the envelope.

"This is great," she says. "It's what you came for. We can start moving you in tomorrow!"

So far, we've painted the place and moved in a couple of new pieces of furniture, like a pullout couch for the living room and a new TV. Maxwell and Garrett have been invaluable, helping me carry the heavy things and hanging up new light fixtures.

"Tomorrow," I say, trying for a smile. "Will you check where the storage space is?" I look up at the building for a second as I steer the car into the street. It's surreal knowing that I'm never going to see him again.

"Ice cream tonight sounds good," I say, still waiting for a response. Jo is flipping through a small stack of papers in her lap, an intense look on her face. "Jo?"

"Did you look at these?" she asks.

"No. What's wrong?"

"Nothing," she assures me quickly, "but you should probably pull over somewhere. You're going to want to see this."

Sitting in a little café just down the street from Simon's office, we pore over the papers while our coffees sit untouched at the edge of the table.

"I can't believe he did this," I say for the third time.

"I know. It looks like you just have to fill in a few things, and then sign the papers. The envelopes are even stamped and addressed."

Simon has prepared a petition for me to receive sole custody of Luke, citing Patrick's abandonment as the reason. If they can't find him to serve the papers, I think it means I win without a court case. There's also a form to change Luke's last name to Winters instead of Jones.

"This is amazing," I whisper. "Why would he do this, Jo? He must've done it after we moved out."

"He still cares about you," she says softly. "I thought he was going to kill his assistant when he asked you out."

I bury my face in my hands. I know he still cares. I never doubted that he'd take care of me and Luke. "What should I do?"

"I don't know," she replies, sighing. "I really don't, Abbi."

"It would be so much easier if he were just a complete jerk, but he's not."

"Yeah," Jo says softly. "Do you want to head home?"

I nod, and we leave it at that.

～

"This is really nice of you, Abbi."

I smile at Garrett before turning back to my chopping board. "I don't mind at all. I love cooking."

"Maxwell's going to be so surprised when he gets home."

We're downstairs in Maxwell and Garrett's kitchen where

I'm helping him cook dinner. Actually, I'm cooking and he's drinking wine, keeping me entertained.

"He does all of the cooking. I'm terrible." Garrett continues. "I'm sure he thinks we're just ordering in tonight since he had to work."

"I'm sure you're not terrible," I say diplomatically. "I could teach you."

"Nah. I'm really more of a trophy husband," he says jokingly, lifting the wine bottle to pour another glass.

"No more for me, please. Luke will be home soon."

"You and the little guy have big plans for tonight?"

"Oh, yeah. Homemade pizza and *The Little Mermaid*. He let me pick it out for our date since it's Valentine's Day and all."

"Nice. You know, Max and I wouldn't mind watching him sometime if you ever want to go out on a grown-up date some night."

"Thanks. I'm not really dating right now, though."

"Bad breakup?" He holds up his hand before I can answer. "Sorry, was that too personal? I know you've only just moved in, but I feel like we're friends already."

I beam at him, touching my nearly empty glass to his. "I feel the same way. You and Maxwell have been so great." I drink the rest of my wine without making a face. I'm getting used to the taste of it. I realize the only reason I've started having a glass now and again is because it reminds me of Simon's kisses. If he smoked cigars, I'd probably try that too. I'm a glutton for punishment, obviously.

"Yeah, bad breakup," I tell him. "I'm not really over it."

"I'm sorry. That sucks. Was it Luke's dad?"

I shake my head. "No, he ran off over a year ago. I just sent in papers last week, filing for sole custody. Honestly, I hope they don't find him so I can get this done quickly. Luke never even talks about him anymore." I draw a breath. "I have horrible luck with men—well, romantically speaking, at least. I think I'm pretty lucky in the housemate department."

Garrett grins at me, stretching his arms above his head. "I should really grab a shower at some point. I stink."

"I wasn't going to say it." I tease him, looking over his admirable physique, which is on full display in his workout clothes. "Go. I'll finish prepping this so you can throw it in the oven before Maxwell gets home."

"You're the best," he says, jumping off his stool.

As I'm cleaning up, the doorbell rings. Luke isn't due for another hour, depending on traffic between the school and here, but I open the door anyway, since Garrett is still in the bathroom. I blink in surprise when I see a familiar young man outside my door.

"Andrew?"

"Hello, Miss Winters."

"Hello. What can I do for you?"

"I'm not here to ask you out again," he says quickly. "I'm here on business. For Mr. Thorne." He turns toward the driveway, and it's only then that I notice the U-Haul truck parked there.

"Um, what's in there?" I ask.

"It's your furniture," Andrew says.

"I already got my furniture." Jo, Thomas, and I took everything out of storage, and with the help of Garrett and Maxwell, it took no time at all to get everything moved in.

"Hey, what's up?" Garrett says behind me in his usual cheerful tone. "Oh, you got more to move in?"

"No, it's a mistake, I think."

"No mistake," Andrew insists. "A queen and, uh, a kid's bed that looks like a car, plus some other cartoon stuff?"

"Oh," I whisper, shell-shocked. "I see."

"Well, let's get them in before we freeze to death," Garrett says, clapping his hands together. "I'll just grab my coat and shoes. Hang on."

I finally get my bearings. Part of me wants to say no, but I know Luke will be over the moon, getting it all back. "Look, uh, tell Mr. Thorne thank you for me. I'll just take the race-car bed, please. And the kids' stuff."

"You don't want the queen?"

"No, that's okay. I already have a bed."

The one Simon got me is much more comfortable, but the pullout couch is practical so I can still have company over. Garrett and Andrew insist on carrying everything in themselves, leaving me feeling like a damsel in distress as I watch them quickly set everything up and carry out the cheap used bed I got for Luke, loading it into the U-Haul. Andrew says he'll get rid of it for me, no problem.

"Thank you," I tell him. "My son will love this. Please, tell Mr. Thorne I really appreciate it, and also thank him for the paperwork. He'll know what you mean."

"I will. Have a nice Valentine's Day, Miss Winters."

"You too."

Thankfully, Garrett doesn't ask where the things came from, and I spend the next hour setting everything up before Luke comes home. When I'm done, his room looks almost the same as the one he had at Simon's house, which is both good and bad. He misses Simon, and whenever he asks for Mr. Thorne I feel guilty for have putting him in a situation where he could get hurt emotionally.

While I wait by the window for Luke's bus, I call my mom, wishing her a happy Valentine's Day. I've been worried about how she would handle this day, but she sounds better than I expected and she's looking forward to having me and Luke come up for the weekend tomorrow afternoon after both of us are done with school. I spot Luke's bus and tell my mom goodbye before walking out to fetch him.

"Hey, Mommy!" he yells, sprinting toward me, his schoolbag bouncing on his back with each step. "Look! Look what I've got for you." He runs into my waiting arms, giving me a quick hug before pulling away and thrusting his little hand toward me.

"Happy Valentime's Day," he says with a huge grin, handing me a card. I don't correct him. His way sounds so much cuter.

"Happy Valentine's Day, baby. Is that really for me?"

"Uh-huh. I made it myself!"

"It's so pretty. Did you draw that heart on the front?"

He nods eagerly as I open it.

"To Mommy from Luke. Happy Valentine's Day," I read out loud.

"Ms. Daniel wrote that for me," he says, "but I wrote my own name!"

It's easy to tell, but I act surprised anyway. "You did? That's awesome! Thank you so much, honey. I love it. I'm gonna hang it on the fridge so that everyone who comes to visit will see it."

Luke beams at me.

"Do you want to come inside and help me make the pizza dough for tonight?"

He nods, grabbing my hand as we walk into our new home together.

"And there's a surprise for you in your room," I add, not at all shocked when he lets go of my hand to run ahead of me.

As I listen to his shrieks of excitement when I come up the stairs to our apartment, I smile. Simon has made my son very happy, giving him not only this beautiful furniture, but a great start to his schooling, and I'll always be grateful for that, regardless of how we ended things between us.

"Can we watch another one?" Luke asks, yawning as the credits for *The Little Mermaid* roll across the screen.

"Sorry, buddy. We both have school tomorrow, so we should probably get ready for bed, don't you think?"

"Yeah, okay. We're still going to Nana's after school, right?"

"Yep. The whole weekend."

After I've read him a story and tucked him in, I convert the couch into a bed and curl up with one of the books for my Economics 101 course. I've just started the chapter on supply and demand when I hear the doorbell ringing downstairs. A few seconds later, the sounds of loud voices travel upstairs, followed by an insistent knocking on my door. I jump out of bed and run to it just as it opens, and two tall figures burst through.

"You know this guy, Abbi?" Garrett asks, taking a protective stance.

"Yes," I whisper, staring at Simon, who looks agitated and disheveled as he tries to push past Garrett.

"Hey, cool it, man," Garrett says. "You asked to see her, and here she is. But I'm not leaving until she says it's okay."

Simon's lips curl into a sneer as the two of them size each other up.

"Stop that," I snap at him. "What are you doing here?"

"Get rid of your boyfriend here, and I'll tell you," he says, never taking his eyes off my housemate.

"Boyfriend?" Garrett laughs. "Abbi, do you want me to throw this idiot out of here?"

"No. No, it's okay. Go back downstairs. Maxwell will probably be home soon. I'll handle this." I send him what I hope is a reassuring smile. He throws Simon a warning look before retreating, leaving the door open.

"What the *hell*?" I ask when Garrett is gone, shaking my head.

Simon tugs at his jacket and runs his hands through his hair. "He's not your boyfriend?" he asks, his eyes darting to mine. "My assistant said ..."

"No!" I grit my teeth. "But even if he were, it's none of your business. You come bursting into my home like—Look, you need to leave. I can't do—"

"I want you back."

313

I inhale sharply, my stomach flipping like I'm in an elevator that's suddenly dropped. I shake my head back and forth, walking backward away from him. "No. No, I can't do this again. You can't just barge in here and make demands like that. No. That's not how it works."

"Abigail, I—" Out of nowhere he drops down on one knee, pulling a small blue box out of his coat pocket.

Holy fuck.

"I didn't have a lot of time," he says, lifting the now-open box up toward me. "We can get you another one. Any kind you want."

My eyes dart to the ring he's holding, my mouth going dry at the size of the diamond. I know it's real. If anyone else showed me a ring that big I'd think it was a fake, but not Simon. I feel as though the room is spinning.

"Abigail, will you—"

"Mr. Thorne?!" Luke's excited voice is clear even through the door to his room.

Oh, no!

I barely have time to pull Simon up off the floor before my son comes out, looking lit up from the inside as he runs to Simon, throwing his arms around his legs.

"Hi, Luke." Simon runs his large hand over Luke's rumpled hair. The sight of it makes my insides feel all jumbled and my throat raw.

"Luke, you should be in bed," I say as calmly as I can, noticing how Simon discreetly puts the ring box back in his pocket, my son none the wiser. "Big day tomorrow, remember?"

"We're going to visit my Nana for the whole weekend," Luke announces. "And look, I made Mommy a card for Valentime's Day." He pulls Simon over to the fridge, showing off his card.

"That's very good."

"Did you get Mommy a card?" my son asks, tilting his head

back to look up at him. "You're s'posed to do that today. Or flowers."

"Oh, I didn't think of that," Simon says. "I'll remember that for next time. I promise."

Luke's smile is radiant, but my stomach feels as though it's filled with acid.

"Back to bed with you," I tell him. "Say goodnight."

"Okay," Luke grumbles. "Goodnight." He makes a show of walking into his room at a glacial pace before closing the door just as slowly. He leaves it a few inches open, and I can still see him standing right there.

"To bed," I say firmly.

The door finally closes all the way, and I drop my head into my hands for a few seconds. "You can't say stuff like that to him."

"What do you mean?" Simon asks, approaching me slowly.

"Promising him a next time," I bite out. "That little boy has had enough disappointments to last him a lifetime. But no more. We're in a good place, and things have just settled down. I can't do this—" I gasp as his hands gently cup my cheeks.

"Please. I know how badly I fucked up, Abigail. I know I hurt you."

His left hand still cradles my cheek as he moves his right down the length of my hair, settling on my waist. I stare hard at the buttons of his shirt, willing myself not to yield. This is too sudden, too unexpected. What if he changes his mind?

"I'm sorry," he whispers, his breath tickling my forehead before his lips brush over the same spot. "I'm so sorry. I *never* meant to hurt you. I thought ... I thought I could ..."

"Mommy, I'm thirsty!"

I take a step back, running my hand across my face. "In a minute, Luke." I turn to him again. "Look, Mr. Thorne—"

"Simon," he says immediately. "No more 'Sir,' no more 'Mr. Thorne.' Just Simon."

"Simon." I look up at him, forcing myself not to get my hopes up. "I can't marry you."

He winces, pain etching his features. "Am I too late? I don't want to live without you. I thought this was what you wanted."

"Marriage? I just wanted you."

"Wanted? Not want?"

I draw a deep breath. I do want him, but does he really know what he's saying? "We don't really know each other and getting married ... this is all really crazy." I shake my head, unable to stop myself from smiling a little. This whole situation is beyond bizarre.

His lips twitch, his posture relaxing as the line between his eyes eases away. "I thought you had a new boyfriend. I wanted to steal you away from him."

"I don't. Garrett is gay. He lives downstairs with his husband."

"Oh. Don't I feel like an ass now."

"Mommy!" Luke shouts from his room.

I look up at Simon, still desperately trying not to get my hopes up. "I can't do this with you right now."

"But later, can we talk?" he asks. "Please, Abigail."

"Okay." I nod my head, trying to buy time so I can think clearly. "Okay. We can try to talk."

"Mommy! I have to pee!"

I chuckle, knowing all of my son's sudden, pressing needs are excuses to get back out here. "I should ..." I point my thumb over my shoulder toward Luke's room.

"Yes, I'll go. But we'll talk?"

I nod, following him to the door.

"May I ..." He takes a small step toward me, his gaze trained on my mouth.

I shake my head. I can't have him kissing me tonight. As far as I'm concerned, nothing has been resolved besides the fact that we'll talk soon. Still, despite my best efforts, I can't deny the tiny ember of hope in my chest. I'm such a fool for him.

"Goodnight, Simon," I say softly.

"Goodnight." He stops halfway down the stairs, looking back up at me. "Please apologize to your roommate for me?"

I nod.

"And ... I really like your new place."

"Thank you."

"We'll talk?"

"Yes, I promise."

"Happy Valentine's Day," he says softly.

"You too."

"Mommy! I have to tell you something really important!" Luke yells from his room.

I tear my eyes away from Simon and go to my help my son with his dehydration, bathroom needs, and philosophical thoughts. And inside of me, the ember of hope ignites.

CHAPTER THIRTY-THREE

"Nana!"

Luke runs up the steps to my mom's house and into her waiting arms. I wave at her as I unload the car, happy to see her. It's our second visit since Christmas and she's looking even better this time, with a healthy glow to her skin and newly dyed hair. Once we're inside, she hugs both of us and takes us into the kitchen where the table is already set for dinner.

"You made good time getting here," she says, carrying several dishes to the table.

"Yeah, hardly any traffic after we got out of the city. And Dad's car is running great."

She smiles at me. "How's school going, Luke?"

"Good! I can write my name now. Oh, wait!" He runs out into the hallway and comes back a few seconds later, carrying his bag, already tugging at the zipper. "I made a Valentime's Day card for Mommy, and here's yours, Nana." He pulls it out of the bag and hands it to her. I sit back and smile as my mom gushes over it, hanging it on her fridge, just like I did with mine.

"Let's eat," she says, bringing her hands together.

Luke carefully folds his own hands. He and I smile at each other as my mom says grace. It's not something we do at home, but it makes my mom happy, so we join in here.

"Any plans for this weekend?" she asks after dinner while I'm helping her do the dishes.

"Not really." I shrug. "Why?"

"I was talking to the Hansons at church on Sunday. Their son Tim is home for the weekend too." She gives me a quick glance.

"Mom, whatever you're thinking, no."

"It would just be a casual dinner, and I could watch Luke for you. He's a very nice young man."

"I'm sure he is. But I'm not interested." I hold her gaze when she looks over at me again, but I'm not backing down. I can't imagine dating anyone, considering how I feel about Simon. That would've been true even if he hadn't shown up at my apartment last night.

"All right." She sighs, turning back to the sink. "I suppose I'll give his mother a call."

"You do that." I put my arm around her, giving her a small squeeze. "It's not that I don't appreciate it."

"I don't want you to be alone in the city," she says.

"I know. And I'm not. I have Luke and my two house-mates, Garrett and Maxwell."

She stares at me, eyes wide. "You're living with two men?"

Oops. "Okay, about that, Mom. Please remember that it's the twenty-first century, and not everyone is as conservative as you."

"I'm not *that* conservative," she answers with a huff.

"All right. Yes, I'm renting an apartment in a really nice house in a really nice neighborhood, and the owners are a nice married couple, who also happen to be men."

Her eyes dart back and forth as she processes this information, pursing her lips. "You like living there?" she finally asks. "And Luke?"

"Very much. They've been nothing but friendly and helpful."

"Well, okay, then"—she continues washing dishes—"as long as you're happy."

I smile widely as I take the soapy glass she hands me and wipe it off. "Thanks, Mom. We're all moved in now, so you can come visit anytime you want."

"I'd like that. See where you live."

"Anytime," I say again. "Let's finish up here, and then how about a rousing game of Candyland before Luke gets too tired?"

She chuckles, nodding her head. "Sounds good. I'm really glad you're here, Abigail. That you let me into your lives." She blinks a couple times, her eyes on the glass in her hands.

I put my arm around her again and give her another squeeze. "Me too, Mom."

The following afternoon, I get an unexpected text.

Can I see you?

It's him. He's texting me. My heart seems to skip a beat, and I have to take a deep breath before I can write back.

I'm at my mom's house. We won't be back until tomorrow afternoon.

His reply is instant.

Can you get away for a little while? I'm parked at the diner.

My heart jumps in my chest. He's in Pinewood, and wants to meet right now? I'm not prepared for this, and I can't believe he drove all the way here.

Is everything all right?

Yes. I just couldn't wait.

He texts again immediately.

But I will if I have to. It's up to you.

"Mom? Can you watch Luke for a little while?" I call out. She's in the living room with him.

"I already am," she replies cheekily.

I grin, walking into the room. The two of them are curled

up on the couch, watching some kids' show on TV. "Is it okay if I go out for a little bit?"

"Mmhm," she hums. "Where are you off to?"

"Oh, uh, just a drive ... to clear my head." *I'm such a bad liar*.

She looks at me, and I remind myself that I'm an adult and I don't have to tell her everything.

"Okay, drive carefully," she says.

"I will. I'll be back before dinner."

"Bye, Mommy," Luke says, eyes glued to the screen.

I text Simon back, asking him to meet me down the road from the diner. It's not that I don't want to be seen with him, but Pinewood is a really small town, and word would undoubtedly get back to my mom if I go into the diner with him. In the bathroom, I quickly brush my hair and put on a touch of makeup. I didn't think I'd be seeing him today; I didn't bring any nice clothes, so the jeans and black, fitted sweater I'm already wearing will have to do.

I don't know why I'm so nervous when we're just going to talk. But that's exactly it—we haven't ever really talked. Not like this, at least. I inhale through my nose and let my breath out slowly. I can do this.

I spot his car easily enough, parked in a rest area, and pull up behind it. Both of us get out at the same time, and we stare at each other for a few seconds.

"Yours or mine?" he asks, giving me a tentative smile.

"Yours is probably warmer," I say, returning the smile before walking over to the passenger side.

He hurries around his car, opening the door for me to slip inside. It *is* warm, and I unbutton my coat, trying to relax as he joins me.

"Do you want to drive somewhere," he asks me, "or just stay here?"

"Someone might see us here," I say, looking around. "I

321

didn't tell my mom I was meeting with you. I know where we can go."

Twenty minutes later, we're parked again, looking out over the water. Simon exhales, turning the engine off but leaving the radio and the heat on.

"It's nice here," he says quietly. "Did you come here a lot when you were growing up?"

I laugh through my nose, and he turns his head to look at me. "This is, um, the local make-out spot."

"I see." He chuckles. "And you brought me *here*. Interesting."

My gaze meets his, and I blush. That wasn't why I asked him to drive us here. Well, not consciously, at least. We sit in silence for a few seconds. I don't know what to say to him, where to begin.

"I almost forgot." He reaches into the back seat and produces a tote bag. I watch as he pulls out a silver thermos and a travel mug, handing me the latter. "Would you like some hot chocolate?"

"Why did you come here?" I blurt out, completely ignoring the question.

"I was"—he draws a quick breath—"I was worried you might change your mind about talking. I guess I wouldn't blame you if you did."

"I haven't. We should talk."

He nods, pouring me some of the chocolate. I take a sip. Neither of us says anything.

"This is weird," I finally say. "We've never really done this."

"I know. I like being here with you, though." He looks out over the water again. "It's peaceful," he adds.

I lean my head on the seat, studying his profile. He's a beautiful man. I never dreamed I'd find myself in this situation with him, drinking hot chocolate at the beach in wintertime, with so many unspoken things between us.

"That night, when you picked me up on the street ..."

He turns his head to look at me.

"Was that the first time you'd done that?"

"No," he says simply. He places the thermos in the cup holder. "I've done a lot of things I'm not proud of. I won't try to deny that. I'll do my best to be honest with you even if you might not like the truth. I want you to know who I am." He gazes at me, his eyes wider than usual as he scans my face before visibly relaxing. I wonder if he thought this confession would scare me off.

"What is it you want, Simon?"

"I want you back—but not the way things were. I don't want you to work for me. I just want you to be with me." His voice never wavers.

"What changed?" I whisper.

"Nothing. Everything." He lowers his gaze, taking the mug from me before holding my hand in his. "I knew how I felt about you. But I did my best to ignore it, treating it—treating *you*—like it was just about the arrangement. Although I don't think I did a very good job at that."

My heart feels like it's swelled up to double its size, making it hard for me to draw breath properly. I was right all along. It wasn't just an arrangement for him, either.

"It was like you wanted me to feel for you," I whisper.

"I did. *God*, I did." His voice has a rough edge to it, sending pleasant shivers up my spine. I still want him as much as ever. "I wanted you so much, it scared me shitless. The thought that I might actually get you, it thrilled me and it terrified me."

"Why?"

His head snaps up, and he pins me with his gaze. "Because I could lose you again. I'm not easy to live with on a good day, and in case you haven't noticed, I'm pretty fucked up, Abigail." He leans closer—so close I can smell him and sense the heat coming off his body. "But it was like you never saw any of that.

323

You accepted my ways so easily, indulged in my kinks so willingly, embraced it all so openly. I never thought I'd get to have … that I'd feel …" His nose bumps against mine, and I startle at the contact, my eyes fluttering closed. I'm breathing just as hard as he is.

"You pulled the rug out from under my feet," he says, exhaling against my lips. His hand lets go of mine, traveling up my arm to settle on the back of my neck, tilting my head back. I can't suppress a moan as he sucks my lower lip into his mouth, grazing it with his teeth before letting go.

"You have no idea"—his voice is raw, a harsh whisper —"how it feels to cherish you so much, but at the same time want to do such completely filthy things to you. You think we've done a lot now? It's nothing compared to the things I've fantasized about since meeting you, all of the positions I want to put you in, all of the ways I want to use your body and have you worship me as I worship you in return."

I whimper at his words, clutching the thick material of his coat between my trembling hands. My body is a live wire of burning desire. I want everything he says. All of it and even more.

"And knowing that you want all of that too? Look at me."

I draw an unsteady breath, opening my eyes and blinking rapidly to focus. He strokes the apple of my cheek with his thumb, and the intense look in his eyes softens.

"It seemed too good to be true. I was waiting for it all to get ruined, for you to get fed up with me and my demands, and then I ended up ruining everything myself." He brushes his nose against mine before pulling back, giving me some much-needed space. "I'm sorry. I'm getting carried away."

"No." I shake my head. "It isn't just you. None of it was just you."

He smiles. "I could use some air," he says, nodding toward the beach.

"It's freezing outside," I protest softly.

"That's the point." He chuckles. "I think we need to cool off."

We really do, or we'll end up naked right here in this car. God, I want that so much. It still startles me how willing I am to let common sense fly out the window when it comes to him.

We walk by the shore, close together but not touching.

"Things were going really well for us," I say, "And then ... Luke's birthday."

"It wasn't his fault," he says quickly. "His wish—for a split second after he said it, I felt happy. But the very next moment, it was replaced with complete fucking panic." He shakes his head, wetting his lips. This makes sense to me. I understood why Luke's wish shocked him, but I didn't know the full extent of it, why he reacted so strongly, until I found out he had a son.

"Can we talk about Valentine's Day?" I ask.

He glances at me, giving me a hint of a smile. I take it as a yes.

"What happened? After I went to your office, I didn't think I'd ever see you again."

"You would have seen me even if you'd never gone to my office."

"I would?"

"I'm getting some help with my issues. I have a therapist. After you said no to me that night after the funeral, I made a decision. I knew you were right, that it couldn't just be an arrangement anymore, but I wasn't ready. I've talked to her about you, about wanting you back, but she advised me to wait, to give you some space. Obviously, I didn't listen." He chuckles, shaking his head. "I'm in for an earful the next time she comes by."

Same time next week. The woman in his office. She's his therapist. I feel like an idiot for being jealous.

"What made you come by, if she advised against it?" I ask.

"My assistant. I heard what you said when he asked you out, that you were already seeing someone."

"I lied."

He nods, continuing. "Andrew told me you were living with a young man, and I couldn't afford to wait any longer."

"So you barged in and proposed marriage."

"Let's head back," he says, changing direction. "You're getting cold out here."

I do my best to keep up with his brisk pace until we're at the car again, and he opens the door for me. Inside, it's nice and warm, the radio still playing softly. He's quiet, tapping on the steering wheel, seemingly lost in thought.

"What's wrong?" I finally ask.

With a deep breath, he turns to me. "I want you in my life. I want you, Abigail. And I was afraid I'd lost my chance. Obviously, I hadn't thought it all through."

"Simon." I take his hand in mine. "You don't have to marry me to have me in your life."

"I know," he says, playing with my fingers. "Realistically, I know that. All I can hope for is a chance. To do things differently this time." He draws a breath. "I know I don't deserve it, but I still want it. Will you give me a chance?" He lifts his eyes to mine.

"Things will have to be *very* different," I say, still being cautious.

"I know."

"We're not moving back in, and we have to leave Luke out of this—for now, at least. I don't want him getting his hopes up if this doesn't work out between us. I'm not ready to just pick up where we left off before his birthday."

He nods, watching me. "All right. That makes sense."

I smile at him. "You're being very ... accommodating," I say.

He grins. "And you're being very commanding. Quite a change of pace for us."

"You don't seem to mind."

"I don't. I'm taking my cues from you this time around."

He leans closer, caressing the side of my face. "I meant what I said. I want to do things differently with you. Will you give me a chance?"

That's all I've ever wanted from him. I know he isn't perfect, but neither am I. I want him with all his quirks because they make him Simon, the man I love.

"Yes, I will."

His smile is radiant. "What do you want, Abigail? What do you need from me to make this work?"

"Just you," I whisper, blinking back a rush of tears. "You said you're hard to live with, that you're fucked up. Well, you're not. Not to me, at least. I didn't *indulge* you."

He raises his eyebrows, his gaze warm.

"I loved doing everything you asked me to do: dressing up, cooking, serving you, the, uh, spankings, and all the other things we did. You were right about me all along. I feel it whenever you look at me, whenever you touch me. We fit together."

"We do," he says in a gentle voice.

"I want a real relationship with you: talking, sharing, doing things together, and the kind of sex we both like. I don't want that part to change. You can cherish me, like you said, and still want to do really dirty things with me."

He smiles. "I do like the sound of that. But before we start anything, I know I owe you an explanation for how I've been, for why I'm like this."

"It doesn't have to be now," I say softly. "We have time."

"I don't want to wait. You should know everything." He reaches into his inner pocket and fishes out a picture, creased and wrinkled around the edges. "It was a very different time back then," he says, handing it to me. "*I* was very different."

Drawing a deep breath, I hold it up, my eyes sweeping across the image. It's a group photo. A dozen or so young people face the camera, smiling faces all around. Most of them are dressed in faded jeans, T-shirts, and plaid shirts. To the right of the center, there's a young man who catches my eye. His dark hair reaches his shoulders and his smile is happy and relaxed, his arm thrown around the shoulder of the girl next to him. I glance over at Simon. His shoulders are tense and his mouth set in a hard line.

"When was this taken?" I ask.

"It feels like a lifetime ago. I was just nineteen."

I look at the picture again, at the girl next to him. She's petite with wild red hair and a pretty smile.

"Who is she?"

"My wife."

My eyes snap up to his, my mouth falling open in shock. "You were married at nineteen?"

He nods, then rubs his face with his hands. "Remember how I told you about going to school in England? My parents were American, but my father worked abroad most of his adult life. Lots of travel. My stepmother usually joined him, and I was sent away to school. It was easier for them, I suspect. I didn't see them all that much, even during holidays."

"I'm so sorry," I tell him, reaching for his hand again. "Are they ...?"

"Long gone," he says in a monotone. "Good riddance." He looks at me. "He was an abusive bastard, and she couldn't have cared less what happened to me. I don't miss them one bit."

"I'm still sorry—for you," I whisper, "that you had such an awful childhood."

"Thank you," he says softly, stroking my hand before drawing a deep breath. "When I graduated at eighteen, I was more than ready to get away. First chance I got, I put an entire ocean between us and came over here. I'd inherited quite a bit of money from my father's mother. She was nice, as far as I remember. I had a plan all set out. I would start here on the West Coast, buy a car, and drive across the country. But I never got any farther than Seattle."

"What happened?"

"I met Donna." He shakes his head. "It was so strange. I was sitting outside a café downtown, planning my trip, when suddenly this girl comes up to my table and sits down, asking me if I can spare a cigarette and buy her a coffee. She looked hungry and a bit worse for the wear, but still very pretty. I said yes. After that cup of coffee and a few cigarettes, I left the café with her, and all of my plans behind." He glances at me.

"That sounds really romantic," I whisper, trying to ignore the acid in my stomach.

Simon shrugs. "I was an eighteen-year-old virgin who'd barely spoken to a girl before that point, and she was pretty candid about what we'd do if I got us a room somewhere."

I try for a smile. "But it wasn't just a one-time thing."

"It wasn't. For the next three years, I barely left her side. It turned out she was homeless when I met her, and it felt good to save her from that. She was so different from anyone I'd ever met, free-spirited and wild, but with absolutely crazy mood swings. One day she'd be bouncing all over the place and the next she'd stay in bed all day." He shakes his head. "With what I know now, I can see that she was not okay. I didn't realize it at the time, of course. I was too blinded by it all."

"Blinded by love?" I whisper.

He sighs. "I know I'm supposed to say that I've never felt that way about anyone before, but we agreed on honesty."

I nod.

"I did love her—with all the naiveté and excitement of the teenage boy I was. I loved her very much, and married her, but I wasn't at all prepared for what came next." He shoots me a quick glance. "The group of friends we hung out with ... there was a lot of alcohol and pot even in the beginning. We partied hard. But then another guy started hanging around and he brought harder stuff, pills and powders. I guess I was sensible enough not to partake, but I can't say the same for Donna. She took whatever he gave her even though I told her it was a bad idea. The drugs made her different, mean. I thought about leaving once or twice when she was really bad, but ... I loved her. I took care of her as much as I could, making sure she ate, staying with her whenever we went out to make sure she'd be all right. It went on like that for a while. Then we found out she was pregnant. We hadn't exactly been careful all the time."

I chew on my lip as I watch him, dread building up inside me. I know how this story ends, how it changed him from the happy-looking kid in the picture to the man I met in that strip club, closed off and reclusive.

"We never talked about having kids, but I wanted it. So I took action, removing both of us from the party scene. I told her we were done with all that, that we'd be good parents, that we'd give our kid the great childhood we were deprived of, starting immediately. I spent some of my inheritance and got her into a rehab program. We went shopping for baby stuff. For a little while it seemed like everything was going to work out." He stops talking, scrubbing his face with his hands.

"But it didn't," he says, his voice now hoarse. "I'm sorry, I can't."

He's out of the car before I can react, standing stock-still as he faces the ocean, his coat flapping in the wind. I join him, standing quietly by his side and listening to his fast breaths. Eventually he calms down, putting his arm around me to pull me against his tall frame. We stand there for a while, listening to the crashing waves, and even though it's freezing I don't consider moving. I like being here, by his side. This is the first time I've truly felt like his equal.

"Are you all right?" I ask.

"My therapist has high hopes for me," he responds dryly.

I gaze up at him.

"Sorry," he says. "Talking about this brings up a lot of things I'd rather keep buried forever. But you deserve to know." He looks out over the water. "They're both buried in Seattle."

"B-both of them?" I stutter, trying to grasp the magnitude of such a loss. "Donna and your son?"

"I named him Sean," he says softly. "Maybe someday I'll take you to meet him, if you want?"

"Of course I do," I whisper, a thought occurring to me. "Do their deaths have to do with the scars on your stomach?"

"Yes, but not in the way you probably think. They weren't attacked. Just me. After she got pregnant everything changed," he recounts. "Donna did the rehab program and I got a job. It was just part time at a record store. I didn't really need the money at that point because of my inheritance, but I loved it. I loved coming home and having her there. I felt like I finally had a real home of my own."

His expression darkens. "Then she started disappearing," he whispers. "I'd wake up and she'd be gone and wouldn't return for hours. She said she needed space, that I was smothering her—always watching her and hovering over her. We fought a lot. I was worried about her and the baby, and I didn't think she was taking good enough care of herself. She accused me of being controlling, and looking back, I can see that I was. But only because I was afraid—afraid of losing her, of losing everything that meant something to me. She wasn't being careful and I had to take control of the situation. I *had* to. But it didn't work." He pauses, staring into space. A gust of wind makes me shiver and he focuses on me again, leading me to the car. It's still warm inside, but he takes my hands between his, rubbing them gently.

"I have issues with control, as I'm sure you've noticed," he says. "There's a reason for that. The more Donna pulled away, the harder I clung. Or maybe it was the other way around. I don't know. But I suspected she was using again."

"She was pregnant," I whisper.

Simon shakes his head, giving my hands a tug. I know what he needs. He needs me to take care of him now, to show him I'm not going anywhere. He pushes his seat back to make room for me in his lap, wrapping his arms around me as I sink into his embrace. He gives me a gentle squeeze, sighing.

"She stopped coming home for days on end, and I went to see our friends. They told me she was off somewhere—that she'd been coming around a lot lately. I had no idea. I got ... very upset. I asked if she'd been doing drugs. They said yes, like it was no big deal. They were my *friends*. Why hadn't they told me? Or tried to stop her? All of them were so fucked up. Addicts."

He swallows audibly. "She came home that night, and I looked at her, really looked. Her skinny arms and vacant eyes. And that swollen belly she took with her whenever she left my sight. She was hurting our baby and I couldn't do a thing about it. I lost it. I just lost it."

I sniff quietly, my eyes welling up with tears. I've never heard his voice like this before—so raw.

"I screamed at her. I called her *awful* names. I threw things. I accused her of fucking her drug dealer. I knew he'd want payment for whatever he was giving her, and she didn't have a dime. She didn't deny it. She screamed right back at me, hitting me and pushing me. Said she couldn't be a mother, that I hadn't given her a choice, that I was forcing this life on her. She didn't want it, didn't want me."

I can't hold back my tears, but I do my best not to sob, not wanting to interrupt him.

"She was right. I never asked her what she wanted. I only saw what I wanted. I realize that now, but back then I didn't. All I could see was her betrayal. I hated her, and I told her as much. I was so angry with her. She ran out. I didn't follow."

He draws a shaky breath. "It only took me a couple minutes to realize what I'd done. It wasn't just Donna who left —she carried our baby. I looked for her, but nothing. My former friends wouldn't help. I filed a missing person's report and walked all over the city, handing out flyers with her name and picture on it. I was sick with worry."

He clears his throat above me, and I reach up to rest my hand on his shoulder.

"About a week later, in the middle of the night, I woke up to screaming—hers. I remember seeing the drug dealer above me, his face partly in the shadows, and the flash of the knife a moment before he started stabbing me. I managed to roll away from him, and he mostly hit my side. All the while, Donna was screaming at him, telling him she'd already found my money, begging him to stop. At least I know she didn't want him to kill me."

He shudders, his breaths coming faster. "The pain was excruciating. I think I blacked out. I made it into the hallway somehow, and a neighbor found me and called 9-1-1. There was so much blood; I thought I was going to die. Sometimes I wake up and I can still feel the blood clinging to my clothes, to my skin. I can still smell it."

"Oh my God." I can't stop myself from whimpering as I cling to him.

"I was still in the hospital recovering when I got word that she'd OD'd. And the baby ... they tried a C-section, but ..."

"Oh, no." I cry, stroking his head. There's nothing I can say to make this better, but I try just the same. "I'm here. I'm here, Simon."

"I held him." His voice cracks. "He was so little, but so beautiful—even with all the wires and the mask on his face. And he was strong. He fought to live. He wanted to live. I held him and he lived for almost two hours. And I whispered to him that I loved him, that I was his dad, that I wanted him more anything in the world. I held him until they made me let go."

"I'm so sorry. I'm so sorry," I whisper, holding him tighter. No wonder he reacted so strongly when Luke was sick, no wonder he rejected the idea of being in a real relationship for so long, and no wonder he got a vasectomy. After experiencing such a profound loss I'm amazed he survived at all.

He's silent for a long time, his breaths tickling my neck. "I buried them together," he says, his voice hoarse. "She didn't want him, but I couldn't bear the thought of him being all alone in the dark. Do you think that was right of me?"

I nod, pressing my lips against the top of his head. "You did everything right. It wasn't your fault, any of it. You did everything you could to help her. There are just some things you can't control, no matter how hard you try, even if it's unfair and not right at all."

"I know," he whispers. He turns his head away, wiping at his face. Eventually, his stuttering breaths even out.

"Thank you for telling me," I whisper.

"Now you know what kind of man I am," he says, his voice sounding hollow. "The kind who tries to control the people he loves, who loses his temper and drives them away."

"That's not who you are," I say softly, tracing his features with my fingertips. "There's nothing wrong with wanting control. It makes you feel safe. I didn't leave because you wanted to control me. I felt safe within your control. You're good and strong, Simon. You survived, and I'm so grateful you did."

He hugs me to him. "I thought about ending it all. After I buried them, I wanted to die too. But I realized if I were gone, there wouldn't be anyone left to remember him, to love him. He may as well never have been born." He draws a deep breath. "It's been so many years, but I still think about him every day. I remember."

"You'll always be his dad," I whisper. "He was loved."

He nods, his eyelids fluttering as wetness coats his long lashes. "It happened on Christmas. I'd bought presents, even though he wasn't due until February. I've never celebrated since. After the funeral, I left. I went back to the apartment for some papers and a photo album, but I left everything else behind."

"The *Indiana Jones* movies. You said you had them once, but not anymore."

"I lost everything. I had no one. I studied. I worked. I found ... distractions. But I never had anyone until I met you." He opens his eyes and looks at me. "You made me feel again. You and Luke. I didn't want to, and I fought it hard, but it didn't work. I thought I could keep it all separate, that I wouldn't cross any lines. You and Luke downstairs, me upstairs. I thought I could control everything, setting up the rules of our arrangement." He moves closer, touching his forehead to mine. "But you didn't just move into my house. You moved into my heart, both of you."

"Simon," I whisper, leaning in to kiss him softly. "It was the same for me. I tried to convince myself I shouldn't care for you, and I tried to fight my feelings. It didn't work."

He smiles, rubbing his nose against mine. "What a pair we make."

I return the smile, hesitating for a second. "What was different about me? Why did you invite me to your house that first night? Was it because I reminded you of Donna?"

He exhales. "In a way, yes. There's no real resemblance. It was the look in your eyes as you left that club. I recognized that look—sad and lost. You were so thin and pale, but beautiful too."

"Do I still remind you of her?"

"No," he says immediately. "I thought you were troubled and frail, but I couldn't have been more wrong. You're strong and capable, sweet and gentle. I can't tell you how happy I was to realize that, knowing you wouldn't be as reckless as she was. And when I found out about Luke, how you'd do anything to take care of your son ... I was in awe of you. Complete awe. I thought I could help you, maybe even save you, but it turned out to be the other way around. So, no. You don't remind me of her at all. That's not why I want to be with you, Abigail."

"I understand your need for control a lot better now, why you needed me the way you did."

He hums in agreement. "What happened to me—I never

want to feel that helpless again. Having you at my beck and call, knowing you'd do whatever I told you to, it was a complete rush. It's why I wanted an arrangement in the first place, one where I called all the shots. A real relationship isn't like that. I know that I'll have to give up control and trust you to make your own decisions."

"Can you?" I ask softly.

"Yes. I know I can trust you. Please just be patient with me?" He kisses the tip of my nose. "You know what they say about teaching an old dog new tricks."

I smile. "I like your old tricks too. We'll figure out the balance together."

He turns serious. "Abigail, in the spirit of honesty, you need to know. Being with me comes with ... difficulties."

"What do you mean?"

"My therapist thinks I have post-traumatic stress disorder, and my issues aren't just going to disappear—even with therapy." He holds my gaze, continuing. "I have triggers—that's what she calls them. Christmas is one of them. Sharing a bed is another. I don't know if I'll ever be able to ..." He trails off, his tension evident on his face, in its lines.

"I hurt you," he whispers, "that night Luke was sick, and I fell asleep in his room. When you tried to wake me, I hurt you. I didn't mean to, and I'm so sorry, but it happened. I don't know if I'll ever be able to sleep with you, as much as I want to. Can you live with that?" He scoffs and continues before I can reply, "Can I even ask you to live with that? A life with no Christmas and separate bedrooms, not to mention all my other issues."

"Hey," I say softly, "none of this is that much of a surprise."

He blinks, bemused.

"I already knew you had a good reason for the sleeping arrangements, and as for the Christmas thing, I just wish you would've told me. We never would have decorated your house if I'd known. It was meant as a happy surprise for you, to show you what it's like not to come home to an empty house after a long trip. I wanted to show you how much I care about you, how much Luke cares. And you're not a violent person, Simon. When you pushed me away, I was more startled than hurt and I haven't thought of it since. I'm not afraid of being close to you."

He exhales. "That night, I was already on edge. We left things in such a bad place before I went away, and I didn't know what to expect when I got home. I was going to apologize to you."

"You were?" I ask.

"Yes. I felt awful. You gave me so much of yourself the night before I went away. You let me push your limits without hesitation."

"I liked it. All of it." I blush, remembering all the things we did.

"So did I." His stare is intense. "Everything we've done ... I never dreamed I'd find someone like you, but then I ruined it and left you with that envelope. You were so much braver than I was about showing your feelings, and I knew how much you liked us getting closer. I liked it too, so much so that it scared the hell out of me." He gently brushes my hair away from my face before looking deeply into my eyes. "But I'm not scared anymore. I can't promise you we'll be able to sleep together, or have Christmas decorations in the house, but I *can* promise that I'll stay in therapy, and I'll work on my issues. I swear. I want to be with you. What can I do to show you?"

His expression is open and sincere, hopeful even. I've never had much luck and being hopeful has always been a scary prospect. But looking into Simon's eyes, I can see the future, my own personal fairytale come true, and feeling hopeful comes as naturally to me as breathing.

"Ask me out on a date."

CHAPTER THIRTY-FOUR

"I don't know about this dress. Do I look okay?"

Jo nods, watching me with an amused look as I fly around the apartment, pretty much beside myself.

"You look fantastic," she says. "Really, Abbi. Do you know where he's taking you?"

"He just said a restaurant."

"Then you can't go wrong with a little black dress."

It's been almost a week since I saw Simon in Pinewood, but we've talked on the phone and texted every day.

"I've never been on a date like this before. I'm so nervous, I might throw up."

"I don't blame you," she says, taking a seat on my pullout couch. "This is kind of a big deal."

"It's a huge deal." I shake my shoulders, trying to calm myself before flopping down next to her. "What do we even talk about on a first date after everything we've been through? Was it like this for you and Thomas when he came back?"

"Not really. But that was a totally different situation. We'd been in a relationship before, and we have kids together. Just treat it like you would a normal date. I mean, even after everything, you don't really know that much about each other."

I chew on my lower lip. "I'm just nervous. I can't remember the last time I went on a date."

Jo sends me a teasing smile. "So since this is technically only your first date, are you going to ask him up afterward?"

I roll my eyes at her. "Maybe. If it feels right."

"Oh, I'm sure it'll *feel* right," she drawls, leering at me before she starts laughing.

Nerves forgotten, I shoot her a grin. "I really want this to work out, Jo."

"I do too." She stands, pulling me off the couch. "So let me get Luke out of here so you're ready when Mr. Thorne gets here."

"Simon. It's just Simon," I say, unable to contain my smile.

"Just Simon." She grins at me. "Man, you've got it bad."

Laughing, we go help Luke pack his bag, and a few minutes later, I wave them off before running back upstairs to fuss over my dress again—and turn the couch into a bed, just in case.

The doorbell ringing downstairs stops my pacing and my heart jumps into my throat. As I descend, male voices reach my ears.

" ... apologize for what happened on Valentine's Day."

"Hey, man, we've all been there," I hear Garrett say. "Just treat her right, you hear?"

They come into view, and both of them look up at me.

"Oh, yoo-hoo, Abbi. There's a gentleman caller for you," Garrett says in a fake Southern accent, batting his eyelashes. "A tall drink o' water if I ever saw one. Oh, my!" He fans himself, cracking up. I can't help but laugh at his antics.

"And this is why he couldn't possibly be my boyfriend," I say, turning my attention to Simon. He really is a tall drink of water and I can't stop staring at him.

He's in a dark suit, as usual, a crisp white shirt and a char-coal gray tie underneath and a black wool coat on top. The circles underneath his eyes have disappeared, and his cheeks are flushed, giving his skin a healthy glow. He looks me up and down, from my curled hair to the heels on my feet and pauses to admire my dress. It's slinkier and more revealing in the cleavage area than anything else I've owned before or anything he's ever put me in, and it makes me feel sexy. I've slowly but steadily been gaining weight, and it definitely shows in my curves. I'm not so waifish anymore, and I like it. Judging by Simon's blatant ogling, he likes it too.

"You look beautiful," he says, reaching out to help me down the last two steps.

"So do you. I mean, handsome. You look very handsome." I stumble over my words, feeling fluttery and stupid in his presence as I give him a shy smile.

"Oh my gawd." Garrett sighs. "Okay, I need to go call my husband. You kids have a good time." He wags his finger at Simon. "Be sure to have her home by midnight, young man."

"Okay, bye!" I say, narrowing my eyes and giving him a look that usually works on my son. It doesn't work on Garrett. He sends me a dazzling smile before sauntering away, leaving me alone with Simon.

"I brought you these," he says, bringing his left hand out from behind his back. He hands me a bouquet of lilac roses.

"Thank you," I whisper. "I've never seen them in this color before."

"Everyone buys red ones. I wanted them to be, uh, special," he says, fidgeting. "Do you like them?"

It dawns on me then—he's nervous too!

"I love them. They're so pretty."

"Well, I have it on good authority from a very clever little boy that you're supposed to bring flowers."

I smile, remembering. "Let me put them in water. I'll just be a minute."

I hurry up the stairs as fast as I can in heels, and head for the kitchen. I know I have a vase somewhere. Carefully, I place the bouquet on the counter and start searching. I'm standing up on my toes, reaching for the glass vase on the top shelf when I sense him behind me. He whispers my name and places one hand on my waist as his other reaches over me and grabs the vase easily. He puts it next to the flowers, his other hand still touching me as he lightly presses his front to my back. I'm frozen, overwhelmed by his closeness, yet wanting him closer still. I inhale a shaky breath as he leans in to bury his face in my hair before nuzzling my neck.

"God, you smell so good." His voice is husky, sending little jolts of pleasure up and down my spine. "And this dress ..." He trails off, bringing his other hand up to the one I still have raised in the air, caressing the length of my arm with the tips of his fingers and causing my skin to contract beneath his touch.

He presses his lips against my neck and my naked shoulder, gripping me tighter with his strong hands and fully pressing himself against me. I can feel how I affect him and can't help but moan. It's been months since he's touched me like this, and my body craves it like it craves oxygen.

"Simon, oh," I whimper as he nips at my earlobe, his breath hot in my ear. Abruptly, he pulls back, uttering a low curse. I turn, trembling.

"Fuck, don't look at me like that, Abigail," he says, still breathing harshly.

"You started it," I murmur.

He grins, shaking his head. "You did. When you decided to put on that dress."

"I can change," I offer, only half-serious.

"Don't you dare."

We stand a few feet apart, staring at each other. It's obvious what we're both thinking, and it has absolutely nothing to do with going out to dinner.

"I'll just wait for you downstairs," he finally says, although it sounds like a question.

Or you could bend me over, pull up my dress, push my

underwear to the side, and take me right here on my kitchen counter.

"That's probably best." I want this night to be about more than sex. It's our first real date and tonight I want romance. I send him a smile, and he walks away, giving both of us an opportunity to calm down.

After putting the roses in water and briefly considering sticking my head in the freezer to cool off, I head back downstairs. Simon is by the door, and he helps me into my coat wordlessly. Outside, the cold air is welcome, and I draw a deep breath as we start walking toward his car.

"I apologize," Simon says softly next to me.

I stop and look up at him.

"I asked you out tonight, and I honestly don't expect anything except a good meal and your lovely company. I promise."

"Thank you, but you have nothing to apologize for. I was right there with you."

"Still, we'll take it as slowly as you want, Abigail. You're in control."

I raise my eyebrows.

"I'm making progress," he says with a smile.

"You are. I'm proud of you." I stand up on my toes to kiss his cheek. "I'm going to be honest with you. Taking things slowly ... it's going to be really hard."

His eyes spark with humor. "Pun intended?"

I snort out a laugh, quickly covering my mouth in embarrassment. He grabs it so he's holding both of mine in his, looking down on me with warmth in his gaze.

"I like making you laugh," he says softly.

"I like it too."

"C'mon. Let's go to dinner," he says, letting go of my left hand but holding my right one as we walk to the car together.

He drives us to a restaurant downtown, still holding my

hand while using the other one to steer the car. On the way, he asks about Luke's school, how he's doing, and how my mom is faring. It's so unlike our old relationship, so normal—and it's lovely. We walk inside and hand over our coats, and we're seated right away even though I can see there are a lot of people waiting for a table. Simon must be a frequent visitor; the maître d' makes a big deal of him arriving with a date and compliments me excessively. Simon chuckles as I blush, resting his hand on my lower back as we're escorted to the table. It might be my imagination, but I feel eyes on us as we take our seats, the maître d' holding out my chair for me and even placing a napkin on my lap. Nervously, I pick up the menu, looking around the room, and sure enough, I see diners stealing glances at us.

"Do you know everyone here?" I ask, feeling a little uncomfortable.

"No. Some of them probably know me, though. Or know of me, at least."

"Oh. How?" I lean forward, intrigued.

He gives me a smile. "You really haven't ever looked me up," he says, looking pleased.

"Only to find out where you work so I could come see you."

"There was an article a few months back"—he waves his hand dismissively— "most eligible bachelors in the city or something like that. I made the list."

"Oh." I glace around again. "The top of the list?"

He shrugs. "It was good publicity for my business." He leans forward, whispering, "But all the men are most likely staring at *you*, wishing you were with them."

"Yeah, sure." I laugh softly. I don't care about any other men, just the one in front of me.

A waiter appears, asking if we'd like wine. Simon looks at me.

"Er, sure. Nothing too sour, please."

"A glass of Moscato for the lady and the 2007 Sassicaia for me."

"The Moscato is really more suited for desserts," the waiter says apologetically.

"Yes, thank you, I'm quite aware of that," Simon says with a hint of irritation in his voice, raising his eyebrows at the waiter. "But that's what my date wants."

"Y-yes, sir. Right away." He hurries off and Simon just smiles at me before perusing his menu.

I resist the urge to fan myself. When I first met him, I remember how nervous his commanding ways made me feel. Now it just turns me on, seeing him in charge.

The waiter is back almost immediately, pouring the two different wines for us, mine white and Simon's red.

"Abigail?"

I look up from my menu. The waiter is still standing there, and Simon nods toward my glass.

"Thank you?"

He laughs softly, pushing it toward me. "Taste it."

I take a careful sip, happily surprised that it's both sweet and bubbly.

"Mmm, it's good."

He grins at me, and I watch as he does the same thing, tasting his wine and telling the waiter it's all right.

"Would you like to hear tonight's specials?"

Simon nods and the waiter starts talking. A lot. The more he says, the more confused I feel. *Glazed couscous. Fijian albacore sashimi. Parsnip mousseline. Conchiglie.* Is any of that English?

After the recitation is done, Simon looks at me for a moment before turning back to the waiter. "We'll need a minute or two."

I blink a couple times, staring at my menu as I try to make sense of it all.

"Abigail? What's wrong?"

I chuckle, shaking my head. "Nothing, I just have no idea what he said. I've never been to a restaurant like this before. It's so fancy."

Simon leans forward, looking at me intently. "I wanted to bring you here because it's something we talked about but never did. I thought you'd like it."

"We talked about going here?" I ask.

"This is where I ordered from when we celebrated my birthday," he says softly.

"Oh." I think of the wine, the dancing, the lovely dinner we shared, giving him the DVD box set, the marathon sex, and finally falling asleep in his arms for the first time. "I remember."

"That was a good night." He runs his thumb over the back of my hand, gently caressing me. "The best birthday I've ever had."

"Yet," I whisper. "The best birthday you've had yet. I love that you brought me here tonight."

He lifts up my hand, pressing his lips against my knuckles. "Would you like me to order for you?"

I nod, gazing at him as he places little kisses on the backs of my fingers, all the while staring right back into my eyes with so much tenderness, it takes my breath away.

The waiter comes back, and Simon lets go of my hand, ordering with confidence as I watch their interaction in quiet awe. I have no idea what I'm having for dinner, but if it's anything like what we had for his birthday, I know it'll be delicious.

The waiter takes our menus, and Simon raises his glass, giving me an expectant look. I hold up my own, and he touches his to mine.

"To our first date," he says softly. I smile, taking a sip.

"So, Simon," I say, remembering Jo's advice, "this is our first date. Tell me about yourself."

345

He smiles back at me, taking a drink of his own wine. "What would you like to know?"

"Anything."

"Well, the first thing you should probably know is I'm quite a bit older than you." He leans in, whispering conspiratorially, "I'm forty."

"I like older men."

He pretends to wipe sweat off his brow and I grin, elated by his humor.

"I have a knack for numbers," he says, continuing, "so that's what I do for a living. I audit large companies."

"And you're good at it?"

He winks. "I'm the best."

"Modest too, I see."

He chuckles.

"And in your spare time?" I ask.

"I've never had much of that. I travel a lot for work, all over the world—Europe, Asia."

"Wow."

"I told you. I'm the best." He picks up his glass, swirling the ruby liquid around. "But I'm going to try to limit my traveling in the future. I want to be home more." His words settle over me like a warm blanket. I know I'm the reason he doesn't want to leave the city.

"What are you going to do when you get more time on your hands?"

"Spend it with someone special. Stay in and watch movies with her, go out to dinner with her, drive out of the city with her, maybe even travel abroad for fun with her. I think she'd enjoy that a lot." He says it without hesitation, his eyes determined. He's telling me he's all in. My heart soars and my mind buzzes with all of the wonderful scenarios he's laid out.

"That sounds amazing," I whisper. "I'd love to do all of that."

"I'm glad we have so much in common already." Simon grins, falling back into the role-play. "Tell me about yourself."

"I'm a freshman in college," I reveal, noticing the look of surprise that flashes across his face, quickly followed by the dazzling smile.

"Really? Abigail, that's wonderful."

"My dad created a college fund for me. I just started. I'm still getting used to it all."

"What are you studying?"

"Business. And later possibly culinary school. I'd like to someday open up my own shop or be a professional caterer. I really like cooking and baking, you see." I grin.

His gaze is warm. "I'd like to sample your skills someday. I don't cook at all."

I send him what I hope is a mischievous smile. "I could teach you. Really, isn't it about time for a man your age?"

He leans forward, the grin he once did his best to hide away tugging at his lips. "What if I told you I'm old-fashioned about that sort of thing? That I like having my woman in the kitchen, cooking for me?"

I lean forward too. "I'd tell you to join the rest of us in the twenty-first century. But then I might also ask where you are in that scenario."

"Behind her," he answers immediately, eyes smoldering. "Watching her, complimenting her, maybe even distracting her ... with my hands. Just a little."

I draw a shaky breath. I remember how it felt, having him with me in the kitchen. I miss it.

"You're being very forward." I chastise him with my words, not really meaning it. "This is a first date, after all."

"I'm sorry," he says, his grin telling me he's not sorry at all. "I guess I'm just *hungry*."

I laugh, shaking my head. "I just got my first catering job, a small private thing, so others are going to be sampling my skills first."

"You did?"

"A baby shower for a friend."

"Lila?" he asks, breaking character. I nod. "You'll do wonderfully. All of Lila's girlfriends will want to hire you too, I'm sure."

"Well," I say, not wanting to get my hopes up, "since we're talking about it, I wanted to ask you ... Can I borrow your kitchen a few days beforehand? Mine is kind of small."

"Be my guest. It's not like I use it for anything anymore."

"You don't?"

He glances away. "I haven't really been in there much since you left."

Oh, Simon. Underneath his tough exterior he's a lot more vulnerable than he lets on.

"Thank you. I won't be in your way."

"I want you in my way," he says. "I don't want to be without you again."

Warmth floods my chest and I find myself falling completely under his spell, loving every second of our conversation. "I don't want that either."

"Tell me something fun you've done recently," he says, smiling.

I return the smile, taking a sip of my wine, and start up our game again. "Well, I went to Disneyland for Thanksgiving."

"In California?" he asks, acting surprised.

"Yes, with my friends and my son. He's five. His name is Luke."

"I'd like to meet him someday," Simon says softly. His happy expression is contagious.

"I'd like that too."

"So, tell me about your trip. I want to hear everything," he says, his gaze moving toward the two waiters approaching. "Oh, good. Our first course is here."

"First? How many did you order?"

"A few." He grins at me. "You'll need to familiarize yourself with a lot of different courses for when you become Seattle's best caterer."

I laugh. "All right. Sounds good."

Nearly three hours later, I'm in a food coma, languidly reclined in my seat, finishing my third glass of wine. Across from me, Simon looks just as relaxed, although he switched to sparkling water after his second glass since he's driving. We've kept the conversation light and casual as the waiter brought us course after course, ending with cheeses and desserts.

"Full?" Simon asks, smirking at me.

I moan softly. "I couldn't eat another bite. That was incredible."

"Good." He signals the waiter. "Are you ready to get out of here?"

"Mmhm." I'm slightly buzzed in a very pleasant way and feeling warm all over. The waiter brings the bill to the table, and I reach for it, but my movements are slow, and Simon snatches it up, handing the waiter a black card without even looking at the bill.

"I've got it," he says.

"Are you sure?"

"Don't be silly. I invited you, after all. Besides, now you owe me dinner sometime. I'd like something home-cooked." He sends me a cheeky smile.

"Oh, really?" I giggle. "I think we can arrange that."

Simon signs the check, and when the waiter goes to pull out my chair, Simon intercepts, offering me his arm instead. I lean into him, feeling heavy-limbed and content as he wraps his arm around me and escorts me out. The car warms up quickly on the drive home, and my eyelids grow heavier and heavier as I try to keep up with the conversation.

"You can sleep," Simon murmurs.

"I'm not tired."

He chuckles in response.

"Really, it's only"—I look at his dashboard—"a little past

ten. I can't be tired yet. How would it look if I couldn't keep up with my *mature* man-friend?"

His lips twitch in amusement. "Don't think I won't pull over and put you across my knee."

His words send a jolt of excitement through me. I'm wide awake now.

"Yeah, you'd like that," he concludes, satisfaction radiating from him as he keeps driving.

"I would. Maybe our next date."

He smiles. "I had a wonderful time tonight. Thank you, Abigail."

"Thank *you*," I say, reaching over to lace our fingers. "Best first date ever."

"Couldn't agree more."

I manage to stay awake for the rest of the drive. Once we're at my place, he jumps out to open the door for me and offers me his arm again.

"You're such a gentleman," I hear myself say as we start walking with me all but glued to his side.

"I try. That dress of yours is making it difficult, though."

I look up at him, and he's still smiling, so I'm not sure if he's being serious or not. We stop outside my door, and he turns me gently so I'm facing him. His hands are warm on my face as he touches me, and I look up into his eyes.

"May I kiss you?" He exhales. "God, I want to kiss you."

I nod, standing up on my toes to meet him halfway as he presses his lips against mine, hesitantly at first. I feel him relaxing into me, tilting my head to the side as he kisses me again, firmer, better, his soft moan sending my pulse into over-drive as I deepen the kiss, opening to him. His tongue caresses mine, and I press up against him, desperate for more contact until he wraps his strong arms around me, enveloping me entirely. A low whine escapes my throat as I cling to him, letting him take charge. Much too soon, he pulls back, his breath harsh against the side of my face as he holds me close for a few moments before letting me go. I stumble a little, chuckling as I get my bearings. I give him a shy smile, and he returns it.

"I don't think I want you to be a gentleman tonight," I confess. "I know it's only our first date, but I don't want it to end."

"So invite me upstairs," he orders in a rough voice.

I shiver as he tangles his hand in my hair, tilting my face upward before he captures my lips with his. His kiss is demanding this time and makes my heart pound furiously as I cling to him, feeling my knees weaken at the sensations, the soft, warm, and certain glow of happiness radiating through me coupled with the frantic flutters of my heart telling me I'm right where I belong. Abruptly, he pulls back, gazing at me for a moment before he gently caresses my cheek.

"Invite me upstairs," he says again.

I nod eagerly, my fingers trembling as I try to locate the keys in my bag. The house is quiet as we tiptoe up the stairs, and I let us inside my apartment, closing the door to the outside world. I turn to Simon, who's staring at me with that same hungry look in his eyes, noticeable even in the darkness of the room. Before I can say anything, he sweeps me up and carries me to the bed.

"I want to unwrap you like a present," he says, reaching for my stilettos.

I lie still as he undresses me, brushing against my already overheated skin in the process. He stretches out next to me, slanting his mouth over mine, his hands tracing my curves. I moan, arching up, needing more.

"You're so wanting," he murmurs. "So needy."

"Please, touch me," I beg.

His fingers slip between my thighs, gently probing. "So wet already. There's my sweet g—" He stops. "Abigail. I mean Abigail. Fuck, I'm sorry."

"Wh-what?" I draw a breath, dazed. He's frozen above me,

frowning. "Hey." I lift my hand to run it through his hair. "It's okay for you to call me that."

Some of the tension leaves his body.

"I loved being your sweet girl," I whisper. "That doesn't have to change. I can still call you 'Sir,' sometimes. We both like it that way. And you said nothing would be off limits if we both enjoyed it, right?"

His answering smile is brilliant. "You'll still let me dress you up sometimes?"

"Of course. I'll even serve you naked."

"Fuck yes." His voice is a growl. God, it's hot.

"I like dressing up for you, in the 1950s dresses and the aprons." Then I ask a question I've been wondering for a while, but have been too shy to ask. "What do *you* like about it?"

His smile turns into a roguish grin. "It's a fetish, I suppose. Making you look prim and proper, all the while knowing"—he leans down and kisses me—"I can reach underneath to find you naked. Or that you'll bend over for me, equally eager for a spanking or for me to fuck you."

I can't stop a moan from escaping, completely turned on by his words.

"You were right about me, you know," he says.

"About what?"

"I never wanted a submissive, in the traditional sense. I wanted a girlfriend who's sexually submissive, who likes taking care of me. That's what I've always wanted. You. Just the way you are is perfect for me. I want everything with you. I may have been desperate, but I meant it when I asked you to marry me. I want to put a ring on your finger so the whole world knows you're mine."

I stare up at him, wide-eyed. "Simon, I—"

"We can have a long engagement," he interrupts softly. "Time won't change anything. I'll just love you more."

My heart stutters, making me lose my breath for a second. "You love me?"

A flash of surprise crosses his face and he lifts his hand to caress the apple of my cheek. He gazes at me, his expression warm and tender. "Of course I love you, Abigail."

My chest expands with unexpected warmth and tears rush to my eyes. He catches them all, brushing my temples with his thumbs, still watching me. I realize I haven't spoken.

"I wasn't sure," I whisper. "I hoped, because I love you too. I love you, Simon. I've wanted to tell you for a long time." I wrap my arms around him as his lips meet mine, softly at first, then with more eagerness as he starts pulling his clothes off in between kisses. I watch him as he sinks inside me, his face a picture of pleasure, a moan escaping both of us at the same time. I've missed this so much, the delicious stretching and feeling of completion, his weight on top of me. Lacing our fingers, he loves me slowly, only taking his eyes off mine when he leans down to kiss me or to whisper sweet words in my ear. My heart is so full I have to fight not to cry with happiness, freeing my fingers to throw my arms around him, needing him closer. Even quietly and gently like this, our physical connection is breathtaking in its intensity, and he swallows my cries as I come.

Afterward we lie close together, still touching and kissing. Neither of us seems able to stop.

Simon groans a little, shifting around. "Tomorrow we're going out, and I'm buying you a new bed."

"What? Why?"

"There's no way to say it without sounding ancient, so please just let me get you one with a good mattress, or better yet"— he dips his head to kiss my neck —"marry me, move in with me, and let me fuck you in my big bed every night."

"Simon." I sigh as he drapes his arm around me and pulls me close.

"Surrender," he whispers against my lips. "You know I always get what I want."

"Eventually," I say, opening my legs as he moves on top of me again.

His chuckle turns into a moan as he pushes inside. "Eventually, then, but we're getting that new bed tomorrow, you hear?"

"Yes, Sir."

I can feel the effect that one special word has on him, and I gasp as he thrusts—hard, rigid—his physical reaction to my words unmistakable.

"Do you like that?" His hips snap forward again, taking me hard.

"Oh, yes."

"How about this?" He tangles his hand in my hair, pulling my head back to expose my neck, holding me in place.

"God, yes."

"There's my sweet girl." His mouth crashes against mine, his tongue sliding against mine in a hungry kiss.

"Yes, yes, yes," I moan, loving his possession of me just as much as his gentle lovemaking earlier. "My answer is yes."

"Yes to what?"

"Yes to a long engagement. Yes to you and me."

Simon stops moving, his face lighting up. "Yes?"

I nod, crying out as he thrusts again, moaning both endearments and dirty words, promises of great romance and naughty kink in our future together.

EPILOGUE

Three Months Later

"**M**ommy, he's here!"

I smile at my reflection as I put in my earrings, the ones Simon bought for me when we lived with him. They go well with the ring on my finger. "Coming, hon."

I exit the bathroom just as I hear him coming up the stairs, Luke almost knocking me out of the way to get to him first.

"Mr. Thorne!"

"Hello, Luke," Simon says, stroking his hair. "You know, you can just call me Simon now."

Luke frowns. "Why?"

"Well, that's my first name. And I'm not your mom's boss anymore. I'm her boyfriend."

I accepted Simon's marriage proposal and his ring, but I only wear it around him. We're still taking things slowly, enjoying our long, secret engagement as we truly get to know each other. Soon, we'll tell Luke, and I know he'll be ecstatic.

Simon and I haven't discussed it yet, but it's my hope he'll want to adopt Luke as his own when we get married. They need each other too: a boy without a father and a man without a son.

"But my teacher says you're supposed to call grownups Mister and Missus. It's, uh, respectful—especially to old people."

"*Old* people?" Simon gives him a look of mock horror, making my son grin from ear to ear.

"Where are we going today?" Luke asks. "Mommy said you're taking us out."

"I thought we'd go to the zoo. Is that okay?"

"Awesome!"

"Why don't you go find your shoes and jacket?" I suggest, the words barely out of my mouth before my son runs off, eager to get going. Simon comes over to me, pressing a kiss to my lips, followed by another one.

"Hello, sweet girl," he whispers in my ear. "Thank you again for last night. And early this morning."

I look up at him, unable to hide how my face warms. Luke was at my mom's house and I was with Simon. Kneeling for Simon. Bent over for Simon. Tied up for Simon. I shiver with pleasure, remembering, and he smirks, giving my ass a quick squeeze. We're still working on our sleeping arrangements, and for now I spend the night downstairs in my old room when I sleep over at his house. I don't mind. This is what Simon needs right now. Besides, I love having him sneak into my room in the early morning hours, waking me with kisses and caresses, unable to stay away from me a minute longer than he has to. We haven't spent a full night together yet, but I know we'll get there one day.

"Come on, let's go!" Luke hollers from downstairs, bringing both of us back to the present.

On our way out the door, Simon puts his arm around me,

and my heart does a somersault, seeing how Luke slips his little hand into Simon's. The two of them smile at each other.

I think of everything that's happened to bring us to this perfect moment, and I know in my heart I would do it all over again. Some lines are worth crossing.

The End

ABOUT THE AUTHOR

Although she is a native of Denmark, SJ Hooks has always had a keen interest in the English language.

She has a BA in English Literature and an MA in American Studies. As a single working mother of two special needs children, her days are busy.

At night, when she isn't passed out on the couch, she's in front of her computer, writing stories of love, humor and passion-- the best things in life.

You can find SJ Hooks on Facebook, Goodreads and Instagram.

Made in the USA
Monee, IL
02 June 2020